Twelve Quiet Men

An Historical Novel of the Vigilante Raids of 1883-1885 in Montana and Dakota Territory

By

Michael Edward Little

ISBN: 1-4107-0395-9 (e-book)
ISBN: 1-4107-0396-7 (Paperback)

Library of Congress Control Number: 2002096492

This book is printed on acid free paper.

Printed in the United States of America
Bloomington, IN

1stBooks - rev. 01/04/03

ACKNOWLEDGEMENTS

I wish to thank the following fine folks:

Steve Little, Attorney, Mandan, North Dakota, who gave me the time to get the job done.

Lee Ingalls, Rancher, Almont, North Dakota, who kept me honest and challenged me to do better.

John Broyles, Spur-Maker, New Salem, North Dakota, for his insights into spurs and spur construction.

The Range Riders Museum, Miles City, Montana, for giving me access to the original equipment and newspaper articles.

Marshall R. Haferkamp, Range Plant Physiology, Ft. Keogh Livestock & Range Research Laboratory, Agricultural Research Service, U.S. Department of Agriculture, Miles City, Montana, for his insights into native prairie grasses.

J.D. Bauman, Madd Hatter, Mandan, North Dakota, who gave me an appreciation for cowboy hats styles, construction and usage.

Ken Hess, Kickin' Ass Hat Company, Miles City, Montana, for his historical perspective.

John Brown, Saddle Maker, Brown Saddle Shop, Miles City, Montana, who took the time to explain and demonstrate the art of saddle making.

John Paulson, District Supervisor, Wildlife Services, U.S. Department of Agriculture, Bismarck, North Dakota, for his skunk wrangling expertise.

The Miles City Public Library, Miles City, Montana, who took the time to put my nose in the right books in the Montana Room.

Elaine Foreman, Miles City Star, Miles City, Montana, for pointing me in the right direction.

The North Dakota Historical Society, Bismarck, North Dakota, for their eager and helpful assistance.

The North Dakota State Library, Bismarck, North Dakota, for their friendly assistance.

Finally, special thanks to Clarence E. Mulford for writing 28 of the most enjoyable western adventure novels ever written.

Dedicated to the memory of
George Little, Montana Rancher and
a light in the darkness.
Via con Dios

Table of Contents

Forward

Claire Nations

FERGUS FALLS - Claire Boddie Nations, 72, Fergus Falls, died May 23, 1920, at his home in Fergus Falls. Services will be held at 11:00 a.m. Saturday at St. Paul Lutheran Church, Fergus Falls, with Rev. Thomas Hopp officiating. Burial will be at Fergus Falls Memorial Cemetery.

Visitation will be from noon to 9:00 p.m. today at Judson Funeral Home, Fergus Falls, and will continue for one hour before services at church.

Mr. Nations was born Aug. 17, 1847, at Palo Pinto, Tex., to Homer and Constance Nations. Mr. Nations was a working cowboy in his early days and participated in several trail drives from Texas to Montana and Dakota Territories, before settling in Montana, where he worked as a range detective for the Sun River Rangers and later for the Eastern Montana Stockgrowers Association. He next moved to Medora, North Dakota, where he worked on the Elkhorn ranch, owned by Theodore Roosevelt, who later became the 26th President of the United States.

Following his cowboy and range detective career, Mr. Nations moved to Fergus Falls in 1893, where he worked as deputy sheriff until 1898, when he was elected sheriff of Otter Tail County, a position he held until his retirement in 1914.

Mr. Nations demonstrated his bravery several times as deputy and later as sheriff, most notably when he foiled a daring daylight robbery in Underwood during the fall of 1897. He happened on the scene as three armed men exited the Underwood Savings Bank with pistols drawn. Deputy Nations ordered the robbers to drop their weapons, which they refused to do. They began firing on the deputy immediately. Deputy Nations drew his pistol and coolly walked directly into their fire, returning better than he received, killing two of the men and wounding the third. The deputy sustained no injuries.

Although he had no surviving family, those who knew him will miss him. In today's world of bold talk and soaring hyperbole, he was the genuine article. (Judson Funeral Home, Fergus Falls)

Φ

It's not often that providence shines on someone, but it shown on me one morning while attending an estate sale. I spied an old trunk that I thought might clean up nice, and after parting with $46.00, I carried my prize home. The trunk couldn't be opened because the lock was rusty and the key long gone, but using a screwdriver, I finally popped the lock. Inside, I discovered this yellowed obituary. Also in the trunk were several old journals.

I had no idea who Claire Nations was, and the obit from the 1920's didn't tell me much. Over the following few weeks, I carefully went through the journals, and was amazed to discover they contained details of a Vigilante action during the 1880's in Montana and Dakota Territories. The journals told of 12 cattlemen who abandoned their ranches and livelihoods to pursue organized outlaw gangs operating along the Missouri, Judith, Musselshell, Yellowstone and Little Missouri rivers, stealing horses and cattle from local ranchers and selling them in neighboring territories and Canada. Although these events happened more than 125 years ago, I found the journals to be exciting and intriguing.

Using Mr. Nations notes, newspaper accounts of the day and other sources, I constructed what follows. My reason for writing this tale is simple; it's an amazing story that deserves to see the light of day. During my research, I discovered other works that made passing reference to these secret activities, yet none tells the tale in its entirety. Having lived in North Dakota and Montana for many years, I feel I have an obligation to shed light on these remarkable events.

I was able to corroborate some of what Mr. Nations had written. Other details couldn't be substantiated, yet based on what I could verify, I have no reason to doubt his veracity. One mystery remains however. Mr. Nations appears to have had intimate knowledge of these events, yet he doesn't list himself as a participant. If he wasn't involved, how did he gain this secret information? If he was involved, why did he conceal it? This remains a mystery to this day.

Michael Edward Little
Shepherd, Montana

Chapter One - Outgunned

SPANG! The rifle slug hit a rock next to Duncan's head, splattering his sweaty face with rock chips and dust, ripping his worn Stetson from his head. He was lucky and knew it. The jagged and misshapen ricochet would have cut thru him like a buzz saw if he'd been hit. He willed himself flatter, wiping the blood, sweat and grit from his eyes. Lying in a pool of blood from his various wounds, he was still full of fight.

"Missed me, you cross-eyed varmint!" Duncan said, as another shot took the heel off his boot. "Shore happy them devils can't shoot!"

"Well, we got plenty of ammo and the weather's shore improvin'; there's a lot less lead in the air," Black Dutch said, reloading his rifle. "Them last two coyotes is playin' her careful though."

The two remaining rustlers were staying well back, at something beyond 300 yards and the report of their rifles was deeper, more of a "boom" than a "pow." Larger bore, heavier loads, longer range.

"Damn!" Black Dutch exclaimed. Already wounded several times, a bullet entered below his knee and ran the length of his calf. "Ventilated me again! Damn his black soul!"

Black Dutch sighted carefully, adjusting the elevation for the extreme range. At this distance, he had to anticipate his enemy's next move, waiting for the right moment to fire. "Watch me pot that coyote off to the left, Dunc. He don't know I shoots rainbows," Dutch said softly, as he concentrated, held his breath and then squeezed the trigger. POW!

"Take that, you cuss!" The rustler was caught just as he began to move from a small depression and folded up in a heap. "Only one skunk left outa this tribe, Dunc. Yes sir, things is lookin' up!"

Just 25 minutes earlier, the two wranglers had been rounding up horses 20 miles north of the DHS ranch. Set on the eastern end of the Judith Mountains, the ranch occupied the southern end of an open range that stretched 50 miles north to the Missouri River, interrupted only by creek bottoms, folds and creases in the land. To the southwest, Judith Peak, at nearly 6,000 feet, could plainly be seen, as could the ominous countenance of Black Butte directly south. There

1

was surprisingly little wind; the sky was clear and the autumn sun felt good as the two men rode along.

The morning's work should have been a simple task, but when Duncan and Black Dutch suddenly came upon four rustlers putting hot iron to a small herd of DHS beef, hell came calling. An alert rustler fired first, killing Duncan's horse. As the horse dropped from beneath him, the kid jumped clear, but had the presence of mind to jerk his Winchester free. He quickly grabbed Black Dutch's extended arm, who swung the kid up behind him, spun his horse and tried for a break. But before Sarge made three jumps, the kid was hit hard in the shoulder and knocked off, pulling Black Dutch with him. Crouching low, the wranglers ran the 25 yards or so to a low stone outcrop and jumped behind it as bullets struck all around them. Breathing hard, both men began returning fire immediately.

Somehow, Sarge had escaped unharmed, and Black Dutch could see him grazing near a coulee 600 yards away. He was a good horse and would be difficult to replace if lost. Typical of working cowboys, Black Dutch had a small string of horses suited to specific tasks of ranch and cattle work. All but one of the horses in Dutch's string belonged to the ranch, but he'd selected and worked with each and considered them his own, even though he knew if he ever left the outfit, the horses would stay.

The rustlers and cowboys fought it out with rifles, but the advantage was with the rustlers. They were shooting larger, longer-range calibers than the meager 44-40's Dutch and the kid were using. The advantage of the 44-40 was it would fit both pistols and rifles, and while suitable for most situations a cowpuncher may encounter, the small round was a pistol cartridge, lacking range and hitting anything past 100 yards was mostly a matter of luck. Before the rustlers had a chance to get organized and find good cover, Duncan had busted one man in the leg, crippling him. As the man hobbled for cover, several more shots finally settled the matter, and the man hadn't moved since.

"I made that one awful sick, Dutchy. He got the staggers like a poisoned wolf and then laid down for a nap," the kid said, laughing, as he reloaded his rifle.

The three remaining outlaws quickly spread out to encircle the two wranglers, using their numerical advantage and mobility to attack from different angles. Black Dutch was able to drop a second rustler when he became over-confident and foolishly exposed himself, feeling he was safely out of range.

"I just rolled one myself, kid. That's one buzzard that won't be runnin' no sack races!" Black Dutch said, with a grin. Both wranglers were wounded several times but were holding their own.

Now, nearly a half-hour after the gun battle began, Dutch had killed the third rustler. The remaining outlaw was still throwing lead at the two men, but his fire was sporadic.

"Shore wish Harley or Red Mack would come ridin' up. I'm gettin' thirsty," Duncan said, squeezing off another shot. "What you reckon he's shootin, Dutchy?"

"Don't know and don't matter, Dunc. Buffalo gun maybe, but whatever it is, it's more gun than we got. He's got the range on us, but I believe we may squeeze through this knot-hole yet."

Just then, Black Dutch heard a wet slap and knew immediately that the kid had been hit hard. Turning quickly, he was sickened to see one side of Duncan's skull open and exposed, with bits of scalp, bone and brains splattered over his body. *Oh Lord!* Black Dutch looked back, hoping to draw a bead on the remaining rustler but saw him running toward Sarge, holding one hand to his ear. Dutch quickly levered another round into his rifle and fired, but the bullet kicked up dust harmlessly well short of the target. The outlaw continued unfettered toward the horse as Black Dutch fired, levered and fired again, but it was useless. The man was simply too far away. The wrangler could do nothing but watch helplessly as the outlaw stepped aboard Sarge, and with a final look, spurred and whipped the horse toward the west. Dutch swore in frustration, powerless to prevent the escape. The gunfight had lasted only a short time, but what a price had been paid!

He knew the answer before he reached out to touch the boy, but he had to check. Feeling for a pulse and finding none, he wasn't surprised. Dead. The kid had been shot five times, and while the shoulder wound was serious, it probably wouldn't have been fatal.

"Duncan, boy, you shore had sand. Shot to pieces and nary a squeak." Dutch tore the tail off his shirt and quickly bandaged himself as well as he was able. His right calf was his most serious wound, the bullet having traversed most of its length. Another slug had gone through his left forearm and upper arm as it was bent supporting his rifle. Luckily, no bones had been broken. His other wounds were grazing shots, gouges really, which hurt like the dickens but were of little consequence.

Black Dutch then turned to the business of burying his young friend. Lacking a shovel, the best he could manage was to cover the boy's body with rocks so wolves and coyotes couldn't get at it. It was a slow process. Black Dutch could only manage a slow, painful, drag-legged hobble as he carried rocks and placed them carefully on the body. At last, the job done to his satisfaction, he said, "Well Duncan, I done all I can for you, son. Some of the boys will be out to collect you and carry you home. But that'll have to keep. First, I'm gonna kill the skunk that killed you."

Without a single moment's hesitation or concern for his own wounds, Black Dutch turned to the business of pursuing the outlaw. Loyalty was a common feature in this class of men. A wrangler's life was difficult and often dangerous, yet Black Dutch was proud of his outfit, risking life and limb for $40 a month and found. Following emancipation, Dutch took his former owner's name of Hatzenbihler, but almost everyone found it difficult to pronounce or even remember, so people simply called him Dutch, like other men with German names. To eliminate further confusion, the Negro cowboy was subsequently called Black Dutch. Like other freed slaves, he'd drifted into the territory on a trail drive up from Texas following the War of Northern Aggression. Only 14 years old at the time, he held a variety of jobs: freighter, bull whacker and finally wrangler. That was when he met the boss of the DHS outfit, Granville Stuart, and went to work for him. Though older than most wranglers, now 32 years old, Dutch was fortunate in that he had never been busted up real bad and was still in good health. Most cowboys found other pursuits before their thirtieth birthday. Granville treated him with the same respect and held the same expectations of him as any man in the outfit. Race didn't matter, color didn't matter, and the past didn't matter. All that mattered was how a man carried himself and did his duty. Black Dutch liked that and respected his boss for it. Consequently, he would follow the outfit into Hades if need be.

After an hour of painful hobbling, Black Dutch was finally able to catch one of the rustler's horses and lay on food, bed-role, a couple half full canteens of water, extra ammo from Duncan's dead horse and a heavy coat for the cool evenings. When all necessaries were assembled and tied securely to the saddle, he stepped first onto a rock and then climbed painfully aboard the horse. Pointing it west, he soon picked up Sarge's trail and he rode at an easy lope, eyeing the ground as he went.

When dusk settled in and tracking became impossible, Black Dutch made a hasty cold camp next to a small stream, not willing to risk a fire for fear the man he was tracking would see it. He watered the horse, filled the canteens and spread out the blanket tarp and sougan, a heavy quilt preferred by northern cowboys in that cold climate. He found a rotten log near the stream and carefully gathered mold from it, which he applied to his wounds before rewrapping them. He was unsure if the Indian cure would work, but it was the only thing he could do. After making a crude hobble from a short length of rope, he hobbled the horse so it could graze but wouldn't drift far during the night and pulled the saddle, saddle blanket and bridle off. When his various tasks were completed, he sat down to supper. He had found a can of peaches among the outlaw's supplies, which he quickly consumed, along with jerked beef, cold sourdough biscuits and water, lots of water. Loss of blood was making him very thirsty. Once the victuals were consumed, he turned in and quickly fell asleep.

The following morning, he arose very sore but anxious to be on the move just as the sky was brightening to the east. After a hasty breakfast of cold biscuits and jerked beef, he quickly broke camp, watered himself and the horse again. Just as it was light enough to see the faint traces of Sarge's trail, he set off in slow but steady pursuit, aware that the outlaw was probably many hours ahead of him and getting farther away every minute. It couldn't be helped. While Dutch's wounds were growing more painful and more demanding of his attentions, his biggest concern was staying on Sarge's trail. He wasn't the best tracker in the outfit, but he could do a serviceable job, if slowly. *Shore wish Keeps Eagle was here. Now that man can track!* Dutch had once seen Keeps Eagle track three men on horseback while at a dead run!

Late in the day, he came upon a low cabin amongst the cottonwoods set next the Arrow River. He approached the homestead carefully, not wishing to cause alarm.

"Hello the cabin!" he shouted. "Can a fellow get a little food and a drink of water?"

The cabin door slowly opened, and a man stepped cautiously into the light; a double-barreled shotgun leveled at the wrangler. "Who are you mister and what's your business?"

"Howdy. I ride for the DHS brand. Folks call me Black Dutch. Two days ago, over near Armells crick, me and my partner come on four devils stealin' our cattle. We killed three of 'em. The last one killed my partner, stole my horse and lit out. His tracks lead here. I aim to kill him when I finds him," Black Dutch replied. "Maybe you seen him come through here?"

The settler uncocked and lowered his weapon, nodding. "Your man came through here early this morning riding a tired black with a blaze. He took my only saddle horse at gunpoint and forded the river, headin' west. He was missing part of one ear; looked like a fresh wound. Had a bandaged arm too." the man said.

"That's the coyote, all right. I s'pose he kept the black?"

"Yep, put my lead rope on him and away he went." He nodded toward the cabin. "My name's Bill Jeffers. Come on in and eat some supper with us. I'll have the wife dress your wounds. You look pretty used up," the man said, noting the bloody bandages Black Dutch wore.

Dutch dismounted, tied his horse off to the hitch rail and limped into the low cabin. Typical of its type, the one room structure used cottonwood logs taken from the river bottom for the walls and roof supports. The roof was made of a foot of straw topped with a foot of dirt. Dirt had been piled up around outer walls as a measure of protection against the frigid winter cold. The only openings in the walls were two small windows, covered with rawhide, which let a dim light into the interior but couldn't be seen through, and a single door. When his eyes adjusted to the low light, he saw a mean interior with no real furniture; only a crude table, a couple raggedy wore-out chairs and some crude stools spread over a dirt floor. Rough low slat beds with sweet grass for bedding ran along one wall at the end of the cabin. From nails driven into the walls, the family's scant possession hung. Crude shelves held what couldn't be hung. The man's wife was bent over a sheet-iron stove at the opposite end, stirring a large cast iron pot. From behind the busy woman, two small girls peeked out at him, wide eyed, as they clutched their mother's apron.

"Sorry for the kids starring. They ain't never seen a nig...well, they ain't never seen a colored man before," Jeffers explained.

"Happens sometimes, ain't many of us in these parts," Dutch replied, chuckling. "I appreciates the chance to get some food in me. What kind of an outfit you got here, Jeffers?"

"Oh, we moved from the States a year ago or better. We run a few head of cattle. Got a couple hogs too, a good milk cow and a few chickens the coyotes ain't eat up yet. Out back we got a vegetable patch and some berry bushes. We live a little rough but can't complain; all in all, we're pretty well off. You say you ride for the DHS? That's a big spread compared to what we got here. How many head you run over there?"

Dutch bristled. The settler's question was impolite, akin to asking a man how much money he had in the bank. It simply wasn't done. "Some few I'd say," Dutch replied, curtly.

Jeffers and his wife exchanged a look that Dutch noticed but couldn't read. It was a furtive exchange and quick as a flash, was gone.

"Honey, why don't you and our guest go out and wash up? Supper's ready and the kids are hungry," the woman said. "Girls, help me set the table, and make sure your hands are clean. Becky, bring that stool over from the wall so everyone will have a place to sit."

When the men returned and sat down, Dutch couldn't help noticing Mrs. Jeffers features. She was a woman of perhaps 25, but considerably aged. She was probably pretty at one time, but her features were lost to time and endless toil; used up. "This shore is good grub, Mrs. Jeffers. I appreciates it," Dutch offered. The two little girls continued to stare, hardly touching their food.

"Here," said Dutch, smiling, as he held out his hand to the little girls. "Go ahead, touch it. It don't rub off."

Cautiously, the older of the two, reached out and took his hand, running her small fingers over the rough, scarred skin. Slowly she smiled up at Dutch. "See?" he said. "I'm a man just like yer daddy, only a different color."

"How many colors are there?" the younger one asked, finally finding her tongue.

"Oh, shush Martha! That ain't polite to ask," Mrs. Jeffers said, embarrassed her daughter would ask such a question.

Black Dutch laughed. "Oh, they's lots of colors. Red, yellow, green, just 'bout any color you could think of. I once saw a blue man down in Denver," Dutch replied, winking at Mrs. Jeffers. The girl's eyes grew larger at this news. Suddenly they burst out laughing and soon the adults joined in.

"Girls, now stop pestering Mr. Dutch and let him eat. Would you like some more food or some more buttermilk, sir?" the woman asked.

"Oh ma'am, just call me Dutch. I appreciates the good food, 'specially the pie. But seeing as how I ain't had buttermilk since I was a boy, I'd shore like another cup, thank you."

After the meal, Mrs. Jeffers cleaned Black Dutch's wounds, applied a foul smelling poultice to each and wrapped them with clean cotton cloth. "Your wounds look bad, but they ain't sour. This poultice will help them drain and heal," she said. She then quickly made up a sack of provisions and handed it to Dutch. "Here's some bacon, biscuits and such for the trail. I put more poultice in there too, so next time you change your bandages, put some on," she said, with a look that seemed to ask a question.

After an awkward silence, Dutch suddenly caught on. "Err, yes'm, I shore will. Thank you."

He carried the small flour sack of provisions out to his horse and tied it to the saddle horn. Leading the horse over to a chopping block, Dutch stepped gingerly onto the block and then aboard the horse. Addressing the family now assembled at the cabin door, he said, "There's still light for another couple hours tracking, so I'll be on my way. If I can, I'll get your horse back to you, Jeffers. I appreciates your neighborliness and I'll let my boss know what you folks done. Girls, you be sure and mind your folks. And be on the look out for that blue man! So long," Black Dutch trotted away from the cabin laughing, as the girls waved good-bye. As he rode toward the ford, he noticed Jeffers' penned up cows had a surprising number of twin calves.

Sleepering? An easy way to rustle cattle and build up a herd was to put a rope on a unbranded calf from someone else's herd, lead it away from its mother and put it on one of your own cows that already had a nursing calf. This wasn't without its problems though. The calf would bellar for its mother, calling attention to itself. The bellaring could only be stopped if the calf was penned up in the dark, such as in a shed or barn. After a couple days, the new mother would usually accept the little stranger and nurse it as her own. This worked best when the calf was taken from some distance away, because if the birth mother were too close, she would eventually find the calf and reclaim it. All the while, the mother would bellow in a distinctive way as she called to her missing calf, searching. Experienced wranglers easily recognized this cry. This was called "sleepering" and was a fairly low risk method of rustling. With no brand, there could be no proof of the calf's true ownership. Black Dutch was reluctant to even consider that Jeffers might be sleepering cattle, after their kindness to him, and quickly put it out of his mind. He had more pressing business ahead.

Φ

Two days later, after circling south of the Highwood Mountains, Black Dutch rode into the barnyard of a horse ranch just outside of Ft. Shaw, near The Great Falls of the Missouri. Sarge's tracks led to a rough stockade corral 8 feet tall adjoining a stock barn. As he stepped down from the saddle, a man appeared at the barn door with a pitchfork in hand, but said nothing. Dutch tied the horse off, limped over to the corral gate and looked in. There stood Sarge and the settler's horse, easily recognizable by its long untrimmed tail. Cowboys pulled the hair from their horse's tails, making them much shorter and less apt to "load-up" with brush and weeds. A horse with brush tangled in its tail would go off like dynamite when the brush hit the back of the animal's hind legs. The frightened animal would go loco with fear, bucking wildly in its panic. To be thrown from a horse on the open range, many miles from any kind of help, could be a death sentence; the rider could be busted up in the fall and a man afoot could easily die of thirst or starvation.

Turning, Black Dutch walked back to the barn and asked the man holding up the pitchfork, "Who owns the black with the blaze and the sorrel?"

The stable hand pointed past the stockade towards a small grove of aspen and said, "That fellar sleeping over there, past the corral in the quakin' asp. Came fannin' in here yesterday in a lather and asked if we'd look after his horses."

"He owe you money?"

"Nope, he's paid up."

"Good."

Dutch turned and hobbled over to the man, pulled his Colt and killed the outlaw as he slept.

9

"That's one murderin' skunk we ain't gotta worry about," Dutch said to himself, as he limped back to the barn. There, he explained the true ownership of the horses in the corral and recovered them, along with his saddle and effects. Luckily, Sarge looked tired but uninjured.

"Bury that coyote over there when you gets time. Keep his horse and saddle as payment, and whatever you find on him is yours. It's blood money I don't need." Stepping aboard Sarge, he grasped the lead rope on Jeffers' horse and rode away without further comment. He was back at the DHS ranch five days later, after having dropped off Jeffers' horse.

Montana and Dakota Territory held the last remaining open range in the West, all others having been lost to small ranchers and nesters, with their fences and plows, as civilization closed in. When Granville, and his brother James, first entered Montana Territory in 1857, there were fewer than 500 whites in the entire 138,000 square mile territory. As the territory developed and more people moved in, Granville pursued a series of vocations: miner, butcher, blacksmith, grocer, politician and finally rancher. Beginning in 1880, he and his partners, Sam Hauser and A. J. Davis, steadily built up their herd on the nutritious bunch grass that covered the range. In 1883, Hauser and Davis sold their interests to Conrad Kohrs, a wealthy immigrant butcher turned cattleman from western Montana Territory. Granville retained his third interest and stayed on to manage the ranching operations. Known for his public mindedness and fairness, at 49 years of age, Granville was a force in the region, respected and well liked.

Black Dutch rode up the hitch rail, slowly dismounted and was tying Sarge off in front of the Stuart house, when Granville stepped out onto the porch and quickly sized up the situation. He saw the wrangler's several bandages and the look of resignation on his face.

"What happened to Duncan Sides, Dutchy?" Granville asked softly.

"Rustlers killed him, Mr. Stuart. We caught four of 'em branding some of our cattle and they started shootin'," Black Dutch said. "Me and Duncan busted three of 'em before he was killed. I covered him with some rocks and left them three devils for the wolves, coyotes and magpies. I caught up with the last one over near Ft. Shaw and killed him in his sleep."

"You didn't give him a chance?"

"Sir, I never gives a rattler a second chance."

"It's settled then."

"Yes sir, it's settled."

"Thank you for squaring accounts, Dutch. Get Phonograph to patch you up and we'll get Dr. McDonald out here tomorrow," Granville said, then turned and walked away, looking for his foreman.

After Black Dutch tied Sarge off in front of the bunkhouse, he hobbled inside with his gear and sat down at the table, tired and very sore. Phonograph Bill, the bunkhouse cook, came charging in and was brought up short when he saw Dutch's wounds. Drawing a full breath, he quickly launched into a full-scale interrogation, but Dutch would have none of it.

"When everyone comes in, I'll talk. Now quit pesterin' me, you lop eared siwash, and turn Sarge into the corral. Tell Flagg to give him some grain. I'm whipped, Bill."

The disappointed cook grumbled, but did as he was told, which was unusual because Phonograph only took orders from two men on the ranch, and Dutch wasn't one of them.

Early that evening, the wranglers returned to the bunkhouse after completing their various chores. All were happy to see Dutchy had returned and wanted to know what happened to Duncan, but Dutchy held them off until everyone was assembled, making certain Phonograph was present. He then told the tale of Duncan's murder and settling scores with the last rustler. The mood of the men was one of smoldering anger that evening.

After supper, Harley Denny, the foreman, asked Black Dutch outside. As the two men leaned on the corral and rolled their smokes, Harley asked, "You got any idea who them polecats was, Dutchy?"

"Don't know, boss. I never seen 'em before."

Both men smoked in silence for a bit, then Harley asked, "How'd the kid do?"

"He spit in their eye. He was shot full of holes and laughin' and cussin' 'em all the while! I didn't know he was so shot up 'til it was over. He never even squeaked. I was proud of him, boss."

"Shore wish I coulda been there. Damn them bastards!" Harley exclaimed. "How you feelin'?" he asked, after a brief pause.

"Sore and tired. I stopped at a nester's spread over on the Arrow and the missus give me some poultice and I been usin' that. I don't smells ripe, so I guess I'll be fine when the achin' stops," the wrangler replied.

11

"Well, you got no chores 'til you're healed up. Just take it easy and try not to ride Phonograph too hard," the foreman said, walking off through the twilight toward the big house.

Harley Denny was an interesting man. Born in Texas, he was raised on the frontier, early on learning the skills that would save his life many times. He joined the Special Force of Texas Rangers in late 1874 when he was 22 years old. The Special Force was given the difficult and dangerous assignment of curbing cross-border raids in the Rio Grande-Nueces River region, or as it was called in Texas, the Nueces Strip. The raids were the work of the diabolical outlaw General Juan "Cheno" Cortina and the thousands of Mexican brigands under his command. It was estimated that from 1869 to 1874 Cortina's men stole nearly a million cattle and killed an estimated 2000 ranchers and citizens, both Mexican-Americans and Anglo-Americans. These Mexican raiders were vicious in their attacks, murdering men, gang raping women and girls and burning ranches. When confronted by elements of the U.S. Army, the desperados always fled across the border to the sanctuary of Mexico, only to strike at another location a short time later. The Army was not permitted to pursue the outlaws and found the situation impossible. It was into this situation that the Special Force was thrust, and because they were free of the constraints the Army suffered under, they conducted numerous cross-border raids into Mexico. Harley served with valor and distinction until 1879 when he resigned from the Rangers and joined a cattle drive taking a herd of Longhorns north to Montana Territory on the Goodnight-Loving trail. He enjoyed the rough and ready atmosphere of Montana and decided to stay. He'd been foreman of the DHS from day one and had proven to be a tremendous asset to Granville and the ranch.

Later that evening, Katie, Granville's oldest daughter went to the bunkhouse and asked for Black Dutch. When he appeared at the door, she said, "Papa and momma want you to stay with us until you're healed. Please gather your things and we'll go up together."

"But Miss Katie, I'm fine just where I'm at," Dutch replied, nodding at his leg. "This here ain't nothin' special."

"Momma asked that you should come and papa agreed. They want you up at the house."

"Yes miss, but if I does that, these bummers will think I'm bein' treated special and they'll ride me like a wounded animal," Dutch begged. "Please, miss."

"Gather your things and come with me," she said, in a tone that would brook no argument or equivocation.

Reluctantly, Black Dutch gathered his few possessions, announced his retirement to his fellow wranglers, which was met with hoots and a couple thrown boots, and walked with the young woman up to the big house, where they were met by Phonograph Bill. He slowly led the hobbling wrangler to a small bedroom and helped him put his few clothes away. Awbonnie, Granville's wife, and Katie had prepared a hot bath on the side-porch, and Phonograph led the wrangler to it and told him to scrub up. After his toilet was complete, the cook dressed his wounds and gave him clean clothes.

As the black wrangler was returning to his room, Awbonnie called to him from the kitchen. When he entered, she said, "Mr. Dutch, I want you to remain here until you are well. My husband tells me you did your best to save that young man. Thank you," Mrs. Stuart said. "I'll send for Doctor McDonald first thing tomorrow. Good night."

After returning to his room, Black Dutch crawled into the luxury of the featherbed. But his thoughts weren't on the sudden comfort; he was thinking of Mrs. Stuart's words. In the 2 years he'd worked for the DHS, she hadn't said more than three words to him and had never been particularly friendly. Not that she was unfriendly exactly; she just wasn't very sociable toward him. The softening in her manner came as a surprise to the rough cowboy.

Awbonnie was a Shoshone Indian woman, from the Snake band, Granville had married in 1862 when she was just a girl. When the territory was first opening up, white men "marrying" Indian women was quite common, though usually a matter of convenience. As more settlers, particularly white women, moved into the territory, prejudice became more common, and such relationships were considered "improper" by newly arrived whites. The social stigma was undeniable, and although Granville was under some pressure to get shed of her, he remained loyal to his wife until her death years later. This in itself was uncommon; most men who had common-law marriages with Indian women dissolved them without a second thought, abandoning wife and children alike; leaving them to fend for themselves.

13

The following day, Harley sent two men in the Texas wagon carrying a freshly made coffin to pickup young Duncan's body. Wagons used in Texas had a wider track between the wheels than the wagons of the northern plains. Consequently, they couldn't be used on any of the roads because of the rough and bumpy ride they offered. This particular one had come up from Texas with a trail drive and Granville had picked it up for $5 for use around the ranch. If the wagon were eventually destroyed by rough service, it was small loss, and for this reason, the DHS men used it to collect the body of the young wrangler. He would be returning home one last time. The mood of the outfit was a mix of sadness and slow burning anger. Duncan Sides was just 18 years old, well liked and would be missed.

Φ

Two days later, the funeral was held and the young cowboy was buried on a rise above the ranch. The Stuarts, their 9 children, all the hands and other folks from neighboring ranches and other parts of the territory were in attendance. The large turnout was puzzling to the family and wranglers, but when asked who they all were, Granville would only say "just old friends." Reverend Moss, a Methodist missionary, read some words from a well-worn bible and then dirt was shoveled over the young man. Though not known for their sentimentality, some of the wranglers wept quietly as a simple white wooden cross was placed on the grave of the young man.

Following the ceremony, the mourners adjourned to the house to commiserate with Granville, his family and the wranglers. The wives from the neighboring ranchers helped Mrs. Stuart serve drinks and food to the assembly. Granville made a point of speaking to everyone individually and ignored no one, but as he made his rounds, he quietly asked certain men to adjourn to the back porch for a pow-wow.

This was to be a significant meeting. In attendance were Nelson Story, a Montana pioneer and the first man to drive cattle into the territory, Conrad Kohrs, Granville's new partner in the DHS ranch and the first man to introduce Shorthorn and Hereford cattle into the territory, James Fergus, a rancher who settled in the area at the same time Granville did, his son, Andrew Fergus and Pierre Wibaux, a prominent rancher from Beaver Creek in eastern Montana Territory, among others. As the men drank and talked in small groups, one of the neighboring ranchers, Ham Rather, said just loud enough to be heard by all, "...well I don't think it's right that some damn nigger killed a white man..."

Granville, who was at the other end of the porch talking to Harley, Dutch and James Fergus, spun on his heal when he heard the words, set his drink aside and walked briskly through the group to stand nose to nose with Rather.

"I sure hope that's the liquor talkin' Ham," Granville said softly.

"I meant exactly what I said! Ain't no damn nigger got the right to shoot a white ma-"

Smack! Granville hit the man's face hard; it wasn't a punch but an open-handed slap and expressed a certain contempt, as though Ham wasn't man enough to rate a man's response. Ham's face turned bright red from embarrassment.

Before Ham could respond, in a low strained voice, Granville said, "Black Dutch is one of the whitest men I've ever known. I don't mean the color of his skin; I mean the color of his soul. I won't have that kind of disrespect shown to him. He spilled his blood protecting this ranch and has earned my respe—"

Black Dutch quickly ran to Granville's side and interjected, "Sir, I don't takes no offense at this."

Granville turned to Dutch and said, "Maybe you don't, Dutch, but *I* do." He quickly turned back to Rather and said, "I want you to get the hell off this ranch and stay off. Now scat!"

Rather stomped out in a huff and rode away without another word. Black Dutch never felt more awkward in his life and quietly stepped off the back porch and limped around the house, making slow progress toward the bunkhouse. Before he had gone far, someone called his name and he stopped. Turning, he saw Harley approaching.

"Why you sneakin' off, Dutchy?"

"Boss, I feels like a skunk at this picnic. I don't want to cause no trouble."

"Granville meant every word he said to Rather. Every word. He respects you and considers you his friend. If you walk out on him now, it'll be disrespectful. Is that what you want?"

"No! Of course not! But I don't want to cause no trouble. I was embarrassed and didn't know what else to do."

"How do you think Rather feels right now? He will never live this down. Right now, Granville wants you and me with him. He's got some of the biggest ranchers in the territory in there and he's invited us to join them because he trusts us with everything he has, including his life. Every one of those men knows it, too. You don't see no other cowpunchers in there do you? You think that's an accident? I'd call it an honor. Come on, let's go back"

Back on the porch, the conversation of the men was becoming more focused. "I gotta say I'm sick and tired of this outlawry! I damn near gotta sleep with my horses if I want to make sure they're around in the morning!" said Nelson Story. "I'm so damned mad I could bust!"

"Just who are these men and where do they come from?" asked Dave McHenry.

"They're the dregs of society in the States; former raiders of Quantrell's, thieves, thugs and bad men. They're a dangerous lot and most are slippery as a greased weasel," Granville said, "When the railroad came through, riverboat traffic was cut way back and most of them wood hawks working on the rivers was put out of work. Same with the buffalo hunters. With the buffalo all gone, many of them have turned to thieving. We're more than a hundred miles from the county seat and we got one deputy over at Maiden to cover this whole country. There's no way he can handle the job."

"Yes, and them range detectives we hired are all hat and no cattle," said Dave McHenry. "If they learn anything, it's always too late and too little. If things go on like this, I'll be broke in a few years."

"Well, it's gotta stop, and that's flat. Between Indians, wolves and these rustlers, I figure I lost close to 5% of my stock this past year. And as Sides' killin' shows, these sons-of-bitches are gettin' more brazen every day. Question is, what can we do about it? I'm shore tired of sitting around, wringing my hands and squawking like a bunch of old hens," added Reb Peters, another local rancher.

"You're right, Reb. I am tired of talkin' too! Our little protective associations ain't done a damned bit of good. What if we roll all the small cattlemen's associations into one operation that would cover the whole eastern territory like they have over in the west?" asked Nelson.

"That's a good idea. We might get everyone to sign on, seeing how we all got the same problems," added Peters. "We gotta do something, that's certain. I can't go on like this."

"You men know I support law and order first, last and always. Hell, I'm a territorial representative, but you're right," Granville said, "If anything's going to be done, it looks like it's up to us to do it. And I think Nelson's right about roping all the small associations together. It would give us some political muscle we haven't had before and allow us to share information. I think we need to get all the range detectives working together too, so everything they learn can be collected and looked at carefully. Our efforts won't be so scattered."

"That sounds like a good plan, but while we're at it, lets get them ranchers over Dakota way involved. They got the same problems we do and some of the same gangs are workin' over their spreads as well as ours," Pierre Wibaux said.

"You're right. These murderin' devils don't pay no attention to borders, so why should we?" asked Nelson Story.

"I know some of them Dakota men," said Granville. "I met that young Roosevelt not too long ago and I've met the Frenchman too. I'll make a trip and talk to them. It's in their interest to throw in with us."

Granville was referring to Theodore Roosevelt, a wealthy 25-year-old New Yorker who came to the region to seek relief from the twin sorrows of losing both his wife and his mother on the same day. In September of 1883 he squatted on the Maltese Cross ranch and later obtained legal ownership. Although he was unfamiliar with cattle operations, his force of personality, wealth and eastern connections made him a man to be reckoned with and a natural leader.

The Frenchman was Antoine-Marie-Vincent-Manca de Vallom-Brosa, the Marquis de Mores, a 26-year-old French aristocrat who'd come west in 1883 to make his fortune. He planned to ship dressed beef using NPRR refrigerator cars to retail markets and built a huge packing operation and new town where the Northern Pacific Rail Road (NPRR) crossed the Little Missouri River in western Dakota Territory to facilitate his plan. He also bought 45,000 acres of strategically placed land, which gave him effective control of 8,000,000 acres because his holdings prevented access to water. The new town he named Medora, after his wife, the former Medora Von Hoffmann, the daughter of wealthy New York City banker Louis A. Von Hoffmann, and though new to the territory, the Marquis immediately became a power in that region.

"Hold on a minute!" said Conrad Kohrs. "You men know where this is leading? Vigilantism!"

"And it's about damned time too!" James Fergus said. Although the white-haired rancher was 70 years old, he was still active and full of fire.

"That's all we got left. If we just talk about it but don't take it to its logical end, we'll be worse off with every day that passes. Are we prepared to take this next step?" Kohrs asked.

With the issue brought sharply into focus, all the men present, except Harley and Black Dutch, quickly and forcefully answered Kohrs' question in the affirmative. Because the two wranglers were with Granville, he vouched for them and they would ride whatever trail he determined.

When satisfied all were in agreement, Kohrs turned to face Granville and paused before speaking. "Looks like we're all in on this roundup, Gran. Now, I got a question for you. Were you involved with the Vigilante activities in Virginia City? I've heard whispers, but 'til now, it weren't any of my business. If we do this thing, I want to know for certain 'cause we're gonna need a leader and I say experience counts!"

All eyes turned to Granville. There'd been rumors over the years, but no one had ever confronted the man with them or questioned his involvement. Granville stood silent, as if making a difficult decision. Finally, he said, "Yes, I was a member of the Vigilante committee, although I am not particularly proud of everything we did. One man, Joe Slade, was hung for nothing more than disturbing the peace because we didn't have a jail to put him in. I'll never forget the look on his young wife's face when she found him hung. Molly didn't deserve that, nor did Joe. But we did wipe out the Plummer gang. We killed 22 of them once we started rounding them up. It took less than a month."

"Well, I'm relieved to have the truth of it at last," said Conrad. "What you did had to be done. I'd like to think each of us would've done the same. And, while that one fellow's case is regrettable, the overall result was good for the citizens, good for the town and good for the territory. I'll never repeat what you just said or speak of any actions we take regarding our current situation. I'll take whatever I know to my grave."

All the men in attendance quickly affirmed their thoughts in a similar fashion. Secrecy was to be a common feature of the newly formed Vigilante group, and nearly all of the men involved never revealed their activities or involvement. Granville was relieved. "Well, we hung 23 men, and all but the one I mentioned were members of Sheriff Henry Plummer's gang, the so-called 'Innocents.' We never found out exactly how many miners they waylaid and killed, but I'm certain it was hundreds."

"Hundreds? Jesus!" exclaimed Dave McHenry. "How'd the committee start?"

"We just got fed up with innocent men being killed. I had a blacksmith shop at the time, so I wasn't on the miner's court, but I joined the Vigilante committee. But, you men must know if we start this thing, you must be prepared to go all the way. Half measures won't do. And no one can breathe a word of our activities; if anyone does, we'll all hang for it. Our goal should be to drive these thieves from the territory. If that means we have to kill all of them, that's fine, but I think most of these men are cowards at heart, and once we start hanging them regular, those that's left will pull their freight," Granville said.

"Well," said Dave McHenry, "I've never been involved in anything like that Virginia City business, although I'd like to think I have the vinegar to do what's necessary. How were the subjects of those affairs were identified? How exactly did you proceed, once the decision was made to move on them?"

"We made a list. It was simple," replied Granville. "We'd suspected Plummer and we knew his deputies and the men they associated with. We caught Long John Franck and George Hilderman, both Plummer's men, after they killed a youngster named Nick Tiebald in front of their shack. His neck showed they'd dragged him with a rope before they finally shot him. When we confronted them, we found one of Tiebald's missing mules at the shack. George Ives was with them. We tried Ives first and after a trial that lasted several days, he was found guilty and hung. Hilderman was tried next and also found guilty. But because he was old and slow-witted, he was shown mercy and given ten days to clear the territory, which he did. Franck was set free also, because he testified against Ives. Working off our list, we started rounding up the road agents. Some of them revealed everything and named Sheriff Plummer as their ringleader.

We usually tried them in miner's court if they were close by. James Fergus was judge on that court. But we hung several where they were caught in Big Hole, Frenchtown and Hell Gate. As it turned out, our list was complete and accurate, and our efforts were completely successful. Except for the man I mentioned earlier, no one stretched rope that didn't deserve it."

"That's the way it happened," Fergus put in. "If those men hadn't acted, there's no telling how many more innocent men would have been waylaid and killed for their gold."

"If we suspected someone, but weren't completely convinced he deserved hangin', we warned him that he had 24 hours to pull his freight and drift. If we couldn't find 'em, we marked "3-7-77" with charcoal on their tent or shack as a warning. No body ever stuck around to see if we were bluffing. The Vigilance Committee remained in force for the next two or three years and if the law failed to do its duty, the committee got busy."

"What do those numbers mean?" asked Bob Shepard.

"To tell you the truth, I don't know. The miners came up with it somehow. Because most of them came from California, I think it has something to do with that, though I don't really know. Anyway, we put signs with them numbers on all the men that were hung and we used them as a warning to others. Once someone was warned, they drifted fast," Granville replied.

"Tell them about that kid with the two card sharps, Gran," said James Fergus. "I don't want anyone to think the Vigilances were just a bunch of cutthroats."

Granville chuckled, and then responded, "Three gamblers rode into town and set up operations in one of the saloons. The two older men had unusually good luck, often beating some placer miner out of his poke or winning his quitclaim deed. The youngest of the three, just a kid really, couldn't catch a good hand to save his soul. A couple weeks later, a man rode into town and identified the men as having stolen horses from him. Because the kid rode in with them, the committee decided to round all three of them up for trial. One of tinhorns resisted and tried to shoot it out, but was killed quick. The other two were tried before a miner's court, found guilty and were sentenced to hang. Well, the kid had a story to tell. He said he'd met the other two on the trail coming into town and fell in with them, not knowing them or their business. We asked the other one about it and he confirmed what the kid had said. Him, we hung. As to the kid, we gave him 6 hours to get out of town, but he said he was broke and hadn't the means to flee. Because he'd been found guilty, we were obliged to hang him anyway, but someone started a collection and we all chipped in. We scrapped up enough to buy him decent horse and saddle and put $25 gold in his poke. He was well clear of town before his time was up and we never heard of him again."

The small assembly of ranchers was silent for a bit, each man considering the story they had just heard. Finally, Pierre Wibaux asked how they should proceed.

"Well, we need to find out who the ringleaders are and where they hide out. To do that, we need to get the range detectives workin' together as a unit. Then we'll start a list of names and locations and keep adding to it as we learn more. Conrad? Why don't you look to that part of it? I'll talk to the Dakota men and Nelson can organize a meeting to consolidate all the cattlemen's associations. That's about all we can do until we see how things break. Are you all in this then?" asked Granville.

Each man affirmed his commitment to the operation and swore his silence would never be broken. If the matters at hand hadn't been so deadly, it would have looked comical, each man stepping forward to make his pledge, as though it were a Masonic Initiation. There was no laughter during or after the pledges however, and each man took his vow of silence seriously.

That these men were desperate enough to enter into Vigilante activities is an indication of the seriousness of the situation. The cattlemen of Montana Territory had $35,000,000 worth of property spread over 85,000 square miles of mostly uninhabited country. All appeals for increased law enforcement fell on deaf ears. The territorial government, which was controlled by wealthy mining interests from the western part of the territory, claimed to have no funds to support additional enforcement operations.

The U.S. Army had been appealed to, but their role was one of protecting settlers from the depredations of Indians. With most of the Indians bottled up on reserves, breakouts were the primary concern of the military. Just 6 years earlier, the Nez Perce had refused to relocate to a reserve in Oregon Territory, and had gone on a 9 month, 2000 mile long rampage through Idaho into Montana, down through Yellowstone Park and then north through Montana toward Canada.

Though pursued by overwhelming military force, the Nez Perce foiled their best efforts, terrorizing the citizenry as they fled north.

Poor communication, shoddy equipment, inexperienced troops, inferior leadership, lack of ammunition and political meddling hamstrung the military's efforts. Their dismal performance resulted in the military being soundly vilified in the regional press and held in contempt by the settlers, ranchers and townsfolk. After much suffering on all sides, the Nez Perce were finally brought to heel by Col. Nelson A. Miles, just 40 miles shy of the Canadian border, east of the Bear Paw Mountains in the winter of 1877. Several factors contributed to this success. First was the willingness of Army leadership to wage war and fight during the winter months, which was seldom or never done among the Indian tribes. Second was the overall better condition of the cavalry horses compared to Indian ponies or other range stock. The cavalry mounts were grain fed, whereas Indian and range horses were not. With the proper mixture of grain and grass feed, the cavalry horses had better speed and "more bottom." Finally, although the Indians fought bravely and gave better than they got, there were simply too many troops arrayed against them. They were near starvation and most of their horses used up and worthless at the end.

The Indians were being portrayed by the eastern press as a peace-loving friendly people who were being downtrodden by the Army and the "cattle barons." This resulted in the Army becoming overly sensitive to misinformed public opinion. Small bands of Indians frequently jumped the reserves and stole horses, slaughtered cattle and destroyed rancher's property when in the mood. If caught, the renegade bands were not punished, but were returned to their reserve under Army escort. Once there, the raiders were esteemed for their actions, thus encouraged toward further depredations. Worse, the stolen horses were seldom or never returned to the rightful owners. This infuriated the ranchers, particularly when they could prove ownership through known association brands. Consequently, the ranchers universally reviled the Army.

After the meeting broke up, James Fergus and his son Andrew, approached Granville. "Gran, I'm afraid I won't be able to ride along with you when things get organized," the rancher said, in a thick Scottish accent, "but my son, Andrew, insists that he be part of your show. Have you any problem with that?"

"None whatever. Andrew is more than welcome, once we figure out what has to be done."

"Good. I may be able to help in another way though. Once things get started, I'm going to start a campaign of letter writing to all the newspapers in the territory, expressing the need for and support of Vigilante action. I won't be namin' no names, of course, but I think my efforts may prove beneficial. You're going to need public opinion on your side if you are to succeed. At my age, that's about all I can offer," the old man said.

"I appreciate anything you can do, James. We're being picked apart here, and getting public opinion on our side would certainly help."

James Fergus left his native Scotland at the age of 20, going first to Canada and then to the United States where he hopped around frequently trying new vocations as he raised his family. His friendship with Granville began in the early 1860's when both men lived in the Virginia City and Bannack area during the wild and wooly gold rush days. Fergus was appointed judge to the miner's court and took his appointment seriously, handing down fair and reasoned decisions. Although he wasn't a Vigilante, he supported their work. Later he was elected a Territorial Representative, as was Granville, and the two men served together in the legislative body. Finally disgusted with his family situation and prospects, he followed Granville's lead and moved to the Judith Basin in 1880, where he built up a spread north of the DHS outfit. In his lifetime, James Fergus was a successful miner, rancher, businessman, scholar and politician. Later, in 1886, the eastern reaches of Meagher (pronounced Mar) County would be split off to form the 7,500 square mile Fergus County, which was named after him.

Φ

Granville Stuart, Nelson Story and Conrad Kohrs proceeded with their respective assignments. Granville and two of his wranglers, Keeps Eagle and Terry Beard, made the long trip to Medora. When they arrived, they quickly found the Marquis de Mores but learned that Roosevelt was presently back east and unavailable. Granville told Vallom-Brosa of the recent killing of Duncan Sides and of the ad hoc meeting of ranchers. He urged him to organize the ranchers in Dakota

Territory. The upcoming fall meeting of the Eastern Montana Stockgrowers Association was discussed, but Granville advised that the following spring, a territorial meeting would be held to address Montana stockmen's concerns, and that would be a good time to attend, if the Dakota ranchers could be organized and would send representatives.

Vallom-Brosa understood the value of the plan and quickly gave his assurance that he would do all that could be done along those lines. That night, Granville, Keeps Eagle and Terry ate supper at Vallom-Brosa's 26-room mansion, the Chateau de Mores, which sat perched on a bluff overlooking the Marquis' packing operation and his new town. When the two wranglers entered the chateau, they felt they had died and gone to heaven, never having seen such opulence or eaten such fare. Medora Vallom-Brosa, the beautiful Marquise, though wealthy and refined, treated the rough men as though they were visiting potentates. The couple had a French chef who was a master at his craft, and the men were given enough ammunition for many years worth of fireside yarns. The mansion, the Marquise, the 20 servants, the chandeliers, the paintings, the Turkish carpets, the food, the champagne, the empire the Marquis had built: it was enough to make a wrangler's head spin! For the first time, the men heard a real phonograph.

"Yep, while this machine was squeakin', we ate us some scar-gots! Never heard of 'em? Shoot, them's snails! Little curled up rascals that looked like they was sleepin'! No, damn it, we didn't eat no shells! They was coaxed out of 'em and then cooked proper. And we ate the legs off these spidery lookin' things called crabs that we dipped in butter after we skinned 'em! And we ate some taw-taw, that's raw beef with onions. I don't know how them people stand it ever' day!"

The Marquis took immediate action after Granville and his men departed. He organized a secret meeting two weeks later in a home 6 miles south of Medora on the Little Missouri River. In attendance was A.C. Huidekoper, Henry Boice, the Eaton brothers, the Wadsworth brothers and Theodore Roosevelt, all prominent ranchers from western Dakota Territory. Vallom-Brosa related what Granville had said and recommended they organize a Dakota cattlemen's organization along similar lines as that being formed in Montana. The men quickly agreed, since their interests and concerns were identical to those Montana ranchers.

Conrad Kohrs began contacting the various range detectives. At last, the men were given something they could sink their teeth into, and they went at it with a will, spending extra hours scouting, glassing and making their written reports. In Central Montana, rustling operations were centered south of the Missouri River between the Musselshell and the Judith Rivers. In Eastern Montana and Western Dakota, the area between the Little Missouri and the lower Yellowstone River was prime country for outlaw activities. As more information came in, the picture that emerged was shocking, reaching proportions never imagined.

The rustlers stole cattle and horses from northern Wyoming, southern Montana and Dakota Territories and drove them into remote areas, where they were safely hidden from discovery. There, the brands were reworked with running irons, wire or acid, so as to be impossible to identify by the true owner. When the brands had healed, the stock was driven to local settlements, remote rail sidings, out of the territory or into Canada, to be sold. When stock was disposed of in Canada, the outlaws would often steal Canadian stock and drive it south into Montana and Dakota where the process was repeated and the stock sold to unsuspecting buyers. Eventually, this pattern was brought to a halt by the efficient actions of the Royal Canadian Mounted Police.

For his part, Nelson Story quickly gained the interest of the various stockmen's protective associations and a meeting was scheduled to take place in Miles City late that fall. There, the Eastern Montana Stockgrowers Association was formed and Granville Stuart was elected President. Plans were made for a general meeting to be held the following spring in mid-April. Topics to be discussed would be Texas fever, over-grazing and rustling. The representatives were encouraged to carry these topics back to their members and be prepared to address them the following spring.

The cattle industry in Montana was booming during this period and cattle were pouring in from all around the west. Cattle of Shorthorn and Durham breeding were trailed in from Washington, Oregon and Idaho. These were dual purpose cattle, providing both milk and beef, and proved to be more docile and more easily managed than the rangy, wild Texas Longhorns. Hereford cattle were being shipped in by rail from Minnesota, Illinois and Iowa. Like the Texas Longhorns, these other types proved hardy enough to fend for themselves and survive on the open range. Although Texas Longhorns were the first stock brought in, they comprised less than 50% of the range stock during this time.

Another type of cattle operation brought stock to the open and bountiful ranges of Montana and Dakota. Cattle were driven in as yearlings from the south and allowed to mature or "double winter" on the rich prairie grasses. It was found that the Montana and Dakota grasses were superior, being more nutritious, producing faster and healthier growth. Cattle "topped off" in this fashion averaged a couple hundred pounds heavier than their southern cousins and for this reason; the influx of cattle seemed to be without end. In 1880, cattle operations were very limited, with fewer than 100,000 head in the entire territory. By the end of 1883, more than 600,000 head were grazing on the Montana ranges and more were arriving by the day.

English and Scottish interests, cartels and eastern corporations were quickly formed to capitalize on the remarkable moneymaking opportunity the open range presented. Return on investment was typically 25% per year! And yet, no controls existed. No brand inspectors existed. No stock inspectors existed. The situation was ripe for the spread of both cattle rustling and disease.

Southern herds carried with them a particularly pernicious disease the ranchers called Texas or splenic fever, that was ravaging southern herds and causing concern it would spread to Montana stock. Texas cattle were immune to the disease but spread it along the cattle trails as they passed. It was later found the disease was tick-bourn; passing from one animal to another after the infected tick fell to the ground to lay its eggs. After the eggs hatched in 20-28 days, the young ticks would climb up the legs of any passing animal, infect it, and repeat the cycle. Some ranchers in Colorado and Wyoming lost 50% of their herds as a result. This in turn led to quarantines by the different states and territories the herds passed through. As these measures were put in place, the trail drives were shifted further west. Ultimately, a total of 11 states and territories refused to allow southern trail drives to cross their borders without a one-year quarantine. This, along with other factors, brought the era of Texas cattle drives to an end.

Over-grazing of the range was also causing concern. Some feared the native grasses would be depleted to a point where they would no longer support the huge herds, leading to widespread starvation and death. The situation was exacerbated by the influx of huge flocks of sheep, which were also being driven in from the east. Overgrazing couldn't be proven conclusively, and any talk along these lines was often seen as alarmist. Yet everyone knew the resource was finite; there was, in fact, a limit to the amount of stock that could be grazed on the land. The problem was, no one knew what that limit was or was willing to curb their operations to save the range. In years to come, the warnings of these alarmists would prove to be prophetic.

Φ

The chief impediment to settlement of the American West was transportation. The earliest people in the remote wilderness moved in on foot or on horseback. Subsequent discoveries of gold brought a flood of miners into western Montana Territory, again on foot or horseback. As the population grew, stagecoach lines were developed connecting the mining camps with the outside world. As more people continued to move in and settle around the gold camps with farms, ranches and small businesses, the United States Army built forts to protect the settlers from Indian attack. These forts were often built near rivers where they could be supplied by water, and rivers became the highways of the west. Beginning in the 1860's, steam powered riverboats became the vehicles on these highways, moving people and materials upstream from Yankton, a town in extreme southeastern Dakota Territory opposite Kansas on the Missouri River. In 1873, the Northern Pacific railhead reached Bismarck, Dakota Territory, on the banks of the Missouri River, 613 river miles upstream from Yankton. While the financial crisis of 1873 and other factors halted construction on the NPRR for 4 long years, Bismarck became the jumping off point for entry into the western frontier. Because it stood on the banks of the Missouri River, Bismarck was also the point at which goods were transferred from rail to one of the many riverboats for shipment upstream to forts and various fledgling settlements.

Upstream from Bismarck, the U.S. Army built Ft. Stevenson, Dakota Territory (D.T.), Ft. Berthold, D.T., Ft. Buford, D.T., Ft. Peck, Montana Territory (M.T.) and Ft. Benton, M.T., the end of navigation, 620 river miles away. Near Ft. Buford, the Yellowstone River joined the Missouri River, and upstream on the Yellowstone were built Ft. Keogh, M.T., Ft. Alexander, M.T., Ft. Sarpy, M.T., Ft. Pease, M.T. and Terry's Landing, M.T., the end of navigation, off the Yellowstone on the Big Horn River near the junction of the Little Big Horn River, 306 river miles upstream from Ft. Buford.

Riverboats were often contracted by the military for transportation of troops, horses and supplies. In 1876, during the U.S. Army's summer campaign against the Sioux, Captain Grant Marsh commanded the riverboat "Far West" carrying 200 tons of military supplies upstream from Ft. Lincoln, D.T., the fort Col. George Armstrong Custer departed on his journey into history and nearly opposite Bismarck, to Ft. Buford, D.T.. There, the craft served as a floating headquarters for General Terry while the campaign was under way. When Custer's command was wiped out by the Sioux on the Little Big Horn River, the "Far West" transported the wounded and dying soldiers 710 river miles downstream to Bismarck in 54 hours, bringing word of Custer's stunning defeat and thus gaining a small place in history.

The era of the riverboat on the Missouri River and its tributaries spanned just 30 years. The first trip upstream to Ft. Benton took place in July of 1860. The last trip was made downstream in the summer of 1890. During this time, more than 50 riverboats serviced the Dakota and Montana Territories. The "Far West" was typical of vessels of the time. Built in Pittsburgh in 1870, the craft had three boilers, a 33-foot beam and was 190 feet long overall. Empty, it had a 20-inch draft; fully loaded to its 400-ton capacity, its draft was 54 inches. As originally designed, it had sleeping accommodations for 30 passengers in addition to bulk cargo, and on occasion, carried horses, cattle and sheep. The Far West sank in 1883 after hitting a snag just north of St. Louis on the Mississippi River.

The water level of the nautical highways was critical. Abundant winter snows would yield heavy snowmelt in the spring and summer, making navigation of the rivers easier. The Missouri River was usually navigable as far as Cow Island, M.T. and often further. Except when winter ice forced the riverboats to suspend operations, cargo was taken upstream to Cow Island and freighted overland from there. The Yellowstone River was navigable for about two months each year during the "June rise" when melt waters would fill the channels and allow river traffic.

Rivers are dynamic, not static. Submerged sandbars shift continually in the current and channels are rerouted, often with no visible sign of change on the water's surface. Riverboat pilots had to contend with the changing conditions as best they could. Grounding was common, and riverboats used various methods of freeing themselves and continuing on their journey. If at all possible, the riverboat captain would reverse the engines and back off the sand bar and then hunt for the deeper water of the new channel. When the boat was hard aground, sometimes all the passengers and cargo were put ashore to lighten the load so the craft could slip over the bar. If this failed, the vessels would use their boom cranes, normally used for loading and unloading cargo, as "legs" to walk the boat forward. On each side of the boat, the crane booms were lowered into the water and driven into the river bottom. Then each crane was swung to the rear. The paddlewheel was then reversed, forcing more water up under the hull, thereby raising the boat over the obstruction as the cranes pushed the boat forward. In this manner, the boat could slowly walk itself forward a few feet at a time, grasshopper fashion. It was a slow and tedious process, but there was no recourse. All these factors sometimes made riverboat travel tedious; one man said it took him 75 days to travel upstream from St. Joseph, Missouri to Ft. Benton, M.T..

Not only could riverboat travel be inconvenient, because of frequent groundings, high winds or other delays, it could also be dangerous. The boilers that powered the vessels were potential bombs, filled with high-pressure steam. Despite the passage of The Steamboat Inspection Act of 1852, which set standards for both equipment and personnel, boiler explosions still occurred and when they did, the results were often catastrophic, killing passengers and crew with super-heated steam, scalding water, flying debris and drowning when the boat sank. Another menace to riverboats was snags. These were submerged waterlogged trees that drifted downstream and became lodged in the silt that made up the river bottom. Because they didn't float, they couldn't be seen. When a boat struck a snag, often a hole was punched in the hull and the boat would begin taking on water. If possible, the boat captain would quickly back the boat off the snag and ground the craft on the nearest shore to prevent sinking. There, repairs could be made to the hull and after they were completed, the boat would be walked off to continue service. This was not always possible though, and often the boats sank where they were snagged with loss of life, cargo and equipment. Worse, the sunken boat itself would become a hazard to navigation for other riverboats.

If all went well, riverboat travel was an enjoyable mode of transportation. Traveling against the swift current as it struggled upstream, the riverboat sometimes offered unprecedented views of the land at a stately 4 knots per hour. Frequent stops were made to "wood up" and passengers often debarked briefly to shoot game or explore along the river's edge while wood was being loaded aboard. Large steamers, such as the Far West, burned 50-75 cords every 24 hours, so stops were frequent.

While the steamers offered some degree of comfort, not to mention better food, going upstream, they were generally slower than the stage lines, which networked the territory. Stagecoach travel was difficult in the extreme however. The dust, the jolting ride over rutted and uneven roads, the mean conditions of the frequent stage stops and the poor quality of food led many a passenger to regret having ever set foot on a stage. Granville Stuart wrote some particularly scathing reports of the difficulties and hardships of stage travel, saying it would try the patience of Job. Some stagecoach travel was nearly always necessary however. Stage lines serviced the major ports of call for the riverboats and from there, passengers moved into the interior via Concord coach or wagon.

The coming of the railroad supplanted riverboat service near the tracks, but vast areas were not convenient to rail service, and still relied upon riverboats for supply and transportation. The railroad's chief impact was that of bringing countless settlers and immigrants into the territories, many more than previously seen, and the railroad was chiefly responsible for the ultimate settlement and civilizing of the American West.

Chapter Two – Conspirators

"Order! Order! Will you men take your seats?" Granville shouted, struggling to bring order to the contentious meeting. Every member seemed to be on his feet, shouting, arms waving, tempers flaring. The third day of the Eastern Montana Stockgrowers Association Convention threatened to erupt into violence as emotions ran high; each man seemed to have a grievance and was arguing his point with gusto. On the two previous days, the members had discussed overstocking of the range and Texas fever. The final day was devoted to the most contentious issue: rustling.

"Order, goddamnit!" Granville shouted, futilely pounding on the table before him with a bung-starter. As President of the association, it fell to him to keep the meeting moving forward in an orderly fashion, yet bedlam reigned unabated. Finally, his patience at an end, he pulled his Colt and fired three shots into the air. "Will you men sit down and shut up? This ain't a meetin'; it's a damned stampede!"

The rowdy ranchers began to settle down and although it took another five minutes until order was fully restored, Granville was relieved. The meeting had staggered between orderly efficiency and uncontrolled chaos, like a drunken cowboy on a Saturday night, taking a random path down a sidewalk. The President was kept in suspense as to which direction the meeting would turn next.

"That's better! If anyone has anything to say, please stand and be recognized by the chair. That's me, I'm the chair," Granville shouted, scowling at the entire group.

Of the 429 men present, at least a quarter jumped to their feet and shouted to be recognized. Another pistol shot quieted the crowd again and Granville shouted, "Have all you men gone loco? I'll get to everyone in turn. If you aren't recognized yet, sit down! I'll get to you when I can. Now, the chair recognizes Mr. Theodore Roosevelt, representing the Dakota ranchers. Sir, you have the floor."

Roosevelt stood and paused before speaking, making sure his words would be heard. "Mr. President, I'm confused. Initially you spoke most powerfully and persuasively, saying we should take action against the brigands and thieves who're intent on stealing our cattle and spreading lawlessness throughout the territories. Now, you reverse yourself and argue for restraint. It's as though a different person were speaking entirely. I, sir, do not understand you and nor do I understand your backsliding. Sir, you astound me!"

A low murmur rolled through the crowd, as some members voiced their agreement with Roosevelt's sentiments. When things quieted down under the President's stare, he responded to Roosevelt's concerns. "It wasn't my intention to confuse anyone, but to bring into focus both sides of the issue before us. Be assured we will act as the majority sees fit, whatever the outcome. The various reasons for taking action have been expressed ably by others as well as myself; now I will explain my reasons for letting the law handle our rustling problem.

"First, if we take the law into our own hands, it will be illegal and there'll be consequences. The rustlers will have the law on their side.

"Second, these outlaws are hardened criminals and dead shots. My fear is our members will become the victims, rather than the other way 'round. I'd hate to see men crippled or killed because we acted hastily here today.

"Third, these men have heavily built hideouts, fortresses really, and are known to be armed with the latest weaponry. I doubt we can dig them out without great loss of life. These are badgers that shoot back.

"Fourth, the outlaws know the country better than anyone. They've made the Breaks and the Badlands their homes and are able to easily escape any force we send against them. I can't see the percentage in chasing someone around who knows the country better than I do.

"Those are my reasons, sir. If I appeared to 'backtrack' it was only so a full airing of the situation could be made. Now sir, do you have anything further to add?" Granville asked. He'd known Roosevelt since he came to the territory and they had talked privately before this public meeting. When speaking privately to Roosevelt, he spoke passionately of the need for action against the rustlers. This was the method Granville used for determining the easterner's thoughts on rustling. It wasn't surprising that Roosevelt felt he were talking to a different person when Granville now urged restraint.

"I do not, Mr. President, although I can only repeat that I am deeply disappointed," said Roosevelt, before sitting down.

"Does anyone else have something they want to say?" Only about 20 men stood and Granville was quietly pleased the members were more restrained and disciplined. "The chair recognizes Buck Albrecht from White Sulphur Springs," said Granville, recognizing someone he knew would speak for restraint.

Albrecht stood and underscored the President's sentiments, painting a picture of loss, ruination and great suffering. When finished, he sat down; satisfied he had made his points and yielded the floor.

"The chair recognizes Mr. Vallom-Brosa, the Marquis de Mores, another Dakota man. Sir, you have the floor," Granville said.

The Marquis stood and addressed the assembly. "I too, feel as Mr. Roosevelt does. We must take strong action and bring these plunderers before the law to answer for their crimes. They must be held to account. There is such a thing as the rule of law and we must endeavor to bring these ruffians under its influence. It's been shown that the law will not do its duty. Therefore it falls to us to capture these brutes and drag them, if we must, before the proper authorities. That is all I have to say," Vallom-Brosa said and took his seat. Like Roosevelt, Granville had spoken to the Marquis as well, for the same reasons. Both men seemed sympathetic to strong measures, but Granville doubted the ultimate resolve of either man.

"The chair recognizes...."

Granville was careful to appear to balance both sides of the rustling issue, favoring no particular interest. But, as a result of secret meetings over the past several months, he was able to recognize members he knew would appear to support lawful action. However, appearances do not always reflect the truth of a situation.

The meeting dragged on for two more hours in this fashion. The membership was divided among its members as to how to deal with the rustling situation; the younger members urging the Association take some unspecified action immediately. Whether this action was to round up the rustlers and bring them to justice, or something more permanent, as others hinted, was never made clear or brought to a vote. Some few suggested a "rustlers war." Conrad Kohrs, Nelson Story, Pierre Wibaux and the older members, many of them fellow conspirators in Granville's plan, pressed for restraint. When the issue was finally brought to a vote, restraint carried the day.

Granville rapped the table again and addressed the membership. "Gentlemen, those members arguing for improved law enforcement have carried the vote: 244 for to 185 against. The motion is carried and our secretary, Travis Ainsley, will contact the territorial authorities regarding improved law enforcement. If there is nothing further, I suggest we adjourn for the big doin's tonight. This meeting is adjourned."

Before Granville could exit, one of the young ranchers jumped to his feet and shouted, "Mr. President! How many of your daughters will be attending the dance tonight?"

Amid much laughter, Granville returned to the table at the front of the room and said, "Three, but you look like you're stompin' snakes when you dance, so I'm not worried!" More laughter followed and Granville started moving toward the exit, his official business concluded.

The Eastern Montana Stockgrowers Association meeting was held in Miles City, in eastern Montana Territory, at Russell's Roller Skating Rink, the only venue in the town large enough to hold all the attendees. Granville didn't like to be away from the ranch while the spring calf roundup was underway, but it couldn't be helped. The success of the Association was important and necessary to support all ranching operations, address common concerns and provide the ranchers with a united voice in the territory. As a territorial representative, Granville had struggled to push legislation he felt critical to cattlemen's interests, but his efforts had been thwarted at every turn by wealthy and powerful mining interests from the western part of the territory. Granville and others felt brand inspectors were needed to reduce rustling activities and a Livestock Commission was needed to reduce the threat of disease. It was hoped the Association would provide the political power to get these and other reforms implemented.

At the back of the hall, several rough looking characters made a speedy exit at the conclusion of the meeting. Gus Adams, the chief range detective of a secret force that Granville Stuart and other conspirators had created, noted these hasty departures. Adams slowly made his way toward Granville, who had been corralled by a couple talkative friends. Finally, he was able to get near enough to catch Granville's eye. The detective gave a quick nod. Granville appeared not to notice but made a slight nod in response, then continued to meet with people as the huge crowd dispersed.

The meeting had gone exactly as Granville and his fellow conspirators had hoped. They were fairly certain spies would attend the public meeting and consequently stage-managed the entire event, and while it looked like the call for action might actually pass, the conspirators were confident they could sidetrack any serious call for a "rustler's war." The spies could be depended upon to report to their leaders that no action was to be taken and the membership was in confusion. This was exactly the message the conspirators wanted delivered. The outlaws would be lulled into a false sense of security and would feel confident in continuing their depredations. By this public action, the association had distanced itself from what was to follow. It was a masterful exercise in misdirection and was typical of Granville's methods.

When Granville and his brother James had first come to the territory in 1858, they and another man, Sam Hauser, had built a rough cabin in preparation for the upcoming winter. One winter day, James and Sam returned to find Granville sitting before a fresh stack of pancakes, studying a dead mouse on his fork, dripping of molasses. On the table, stood the gallon jar of molasses, the only supply the men had. It appeared the mouse had fallen into the jar and drowned and Granville had just fished it out. The two men said nothing but refused to eat any molasses after that, although Granville had no qualms and ate the molasses with gusto. As spring broke and the molasses were finally finished, Granville asked his two partners why they'd lost their taste for the sweet brown stuff. Both said the thought of a mouse drowning and dying in the molasses was too much for their stomachs. "Oh, that mouse didn't drown," Granville replied, "I found him dead and covered him with molasses just to see what you'd do."

After the general meeting was concluded and the members were going about their various affairs, a secret executive session was held behind closed doors, unknown to everyone except those in attendance. Here, Granville Stuart, Conrad Kohrs, Nelson Story, James Fergus, Bob Ford, Thomas Bryan and other conspirators met to discuss their secret plans. Gus Adams was the only outsider in attendance. He'd had been hired by the conspirators to coordinate the range detective's activities.

During this meeting, Gus reported that the spies had gotten an earful and left immediately after the convention was concluded. Satisfied the first step of their plans had been successful, conspirators proceeded to divide the region from central Montana to western Dakota into three areas of operation. Each would have its own "executive" who would organize and make the raids within his own area. Granville was appointed to head the Ft. Maginnis "executive committee," while another man was responsible for the Tongue River area and a third put in charge of the Little Missouri River area.

Ultimately, the other two "executives" made no moves against the outlaws in their respective areas, often being conveniently out of town or otherwise engaged when the need for action presented itself. The breech left by these two recalcitrants was one Granville felt obligated to fill if outlaws were to be driven from the territory and not simply inconvenienced and shifted elsewhere temporarily.

Φ

Miles City was founded at the mouth of the Tongue River, where it joins the Yellowstone River. In 1875, this was the wintering ground of the Oglala and Cheyenne under Crazy Horse, the Hunkpapas under Sitting Bull and the Minneconjous under Lame Deer. In August of 1876, Ft. Keogh was laid out at this location for the protection of the region and after the defeat of Crazy Horse in January of 1877 at Wolf Mountain, the area was free of heavy Indian attack. Ft. Keogh was an open fort, meaning it had no stockade walls surrounding it. Before the fort was complete, a tent camp of merchants popped up within its bounds to service the soldier's needs. These hustlers, storekeepers, saloon people and prostitutes adversely affected the military order and discipline and drunkenness was common among the men. Finally, Col. Nelson A. Miles, the exasperated post commander, ordered all civilians off military property and the merchants moved 2 miles east on the opposite side of the Tongue River. A tent city was up and running full bore within a day. The new settlement was subsequently named in honor of the fort commander, the man who had thrown them off the post.

The tents were soon replaced by rough shacks and log cabins. These in turn were replaced by wood framed and brick structures as fires periodically claimed portions of the growing town, and buildings were replaced. Called the "Dodge City of the North," Miles City was wide open, with a crude stockade jail (no roof), and a "saloon" sheriff who wasn't overly officious. He tended to let smaller matters sort themselves out, and this was the way the town seemed to want it. Miles City had always been a rough town, initially being populated by soldiers and buffalo hunters. The influx of ranchers and cowpunchers began in 1880, predating the arrival of the railroad by a year.

The Northern Pacific Rail Road, with its grading, bridging and track gangs of 2,000-3,000 men, along with camp followers, was largely responsible for a new surge in lawlessness, bringing with it a rough element of freebooters, cheats, thieves, gamblers, whores, pimps and badmen as the construction passed through the town. The influx of this new rough crowd prompted the Yellowstone Journal, in September of 1881, to warn all *"wicked and dissolute characters"* of possible Vigilante action and of the significance of 3-7-77. Rail service also meant the town was no longer dependant upon the vagaries of the shallow draft riverboats built for service on the Yellowstone River. Prior to the arrival of the railroad, goods that couldn't be shipped via steamboat were freighted in by jerk-line men and their teams of horses, mule skinners with their mule teams or bull-whackers with their teams of oxen pulling heavy freight wagons, often in tandem, which were assembled into "trains" of 10-40 wagons each. For example, four heavily laden freight wagons could be linked one behind the other and drawn by 12 stout draft horses, thus accounting for four wagons in the makeup of the train. Miles City merchants sometimes waited up to 9 months for orders to arrive from distant eastern cities.

The railroad also brought honest hard-working citizens and merchants and over the next couple years, the rough element and the honest citizenry struggled for control of the rugged frontier town. It took several Vigilante hangings to get the attention of the lawless element, but the honest citizens finally wrested control of the town away from the rough crowd and began a slow but steady march toward civilization.

The arrival of the railroad also spelled the end for several ways of life. An upsurge of eastern hunters came west on the train and within a very short time the buffalo were wiped out, leaving the hunters in search of other ways to make a living. The railroad also spelled the doom of the numerous steamboats that plied certain rivers in the west.

When riverboat service was cut back, the wood hawks that serviced them were forced to find other income sources. One method of earning income was as bone pickers; people who collected and sold buffalo bones to companies back east for use as fertilizer. Many tens of thousands of tons of buffalo bones littered the prairies following their near extinction. Bone pickers would drive wagons out onto the prairie and collect the bones of the dead animals, which they then sold for $7 per ton. Other displaced men became wolfers, hunting down, poisoning or trapping the abundant gray wolves that preyed on the cattle and sheep. Ranchers would pay $5 per wolf killed and the wolfers could sell the pelts collected at certain times of the year.

In the spring of 1884, the bustling town of Miles City boasted a population of nearly 3,000 citizens, with dozens of saloons, 5 churches, 3 dance halls, 2 banks, 2 hotels, 1 brewery, 2 billiard halls, a roller skating rink, a school, a volunteer fire department, a newspaper with a steam driven printing press, a post office, a photographers studio, a sawmill, hay and coal scales, an itinerant doctor, stockyards, a Northern Pacific Rail Road Express office and train depot plus a variety of shops including general store, druggist, barber shops, stables and saddle shops, for which the town would become noted.

The merchants offered new potatoes, rice, cabbages, squash and melons in season, coffee, tea, dried apples, dried and canned peaches, sugar, molasses, honey, flour, bacon, butter, eggs, fresh fish, sugar cured smoked ham, mutton, beef, venison, antelope, buffalo, sugar, onions, beans, salt, soap, coal oil, beer, whiskey, tobacco, soda pop, ice, lard, oats, corn, bricks, lumber, firewood, coal, shingles, white lead, nails, strap iron, hand tools, pistols, rifles, gunpowder, lead, lead molds, ammunition, gloves, mittens, boots, wool socks, cotton socks, insulated pants, shirts, jackets, coats, long underwear, dresses, petticoats, hats, bonnets, parasols, combs, brushes, fabric, thread, sewing machines, furniture, oil lamps, clocks, watches, cook stoves, wagons, horses, cattle, mules, barbed wire, farm equipment, real estate and all the various items necessary for taming and civilizing what was still wilderness.

For the Eastern Montana Stockgrowers Association meeting, the town rolled out the red carpet for the three-day-long event, decorating the town with colorful banners, signs and buntings. The opening day of the convention was kicked off with a parade down main street, featuring a brass marching band from the Fifth Infantry at Fort Keogh, carriages containing Granville and the leadership of the Association followed by a wild cavalcade of cowboys on horseback and finally about 150 cowboys marching four abreast in boiled white shirts. The streets were full of rowdy cowboys feeling their oats, racing through town and firing their pistols into the air. The social high point of the convention was the Stockgrowers Association Ball, to be held the evening of the third day at the Inter Ocean Hotel. This was a huge establishment built in 1882 and featured 110 heated rooms, a 40' x 70' dining room, a billiard room and a barbershop.

Granville brought his wife and three daughters with him to Miles City, so they could enjoy the festivities, and the ladies were humming with anticipation. The dance promised to be a gala affair and the social event of the year. Ranchers and their families seldom got into town because the ranches were so remote and the towns few in number. Because the dance was the largest ever held in Miles City; the brakes were thrown off and everyone went at it full bore. The women had been preparing for months, making or buying new dresses in brilliant colors and of the latest fashion. An air of excitement swept through the rugged frontier town.

Φ

In the Grand Central Hotel bar, Granville met with Conrad Kohrs, Nelson Story and Gus Adams for a quick drink, and then went to his rooms in search of the ladies. Anyone who had rooms was lucky; hundreds of people were forced to sleep in stables, alleys or under the stars down by the river in the cottonwood groves. As he entered one of his rooms, there was a flurry of activity, as the ladies primped and preened, helping each other with ribbons, buttons, laces and bows. "I must be in the wrong room," Granville said, smiling as he looked at the four lovely ladies, Awbonnie, Katie, Mary and Lizzie. "A man in the presence of such beauty must surely have gone astray!"

"Oh Gran, please hurry and change. We're meeting Dave and Linda McHenry for supper, and Katie's anxious to see Jimmy," Awbonnie said.

"Jimmy? Jimmy Van Horn?" exclaimed Granville, smiling. "What's one of my cow pokes doin' here at this shindig?"

39

"Oh papa, don't tease! You know you said Jimmy could come," Katie chided.

"Oh, I guess I did. But what of it? You see that bobcat every day around the ranch," Granville said, playing ignorant. Jimmy had been sweet on Katie for some time, though Katie had many suitors. Just how she felt about Jimmy wasn't known. Katie was a beautiful young lady and deserved the fulfillment that Granville knew only love and marriage could bring to his daughter's life. She had her mother's small frame and lovely features, and was quite stunning, but to Granville, her best quality was her pleasant disposition, just like her mother. When asked why he'd married an Indian girl, Granville always said if he'd married a white woman, they'd always be fighting. He wasn't kidding. He felt white women were more trouble than they were worth; offering more complaint than cooperation, more posturing than support. He felt blessed that he'd married Awbonnie. They'd been married more than 20 years and though mixed marriages were scorned by some, particularly white newcomers, Granville was determined to fulfill his obligations as he found them. The couple braved many hardships over the years, yet Awbonnie remained at his side.

Mary, his next youngest daughter, had an equally pleasant disposition and quality of character. Deep down, she was spring steel. Once, when quite young, she was riding in the back of a freight wagon Granville was driving. Traveling too fast around a sharp bend, the wagon hit a chuckhole and bounced hard, throwing her out. She hit the ground in a tumbling cloud of dust and skinned limbs, but was on her feet in a flash, chasing after the wagon, mad as a hornet! She didn't consider her bloody scrapes for a second, and while most little girls would have been bawling like a sick calf, Mary only wanted to catch the wagon and her reckless father so she wouldn't be left behind.

Lizzie, the youngest, was only 14, caught somewhere between being a child and a woman. She'd insisted on attending the dance with her older sisters and neither parent wanted her to be left out. This was her first big affair, and she went through the same preparations as her older sisters, showing the same level of excitement and keen interest as the other women attending the dance.

Granville quickly cleaned up and changed clothes. In his new black suit, polished boots and new Stetson, the 49-year-old rancher still cut a trim and handsome figure. The ladies were absolutely beautiful in their gay finery of satins and crinolines, rustling and swishing with every movement. As the party entered the dining room, Granville felt a rush of pride as all the diners turned and admired his entourage. The Stuarts quickly settled in with the McHenry family, who were already seated, and exchanged the requisite pleasantries, as though they hadn't seen one another in weeks, although it had been just hours. As the ladies chatted amiably, complimenting one another on their attire and such, Granville and Dave entered into their own conversation.

"We were successful, Gran?" asked McHenry. "The meeting went according to expectations then?"

Granville casually looked around to see who was near and might be listening. "Yes," he replied, "the meeting was a good one, I think. I was relieved that the young hot-heads were able to see reason and let the law do its job."

"Well, you know these young fellars. Full of pis...err feelin' their oats," McHenry said, forgetting himself briefly.

Just then, the waiter arrived and all took their orders. The arrival of the railroad put an end to dull range fare, and many restaurants had extensive menus including fresh vegetables, fruit and delicacies such as fresh oysters at $.50 per dozen in season. After the food was served, the men dug in with a will. The ladies, for their part, ate like birds. When the meal was finally concluded, Granville said the words the ladies had been waiting anxiously to hear, "Well ladies, shall we go to the dance?" In a swirl of color and hiss of fabric, the group swept out of the restaurant and set a course for the Inter Ocean Hotel, 4 blocks away, where the dance was to be held. It was a fine night for a walk.

"Check you guns, gentlemen. Please check your guns," the two ladies at the entrance table said. Granville reluctantly complied, feeling naked without his constant companion. He was somewhat relieved to see many others had done the same before him. After he and Dave checked their Colts, they followed the ladies into the hall. The interior had been decorated with colorful ribbon streamers and the light of many colored lanterns shimmered and sparkled. Fresh sawdust had been sprinkled liberally about the floor to aid the dancers and even the brass spittoons had been cleaned and polished! Katie, Mary and Lizzie were equally thrilled with the festive décor, and along with their mother, quickly found the ladies from the decorating committee to express their wonder and pay their compliments. As more people entered the hall, the ladies in their most colorful costume and the men duded up, the festive atmosphere blossomed.

Soon the band began to play; a collection of fiddles, banjo, guitars and piano jumped into their first number and the hop began in earnest, the musicians quickly getting a strangle hold on the crowd. The four women returned to Granville, to stand with him and watch the first dancers take to the floor and practice dance steps nearly forgotten. Laughter seemed to be universal and there were smiles at every turn.

Suddenly, Katie spotted Jimmy entering the hall with his friends. She was surprised. He wore a new blue suit with a boiled white shirt and black string tie, fancy gray and blue boots and a new gray Stetson. When Jimmy saw Katie, he was equally taken aback. Katie wore a blue and black striped satin dress with a gathered bodice and scoop neckline. The beautiful dress was set off by ribbons of the same colors in her hair, which was pulled up on top of her head. She was beautiful! Jimmy's heart skipped a beat when he saw her, and as a bee is drawn to the sweetest flower, Jimmy quickly made his way across the hall, wearing a huge grin whose corners threatened to meet at the back of his head.

Jimmy was just 24 years old and already one of the best hands on the DHS ranch. A protégé of Harley Denny, he was respected by Granville and the other hands, very fast with his guns and fists. Granville called him a bobcat and that wasn't far from the truth. His lightening reflexes had saved him in many a tight scrape. Originally from Kansas, he'd been on his own since he was 12 years old, making his way in a very tough and dangerous world. Under Harley's guidance, he lost the chip on his shoulder and the need to constantly prove himself tougher than the young roosters around him. He was becoming more steady by the day under Harley's influence.

"Hello, Mr. and Mrs. Stuart," he said, "Hello Katie. My, you look beautiful tonight! You must be the purtiest gal in the territory!"

"Hello Jimmy," Granville said, somewhat formally, pulling the kid back from his reverie. "What a surprise to see you here!"

Awbonnie elbowed Gran in the side and said, "Hello Jimmy, don't pay any attention to Gran. He thinks it's funny to make young men squirm."

"No ma'am, err yes ma'am," the young wrangler replied, stuttering nervously, then turning to give Katie his complete attention.

Katie was laughing as she looked on, her eyes sparkling like diamonds. "You look very handsome tonight, Jimmy."

Jimmy was embarrassed, but secretly pleased Katie approved of his expensive attire. The rig had cost him two months wages but he knew he must make a serious effort if he were to win her heart. "Do you want to dance, Katie? I mean if it's okay with your folks?" he said, asking permission to dance with their daughter without actually asking.

Granville and Awbonnie both laughed. "You youngsters go show 'em how it's done and enjoy yourselves," Granville said. As the two young people headed for the dance floor, Awbonnie said, "I have never seen Katie so happy! And Jimmy is so handsome! If I hadn't seen it, I wouldn't believe it."

"That boy cleans up pretty good, alright. I was afraid Jimmy's face would split in half, with that grin of his," Granville said.

"Gran, do you think Jimmy's a good man? Could he make Katie a good husband?"

"Well, he's a hard worker and he ain't got any quit in him. Harley likes him an awful lot too. Being an orphan, he's had a rough life, but I think he's a good man," Granville replied. "I'm sure he would do his best, but I don't know how Katie feels about him."

As the evening progressed, the hall came alive. The bright colors, the swirling movement; the effect was hypnotic. The band worked the crowd like a pump handle, taking them through slow sentimental ballads and waltzes into fast paced square dances and reels, and back again, cycle after cycle. Those men with a lady on their arm were a fortunate minority; women were in short supply and every woman a treasure and shown every courtesy. Jimmy felt ten feet tall with Katie on his arm. Finally the band took a well-deserved break. Jimmy offered to get Katie a cup of punch but she declined; she looked as fresh as the moment she'd entered the hall while Jimmy was blowing and lathered up, having put his all into every dance. What the young man lacked in skill, he more than made up with enthusiasm.

"I think I better step outside and get some fresh air. Do you want to go outside or will you be alright here?" he asked.

"I'll be fine right here. Take your time, Jimmy," Katie replied with a smile, looking up at him. Watching him walk over to his friends, and then follow them outside, she wondered what her feelings for him were. She was quite sought after, and never lacked for the attentions of young men in the area. For the various social events in the area, young men often asked her for a date many months in advance. Being popular was so confusing! She walked slowly toward the refreshment table in a daze, thinking of nothing but the future and all the possibilities it held. Suddenly, a man stood in front of her, blocking her path. She turned to walk around him, but he stepped in front of her again and wouldn't let her pass.

"How 'bout a dance, sweetie?" asked the cowboy in a drunken slur, "Ain't I good enough to dance with?" His tone was insolent and Katie sensed he wasn't as drunk as he appeared, as if he were play-acting.

"There's no music," Katie said, "and I'm with someone else." Again, she tried to walk around him but he suddenly spun her around and pushed her hard into the wall behind her. The man gave an ugly smile and moved in on her.

"You breeds shouldn't act so damned uppity," he said, reaching out with both arms to trap her against the wall.

Quick as a cat, Katie bent low, ducking under an arm before he could press his advantage. As she dipped past him, she deftly grabbed a spittoon from the floor. Straightening up, she whirled around; the spittoon in her right hand, her arm fully extended. The full force of the movement caught the side of the man's head. Whack! He dropped as if pole-axed, unconscious, unmoving, and uncaring. She glanced around, but no one had seen the blow in the darkened area of the hall. She bent down and set the spittoon back on the floor, then leaned over the man. She whispered, "Be happy I'm not my mother. She'd do more than tap you with a brass pot." Just then Jimmy returned to find her hovering over the sprawling stranger.

"What happened?" Jimmy asked, bending down next to Katie.

"I don't know," Katie replied. "Maybe he had too much to drink."

Jimmy looked closely at the man. "He didn't get that knot on his head drinking. What happened?"

Katie stood up and Jimmy followed. "He got a little frisky and I had to cool him down," she said. "Do you know who he is? I've never seen him before."

"Frisky? Cool him down? What happened Katie?" Jimmy asked, getting angry as he considered different possibilities.

"Jimmy, do you trust me? He was drunk and wanted to dance. I said I was with someone. He insisted, so I hit him with that spittoon," she said, nodding at the weapon. "I'm not hurt and no harm's been done, other than that lump on his head. Now, come on. We're wasting the evening." She took Jimmy's hand and started leading him towards the dance floor just as the band got wound up again.

"How could he dance? There weren't no music," Jimmy said, not willing to accept her illogical story.

"That's exactly what I said to him! Come on cowboy, I'm not wastin' the best dance of the year on some drunk I've never seen before."

Though still not mollified, Jimmy put up no protest. He *did* trust her, and whatever had happened couldn't have been too serious because she was unhurt and seemed in good spirits. Inwardly, Katie was shaken, remembering the man's tone and the look in his eyes, but was determined to not let on. Her only fear was that Jimmy would play the cock rooster and challenge the man to fight, or worse. She was determined to avoid that at all costs, so she screwed up her courage, reined in her raging emotions, and forced herself to act natural.

The band started in again, but before they started dancing, Katie said she needed to get some fresh air.

"I'll go with you," Jimmy said, feeling on edge and protective.

"No, I'll go find my mom and we'll go out together. You find your friends until I come back in. I won't be long," she said, and then went in search of her mother. Jimmy watched her walk away, still torn between the story Katie had told him and the puzzle of the prostrate man at the side of the hall, but he had no choice; if he trusted Katie, he would have to ignore the man and leave him lay. Reluctantly, he went in search of his friends.

Katie found her mother talking with some other women. "Where's papa?" she asked. Her mother pointed him out, talking with several ranchers, and she quickly walked to his side and put her hand on his elbow. As he turned toward her, she pulled him aside and said, "Papa, there's an unconscious man over against the far wall. Will you find out who he is, please?"

"Why Katie? What's this about?" he asked, suddenly concerned.

"Please papa," she begged, "just find out who he is?"

45

Katie would tell her father about the man's advances the following day. The experience seemed queer; particularly the man's drunken act, and she felt her father should know.

Granville was able to find Gus Adams quickly and asked him to find out what he could about the man lying unconscious. As the detective turned to his business, Granville was pleased and somewhat relieved to see Katie and Jimmy dancing. Whatever the cause of Katie's request, it seemed a small thing. She wasn't hurt or upset as far as Granville could tell. He stood watching the young couple as they danced when he felt a nudge in his side. Turning, he saw his wife standing at his elbow, smiling up at him. Granville thought she had never looked more beautiful.

"I'm sorry I've been too busy politicin' and haven't had the chance to dance with you," he said. "Will you do me the honor of the next dance?"

"I was afraid you wouldn't ask," she responded, beaming. "I'd hate to dress up like this and not have you notice."

"Not much chance of that. Let's show these youngsters how it's done."

The remainder of the evening was uneventful. The Stuart family, accompanied by Jimmy and the McHenrys, returned to the hotel following the dance. As the ladies retired to their rooms, the men stepped into the bar for a nightcap. As they sat at a table sipping their drinks, Gus Adams came in, spotted Granville and pulled a chair next to him. Leaning over, he spoke softly into Granville's ear, "The man's name is Zeke Tyler, a local bad man thought to associate with John Stringer and other rough elements. Strictly a rattler, spent 4 years in Ohio State Penitentiary for manslaughter, killed a man in a fight and claimed it was accidental. The sheriff knows all about him."

"Anything else?"

"Got a knot on the side of his head the size of an turnip. How did he get it?" asked the detective, curious. "Someone popped him good. He was out for nearly an hour."

"Where is he now?"

"Came around a short while ago and wandered off. Why?"

"I'd like to know what he looks like."

"He's a regular looking fellar, 5 feet 10 inches, dark brown hair, blue eyes, weighs maybe 170 pounds. He's got three long scars on his left cheek running from near his eye down to his chin. Looks like someone raked him good. He's mean as a snake. Last summer he shot a boy's dog just for fun. The more the kid cried, the more the devil laughed," the detective added.

"Thanks Gus. Get yourself a drink on me," the rancher replied as he stood. "I'm calling her quits," he announced. "Good night."

The following morning, Granville and the four Stuart women, along with Jimmy, set out for the DHS ranch in the company of Dave and Linda McHenry. It was a long, rough 210-mile journey in the spring wagons. They would be stopping along the way to spend the nights with various friends and would arrive home a week later.

Overall, Granville was pleased with the convention; public attention had been diverted from the Stockgrowers involvement in future Vigilante activities and the outlaw gangs had been misled as to the cattlemen's intentions. He was anxious to take the offensive.

Chapter Three - The Roundup

From the foothills of the Rocky Mountains in western Montana Territory, east into Dakota Territory, vast rolling grasslands are broken by low mountain ranges, benches and buttes, folds and creases, river bottoms and areas so rough and inhospitable as to be called "badlands." These hostile areas were created primarily by water erosion. The badlands of central Montana Territory along the Missouri River feature shear escarpments hundreds of feet high in places, while the badlands further east in Dakota Territory are lower formations, banded horizontally, wind and water having swept away softer materials to form hills, hummocks, ridges, ravines, canyons, cliffs, hillocks, draws, gullies, arroyos, coulees, washes and cuts whose sides reveal plainly the different materials which make them up. Bands of tan, gray, brown, black and red correspond to the different base materials of clay, stone, shale, sandstone, earth, coal and scoria and are presented to the onlooker layer-cake fashion. The badlands looked like "hell with the fires put out," as General Crook said, and navigating this rough maze-like landscape was nearly impossible. For this reason, the badlands made excellent country in which to hide stolen livestock and elude any possible pursuers.

Surrounding these rugged areas, the open range stretched mile after mile with few impediments to grazing cattle, which drift wherever the grass is greener, mixing freely with cattle from the other herds sharing the range. The DHS and other ranches on the Maginnis Range held three cattle roundups every year; the spring calf roundup, usually occurring in April, was needed to brand and ear notch the new calf crop, castrate young bulls to maintain the proper bull to cow ratio, determine losses from the preceding winter and return each herd closer to its home range. In September, another calf roundup was held for branding, ear notching, castrating and returning the herd nearer the home range. Bulls were not segregated on the open range; consequently calving was on going, forcing the ranchers to mark stock and cull excess bulls twice a year. Finally, a beef roundup was held in October, and all marketable beef, generally 4-year-old steers, were shipped to the various markets, primarily St. Paul and Chicago. With more than 60,000 cattle sharing the Ft. Maginnis range, the DHS ranch and the 9 other outfits on it, must, by necessity, work together during each roundup. These were huge, far-flung affairs lasting 3 to 4 weeks. Each ranch sent their representatives, or reps as they were called, to work the roundup and do their fair share. The number of reps an outfit sent was determined by the size of their herd; normally one wrangler being provided for each 1000 head of cattle being grazed. A roundup boss was appointed annually to supervise the three roundups from one of the participating ranches, and like the captain of a ship, his word was law until the roundup was concluded. Each wrangler was expected to obey the roundup boss' orders so the roundup might succeed and be quickly and successfully completed.

As the Eastern Montana Stockgrowers Association meeting was being held, the spring calf roundup was in full swing. The wranglers on the round-up were typical of their class, with most sporting wool plaid shirts, canvas pants, "imported" (mail order) tight fitting cowboy boots with high riding heels, heavy functional spurs with small rowels, chaps when needed for brush work, an expensive stiff beaver felt Stetson hat and a bright silk bandana tied around the neck. All were armed with a holstered revolver, generally a Colt, but sometimes a Remington, Marlin, Smith & Wesson or other make. The vast majority carried only a single sidearm, although some carried two pistols, the second usually smaller in size and caliber, and was often carried in a pocket or a shoulder holster under the arm. Some few were two-gun men, such as Harley, although this was a rarity on northern ranges. Two-gun rigs were more often found in the southwest and were used by bonafide "shootists." On their horse, most wranglers carried a Winchester or Marlin lever-action repeating rifle in a leather scabbard. Contrary to popular opinion in the east, cowboys generally took a great deal of pride in their dress and the fittings for their horse, often going to the expense of a fancy silver bit and bridle.

Cowboy saddles were purpose-built and of quality construction, but relatively plain. Just as clothing styles change over time, cowboy saddles also changed, evolving to suit specific needs. Early examples were simpler, with a smaller horn and swell but a taller cantle than seen today. The seat jockey and back jockey were often the same piece of leather, and these working saddles often had no skirt. The tree or frame was made of soft wood so it would accept nails without splitting. The different pieces of leather used for saddle construction came from different specific areas of a cowhide, depending on the intended use. Saddles were sized to match a rider and horse; saddles used for the smaller Spanish and Indian cow ponies would not fit the larger Kentucky or Natchez breeds, and would make the animal sore if used. A good working cowboy's saddle weighed roughly 45 pounds. This is in contrast to an Army or McClellan cavalry saddle, which weighed less then half that, had a tiny swell and cantle and often no horn or skirt. Small or no fenders were also the rule for military saddles. These were purpose-built for a different use than a working wrangler's saddle.

The DHS ranch sent 12 working wranglers, a cook with chuck and blanket wagons and a horse wrangler. Each working wrangler took 7 or 8 saddle horses with him, driving them to the pickup point where the roundup would begin. All the horses were placed in a horse herd called a remuda or cavvy. During any given day, a wrangler may ride 2 or 3 different horses, sometimes more, exchanging a tired mount for fresh, as need demanded. Each wrangler's string included horses with specialized skills.

An agile and intelligent cutting horse was needed for cutting cattle from the herd and a good cutting horse showed an uncanny intelligence that was almost human. Once the rider put him on the animal needed to be cut, a good cutting horse would stick with him no matter what tricks the critter tried. The rider's only work involved staying on the animal as he darted and jogged in response to the selected animal's evasions. Good cutting horses worked quietly and didn't excite or make a herd nervous as he moved among the stock doing his job.

A steady sure-footed horse was needed for night herding. These were usually able to see in the dark better than other horses, a trait necessary to avoid gopher holes, obstacles and drop-offs. Some were known to stop entirely and probe the ground before them if the night were particularly dark and they were unsure of what was immediately in front. Sometimes they would come to a complete stop, even to the point of not breathing so the saddle leather wouldn't squeak, and listen intently for movement of the herd in the darkness. They were light on their feet and made very little noise as they circled the sleeping herd so as not to alarm them and cause a stampede. Finally, a good night herding horse wouldn't nicker to his mates in the remuda as he circled the herd repeatedly. This too could cause a stampede in a skittish or edgy herd.

Good roping horses were needed to carry the rider close enough to the selected animal so it could be roped. If the horse got too close to the animal, a good roping horse would back off to the proper distance without any actions from the rider.

Circle horses were used for rounding up cattle and often traveled 20 miles from camp in search of strays. These horses were long legged and deep chested with plenty of "bottom" and loved to run. Known for their endurance, they would set their own pace, never seemed to tire and would carry a rider all day with untapped reserves always at the ready.

Each day, after breakfast was finished and the wranglers had ridden off on their various assignments, the cooks and helpers would break camp and follow the horse herd to the next camp location; finally selecting a spot with good wood and water for the noon meal. The horse herd would graze within sight of the wagons until the wranglers came in for their dinner. The remuda was then driven into a temporary rope corral close to camp so tired horses could be exchanged for fresh. Following dinner, after the wranglers had ridden off, the horse herd would again be moved on ahead, the chuck and blanket wagons following, to the supper camp sight, where the last meal of the day was prepared. Again, the remuda was corralled near camp so tired stock could be turned in. Finally, the nightriders would select fresh stock for their two-hour tricks. At night, the remuda was driven away from camp under the watch of the horse wranglers until the following day, when the process would be repeated. By this method, the roundup was constantly moving forward, traveling 10-15 miles each day across the open range. This routine would be repeated day after day, until the entire 150 mile long range had been swept clean, the herds separated out, accurate tallies taken and all calves branded, notched and castrated as needed.

The chuck wagons were the nerve center of the roundup, where wranglers took their meals, got their orders for the day and slept following their trick. One four-horse chuck wagon and cook usually fed 10-12 men. The chuck wagon often towed a small two-wheeled blanket wagon, which carried the men's bulky bedrolls. For this spring roundup, seven chuck wagons were used, along with their blanket wagons, to support the 63 working wranglers. The cooks and helpers drove the wagons from site to site, setting up camp, cooking and cleaning up the wreck after each meal. Later roundups also carried tents for eating and sleeping, although this one did not.

Good trail cooks were valuable, and outfits would go to considerable lengths to obtain and keep one. Rain, wind, snow, blazing sun, stampede and come what may, a culinary Ganymede could lighten the mood of any outfit, improving morale through his efforts. One trait that most cooks shared was general contempt for all humanity, particularly cowpunchers. The cook was always subject to the wrangler's ire; if he burned the biscuits or committed some other culinary sin, he could expect abuse from the wranglers, sometimes jokingly and sometimes not. With no ice house to keep food from spoiling, the challenge of adding variety to the basic stocks of beans, bacon, flour, molasses, corn meal, salt, occasional fresh beef and coffee was daunting. An experienced cook would use cammas root, wild onion, sage, lemon grass, mint, dried peppers and anything else that came to hand to add variety to the dull and repetitious fare.

When the crew from the DHS arrived, they found Lem Slocum, foreman of the Double S, Ham Rather's outfit. Slocum, as roundup boss, was dressing down one of the cooks for some unknown infraction. When he finally ran low on pressure, he turned to the newly arrived wranglers, eyed the **D-S** brand on their mounts and made a sour face. "Throw yer chuck wagon in with the others and put your mounts in the remuda off to the west. Get some grub. Tomorrow morning, we starts proper," he said, then spun on his heel and returned to abusing the cook.

"That Slocum's a crusty old coot," Tom Burns said, as they rode away. "You see the sour look he made? Wonder what that's about."

"Granville slapped Slocum's boss at Duncan Sides' funeral last fall and ran him off the place. Things has been a mite thin 'tween that outfit and ours since," Red Mack said.

"Slapped him?" Tom asked, "What happened?"

"Don't matter what happened. Slocum's the roundup boss now. That's all you gots to know," Red replied.

"Well, I'd hate to be that poor cook right about now. Wonder what he done."

"Drop it kid. What Slocum says, goes, and that's flat," Red said.

"That cook looked like he could take 'bout anything Slocum could dish out," Buster Burns said, coming to his younger brother's rescue. "Seems to me I seen him somewheres before."

"He was cookin' for Two Bar 'til last fall. We seen him on other roundups," Ed Spencer offered.

"I shore hope them cooks knows what side of a skillet's up," Dave Thomson offered. "Nothin' worse than a cook gone loco. I saw a cook down in Abilene get his self hung for feedin' bad grub." Dave got nervous if anything threatened his cherished viands. He could take any form of rain, wind or weather, but couldn't abide bad food.

"They hung a cook for fixin' bad food?" Tom Burns asked, incredulous. He was green as grass, new to the outfit and this was his first roundup.

The men burst out laughing. "Some they shoots, kid. Sorta motivates 'em to do a good job!" Dirty Bill said, chuckling.

"On a drive down in the Nations, they shot four cooks in a row, 'til they got a good one, and he was a mite nervous. We called him Shaky Bob. Shook all the time. He was so scared, he slept with both eyes open. Had to retire and raise ducks when the drive was over," Red added, winking at Buster. "Besides, we got Phonograph with us and I reckon he's about the best cook in the territory."

"Shore hope he don't pick up no bad habits from them other pot wrestlers," Dave said. "We got him trained just about right."

The men quickly found the large remuda and turned their horses, along with Ed Spencer, over to the head horse wrangler, a man named Hump Benson, who rode for the Triple C. He recognized Fargo Charley Hill from previous roundups and asked, "How you doin' Fargo? How's that buggered-up laig doin'?"

"Hello Hump," Fargo replied, smiling. He'd broken a leg when a horse fell on him the previous year. "Laig's all healed up an' ready for dancin'! How many cayuses you got in your nest anyways?"

"Oh, got close to 550 or so," Hump replied, watching Ed Spencer and the other horse wranglers loose herd the large remuda.

"And how's your sidekick, Roberts?" Fargo asked. "He 'round here somewheres or is he stretched out in some whorehouse down in Miles City?"

"No, he got tied up with a chinee girl last year and that cured him," Hump said laughing. "Her husband showed up sorta previous and started throwin' lead and screamin' in chinee, so Roberts figured it was time to get back to ranchin' where it's safe!"

Fargo laughed and said, "Where in hob did he find a chinee girl?"

"Oh, she left her husband in Helena and just showed up one day. Roberts can tell you all about it. He's around, but I couldn't say where just now," Hump replied, laughing, then turned to the business at hand. "I'll see you fellars at supper."

There were a surprising number of Chinese in Montana. They'd drifted in when gold was discovered and established themselves in all the larger towns were they operated restaurants, laundries, shops and opium dens, among other things. Some had been caught involved in illegal operations, a few involving murder, and as a community, they were no strangers to the taut rope of Vigilante justice. Yet they prospered, most being hard working and industrious. Sometimes the strain of living and surviving in a strange land was a burden some could not bear and these turned to the pipe for comfort. Early Miles City records show the majority of arrests of Chinese were made for illegal operation of opium dens.

"I gotta find Roberts and see about that chinee girl," Fargo said, as the men rode back toward the roundup.

"Sounded like she left for other parts," Red said.

"Yes, but Roberts don't scare easy. I'm curious to see just what happened," Fargo said. "It musta been hair-raisin' to run him off!"

An oddity of a cowpuncher's language was they generally considered any word ending with an "ess" sound to be plural. Thus, a single Chinese person was call "chinee", just as wranglers around the Medora area called the Maltese ranch, the "maltee." Fargo was no different. Although most of the wranglers came up from Texas, Fargo was from the Dakota Territory. He'd been with the DHS for several years and was a permanent hand, working year round. Ranches in the north country, because of the extreme winter weather, seldom kept a full crew through the cold months, when there wasn't much to do since the cattle were left to fend for themselves. Consequently, the wranglers were either full time or seasonal, depending. Those men laid off in late fall were left to their own devices over the winter months; some took menial jobs in town, some rode south to work distant, warmer ranches and some rode the grub line, taking their meals and shelter where they could. It was considered low form not to offer a stranger a meal and a bed, so those who rode the grub line were able to survive, drifting from ranch to ranch, living on handouts. Grub line riders were generally welcome because they often brought news of happenings elsewhere. When spring broke, they would again find ranch work that suited their skills and temperament, sometimes on the ranch they worked the previous year, sometimes not.

That evening, following supper, Slocum gathered all the men around and said in a loud voice, "My name's Slocum. I'm the boss of this here outfit and what I says goes. Don't give me no sass and do your job and you won't have no trouble from me. Cross me or slack off and you'll have more trouble than you can handle. Tomorrow we starts the roundup proper. I've made assignments for everyone and the list will be on the tailgate of the Double S chuck wagon. Anybody got any questions?"

"I got one," replied Dirty Bill. "What we gonna do if we finds stray cattle from the Moccasin or Powder Range?" These were open ranges on either side of the Maginnis Range, and although not common, occasionally stock from the neighboring ranges would drift in.

Slocum frowned at the DHS wrangler. "You new to this line of work? I thought you DHS ladies had experience. Mavericks we keep and auction them off at the end of roundup."

"I'm askin' what we do with strays, not mavericks, if we finds any," replied Dirty Bill, ignoring Slocum's insulting tone and reference.

"Drive in all cattle you find! We'll figure out what to do with 'em after that. That answer your question?"

"Us ladies from the DHS thanks you," Bill said, sweeping the hat off his head and making an exaggerated bow with mock formality. Everyone laughed.

The roundup boss looked like he'd swallowed turpentine, but controlled his fury. "We got a long day tomorrow," he shouted, "Check your assignments and turn in. We're up before the sun!" Slocum turned and walked off to talk to the horse wranglers. The men retrieved their bedrolls from the wagons and set up their "beds" under the stars. Because of the cold climate, the bedrolls used by Montana and Dakota wranglers were unique. First, a waterproof ground tarp was laid out flat on the ground. This tarp was of oiled or waxed cotton canvas, 10 feet wide by 20 feet long. The wrangler then put down a sougan, a thick, heavy quilt roughly 10 feet square. If the wrangler was sharing his "nest" with another man, a second sougan was laid over the first. If sleeping alone, the single sougan was folded back on itself, so the wrangler would have a layer of the quilt above and below him. All the wrangler's gear, including saddle, bridle and rifle, was put on the tarp, either at the head or foot of the sougan. Finally the tarp was folded back on itself, covering the sougan and gear, and all the sides pulled in. The completed package was roughly 9 feet long and 4 feet wide, and would keep the wrangler and his gear warm and dry in any weather.

The following morning, the men were up at 3:00 AM and had finished eating by sunup. Fresh mounts were roped and because most of the horses were half-wild, they tried to escape the thrown lariats, ducking and bolting wildly. Once saddled and mounted, many bucked and pitched, crow-hopping in protest over their unwelcome guest's presence. It was an exciting time of day, for about fifteen minutes. When things calmed down, the circle men rode out in pairs, making huge sweeps to locate stray cattle and drive them in, where other cowpunchers would loose herd the captives.

While this was going on, the branding crew would build the branding fires from scrub oak and ash, good hot hardwood fires that would last longer and burn hotter than pine or cottonwood fires. When the irons were up to proper temperature, the ropers would then move through the loose herd and rope any unbranded calves. Montana cowboys used a "dally" to secure the rope to their saddle horn. A dally was a few quick turns of the rope around the saddle horn that could be released easily if need be. This style originated in Oregon Territory and was found to be superior to the method used in Texas, where the rope end was actually tied to the saddle horn, making a quick release impossible. More than one Texas cowboy died because he couldn't release his rope and was pulled over a cliff or steep bank by a rampaging steer or bull.

As the young captive was taken away, the mother was certain to follow closely, bellowing in protest. The roper would lead the calf near the branding fires, where several branding irons from each outfit were heated to red hot, and shout out the mother's brand, which would be applied to the calf: "Circle Dot!" "Lazy S!" "X Bar R!" Two flankers would grab and quickly throw the calf on a certain side, flip the rope off and hold the animal down so the brander could do his work, shouting "hot iron!" as he moved toward the bellarin' calf and applied the smoking iron. Not only was each brand distinct and unique, it was applied to a specific location on the animal; left shoulder, right shoulder, left flank, right flank, left hip or right hip. Some ranchers chose to brand in two locations, making brand altering more difficult. As the calf's cries became more frantic, the mother often charged the ropers horses, the flankers or the branders, so everyone had to stay alert. Following the branding, the calf's ears were notched in a fashion specific to the particular brand just applied. The notches corresponded to the brand and were used as a further deterrent to rustling. The heat, dust and sweat, mixed with the shouts of the men, the clouds of smoke, the smell of burning hair and the bawling of the cows and their calves, created perfect pandemonium.

After the calves had been branded and notched, any young bulls found would be castrated so the proper bull to cow ratio could be maintained for that particular range. The ratio varied from range to range depending on the lay of the land. Rough country required more bulls to cows because of the uneven footing, but generally ratios fell between 10 bulls per 100 cows to 6 bulls per 100 cows for range stock. The castration process was attended by more bellarin' and commotion; the rough operation being painful and bloody. Quickly performed with three small cuts from a sharp knife, the ordeal was soon over, and the steer released, sore but otherwise healthy. Men who pulled this assignment were fairly covered in blood at the end of the day. Following this final indignity, the calves and their mothers were reunited and thrown over into separate herds for each ranch, so they could be tallied.

An accurate tally was vital so the ranch would know where they stood regarding their calf crop and any unusual losses during the previous six months noted. The men responsible for tallying each herd were proficient at making a fast and accurate count; it wasn't unusual for two good tally men to count thousands of cattle as they were driven past and not be more than one or two cows different from each other. These men used tally strings hung from the horn of their saddle as an aide so as not to lose count. Each time an additional 100 head were counted, another knot was tied in the tally string. On a large roundup or cattle drive, the tally string might easily represent many thousands of cattle. Mexican vaqueros used a similar system except they shifted small pebbles from one hand to the other with each pebble representing one hundred head of cattle. During a range roundup, when an outfit's herd reached 1000-2000 head, it would be driven off some distance and released into an area already swept so its members wouldn't be counted twice. Later, at the conclusion of the roundup, the herds would be driven back to their home range by each respective outfit.

Adding to the general chaos, each cow puncher tried to out do the other; the branders trying to get the holders to move faster and get more cattle thrown and ready for the hot irons, the flankers goading the ropers to pick up the pace and bring in more calves, the ropers yelling at the circle riders, challenging them to bring in more stock and questioning their riding abilities, family linage and general worth as a human being. The circle men would sweep out and drive back any cattle they found. The competition between the various crews made the hot exhausting work more interesting and enjoyable, and in this way, the roundup would cover a strip of range up to 40 miles wide, sweeping the range as clean of cattle as possible.

By the 1880's, the roundup process had changed considerably from the early days in the 1860's, when the majority of range cattle were longhorns of the Texas variety. These formidable beasts had been left to run wild while the War of Northern Aggression was in progress and consequently, they were ill tempered and dangerous to work with, not being afraid of man nor horse. A sudden charge could leave a man or horse badly gored and dying on the prairie. If a man were put afoot and was lucky enough to make it up a tree, a longhorn would sometimes outwait the helpless wrangler, charging and killing him when he finally came down because of hunger or thirst. Following the roundup, jackpot rodeos were often held to celebrate the conclusion of the difficult work, with the cowhands competing in contests of bronc riding, calf roping, bull riding and horse racing. During the rodeo, it wasn't uncommon for a man riding a ringy longhorn bull to be raked off the animal's back. The wily critter would turn its head sharply and use its horns as a tool to scrape the unlucky cowboy off. When this happened, men on horseback would jump into the fray and distract the beast before he could attack the downed rider. The newer varieties of cattle were more tractable and less ornery, making cattle operations safer and less life threatening.

The custom of branding livestock dates back some 4000 years, when Egyptians and others began branding their stock. These operations were not always limited to livestock; in Europe slaves, thieves, prostitutes, debtors and others were often branded. This was the custom in England until 1822, when it was finally banned. Branding livestock in the United States and its Territories began in the southwest, where it spread north from Mexico, following its introduction by the Spanish when they invaded that land. In Texas and New Mexico "dot branding" was used originally. This early style of branding needed three different shapes of irons and from these, various brands could be made. A complete set of dot irons consisted of a small half circle iron; a large half circle iron and a straight line iron, called a "straight edge" that was 3 or 4 inches long. Using these simple shapes in different combinations, cattle could be branded with unique marks. The Ace of Clubs, the Dumbbell, The S Bar, The Rocking C, The Lazy S and many other brands could be made, depending on the owner's imagination. This style of iron was replaced by "stamping" irons, where all the elements of a brand were incorporated into a single iron. Stamping brands were faster and gave more consistent results.

Some care had to be used when creating a stamping brand. Closed areas of certain letters and numbers tended to overheat the animal and roast him in that one spot. An example of this would be the letter R; the closed loop at the top would hold the heat longer than the two legs below it, thus overheating the animal when applied until the legs had burned the animal sufficiently. Another problem area with stamp brands was figures that brought two elements together, such as the intersections of the letters X, K and T. These areas held their heat longer than the outer ends of the straight sections and were often avoided. As an example, the **DHS** brand was pronounced D H S but actually shown as **D-S**, thus eliminating the heat buildup if all three letters were used. Symbols were often used to augment simple brands. These could include a quarter circle above or below a letter or number, a slash between two letters or numbers, a bar above or below numbers or letters, etc. Further variety was added when the letters or numbers were turned on their side, making the figures "lazy." Finally, easily recognizable symbols such as "Sowbelly", "Quien Sabe", "Camp Stool", "Hash Knife" and "Elkhorn" were also used, often in conjunction with numbers or letters. If this weren't confusing enough, different states and territories had different customs for creating and reading brands. For instance, a Wyoming slash leans in the opposite direction as a Montana slash.

Once the rancher selected a brand, he registered it with his local cattleman's association, where all the brands in that particular area were compiled in a brand book. It wasn't unusual for a rancher in Montana to have the same brand as a rancher in Colorado or Dakota. What set these brands apart was where they were applied to the animal and the style of ear notch used. The chance of the brand, location and notching all being the same was extremely remote and ownership was easily determined.

As the days rolled by, it soon became obvious that Slocum had a bone to pick with the DHS men and with Dirty Bill in particular. Bill didn't help the situation, crowing about his ranching skills, and bragging about his accomplishments, as if daring Slocum to respond. For his part, some of Slocum's snide comments bordered on insult. Disputes between wranglers during a roundup were held off until the roundup was complete, so as not to slow the process. Once things were put to rights, any smoldering quarrels would be dealt with man to man. So it was with Slocum.

A week into the roundup, Fargo and Red Mack were partnered up for circle riding. They left camp following breakfast, heading west, to start the morning's sweep. As the two men rode along, their talk turned to Harley and the other absent DHS wranglers.

"You got any idea what the boss is up to, Red?" Fargo asked.

"I can't say for certain, but I think it has something to do with Duncan being killed. Seems to me, Granville's been actin' different since that happened. More secretive," Red replied. "Something's in the wind, that's certain. I never seen such a string of visitors to the ranch and if someone ain't visitin', Granville's off somewheres gadflyin'."

"I hadn't looked at it that way, but you might be right. There's shore been lots of comin' and goin' alright," Fargo said, as both men spotted a group of 50 or 60 cattle grazing near a creek bottom. Many new calves were lying down, resting in the warm sun. They often lay so flat while they slept, it was difficult to tell if they were dead or alive, but moving closer, the rider would be gratified to see one ear sticking up as it slept, a sign that the calf was alive and kicking.

As the two riders turned toward the small herd, Red said, "I heard Harley was supposed to be roundup boss this year, but Granville pulled him. Maybe he's gonna get even."

"Get even? I thought Dutchy killed 'em all," Fargo said, as the men swept around the small herd and began checking a nearby creek bottom for more cattle.

"He did, but maybe those four was part of something bigger; an organized gang maybe. If they was, there's more snakes that needs killin'. I been talkin' to some of the boys from the other outfits and most feel they're losing stock," Red said, as the riders eased down through the heavily wooded draw.

"I been hearin' things too, but with an open range, it's hard to tell for shore. I hadn't thought about organized gangs, but you might be right. If they was takin' just a few head from every outfit, that would add up to quite some herd without causin' any fuss. Whatever's goin' on, I sure hopes the boss cuts me in on it. Duncan was a good kid."

"Did you know he was the one that put the lye on one of the outhouse seats last summer?" Fargo asked, chuckling to himself. "I remember Terry runnin' out like a shot. He didn't even get his britches pulled up! And then he drops into one of the cook's washtubs! Lord, that was funny! I thought Phonograph would bust!"

Red laughed, and said, "I didn't know who done it, but it shore was somethin'! I think if Terry could have found the culprit, he'd have plugged him! And Phonograph goin' on the prod, sayin' his tubs was fer dishes, not asses!"

The life of a wrangler was mostly long hours and hard work, with few pleasurable diversions. Despite the exhausting 12-14 hour days, the younger men still found energy to pull practical jokes, taking great delight in someone else's misery. Duncan, Ed, Jimmy and Dirty Bill were known for their pranks and loved nothing so much as tormenting the other wranglers and each other.

Finding no strays in the draw, the two wranglers returned to the small herd and started driving them in, picking up additional cattle as they went. This effort was hampered by the fact that calves often tried to return to where they had been fed last, so the wranglers were kept busy turning them back into the herd. This was why no cow-calf units were taken on trail drives; it was simply too much work, constantly returning calves to the herd. Any calves born during the drive were shot. A few drives had a wagon follow the drive, collecting young calves too weak to keep up. They were released every night into the herd to be fed by their mothers and collected the following morning after they'd eaten. By the time Fargo and Red arrived at the new campsite and dropped the cattle off with the loose herd, they had well over 400 head. Riding toward the remuda, where they would get fresh mounts, Red said, "I'm goin' to keep nosin' around. You do the same. This range covers a lot of territory, and the men here pretty much know what's happening on it. We better keep our nosin' pretty quiet though. No telling' who's involved."

"Alright, I'll talk to the men I know pretty good, ones I been on roundups with before. We oughta talk to our men too. Who knows? Maybe one of us'll kick over the right rock," Fargo concluded, as the two men arrived at the remuda.

Texas Red Mack had been with the DHS since its start, hiring on less than a month after Harley. And like Harley, Red was originally from Texas, where he grew up in the saddle, working cattle drives and herding for various outfits, including Charles Goodnight. Some men are rough on stock, both horses and cattle, but Red was one of the gentlest men on stock to ride the Montana range. He would push himself until he dropped from fatigue but never abused livestock if there was a better way. He was rock steady in a tight situation and could keep his mouth shut as a matter of course. While his cowboy skills were on par with Harley's, he didn't have the Ranger experience his foreman did, but his life on the range had taught him to be naturally suspicious when things didn't feel right.

Some losses were natural with cattle and horses. They died from exposure, disease or accident. Grey wolves also took a toll. These large predators were native to the plains and had survived for thousands of years feeding off the huge buffalo herds. When the buffalo disappeared, they quickly developed an appetite for cattle and horses, often attacking and killing the young and less able.

The following week, as the roundup progressed, the DHS men made their quiet inquiries. Nothing came to light immediately, other than nearly all the outfits felt they were losing stock. This was most apparent in their various horse herds, because they were fewer in number and the losses more obvious. Because horses were more valuable than cattle, they were prime targets for rustlers. With cattle herds strung from hell to breakfast, unless the rustlers were caught in the act, there was little to go on other than an uneasy feeling that things weren't quite right.

Two weeks later, Red Mack was loose herding the gathered cattle, waiting for the calves to be processed. He was riding with Arty

Quinlan, one of the Circle T wranglers, talking on various subjects. Red carefully turned the conversation to rustling and Arty gave him a queer look.

"You shore took the long way around the barn," Arty said, laughing. "I know you and yer boys is askin' questions and I figured it was my turn. I was wondering when you'd get around to it."

Red laughed. "You caught me, I guess. We been tryin' to be careful, but maybe we ain't careful enough. Why did you let me ramble on so?"

"It was sorta fun watchin' you loose herd me!"

"Damn! You shore could have saved me some work if you'd cut me short," Red said, embarrassed that his efforts were so transparent.

"And miss the fun? Not on yer life!" Arty said, laughing heartily. "What's all this about anyway?"

"Duncan Sides was a good kid and a fine wrangler. When some rustlers killed him, it was sorta personal for most of us. Black Dutch killed the men what done it, but I think there's others involved in the thievin'. If there is, well, there's more varmints that needs killin'."

"I know of one operation you may be interested in," Arty offered. "There's a fellar over on Spring Creek named Larry Hoyt. We calls him Moyt 'cause of his harelip. Got hisself a small dugout. Claims to be a wolfer, but I ain't seen many hides 'round there. Been in these parts about two years. I sees him lots of places where I wouldn't expect; seems to always be turnin' up. Anyway, I seen him several times pushin' small strings of horses, headin' somewheres to the North. I figured he was horse tradin' or helpin' someone out, so I never bothered to get close enough to check the brands. I can't say for certain they was stole, but now that you mention it, it do look sorta queer."

"What's this Moyt look like?" Red asked, interested in certain possibilities.

"He's a breed, about 6 foot tall, and you can't miss the harelip. I been by his dugout several times and he hangs out with some rough types," Arty said. "His place is just up Spring Creek from where it joins the Armells, about 10 miles south of the Missouri. Know it?"

"I know 'bout where it is, though I never been there. I appreciates the information. Thanks," Red answered, and then turned to ride away. Before he had gone far, he heard a shout.

"Hey!" Quinlan yelled, riding over to where Red had pulled up. "If I was you, I'd keep an eye on Slocum and that Double S bunch. There's something not quite right there and I know Slocum's got it in for Bill Rosser. Keep yer eyes open 'round them."

"Thanks for all yer help, Arty. And next time we gets together and you see me takin' the long way around the barn, for God's sake, hobble me!" The two men separated, laughing.

That evening, the weather turned ugly, clouds stacking up off to the southwest, the horizon growing dark and ominous. The rain crows were making their odd cries and men and animals knew a storm was coming. All day the winds had been blowing from the northeast. As the wind began to build, the cattle hunkered down and prepared for a serious blow. Just before 10 o'clock, the storm hit like an explosion; winds gusting to 80 miles per hour swept through the roundup camp, blowing over several chuck wagons and scattering bedrolls, hats, tin plates, coffee pots, cups, pans, wash tubs, saddle blankets, loose clothes and hot embers across the landscape. Heavy rains immediately followed, accompanied by large fist-sized hail that lasted for 15 minutes, pounding everything unmercifully. Wagon tarps were destroyed. Livestock and men were bloodied. Those wranglers who found shelter under the few nearby trees were only slightly better off. Experienced roundup hands sought shelter under the chuck wagons or stripped the saddles from their horses and held them above their heads. The storm lasted less than an hour and after it passed, the landscape was a ghostly white with dark splashes of stripped off leaves beneath the denuded trees. The entire landscape had a freakish, unreal wintry aspect in the moonlight.

It took two days to recover the scattered livestock, many wranglers spending more than 30 hours in the saddle with no sleep and little food. Of the herd, 17 head were killed outright or died of wounds from the hail. At least half that number drowned in flash floods along the creek beds and dry washes. It was a trying time for all. The range cooks kept a steady supply of coffee coming; along with what meager rations they could scrape together from the wreckage. At last, things were set to right, new supplies brought out and new equipment provided as needed. The roundup was back on track.

On the final day of the roundup, most of the men completed their chores by mid-morning, the last calves branded and the last cattle thrown over into the proper herds. The roundup was complete. While the wranglers sat around, swapping yarns and relaxing, Slocum walked up to Dirty Bill and said, "You been shootin' yer mouth off about what a great rider you is and what great horses you got. I seen babies that rides better than you!"

Dirty Bill grinned, and casually replied, "That may be, but I can damn sure run you outa *your* diapers! And I'll put $50 gold on it," Bill paused for just a beat, "*if* you thinks you can *stand* it."

"I can pick any mount?" Slocum asked loudly, with a smile like a fox. *This is too good to be true.* "I hates to take candy from infants, but you keep flappin' yer lips and I just might! Hey boys, this here infant thinks he can out-ride me!" the roundup boss shouted, as he looked around, rolling his eyes like the very idea was beyond belief. Other wranglers quickly became interested, and circled around the two men, anxious to see what would happen. Because the wranglers took such pride in their mounts, horse racing was one of their favorite sports and a pleasant diversion. Most races were relatively short, 400 to 600 yards being a good average.

"You been doggin' me long enough. To Table Top Butte and back. Now put up or shut up," Dirty Bill said quietly. He wasn't smiling now.

"Table Top Butte and back sounds fine. It's about time you learned who's the bull-of-the-woods!"

Each man walked into the remuda and roped his mount. Slocum picked a sleek racer, with a deep chest, strong legs and glistening coat. Dirty Bill roped a buckskin gelding, deep chested and heavily muscled, but otherwise unremarkable. When both men had their mounts saddled, they led them out to the men who'd gathered to watch the fun.

Slocum addressed the crowd. "You men all heard it. The bet is $50 that I can out-ride this tadpole to Table Top Butte and back."

As Slocum was climbing aboard his horse, Dirty Bill jumped Indian style astride the buckskin in a flash and grinned at the other wranglers. "Yep, it's the babies against the knot-heads. Red Mack, how 'bout startin' us off?"

Before Slocum could make another boast at Bill's expense, Red drew his Colt and fired into the air. Dirty Bill spurred his horse and it leaped forward, several men quickly jumping clear as he shot past. Slocum was left at the start, open mouthed and shocked, it happened so fast. He dug his spurs into his horse with a vengeance and began whipping it with the reins, lashing them back and forth rhythmically to the horse's strides as it charged forward.

Dirty Bill Rosser didn't get his name because of poor hygiene or filthy attire. He'd been busting broncs one spring day and a particularly rank animal swapped ends several times, curled up and then bucked him high into the air. It seemed to him that he stayed up most of the day. He finally lit in a deep pocket of mud and manure and was covered with muck and mire from soda to hock. As he sat there laughing and feeling foolish, for he rarely got thrown, one of the fence-setters called him Dirty Bill and the name stuck. Though just 23 years old, the Texas cowpuncher was an expert rider and felt he could ride anything with hair.

Slocum soon passed him and Bill let the boss get a short distance ahead before he picked up the pace to roughly that of the other rider. As the two men thundered along, Slocum would occasionally look over his shoulder to see if he had gained any distance on the kid, but Bill was always there, with little apparent change in the gap between them.

Slocum continued to whip and spur his horse viciously, trying to pull away from the kid, but he could make only a slight improvement, no matter how hard he urged the horse on. For his part, Dirty Bill was careful to slacken his pace when going down into a draw and up the opposite side, preferring to save his mount's best efforts for the expansive flats over which they rode. Although Slocum moved slowly but steadily away, the kid wasn't worried because he had an ace up his sleeve. He knew he only had to run half a race.

When the roundup began, Slocum started riding him about small, insignificant issues. Dirty Bill was curious and began carefully taking the man's measure, noting Slocum was a braggart, a loud talking blow-hard who enjoyed intimidating others with his size and loud talk. And Bill suspected that down deep, the man was a coward. Slocum wanted desperately to be a big man and constantly tried to impress those around him. He always did this at the expense of others, contrasting his soaring abilities against their apparent stupidity, treating others like they were ignorant children. Seeing this flaw, Dirty Bill began to work on it, crowing about his riding prowess, bragging about his ranching skills and baiting Slocum, goading the man into just such a race as this. Having read the man carefully and having studied Slocum's string of horses, he knew if the man could be prodded into a race, he would pick the fastest and most expensive horse in his string; the very horse he was riding now. The roundup boss had already lost the race but didn't know it.

Slocum was finally able to put a half mile's distance between them. He knew his mount was faster than any horse on the range, and he felt confident he would win but by how much? It wouldn't do to win by a small margin. No. Others might still talk. He wanted to show the kid up, to humiliate him, so no one could possibly doubt his victory. Up ahead, he could see Table Top Butte. He again turned to check on the sprout, but was surprised the gap between them hadn't grown as he expected. Slocum went to his spurs again, driving the horse to greater exertions, cursing the animal with every stride, slapping its ears and head when it failed to deliver the speed he knew it possessed.

The horse was heavily lathered with white foam running off the straining animal, snot and drool flowing freely from its mouth and nose, but it pressed forward and increased its exertions in response to the Slocum's demands. Blowing heavily with each stride, the horse couldn't slacken or slow. It didn't know how.

The kid had correctly taken the measure of the sleek racer and smiled as he thought about it. The horse was certainly fast, but it had one fatal flaw: it was a hot-blooded thoroughbred. There were two types of horses common to the region, hot-blooded and cold-blooded. A hot-blooded horse would run and run and run, giving it's all with every stride, running until its heart burst and it collapsed. It would not slow or slacken its pace, though its life depended on it. By contrast, a cold-blooded horse, like the buckskin Dirty Bill rode, would ease its pace as it became more fatigued, until it could finally only manage a feeble wobbly walk. A cold-blooded horse would never run itself to death. Never.

Approaching the base of Table Top Butte, Slocum's horse suddenly heaved and its legs collapsed, throwing Slocum over the saddle as his horse suddenly fell from beneath him and tumbled. The boss somersaulted to a joint-wrenching halt. Dazed, he shook his head to clear it and tried to stand. Though bent and sore, he was relieved to find no bones were broken. Finally on his feet again, he walked unsteadily back to the horse and saw the horse wasn't breathing. Dead.

When Dirty Bill saw Slocum's horse go down, he slowed his own pace; all need for haste now gone. He steadily slowed until he came upon Slocum at an easy walk as the boss was stripping his saddle from the dead animal.

"Give me a ride, kid. You win," Slocum said, reaching out to catch the bridle of Bill's horse.

Dirty Bill wouldn't let the boss get near enough to catch hold, moving away every time Slocum made a futile grab.

"You been ridin' me for a month, Slocum. I say it's about time you walked!" the kid said, laughing and then turned his horse back toward camp. All Slocum could do was watch as the kid rode away, his horse blowing and lathered but showing no signs of collapse.

Slocum dropped his saddle and bridle next to the dead horse and started walking. It was nearly 20 miles to camp and a long painful hike in anyone's book. In tight fitting cowboy boots with high riding heels, the walk would be pure torture.

Two hours later, the kid rode into camp, to the cheers of his fellow DHS wranglers. He quickly put his mount with the remuda and returned riding a fresh horse.

"What'd you do with the boss, kid?" Red Mack asked, grinning.

"Oh, he's out tryin' to find some babies to race," Bill replied. "Hey Phonograph! How long before we eats?"

"You can have yours right now, if you wants. Anybody that put that skunk in his place has got a plate at my table *anytime*," the cook happily replied. Phonograph had his own troubles with Slocum, and seeing the DHS wrangler best the tyrant put a song in the crusty old cook's heart.

After Bill grabbed a plate of food, he sat down next to Red Mack and filled up. When the meal was a memory, Red Mack asked him, "That racer dead?"

"Yep."

"Figured that was the play, you sneaky devil. You been plannin' this fer weeks!" Red said, laughing.

"Well," replied Dirty Bill, "he asked for it and he got it. And he's got a 20-mile walk back to think about it. There won't be no more talk about 'babies' or 'bull-of-the-woods' around here, that's certain!"

Red Mack, along with Phonograph and the few wranglers within earshot burst out laughing, picturing Slocum walking in, dragging his damaged pride behind him. Others quickly learned of the situation and laughter became widespread. The kid left Slocum with a 20-mile walk!

Sometime after supper, the roundup boss hobbled into camp and collapsed onto his bedroll. Someone pulled the man's boots off for him, got him some food from the nearest chuck wagon and a canteen of fresh water. Slocum didn't say a word; didn't crow, didn't cackle and didn't try to impress anyone with his importance. He seemed to be a chastened man.

Following breakfast the next morning, as everyone was breaking camp, Slocum approached Dirty Bill and the DHS hands, walking very tenderly. As he drew near, he reached into his pocket and withdrew $50 dollars in gold coin and tossed it on the ground in front of Bill. "Here's yer money. Now get the hell outa my camp!"

Dirty Bill laughed. "Your camp? This here roundup's over, you ain't boss no more and this damn sure ain't *your* camp! Yer just another tenderfoot!" Everyone in earshot laughed.

Slocum's face reddened. "I don't take that kinda talk from nobody! Specially no sprout from an outfit full o' niggers, redskins, breeds, greasers and squaws!"

Suddenly, the smile was gone from Dirty Bill's face. Eyes narrowed, he slowly separated himself from his friends and stood poised on the balls of his feet, facing Slocum. "I'm gonna make you eat them words, handle first, and then I'm gonna kill you."

Everyone in camp stopped their various activities; all eyes were on the two men. Up to this point, it had just been Slocum trying to buffalo the kid. Now it was something entirely different. Slocum looked around, hoping someone would intercede; hoping someone would save him from the fix his hot temper and bluster had gotten him into.

"If yer lookin' for the door outa here, Slocum, it's right behind you. Now get your yeller ass outa *my* camp," Dirty Bill sneered.

This was more than Slocum could stand. He couldn't let the kid's words pass if he wanted to stay in the territory. If he failed to act, he would be forever branded a coward. Slocum's pride wouldn't allow that.

The boss' hand streaked to his gun, and jerked up, trying to clear leather. Suddenly Dirty Bill's pistol flashed out and fired in a roar of powder smoke and hot lead. Slocum's pistol hadn't cleared his holster when the kid fired, blowing the man's thumb into oblivion. Slocum screamed and fell back, clutching his maimed right hand with his left. Before anyone could react, Dirty Bill holstered his pistol with a flourish and said, "You can't ride, you can't shoot and now you can't eat!"

"You rotten son-of-a-bitch! I'm gonna get you for this!" Slocum screamed.

"How?" the kid asked calmly, stepping through the powder smoke to stand over the wounded man. "Now get your 'bull-of-the-woods' carcass moving!"

Torn between rage and fear, Slocum struggled to his feet and walked away, pale and impotent, blood soaking his shirt and pants, spilling over his boots into the dust. Though beaten, he wasn't broken. Not by a long shot! This wasn't the end of it. He'd make the kid pay a hundred times over for this. He'd make the kid regret the day he was born, if it was the last thing he ever did.

Chapter Four - Blooded

Conditions continued to worsen in the region. The rustlers and outlaws increased their violent activities and created an atmosphere where no man felt safe. The regional newspapers were quick to recognize and reflect the conditions of the day.

The River Press, published at Ft. Benton said of the widespread thievery: *"It is about time the Vigilantes were getting ready for business."*

A few days later, the same newspaper said: *"Some more cold lead and twisted hemp are badly needed on the Musselshell."*

The Mineral Argus, published at Maiden, just a few miles from the DHS ranch, said of the outlaws: *"The most speedy and safe cure is to hang them as fast as captured."*

Φ

In the spring of 1884, having gotten a clear mandate from the Stockgrowers Association, and with the roundup now behind him, Granville turned his full attention to eliminating the rustlers and outlaw gangs. He called Harley into his office, where the foreman saw a territorial map spread out on Granville's desk.

"Me, Kohrs, Story and some others have decided to go on the attack against these rustlers. Your experience with the Texas Rangers qualifies you, more than any man I know, to lead the charge. I'd like you to take command, if you're agreeable." Granville said to his foreman. "I know you weren't hired for man-hunting, but things have gotten a lot worse since the day you signed on. When Sides was killed, well, that showed me we got no other choice."

"You're the whitest man I ever met. You gone way outa your way for me more than once and I appreciates it. I'd be proud to lead this thing, if you wants," Harley replied.

"I was hoping you'd say that," Granville said. "This won't be an easy job though. There's so damned many rats, I expect it'll take lots of work to thin the herd. I've asked Gus Adams, the range detective the association hired, to start coordinating the various range detectives activities and start a list of known rustlers, their hideouts and their

71

methods of operation. He's been working on it since the Stockgrowers meeting in Miles City. It looks like he's found a pattern that involves horses being stolen in Wyoming, trailed north into Montana and finally driven over the border into Canada. The rustlers seem to be using remote ranches as layover points while brands are altered and given time to heal. It's a well-organized bunch. He's been watching the ranches real close and I expect him any day with his list. If we can pin them down, those ranches will be our first targets.

"You can use any of our men you want, if they're agreeable. Naturally, I want to keep the number of people involved to as few as possible. On the other hand, you're gonna need enough men to do the job right. Andrew Fergus has asked to ride along and do his part and I've told him he's welcome, once we have things sorted out. How many men you think you'll need?"

"I'll need twelve quiet men."

"Sounds like a jury."

"It will be."

"Good. The territory from central Montana into western Dakota has been divided into three regions; I'm responsible for the western-most area. Of course, we'll have support from a number of ranchers, as far as fresh mounts and supplies go. And you'll have some of the range detectives around to guide and back your play," Granville said.

"Where do you want to start? You said Gus is making a list?"

"When Gus shows, we'll know which way to jump. Until then, figure out who you want to take along."

The following week, Gus arrived at the DHS. Granville met the detective on the porch and asked him to have a seat in one of several rocking chairs scattered about and took one himself.

"Well, Gus, how goes the battle?"

"It's the damnedest thing. Them ranches we been watchin' didn't pan out."

"What happened?"

"Well, for instance, three of us was watching an outfit down toward Forsyth; and we was bein' real careful. I'm pretty sure no one saw us. Anyway, them jaspers suddenly stopped everythin'. Ain't been no horses through there in some time. I can't explain how, but it looks like they figured they was bein' watched."

"Hell! You don't know who they were working with?"

"Not for certain. There's a devil named John Stringer up in the breaks that I got my suspicions about, but I can't prove they's connected. He's got a large gang and seems well organized, so I have my suspicions, but I can't prove it. However, I can prove he's been stealing stock. I just can't rope these ranches into his game."

"Well, there's nothing for it; let's focus on what we know for certain. You said you were putting a list together. You have it?"

"Right here," Gus said, pulling some papers from his pocket.

"Well, let me get Harley Denny up here. He's my foreman and spent several years with the Texas Rangers down on the Mexican border. Tougher than nails too. He'll be leading this charge. Hold tight."

After Harley joined Granville and Gus on the porch, and introductions were made, the men got to work. Gus was struck by the Ranger's cool blue eyes. They didn't waver or look away. Gus was an honest man, but Harley's eyes made him uncomfortable, as if he'd done something wrong, even though he knew he hadn't. The men spent considerable time reviewing the list, discussing various alternatives and finally settled on a plan of attack for taking several gangs along the Missouri River.

When everything was ready, Harley called in the men he wanted to ride with him; Jimmy, Keeps Eagle, Second Bob, Terry Beard, Black Dutch, Buster Burns, Ed Spencer, Dirty Bill, Fargo, Red Mack and Dave Thompson went to the big house and were shown into the study. When all the men were assembled, Harley addressed them.

"All the big cattle outfits in Montana and Dakota has been hit hard by rustlers and it's gettin' worse. The cattlemen, Mr. Stuart among 'em, want to either run these men off or wipe 'em out, once and for all, and I'm leadin' the charge. Mr. Stuart will be goin' on some of the raids 'cause askin' anyone to do what he won't ain't his style. And Andrew Fergus has asked to do his part and will be goin' with us. Those that we hang, we're gonna put signs on 'em with the numbers 3-7-77 as a warning to others.

"I picked you men 'cause you all got experience and you can keep a tight lip. The law will view these operations as nothing less than pure murder, and any man who's caught ridin' with us may swing for it, if word gets out. Neither me or Mr. Stuart will order you to help out. If you wants to be in on this game, you got to deal yerself in. That's the way she lays; what's it gonna be?"

73

Buster Burns stood and asked, "Harley, my brother weren't picked for this crowd. Why not?"

"It's gonna be risky work and Tom doesn't have the experience. I'd hate to see him get killed 'cause he got into a situation he couldn't handle. These are dangerous men we're after."

"You're probly right, Harley. I'll sign on," Buster replied, sitting down.

All the men present quickly affirmed their willingness to ride along and Harley was heartened by their loyalty. "Granville got new Winchester Model 1873 rifles in 50-95 caliber for everyone. We learned a powerful lesson when young Duncan was killed last fall. He and Dutchy was simply out-gunned. That won't happen again. I want every man to practice and get comfortable with the new rifles. You'll each have 200 rounds to play with, so make sure you do. We don't have much time 'cause our first raids start in two days."

Granville's decision to move to the heavy 50-95 caliber was logical, although not without a significant drawback. The massive round was accurate to 600 yards, much further than the weak 44-40's Duncan and Black Dutch had been armed with. Originally developed for the heavy single-shot Sharps falling-block and Remington rolling-block buffalo guns, the round would kick like a mule in the Winchesters, which weighed less than half what the heavy buffalo guns did. The new rifles had the advantage of being repeaters however, and subsequent follow-up shots were readily at hand.

The next day, as Gus was leaving, Andrew Fergus arrived with all his traps. Like the other men, he was given a new Winchester, along with several boxes of ammunition and stepped out to practice. A short time later, Gus Adams returned to the ranch in a lather and went immediately to find Harley. He found the Ranger talking with J.D. Flagg in the tack room, discussing their needs for the following day.

"I just saw one of the men on our list, Harley. Sam McKenzie was ridin' towards Ft. Maginnis," the range detective said. "If we shake a leg, we can catch him."

"Let's go at it then," Harley replied. Four more wranglers were quickly rounded up and the raiders set out toward the fort at a steady gallop, with Gus in the lead. Coming over a rise, they saw a lone horseman ahead, riding along Ford's Creek bottom. Before the rider was aware of their presence, the six men split up and worked behind the folds in the land to encircle the outlaw. After a brief run, two men popped up over a rise in front of McKenzie, and rode directly at him. Seeing the two men suddenly come into view, McKenzie became alarmed and spun his horse to flee, only to find other riders appearing on all sides, blocking any realistic chance of escape. The riders swept down and quickly had him surrounded. After disarming him, Harley asked Gus if it was the right man.

"This is him alright. This is the notorious Sam McKenzie, famous desperado and horse thief deluxe," Gus replied.

"You men got nothin' on me. The court in White Sulphur Springs cleared me on them charges," McKenzie said, gloating.

"Yeah, 'cause the only witness disappeared," Gus responded.

"You can't hang that on me. You ain't got no proof," McKenzie responded.

"Well," Harley said, "you'll find our standards is a bit less demandin' than them folks in the Springs. Tie his hands, Fargo."

When the outlaw's hands were tied securely behind his back, the men led him to a large cottonwood in the creek bottom nearby. A rope was quickly tossed over a sturdy limb and a simple loop placed around McKenzie's neck. While Black Dutch was tying the other end off to the base of a nearby tree, Harley asked if the man had any final words. McKenzie didn't say a word, but simply stared contemptuously at the Ranger.

Harley gave a nod and Keeps Eagle slapped the man's horse. The outlaw was left kicking and twisting, as he slowly strangled. Five minutes later, the man was dead.

"We got nothing to mark him with, so I guess we'll leave him like he is," Harley said. "Let's get back to the ranch."

Φ

"Clean and oil your weapons tonight," Harley said. "Check your tack too, and bring your bed-rolls along. We'll be spending a few nights on the range. Every man should take two boxes of pistol ammunition and four boxes of 50-95's. That's one hundred and eighty rounds per man. And make damned certain you pick up all your rifle brass when the shootin' stops. Them cartridge cases could lead some curious soul right back to us.

"We'll leave early tomorrow morning and we got nearly 100 miles to make before sundown, so it's gonna be a long day. Pack yer things tonight. Don't wear yer white shirts 'cause we need to stay secret and don't want anyone to know who we are."

Harley talked with Phonograph Bill and arranged for the supplies the raiders would need while away from the ranch. Next, he found J.D. Flagg and confirmed his wants with the horse wrangler.

Early the following morning, the raiding party set out with two loaded packhorses in tow, spending most of the day in the saddle and finally arriving at their campsite just before sundown. The raiders camped 6 miles upstream from the mouth of the Musselshell River on the Missouri, the location of their first target, a rough trading post known to hold and support rustlers.

After surrounding the suspected hideout the following morning, Harley yelled for everyone to come out with their hands up. Nothing happened for several minutes. Finally, Billy Downs and California Ed walked out into the early morning light with their hands high above their heads.

"Who else you got in there?" Harley shouted.

"No one!" Downs yelled. "There's just the two of us."

Granville, Gus and Harley stepped out into the open, walking forward with their Winchesters at the ready. As Gus and Harley kept the two men covered, Granville entered the trading post. No one else was in the building. When Granville came out, he called to the remaining raiders to step out.

"Gus, keep these two jay birds covered while we look around," he said.

In the corral were 26 horses with well-known brands. When Harley asked who they belonged to, Billy Downs said they belonged to him. When asked where he had gotten them, Downs replied that he had traded for them with some Indians and didn't know where they came from.

"All these is local brands. You tellin' me you don't recognize 'em?" Harley asked.

"Like I said, I traded for 'em. They didn't say where they come from."

Fargo stepped from the trading post and said, "Harley, you gotta see all this meat curing in here. Shore is a mess of it."

"That's buffalo! Ain't no crime for killin' buffalo. We shot a bull yesterday," California Ed said, over his shoulder, as Harley entered the building.

"There ain't been buffalo on this range for almost two years," Granville said. "Where's the hide and horns?"

"We dressed it on the range. The scraps is out where we left 'em," California replied.

"Looks to me like you got 'slow elk' here," Harley responded, stepping out into the sunlight.

'Slow elk' was a term used to describe stolen beef. It was common for outlaws to kill cattle and jerk it so its nature couldn't be proven. If asked what it was, thieves often claimed it was elk.

Inside the trading post, Red Mack found a stack of fresh steer hides on the floor. They were salted and looked ready for shipping down river. Lifting and flipping them, Red Mack discovered that all the hides carried the **F** brand, which was owned by the Fergus Stock Company. He carried one outside and asked Andrew Fergus to identify it.

"Yes, that's our brand alright. How many are there?" he asked.

"Looks like 25 or 30. They're salted and ready for shipping."

"Well boys, you got something' you wants to tell us?" Harley asked.

"We stole them horses from some Indians! We admits it!" Downs cried. "You ain't gonna bother 'cause we skinned some Indians!"

As the men were talking outside, Jimmy was nosing around and came upon a barrel of what he assumed was whiskey. Grabbing a dipper from the counter, he scooped some up and took a long pull, only to spit the vile liquid out, gagging and coughing. "Holy hell! Red!" he shouted. "Get in here and try some of this! What is it, medicine?"

Red Mack walked back into the dark interior, grabbed the dipper Jimmy still held, smelled the contents and chuckled. "This here's Indian whiskey kid. Grab that axe by the door and knock the hoops off this barrel and any others you finds. This stuff's worse'n poison!"

Unscrupulous white traders commonly sold "Indian whiskey" to the local tribes. Made from water, alcohol, strychnine, plug tobacco, red pepper, lye soap and sagebrush, it was cheap to produce and consequently, the profits were huge. It had a devastating effect on those who drank it, making them loco and very sick. It was relatively common for an Indian or an entire clan to go on a drunk with the foul stuff, often trading everything they owned to get more, as they became more intoxicated. Blankets, robes, knives, hides, guns, horses, wives and children were traded away when under its demonic influence. When the poor wretches awoke without a thing to their name, they would turn to stealing and sometimes murder to replace what they'd traded away while drunk. If they couldn't get what they desired locally, they often jumped the reserve to steal horses or cattle from nearby ranchers to trade for what they'd lost. Or trade for more rotgut whiskey.

Making and selling the foul swill was illegal and those who did so were considered the lowest of white trash. Some, for the manner they preyed on the Indians, called them ghouls. Ranchers saw the effects of this trade on the Indian culture and felt the impact through missing stock and raids on their ranches.

"Harley!" Red Mack shouted, stepping out of the trading post, "we got us some Indian whiskey traders here. Jimmy just got his first snort."

Harley laughed. "Well boys, that cinches it. You got horses you can't prove you own. You got the hides of stolen cattle. You got 'buffalo' dryin' when there ain't been any in these parts for years. And you been selling rotgut to the Indians. I'd say that qualifies you two as just the kind of skunks we likes to hang. Dirty Bill, tie these two polecats up tight. Jimmy, get out here and get two horses on lead."

"Please, them hors—"

"Save your breath for prayin' son. We got four good reasons to hang you. You may squirm out of one, maybe two, but not all four. We got you cold," Harley said. "Of course, if you told us who was in this with you, we might be willing to give you 24 hours to get out of the territory."

Downs started to speak but California Ed told him to shut up. "We got nothing to say," he said.

"Suit yourself. If you men is determined to hang, we'll shore accommodate you," Harley said, turning to the other men. "Jimmy, you and Buster burn the stock barn and the trading post while we hang these two bad men."

The two outlaws were put roughly on horseback and taken into the nearby woods. Two stout ropes were tossed over thick cottonwood limbs and simple loops were placed around outlaw's necks. When all was ready, one of the raiders slapped the horses and they bolted out from beneath the two men, leaving them swinging, kicking and jerking, until life passed them by. Men hung in this way didn't drop any distance, which would have broken their necks and ended their lives quickly. Instead, they slowly strangled to death as the men struggled to live. When the men were finally dead, signs bearing the numbers '3-7-77' were placed around their necks as a warning to others.

The surrounding area was searched thoroughly for additional stolen stock. When none were found, Harley ordered two of the raiders to drive the stolen horses back to the DHS ranch, where they would later be returned to the rightful owners.

Φ

When the work was done, the remaining raiders rode a short distance, forded the Missouri River and rode upstream 15 miles to Rocky Point, whose inhabitants were widely known for shading the law. The marginal settlement consisted of a crude collection of buildings with two mean saloons, a few marginal businesses, a woodlot, a steamboat landing and a telegraph to Ft. Maginnis. One of the saloon owners, Melton Marsh, was a secret informer and was being paid $50 a month by the Eastern Montana Stockgrowers Association to report on any rustling activity he overheard. He was just one of many people working secretly for the Vigilantes and the raiders were now at Rocky Point as a result of a telegram Marsh sent to Granville. Based on this information, the raiders rode up to a rough log ranch house on the western edge of the settlement, the residence of James Jones, a young man heavily involved in rustling activities.

After surrounding the cabin, Granville ordered Jones to come out with his hands up. Jones responded with gunfire through a loophole, and the raiders quickly took cover, returning fire at the log home. Harley ordered Terry and Fargo to fire the house, which they promptly did. With the structure engulfed in flame, the door was suddenly thrown open and two men charged out, firing as they ran. They were quickly cut down by rifle fire and the matter concluded within a matter of moments.

As the cabin burned furiously, sending a pillar of ugly black smoke into the sky above, Harley and Gus checked the two dead men in the yard. Rolling both men over, the Ranger asked if the detective knew who they were.

"This young one is Jones. The other one, I can't say." the detective replied, as Granville walked up.

"Well, pick 'em up and put 'em on horses," Granville ordered. "Whoever he was, he won't be missed." Then, looking around, he said, "Let's leave a message for this nest of snakes. Destroy everything."

Harley gave the necessary orders and over the next several minutes, the raiders killed Jones' mule and his dog, set fire to the nearby sheds and the two wagons in the front yard. The raiders destroyed completely anything of value.

With the limp bodies of the dead men slung over two horses, several men moved upstream a short distance, where they hung the bodies from a large cottonwood tree and put signs on them.

"We been going all day and not a bite to eat. Let's cook up some bacon and beans. Them cold biscuits Mrs. Stuart sent along would be good too. Killin' snakes gives me an appetite," Harley said to Granville and Gus.

The plan was quickly seconded and two men began unloading a packhorse, only to find all the food soaked with muddy river water. "We ain't gonna be eatin' any of this, Harley. It got soaked through when we crossed the river," Red Mack said.

"Shoot! That's our only food and we just burned everythin' Jones had," Harley responded.

"You think anyone in the settlement would sell us some food?" Jimmy asked.

"Not much chance of that; only way we'll get anything' from them is to steal it, and I ain't prepared to be no thief!" Harley replied.

As Granville and Harley were discussing the food problem, they heard the shrill whistle of a steamboat from downstream. A short time later, the "Bachelor," moving upstream from Ft. Peck, passed the site of the attack. Lining the rails, staring in silence, the amazed passengers saw the smoking ruins of the cabin, sheds and wagons. They saw the dead hound in the yard and the dead mule lying at the edge of a small cornfield. And then, though obscured by dense foliage, they could just make out two men hanging from a tree. A short distance away, stood a group of stern-faced cowboys, under strong discipline, motionless and silent, staring at the riverboat as it slowly passed. A short distance upstream stood a dignified individual known to many, obviously the leader.

"Pull into shore!" Granville shouted.

The captain ignored the order and stared straight ahead, continuing on his course. Granville raised his rifle, took careful aim and fired a round into the ships bell, knocking it from its mount into the river. "I said to pull into shore!" Granville shouted again.

Having gotten the captain's complete attention, he hastily complied, backed the engine to slow and pulled into shore, where the gangway was promptly lowered. Granville stepped aboard and asked the captain for a sack of provisions. The nervous captain quickly showed him his stores and told him to take anything he wanted.

"What's your name?" Granville asked, as he stuffed two flour sacks with foodstuffs.

"T-Todd. Captain J-Joseph T-Todd," the nervous man replied.

"Now listen close Todd; you seen them men hangin' outa the trees? That's what we does to those who crosses us. You hobble your lip regardin' what you seen here today," the boss said, in a voice loaded with menace. "Savvy?"

All the frightened captain could do was bob his head rapidly, his teeth clicking but his voice failing to function entirely. He seemed overcome with nervous twitches and tics.

"If anybody asks, we're just some cowboys who had a run of bad luck and lost our food. This is for the groceries," Granville said, flipped the frightened man a $10 gold piece and then stepped ashore, silently disappearing into the brush and undergrowth.

"Away g-g-gangway!" the captain shouted, and the gangway was quickly retrieved. "All b-back full!" the captain yelled, and the boat pulled back into the current, to continue its journey upstream to Ft. Benton.

The raiders returned to the still smoldering ranch and carefully swept the area, picking up any rifle brass they'd missed earlier. When this final task was complete, Harley ordered everyone to mount up and the raiders moved several miles away from the Missouri River valley and set up a new camp on Crooked Creek.

Φ

Early the following day, the raiders set out for the DHS ranch. A couple hours later, they saw a distant rider approaching and waited until he could catch up. He explained that he was trying to contact Granville Stuart and asked if anyone knew where he might be.

"I'm Stuart. What's on your mind?"

"My name's Floppin' Bill Cantrell. Used to hunt buffalo in these parts, but when they got scarce, I started wood-hawkin' on the Missouri. Well sir, there's so damned many outlaws and rustlers hangin' around where I'm at, I gotta give it up. I don't like them types. If you could help me get outa this mess, and find some honest work, I'll show you where them devils are and help you catch 'em."

"Harley, you hear this?" Granville asked the Ranger.

"Shore did. How many men we talkin' about?" Harley asked.

"Oh, 10 to 15, dependin'. Stringer Jack leads 'em. You heard of him I guess? They post guards around, so we'll have to be careful but I can help get you past 'em," Floppin' Bill replied.

"Well, if you can do what you say, I'll damned sure find some honest work for you. Let's go," Granville said

The raiders turned back to the northeast and rode until near sundown, with the new recruit leading the way. Gus, Granville and Harley hadn't planned on hitting Stringer Jack's operation yet, but circumstances seemed too perfect to ignore. They finally reached a point where Cantrell said they should camp for the night.

After the new camp had been established and everyone had eaten, Granville, Gus and Harley conferred with Floppin' Bill for some time. Finally, Harley called everyone together. "About 20 miles below the mouth of the Musselshell on the Missouri, is Bates Point, also called the James wood yard. We're about five miles south of there right now. It's being used as a hideout for a former buffalo hunter and tinhorn gambler what calls hisself Stringer Jack. We expect 10-15 buzzards to be in this one nest. To make our play work, we need to catch 'em unawares. If we don't, this'll shore be a busted flush. We'll move into position well before dawn, so make certain you're fixed right. Since they post guards, don't do no smokin' 'til after the gunplay's over, as cigarette smoke can carry a long way if the wind is right. And don't do no talkin' on the way in, unless you have to, and then only in a soft whisper. Use Indian sign if you can. Make certain you leave your chaps and spurs where we leave the horses. Don't need no jingle-jangle while tryin' to sneak up on these devils.

"Cantrell says they post look-outs round the clock, so we gotta put out scouts and find out where they are. Once we locates 'em, we'll sneak in around 'em. At the woodlot is a log cabin at the base of a bluff, an adjoining corral and a stock barn on the opposite end. About 100 yards away, closer to the river, there's a large makeshift tent they use too. We expect most of them to be staying in the cabin. Therefore, most of us will cover that and three men will cover the tent.

"We'll ride to within half a mile, leave the horses and work our way in on foot. We've assigned positions for everyone, so make sure you look close at this map so you know where you need to situate yourself," Harley said, pulling a hand-drawn map from his pocket and opening it up so everyone could see it.

"Remember," Gus added, "if we don't take 'em by surprise, this will sure be a mess. When you move into your positions, be extra quiet. No breaking branches, scraping of fabric, nothing rattling. We should arrive about 30 minutes before daybreak, so you'll have plenty of time to move in slow and easy."

As the men set about their various preparations, Keeps Eagle and Harley set out to locate the guards. Three hours later the two men returned and reported that the guards had been located. After marking their positions on the map, Floppin' Bill described a route the raiders could take to the hideout to avoid discovery.

Early the following morning, well before sun-up, the men saddled their horses and began their quiet ride toward Bates Point. Leading the way, Floppin' Bill took the group on a circuitous route through various draws and depressions until the party reached a point a half mile from the hideout, where the wood-hawk signaled for a halt and everyone dismounted.

Terry Beard was to hold the horses. Before the men moved forward, Harley leaned close and whispered, "When the shootin' stops, bring the horses up and lend a hand. See you there."

When the group arrived near the hideout, Harley signaled for the men to split up into the two assigned elements. Granville, Gus, Black Dutch, Andrew Fergus, Floppin' Bill and the others were responsible for covering the cabin, while Harley, Jimmy and Second Bob would cover the tent. Silently, the men moved into their positions and waited for the action to begin.

As the light of dawn brightened the landscape, old man James opened the cabin door and stepped out with bucket in hand and proceeded toward the stock barn. When even with the corral gate, Granville stood and shouted, "Throw up your hands, you son-of-a-bitch, you're under arrest!" The man dropped the bucket and put up his hands. "Now, turn them horses out of that corral and be damned quick about it!" The man did as he was told, swung the corral gate open and set the stock free. Despite Granville's orders, James slowly back-stepped into the cabin, and slammed the door and fired immediately through a loophole. Gunfire quickly became general, each man pouring fire into his respective target. Return fire from the various loopholes around the cabin was intense but poorly aimed, the outlaws not having a clear understanding of where the raiders were hidden.

The tent erupted as those within opened fire, shooting indiscriminately, firing through the canvas covering. As Harley, Jimmy and Second Bob returned fire, shooting blind into the tent, those within slipped under the bottom of tent and disappeared into the thick grass and dense undergrowth. Stringer Jack made his escape in this way, taking refuge in a dense clump of willows, but Harley saw the man slip away and followed close on his heels. The two men fought it out at close range, and Harley was able to wound and finally kill Stringer Jack in the exchange.

As Dixie Burr fled from the tent he was hit in the arm, breaking it, but still managed to escape into the brush where he jumped down an abandoned dry well and remained hidden until nightfall. Paddy Rose escaped from the tent into the brush, working his way around behind the raiders busy firing into the cabin and hid in a dry wash until dark. Silas Nickerson, Orvil Edwards and Swift Bill reached the river, where they hid under the riverbank until they could burrow into a large pile of driftwood and debris.

As gunfire continued to pour out of the cabin, Granville shouted for Black Dutch to set the corral and the haystack within ablaze. Soon the stock barn and the cabin were engulfed in flame, yet the firing continued for some time, finally slackening and then stopping altogether, as the cabin burned to the ground. All within it were killed by gunfire or died in the flames.

"Ho! Ho! Hold fire, boys," Granville shouted.

"Lets see what kinda critters we caught in this trap," Gus said, walking up to Granville and Floppin' Bill, and the three men moved forward, entering the smoldering ruin of the cabin. Floppin' Bill Cantrell identified the five dead men within; old man James, his two sons, Frank Hanson and Bill Williams lay dead. Stringer Jack was not among them.

"Stringer ain't in this bunch, Mr. Stuart. Maybe he slipped the noose," Cantrell said, coughing.

"Might be in the tent; let's check" the rancher said, hopefully.

At the tent, they found Harley dragging the body of Stringer Jack into the open. He was the only outlaw killed there; all other men, though some were wounded, escaped into the brush and undergrowth.

When he heard the shooting stop, Terry brought the horses up and arrived in time to help search for those who escaped, and although blood sign was seen in several places, no more rustlers were found. The men quickly set to collecting the rifle brass from their various firing positions. After the men had thoroughly cleaned the site of evidence, the raiders put the six bodies on horseback, took them into the trees and hung them. Jimmy placed signs on the dead men.

As everyone returned to the scene of the action, Harley said, "Let's see just what those men have hidden around here. Should be plenty of stock, if we can find it."

Within two hours, the wranglers had recovered 284 horses from makeshift corrals hidden in various dry washes around the area. No cattle were recovered.

There was some speculation that the outlaws had somehow discovered the approaching raiders, thus explaining how several men were able to make their escape. Granville dismissed this thought though, reasoning that if they'd been warned, six of their number wouldn't have been killed. "We just didn't expect the snakes to slither out on their bellies; pure and simple."

The raiders split into two parties, one group driving the recovered horse herd back to the DHS ranch while Granville, Harley, Red Mack, Fargo, Jimmy, Black Dutch, Floppin' Bill and Gus continued looking for those who'd slipped the trap. After spending the balance of the day searching, none of the rustlers were found and the men widened their search.

While the raiders searched in vain, that evening Silas Nickerson, Orvil Edwards, Swift Bill and a wounded Dixie Burr built a makeshift raft from driftwood and floated down the Missouri River, where they were discovered by soldiers two days later in a swampy bog near Ft. Peck and promptly arrested. The soldiers didn't know what the men had done, but they were very suspicious because of the haggard, mud-caked appearance of the outlaws, their torn and ravaged clothing and the bloody bandaged gunshot wound in Burr's arm.

Telegraph inquiries were sent to various towns and forts in the territory. The military soon discovered one of the four men was wanted in connection with the attempted robbery of an army paymaster in which a guard sergeant was killed. Samuel Fischel, Deputy U.S. Marshall, left Ft. Maginnis immediately and arrived at Ft. Peck two days later to take custody of the prisoners and take them to White Sulphur Springs for arraignment and trial.

While the deputy escorted his prisoners west, Harley and the raiders were riding east, still on the lookout for the missing rustlers. Ahead of them, they saw several riders approaching. As they drew near, the raiders were shocked to discover the rustlers they sought were before them, in the custody of Deputy Fischel. After some conversation, Harley persuaded the Deputy Marshall to turn the prisoners over to him and his "posse." The Vigilantes made for the DHS, but stopped along the way long enough to hang the four men from a couple stout cottonwood trees.

While camped out that evening, the raiders reviewed their actions to see if they could make any improvements on subsequent raids.

"How did we do on our brass? Did we find all the cases?" asked Granville.

"I took a count of the rifle ammo remainin' and the cases we recovered. We lost two of 'em somewheres," said Black Dutch. "In the thick of the fightin' it's easy to lose a few."

"We need to do better, 'cause them cases are direct evidence we was there," Harley said. "We gotta cover our trail proper if we don't wanna swing."

"All in all, we did pretty damned good though," Black Dutch said. "Fourteen of them thievin' skunks hung!"

"Fifteen, if you counts Sam McKenzie," Red Mack said. "He sorta kicked the whole thing off for us."

"Damnation! That will shore be a warning to all the sneaks in the territory!" Jimmy exclaimed.

"The way I see it, there's only a few of them egg suckers we didn't catch. Paddy Rose ain't been found yet, and them lookouts shore took to their heels," Harley said.

"If only two or three flew the coop, I'll be satisfied if they stay gone. And as Jimmy said, this certainly will be a powerful warning to others," Granville said.

"What's our next play gonna be, Mr. Stewart?" Jimmy asked.

"Harley, Gus and I gotta go over the list when we get back to the ranch," Granville replied. "We got a long list and we're just starting."

"I gotta question, Mr. Stuart. While we was on roundup, Arty Quinlan told me some wolfer named Hoyt over on Spring Creek was seen running horses several times. How 'bout we pays him a visit?" Red Mack asked.

"Hoyt? Let's see if he's on the list," Granville said, pulling several sheets of paper from his shirt pocket. "Yep, here he is. What do you know about him, Red?"

"Only what Arty told me. Said he saw him several times running small strings of horses north towards the Breaks. Said he was a wolfer, but never seemed to have many hides around."

"When we get back, you, Floppin' Bill and anyone else you need can take care of it," Granville said.

Φ

Red Mack glassed the suspected dugout from a mile away. Even at this distance, the raiders were careful not to skyline themselves and always peered around the sides of rocks and outcrops, rather than over the top. Using binoculars, Floppin' Bill, Fargo and Red Mack kept careful watch 24 hours a day for nearly a week, until one morning, well past sunup, a man rode up to the dugout, dismounted and tied is horse off. Hoyt came out into the sunlight and the two men talked briefly. Hoyt quickly saddled a horse and together, the two men rode off toward the southwest.

The three raiders quickly mounted up and followed from a distance, using draws and depressions to remain hidden whenever possible. Just before noon, the raiders watched as Hoyt and his friend met three more men at an abandoned soddy. From there, the group rode directly south and again, the raiders followed, carefully keeping their presence secret.

An hour later, the raiders watched, fascinated, as the five men swept down on a large horse herd, driving the lone wrangler away in a hail of lead. Puffs of smoke indicated the rustlers were firing at the fleeing man, though the sound could not be heard from that distance. As the wrangler fled south, the rustlers quickly gathered the horse herd and started driving them north, toward the Breaks.

"Well, I'll be damned!" Floppin' Bill said. "Must be 500 horses in that herd. I bet that fellar they run off went for help, but by the time he gets back, them devils will be in the Breaks and gone."

"Well, we ain't gotta wonder if Hoyt is guilty. But if they's gonna be stopped, it's up to us to do it," Fargo said.

"I says it's Winchester time. How good are you with that smoke-pole of yours, Bill?"

"I ain't no trick shooter, Red, but I can damn shore shoot! Bad shots don't last long huntin' buffalo. What you thinkin'?"

"You and Fargo stay here and bust 'em when they comes by. I'll high tail it across this little saddle and hit 'em from the other side," Red said, jumping onto his horse and quickly riding away. Fargo and Floppin' Bill quickly grabbed their rifles, along with extra ammunition, and took up concealed positions along the rim of the butte they were on.

Fargo looked expectantly across the small valley, searching for sign of Red Mack, but couldn't find him. To the south, he saw the rustlers moving the horse herd into the narrows, with two men riding left and right point and two men behind riding left and right flank. The rustlers didn't have the manpower to provide swingmen. The fifth man rode drag, driving the large herd at a fast walk. Behind them, no one else was in sight; the wrangler who'd escaped had a long ride to his ranch and it would be several hours before he could return with help.

"What you shootin' Bill?" Fargo asked, as he checked his rifle and set his extra ammunition close where he could reach it easily for reloading should it be necessary.

"Aw, I shoots 45-70. Same as I used huntin' buffs. How 'bout you?"

"All us DHS riders carry 50-95's," Fargo replied, as he carefully adjusted the rear sight for the 600-yard maximum range. "How you wanna take these coyotes?"

"Well, you got some range on me. Let's let the point riders move past us and when they gets at the limit of my shootin', I'll bust the one on our side and you take the flank man behind him. After we drop them two, we can worry about them others."

"Sounds like a plan. We can depend on that red-headed Irishman across the way gettin' at least one, so that'll leave just two of 'em," Fargo responded. Across the narrow valley, he was gratified to see Red Mack finally moving into position. "Red's in position. Here they come."

As the point men drifted past, Floppin' Bill took steady aim on the one nearest him. Fargo did the same on the flank man nearest him. When his man was about 430 yards away, Floppin' Bill let fly and the air was suddenly split by the powerful blast of his rifle. This was followed quickly by another blast and then a third blast, as the DHS raiders each fired in turn.

Bill's shot had caught the point man low in the back, entering above his belt and exiting near his groin, passing through his saddle and finally into his mount's shoulder. The man tumbled out of his saddle and collapsed on the ground, mortally wounded.

"Damn, hit him about 6 inches low! Must be further than I thought," Floppin' Bill said, as he dropped the breech, pulled the spent case from the single-shot rifle and slipped another round into the breech.

Fargo's shot caught the flank rider high in the shoulder, passing down through his chest and exiting below his short ribs, blowing a red mist into the still air. The man never knew what hit him, and his body slipped from the saddle, dead and lifeless.

Red Mack's shot was low as well and caught the point man on his side of the herd high on the thigh, the bullet passing through the saddle fender and skirt, finally burying itself in the horse's chest, blowing the animal's heart out. The animal suddenly rolled and collapsed, pinning the rustler's good leg beneath it, leaving him helpless, unable to push himself from beneath the dead horse with his ravaged leg.

The two remaining rustlers were momentarily confused and unsure what to do. They'd just seen three of their fellows shot out of their saddles, and didn't know if they should fight or flee, save the herd or save themselves. As the three raiders redirected their fire on the two remaining outlaws, their confusion quickly cleared, and both men raced south in a hail of lead, abandoning the herd in favor of survival.

The man who'd been riding flank on Red's side was closest to them and all three raiders directed their fire at him. Suddenly the man was thrown over the front of his saddle, hit hard in the upper back. His body tumbled to the ground in a heap as his horse raced past. It was never known which of the raiders was responsible for the remarkable running shot. The last man, who'd been on drag, was riding fast and was well out of range, but showing no signs of slowing. He dropped over a distant fold in the prairie, and that was the last the raiders saw of him.

The men quickly mounted up and rode down into the narrow valley to see who their victims were. Two of the outlaws were cold as Christian charity and would do no more rustling in this lifetime. The one gut-shot man was still alive, though not for long. The nature of his injuries left little doubt that he would soon bleed to death. The fourth rustler was left to die where he fell, under his dead horse. He pleaded for help but his entreaties fell on deaf ears. Floppin' Bill identified the men as Larry Hoyt, Diamond Bob, Cush Taylor and Horace Humocker, all rough customers and suspected thieves.

"Well, here's four bad men we can take off the list Gus made," Red Mack said, chuckling.

Sometime later, the wrangler who'd been driven off returned with six other riders. The men were surprised to find four of the rustlers dead and the horse herd still intact. Because no trees were handy, the four dead outlaws had been tied to a rocky outcrop overlooking the small valley where they died. All had crude signs placed on them.

"Well, ain't this somethin'," the returning wrangler said. "Them Vigilantes done our work for us and they only let one skunk get away!"

"They shore is makin' a clean sweep of the territory! These devils won't be doin' no more rustlin', that's certain!" another wrangler offered.

After the three raiders returned to the DHS ranch and reported their actions to Granville and Harley, the boss of the DHS was good to his word and got Floppin' Bill Cantrell a job with the Eastern Montana Stockgrowers Association. He proved to be an efficient, reliable and able Stock Inspector.

Φ

Shortly after the Missouri Breaks raids, a Deputy U.S. Marshall from Ft. Benton arrived at the DHS with a Canadian Stock Inspector and two Royal Canadian Mounted Policemen. They were hoping to recover horses stolen from Canadian ranchers and the Mounties themselves. Harley showed the four men where nearly 300 recovered horses were being pastured.

"You fellars got quite some herd here. All these was recovered from rustlers?" the Deputy asked.

"Yep. Some of them brands has been blotted, so I don't know how you'll be able to tell what's what, but you can stay 'til you get it figured it out," the Ranger offered.

The three Canadians rode forward into the horse herd as Harley and the Deputy talked. In less than 20 minutes the three men identified and cut out 13 horses belonging to the Mounties. These were easily identified because the Royal Canadian Mounted Police branded their horse's hooves with the **MP** brand. Of the remaining herd, the Stock Inspector found 19 that still carried their original Canadian brands. These were quickly cut out from the herd. The remaining horses were more difficult to identify because many had blotted brands. Where positive identification could not be made, the horses were left with the herd. Only 7 more horses were recovered where Canadian ownership was fairly certain.

"Well, Harley," the Deputy said, "we got 39 horses, which is more than I figured. What are you going to do with these critters if you can't find the owners? The way some of these brands are blotted, you might never get shed of them."

"We'll auction 'em off and give the money to the Stockgrowers Association so they can hire more Stock Inspectors, I guess," Harley replied. "We been lettin' folks know we got 'em and we're hopin' they all gets gone so we won't have to hold no auction."

Following a good meal, the four men thanked Harley for his help and headed the small horse herd north toward the Canadian border. Over the following three months, more horses were identified and returned to their thankful owners. Finally, all unclaimed horses were sold at auction and almost $7,000 was donated to the Eastern Montana Stockgrowers Association.

Φ

Orin Winkler's delivery boy rode onto the DHS in a hurry and slid to a stop in front of the Stuart home. He jumped from his horse and scrambled up onto the porch where he pounded on the front door until it was opened by one of Granville's daughters.

"I got a message for Mr. Stuart," the boy blurted, breathing hard and out of breath. The girl disappeared and moments later Awbonnie appeared at the door. The boy hastily repeated his message and held out a telegram to her.

"Thank you," she said, giving the boy two bits and closed the door. Inside Awbonnie read the telegram and sent Katie to find Harley. Five minutes later, Katie and the Ranger stepped onto the porch where Awbonnie met them at the door.

"As you know, Gran is in Billings. This message just arrived for him but with him gone, I think you should take it."

Harley took the single sheet of paper and read it: *TWO MEN WITH STOLEN FERGUS CATTLE WINIFRED STOP WILL SHIP FROM JUDITH LANDING STOP COME SOONEST STOP FQ*

"Well if this don't beat all. Tell Granville me and one of the men went to Clagget," Harley said, handing the telegram back to Awbonnie and racing off toward the corrals.

Fifteen minutes later, Harley and Second Bob rode north at a gallop, each leading a spare horse. The men had chosen their mounts carefully, each taking two horses that were long-legged and had plenty of bottom. On their saddles were tied their bedrolls, their war bags and sacks of provisions. There was no telling where they would be staying or how long they would be gone.

"I shore hope Andrew Fergus is home. We'll pick him up if we can and then go on to Clagget," Harley said in Spanish, something he always did when alone with the Mexican wrangler.

"What will we do if he isn't at his home?" Second Bob replied in the same language.

"We'll go on alone if we must, but it would be better if he was with us since it's his stock."

The two men rode on, the silence only broken by the rhythmic sounds of their horses and the squeak of saddle leather. They maintained the same steady pace, slowing only briefly when dropping down into a draw or creek bottom, then resuming their previous speed when they were clear of it. As they traveled, Harley reviewed the telegram in his mind. He had no idea who "FQ" was, but knew Granville had spies throughout the Territory. The fact that the stolen cattle were in Winifred heading for Clagget, also known as Judith

Landing, meant the stock was probably being shipped downstream by riverboat. It was a race against time and they had to get to the landing before the boat pulled out.

A couple hours later, just past noon, the two men rode up to Andrew Fergus' home. Luckily, the man was home and when the situation was explained to him, he gathered his equipment as the two DHS men ate a hasty meal of cold biscuits and bacon. Following this, the DHS men swapped horses, saddling the mounts they had been leading. When Fergus had his necessaries assembled, and two fresh mounts ready, the men hastily departed, riding northwest toward Clagget. The tiny settlement was 40 miles from the Fergus outfit, and the men would have to step lively if they were to stop the shipment.

As they rode, Andrew and Harley discussed the telegram. Second Bob was necessarily left out of the conversation because his English language skills were poor. Second Bob, whose real name was Roberto Alvarado, was a Mexican vaquero who'd made several long trail drives north from South Texas until he'd finally decided to stay. He'd gotten his odd name because there was already a fellow called Mexican Bob over by White Sulphur Springs, and to eliminate any confusion, he was simply called Second Bob. One of the reasons he went to work for the DHS was Harley's facility with Spanish. The former Ranger spoke the language like a native, having grown up in a home where both English and Spanish were spoken. The young vaquero found life difficult and lonely in Montana, and the fact that he could speak Spanish with someone took the edge off his humble existence.

Harley was peculiar about it though, and would only speak Spanish when the two men were alone. He wanted Bob to learn English and encouraged him to make the effort, but so far, Second Bob refused, and could only speak and understand enough of the language necessary for basic communication needs. Harley's personal feeling was that if someone came to his country, they had an obligation to learn the language and customs, but he didn't force the issue. If Second Bob didn't want to learn the lingo, that was his business.

Harley's relationship with Second Bob was unusual. Most Texans hated Mexicans passionately. The slaughter of 189 Texans at the Alamo on March 6, 1836, during the struggle for Texas independence, had infuriated most Texans. The massacre at Goliad, 21 days later, was the blackest day of Mexican-Texan relations. There, 300 plus Texas Volunteer Army prisoners, under the command of Colonel Fannin, were promised safe passage in exchange for their surrender. After the men laid down their arms, they were lined up and shot by Mexican firing squads at General Santa Anna's orders. Although the Texans subsequently won their independence, relations between Mexicans and Texans remained strained. A murderous series of bloody cross-border raids years later only added fuel to the fire, and many Texans considered "greasers" as worthy only of stopping bullets. Despite these hatreds, Harley found most Mexicans to be honest and hard working, and blamed most of the problems on corrupt and vainglorious Mexican leaders, who had little concern for the welfare of *peons* and *compasinos*. During his days as a Ranger, Harley was just as quick to arrest Americans for shooting Mexicans as the reverse, and lived by a fundamental standard of fair play.

Five hours later, the three men dropped down into the rugged Breaks and soon arrived at the tiny settlement on the banks of the Missouri River. Harley checked to see when the next steamboat was due to dock and was told the Coulson Steamship Line's riverboat, Josephine, was enroute from Ft. Benton, and would arrive the following morning. Judith Landing was one of numerous sites along the Missouri River where the shallow-draft vessels stopped to load and unload freight and passengers, as well as take on fuel for the wood-fired boilers. After reporting back to his friends, the men decided to spend the night there and hunt up the stolen cattle the following day. After a good meal and a few drinks at the settlement, the men rode downstream about a mile into the Breaks and setup camp.

Early the next day, the raiders returned to Clagget, and while enjoying a good breakfast, they discussed the situation. Finally, they agreed their best course of action was to ride easy toward Winifred to see if they could locate the stolen herd. Less than two miles from the settlement the raiders spotted a herd of about 140 cattle being driven slowly north toward Clagget. The two men who worked the cattle through the river bottom seemed relaxed and unconcerned.

Harley told the raiders not to make a play until he had control of one of the two men with the herd. He then sent Andrew Fergus and Second Bob along the east side of the approaching herd, as he rode along the west side, nearest the river. As Harley began to pass the herd, and finally drew abreast of the man nearest him, he pulled his Colt and ordered the man to put up his hands. The man started to make a feeble attempt to pull his pistol, but when Harley cocked his weapon, the man realized it was a foolish play. Seeing the situation was impossible, the man raised his hands. Harley quickly disarmed him, shucking his pistol and rifle, and ordered him to step off his horse. Harley quickly had the man's hands tied behind his back and walked him toward the other raiders.

As Harley gained control of his man, Second Bob and Andrew Fergus suddenly pulled their weapons and got the drop on their man. As Fergus kept the man covered, Second Bob moved forward and disarmed him. After being ordered to dismount, his hands were tied securely behind his back and he was ordered to sit on the ground.

As Harley and his man came marching up to the others, Harley said, "This was too easy. I was hopin' these jug-heads would put up a fight."

"Have a seat next to your pardner," Fergus ordered. "Let's have a look at these cattle."

As Second Bob kept the men under guard, Harley and Fergus inspected the brands on the cattle. They couldn't believe what they saw. The cattle all carried an **F** like the Fergus brand but with a bar below it, making the brand read F Bar. Comparing one brand to the next, the men discovered the bars were of different lengths, widths and placements. Some were tapered, and others were squiggled. In fact, no two brands were the same. It looked like poor running iron work to Harley.

Returning to the two prisoners, Harley said, "You idjits ain't even clever. You steal Fergus cattle and then use a running iron to brand a bar under the Fergus brand. And a sorry job at that!"

Running irons were a popular tool among rustlers and illegal to own. Their straight shape allowed the user to draw any shape brand on a stolen animal if the they had the necessary skills. They were commonly used on unbranded steers and for altering existing brands.

"Thems our cattle and that's a legal brand. I got papers in my saddle bags to prove it!" one of the men said, looking up at the Ranger. "You got nothing on us!"

"No? We'll see." Harley went through the man's saddlebags and found papers that purported to prove ownership and proper brand registration with the Sun River Cattlemen's Association. Turning to Fergus, Harley asked, "These look like your cattle?"

"They look like 'em but it's impossible to tell. These bar brands don't look recent."

"Well, there's only one way to find out for certain."

Harley pulled his Colt and killed the nearest steer. The animal collapsed in a heap. He hated the idea of killing an animal to prove ownership, but it was the only way to be certain. After Harley holstered his pistol, he pulled his ever-present Bowie knife and walked over to the dead animal where he cut the branded hide area off the still warm animal. Turning the hide patch over, the inside of the skin showed red inflammation where the bar brand was recently made. The wound hadn't entirely healed. Looking at the carcass, the bar brand area also showed signs of recent branding.

"This proves it. That bar was put on recent, much later than the F, which is completely healed. This here's stolen beef and you is the two thieves that done the stealin'.

"Mister, we didn't steal them steers!"

"Who did? Who'd you get 'em from?"

The man was silent, as was his partner. Neither man could or would answer Harley's question, or identify who they'd gotten the cattle from. As the dejected men sat and considered their fate, Andrew Fergus walked to the horses and returned with two ropes, which he quickly tossed over a stout limb of a nearby cottonwood tree. Harley gathered the men's horses, helped them into their saddles and led them over to where the ropes were now dangling, swinging in the breeze. Second Bob slipped loops over each man's head and then tensioning the ropes, and tied the free ends off to a nearby tree.

When the two men were prepared for their journey, Andrew Fergus slapped the horses from beneath them and they were left to strangle, kicking and jerking as they slipped over the Divide into eternity. Second Bob hung signs on the dead men and their bodies were left beside the trail, their feet swinging free 24" off the ground as a warning to others of similar persuasion.

The herd of stolen beef was rounded up and over the next few days driven back to the Fergus ranch, where the cattle were released back onto the open range. Harley and Second Bob returned to the DHS ranch, where the foreman met Granville who'd returned from Billings.

"Did you do any good?" Granville asked the Ranger.

"If the river rises, they'll be nice and dry."

"Good. I like dry rustlers. No problems along the way?"

"None. But I got a question. Who is FQ?"

Granville laughed. "He's a swamper at Mackle's in Winifred, one of our informants. Why?"

"If I ever see that mop-herder, I'll buy him a drink."

Φ

Following the Vigilante raids into the Missouri Breaks, much ink was spilled in the regional press concerning the hangings, the victims and the unknown perpetrators. Word was carried throughout Montana and Dakota of the anonymous Vigilantes, who stuck the outlaw gangs like lightening, and wiped them from the face of the earth. Naturally, the notoriety attracted the interest of both Roosevelt and Vallom-Brosa. Each man suspected Granville was involved and asked if they could join in the Vigilante operations, but he wouldn't permit it, feeling as outsiders, the two men could duck out at any time, leaving him and others "holding the bag." Both men continued to press for acceptance however, and finally Granville allowed them to join as "honorary" members, and this seemed to placate both of them. Neither was ever permitted to participate in or have any direct knowledge of actual Vigilante operations, but they did provide support in the way of supplies and funds. Surprisingly, neither man pressed Granville for a more active roll.

Φ

The regional newspapers had few specifics, but recognized the Vigilantes as the only force capable of bringing order to the territories.

The River Press said of the hangings: *"The law is powerless to deal with them, and it was left for exasperated and determined stockmen to put an end to their career of lawlessness. The action of the stockmen on the Judith at Clagget ought to be repeated whenever the occasion offers. It is the only way to put a quietus on this business."*

97

Chapter Five - The Range

Summer was approaching; the wet months of April, May and June were nearly gone. With an average annual rainfall of only 13 inches, the frequent rains during this period nourished and rejuvenated the arid land and now it came alive, the brown range grasses turning green and lush, thick with new growth. Mobs of wildflowers bloomed in confetti colors, and songbirds made their tunes heard in ways never discordant. The early summer sun shown down on the rugged land, bringing welcome and nourishing warmth after the cold of winter and the fickle, damp weather of spring. The first fine days of summer made it seem as if all things were possible, all dreams could be fulfilled. There is no place on the earth where the first tendrils of summer are so life affirming, so pregnant with possibility, as in Montana. Here, the world comes *alive* with the passion and mystery of life. And yet, in these careful surroundings, humanity's struggles continue.

Early one morning, just before breakfast, Reb Peters came fanning onto the DHS as though his tail were on fire. He slid to a stop in front of the big house, raced up onto the porch and pounded on the door. Granville soon opened the door, half dressed, surprised to see Peters before him.

"What's the trouble Reb? I don't guess this is a social call?"

"You're damned right, it ain't! Some low son-of-a-gun stole Yellow Jacket right out of his stall!" Peters exclaimed. "It's getting' so you gotta sleep with your critters if you wants to keep 'em!"

"Stole your race horse?" asked Granville, not quite believing what he had heard. Peters owned a beautiful Kentucky stallion he bought for racing and breeding. The horse cost him nearly $5000 and he had big plans for the animal. Reb's excitement over the loss was understandable.

"Yep, the damned skunk! Can I borrow Keeps Eagle and maybe one of your other hands to go after 'em and get my horse back?"

"I got no problem with that, if it's square with Keeps Eagle and whoever he wants to go along," Granville replied.

Just then, Harley came walking up onto the porch. "Howdy Reb. I seen you come sailin' in and thought there might be trouble. What's goin' on?"

"Someone stole Yellow Jacket out of Peters' stable. Reb wants Keeps Eagle to track him down and bring the horse back. Is Eagle around?" Granville asked.

"Hold tight," Harley replied, and dashed off the porch toward the bunkhouse.

A few minutes later, Keeps Eagle and Harley came loping up.

"Hello Mr. Peters. I understand you need some trackin' done?" Keeps Eagle asked.

"Eagle, some skunk stole Yellow Jacket out of his stall last night. I want you to track him down and bring my horse back. I'll pay you, and any man you want to take along, $500 each to get my horse back. I ain't no tracker, not like you are, so I'm askin'. Will you do it?"

Keeps Eagle turned to Granville, who nodded his approval to the young Indian wrangler. Harley also assented.

"How 'bout if I go alone? Do I get all the money?"

"I don't give a hoot in hell how you do it! Take an army if you must. Just bring my horse back, in good condition if possible. You can split the $1000 any way you wants," Peters said, clearly desperate and anxious to see some action being taken.

"I'll be at your ranch in less than an hour. I gotta get ready and pack some supplies," Keeps Eagle said, excited at the possibility of earning two years wages for tracking and bringing a horse back.

Keeps Eagle cornered Phonograph Bill and told him his wants in the way of food for the trail. He then went to the bunkhouse to pack his war bag and just as he was finished, Bill set a sack of food on his bunk. Next, Keeps Eagle talked with J.D. Flagg, the DHS horse wrangler, and asked to have three horses from his string roped. Ranch etiquette demanded that Flagg be asked, instead of being told or simply taking the mounts without his permission. Despite the fact that Granville owned most of the riding stock, even he was obliged to ask for a mount when needed or inform J.D. when he was in the mood to do some horse trading. The horses were J.D.'s responsibility and he took his job seriously. He would pitch an absolute fit if proper custom were not observed.

The horse wrangler quickly roped the mounts Keeps Eagle requested and helped the young Indian saddle one. Eagle tied on his

Winchester in its scabbard, his war bag, his bedroll, two two-quart canteens, the sack of grub Phonograph had prepared and a sack of grain for the horses. Mounting up and leading the two spare horses, he was on his way.

Keeps Eagle was a Blackfoot Indian who'd come to the DHS in 1881 and asked Granville for a job. He proved to be an excellent wrangler and was particularly good with the horses. He was determine to keep the Indian ways alive, and with Granville's approval, spent two months of each year on the reserve learning the old ways. Thus he was an excellent tracker and plainsman. Some said he could track birds through the sky. Granville considered him a genuine asset to the DHS.

The Blackfeet had lived in the region for eons and were known for their ferocity as warriors. They were the first tribe to trade with the French for firearms and the first northern plains tribe to get horses from the south. These two factors, and their ferocity in battle, made them one of the most feared and hated tribes on the plains.

At Reb Peters' ranch, Keeps Eagle studied Yellow Jacket's stall briefly so he could identify the shoes the sleek racer wore. Shod horses were fairly uncommon in central Montana and this in itself would make the tracking much easier. After asking for and receiving a $50 advance from Peters, Keeps Eagle set off after the thief and the stolen horse, following the trail south toward the Snowy Mountains. As he galloped along, Keeps Eagle was careful to follow the stolen horse's trail, despite the fact that he was fairly certain the thief was heading for the Judith Gap.

The rustler surprised him though, going over the foothills between the Big Snowy Range on the west and the Little Snowy Range to the east, staying on a southerly course. Later in the day, Keeps Eagle saw where the man had dismounted and changed horses, now leading the horse he had been riding. Frequent changes of horses became a routine feature of the journey that Keeps Eagle followed himself. He also noticed the horse now being led had a fair amount of cow-hock in its rear legs. This could prove helpful because the animal might fatigue quickly.

As he rode along, Keeps Eagle considered the facts. Yellow Jacket was well known in the territory having been run at the big money races in Miles City, Helena, Billings and Bozeman where he won a $3,000 stakes race. Because the horse had been shown often, the thief would be foolish to keep him or sell him anywhere near Montana Territory. Therefore, he must be planning to take the horse some distance away. Heading south, he might be going all the way to Denver, maybe even Salt Lake City! This could turn out to be a long pursuit, but that's why he was being paid well to recover the animal.

He rode on until it was too dark to follow the trail, and was forced to stop for the night on the north side of the Yellowstone River. Having ridden nearly 110 miles that day, his horses were in need of rest. He watered and hobbled his mounts after stripping his saddle, saddle blanket and bridle off. From one of the flour sacks he carried, he dumped some grain on the ground for his three horses to eat. Feeding them grain improved their endurance and that was certainly something they were going to need. Keeps Eagle ate a sparse supper of jerked elk, cold sourdough biscuits and Red Seal canned tomatoes before turning in.

The following morning he forded the Yellowstone River but couldn't find the trail where the thief exited the river. He rode slowly, studying the rocks and silt in the river bottom carefully, looking for overturned or disturbed rocks on the bottom, which would show a different color through the shallow water. A half-mile downstream, he found a trail underwater that ran parallel to the shore for nearly a mile and then exited to the south. Checking the tracks leaving the water, he was gratified to see Yellow Jacket's as well as the other horse the thief rode. Based on what he saw, Keeps Eagle felt the man was 8 hours ahead of him and whoever the thief was, he was pretty good at covering his tracks, but not good enough. Keeps Eagle Crossed over the Northern Pacific Rail Road tracks and south, moving along at a steady gallop, a pace his horses could maintain all day. The trail continued south, past the Crow Agency and Pryor Mountains to the east and around noon, he took a short break. He watered his horses from his canteens and fed them more grain before changing mounts and continued on. He was unfamiliar with the area and didn't know when he would find water again but this couldn't be helped; he had to keep his horses watered and fed if they were to be fit for the chase.

He rode on, entering some badlands, where he was forced to slow his pace to save his horses. He hoped the man he was following would be doing the same. Stealing a prized racer only to kill it by riding it too hard seemed too silly to be even considered.

Two hours later Keeps Eagle came to a narrow river that smelled of sulphur, flowing from west to east and figured must be the Stinking Water River. He knew the foul smelling river flowed from near Yellowstone Park in northern Wyoming Territory. The park, which covered more than 2 million acres, was established 12 years earlier on March 1st, 1872 when President Grant signed it into existence. This was done primarily to prevent commercial exploitation as had happened to Niagara Falls in New York State. He fed and watered his horses before changing mounts, and while the water was heavy with sulphur and foul smelling, it was tolerable with no alternative available.

On he rode, coming to another river 30 miles south, which he forded easily. Again the thief's tracks failed to exit opposite where they entered the river. Keeps Eagle was forced to repeat his actions of earlier in the day, carefully studying the rocks below the water. This time he found the underwater trail upstream from the entry point. He followed the disturbed stones for nearly two miles before they exited to the south. Here he set up camp again, dumping what was left of the stinking sulphurous water and taking on fresh from the stream.

Keeps Eagle studied the tracks of the horses he pursued carefully. He bent low to the ground until he could see tiny insect tracks that crossed the sign after they were made. In this way, he could get an approximate time the tracks had been made. With too little daylight left for tracking, he was ready for a well-deserved rest, fairly confident he was about now 6 hours behind the thief and the horse he'd stolen. He was slowly catching up.

The following day was much as the day before with long hours in the saddle following the sleek racer, short breaks for food, water and horse swapping, then more riding south, steadily to the south. He was now being more careful and kept a sharp eye on the trail ahead, hoping to catch sight of the man. The trail led up onto a long expanse of rocky flats. The outlaw was taking no chances and had chosen a path over bedrock to prevent anyone tracking him. By studying the smaller pebbles and stones, Keeps Eagle was able to see the man's track fairly easily. Just as at the river crossings, he searched for the discoloration of rocks being kicked over to reveal a bottom side that had been out of the sunlight for eons and thus a darker color. These rocks were "upside down" and Keeps Eagle spotted them easily. Finally, as small stones and pebbles grew more scarce, he was forced to dismount and search for tiny burnish marks left by Yellow Jacket's iron shoes, barely visible but there none the less.

Darkness forced him to call a halt to his efforts and make another cold camp along the river he had been paralleling for most of the day. It was rough and wild country and he'd been forced to slow his pace accordingly. He estimated he had covered at least 350 miles since leaving Peters' ranch and he had yet to catch sight of the man he followed. Again, he bent to the ground to study the horse's hoof prints, looking at the telltale insect tracks and was somewhat relieved because he believed the man he sought was only 3 or 4 hours ahead of him.

The next morning the trail dropped down into a narrow canyon where the outlaw forded the river. As the tracks led up out of the river bottom, they changed to a southeasterly course as the country changed around him. The ground was now loose sandy soil, making tracking easier and Keeps Eagle felt it was time to pick up the pace; his horses were in good condition and he was confident he could now press them harder and finally close on the man he sought.

Keeps Eagle rode hard all day, the trail finally leading into a long valley between two rugged mountain ranges. When the light grew too faint to track, Keeps Eagle had to make a decision. If he continued the way he was going, he would over-take the man some time the following day. He would also run the risk of riding into an ambush. If he rode through the night, he most certainly would get in front of the outlaw but he might miss him entirely if the thief doubled back. But he doubted the man would double back because Keeps Eagle was fairly confident the man he sought didn't think he was still being followed. Finding a clear set of prints, he studied them carefully and estimated the thief was only two hours ahead of him.

After careful thought, Keeps Eagle decided to risk it. After a cold supper and a brief rest for his horses, the wrangler saddled his freshest horse and led his two other mounts well off the trail and hobbled them near a small stream, leaving them so they could graze and water themselves. Before remounting, he pulled some heavy bull hide boots from his war bag and slipped them over the hooves of his horse and tied them in place. This precaution was taken to muffle the sounds of his mount as he rode down the rough valley in the moonlight. Careful to stay well off the establish trail, he chose instead to follow game trails when he could find them. On he rode through the night, slowly making his way down the long valley, watching carefully for campfires or any other signs of life. Several times he detected the faint odor of wood smoke and once he saw his horse's ears turning to one side, as he listened to something ahead and to the right. Whatever it was, Keeps Eagle couldn't hear it but knew a horse's hearing was far better than a man's. Trusting his mount's superior senses, he cautiously skirted the suspect area and continued down the valley.

Finally, as the sky began to brighten in the east, Keeps Eagle began searching for the main trail. The two ranges had closed in considerably since he'd entered the valley and the valley bottom was much more narrow. A short time later, he cut the main trail running through the shadows on the east side of the valley. Carefully he searched for signs of Yellow Jacket's passing but found none. Riding on, he found what he considered a good ambush position behind some large rocks with low overhanging trees above them. He picked this spot because he would be hidden in the deep shadows and nearly impossible see. Also, the outlaw would have to ride close to him if he wanted to continue toward Denver. If the man turned and ran, he would have to travel all the way to the head of the valley before he would be in the open, leaving plenty of time for Keeps Eagle to catch him. After pulling the bull hide boots from his horse, he hobbled the animal out of sight behind a huge stand of boulders. Keeps Eagle finally slipped into his hide with a canteen of cool mountain water and extra ammunition and from his position, he had command of the trail for more than 800 yards to the northwest. After checking the action of his Winchester and making sure a fresh round was chambered, he eased back into the deep shadows to wait.

At just past 8:00 that morning, a horseman came down the trail, riding easily in no apparent haste. He didn't have a spare horse and he wasn't riding Yellow Jacket. The Indian relaxed and continued to patiently wait. A short time later, two more riders came down the trail and passed close-by, but again, Yellow Jacket wasn't with them.

About mid-morning, a rider came up from the Denver direction and passed close by without seeing Keeps Eagle, continuing on his way unawares.

Just before noon a man rode into sight leading a horse. It was Yellow Jacket. Keeps Eagle studied the man as he drew closer. The horse he was riding was cow-hocked as the signs had shown him and the horse was showing signs of tenderness as he suspected it might.

The thief kept urging the horse on, aware that it was in some pain but willing to sacrifice the animal to save the racer. Yellow Jacket appeared tired but uninjured.

Keeps Eagle brought his Winchester up and adjusted the rear sight for a midrange shot and carefully sighted through the buckhorn sights and waited. When the man came within 300 yards, the Indian cocked the hammer and sighted carefully. The rifle barked, and through the powder smoke Keeps Eagle saw the man hit the ground hard. As he moved to close on the thief, he saw the man reach for his horse's stirrup, hoping the horse would drag him to safety, but the horse shied, possibly from the smell of blood, and the outlaw missed his hold as the horse backed away.

Cautiously Keeps Eagle moved forward, slowly approaching the downed man, keeping his Winchester at the ready. The outlaw was showing signs of movement, trying to crawl off the trail but was able to move only a few feet before Keeps Eagle walked up on him. The Indian quickly took the man's pistol and tossed it off the trail.

"I might have known they'd send a damned red-skin to track me," the outlaw said, breathing heavily. "Just my luck."

After setting his rifle aside, Keeps Eagle quickly inspected the man's wound, and then searched his pockets, retrieving a leather poke full of gold coins and some papers. These he quickly stuffed into his pockets.

"Who are you and why'd you steal the racer?"

"My name's Logan. Met two fellers named Rather and Slocum in Montanie. They paid me $500 to steal the horse and deliver him to kin of Rather's in Denver. Said it would be a dead-eye cinch."

"$500? You was killed awful cheap, mister."

"You're right about that. I'm a goner, that's certain. How about leaving my pistol so I can finish myself off?"

"You want to be finished off?" Keeps Eagle asked.

"I don't want to linger here gut-shot. Dyin' like this could take hours," the thief said, obviously in a great deal of pain, "so how about it? Please, I don't want to die like a dog."

"Well, you lived like a skunk but I guess you can die like a man if you got the nerve," the Indian replied, then retrieved the dying man's pistol. He emptied all the cartridges from the pistol except one and handed the Colt to the wounded outlaw.

Keeps Eagle turned and soon recovered a very tired Yellow Jacket, along with the outlaw's sore horse. Just as he turned, he heard the dull report of a pistol shot. Walking back to the man, he saw the man had shot himself in the heart.

"You had more sand than I gave you credit for, Logan. But you can still do some good," the Indian said as he pulled his knife from a pocket, opened it and bent over the man. On the rustler's forehead, Keeps Eagle carved "3777."

"That'll be a warning to any other thievin' sneaks that comes this way."

Keeps Eagle gathered up his own horse and after watering Yellow Jacket and Logan's horse, mounted up. Some time later he recovered the horses he'd hobbled out and leading the four horses, he rode the back trail and began the long journey. He'd ridden nearly 500 miles and although bone tired, he was anxious to get home.

The following week, as the sun was just beginning to slip below the horizon, Keeps Eagle rode up to Reb Peters house. Knocking on the door, he asked for Mr. Peters. Soon Reb stepped out, saw Keeps Eagle and then saw Yellow Jacket.

"You got him, Eagle! You got him!" Reb shouted, fairly dancing with excitement. "I'll be danged!" He carefully looked the horse over, sliding his hand down its legs to feel for swelling and heat in the joints, checking its hooves, leading it in circles to check the gait and confirmed that the horse was in good condition. "Shoot, he ain't even hurt!"

Keeps Eagle laughed, happy that a difficult job was now behind him and glad to see Reb's reaction to the return of his prized horse. Peters had always been friendly to Keeps Eagle; the Indian judged him to be a good man and was warmed to see the rancher happily reunited with his prized horse.

"So, tell me where you went and how you got my horse back," Reb said, smiling and patting Yellow Jacket's neck.

Keeps Eagle explained that he rode almost to Colorado before he caught up with the thief, how he had shot the man and what the man had said regarding being paid to steal and deliver the horse to kin of Rather in Denver.

"I took this money and these papers off him," Keeps Eagle said, handing the items to Peters. "I ain't looked at any of it."

"Ham Rather and Slocum? It don't seem possible!" He opened the poke and spilled the gold coins out into his hand. He quickly counted the double-eagles out then stuffed the coins back into the sack. "Yep, there's $500 alright, 25 eagles. You better keep this money though. Consider it a bonus. But Rather and Slocum?" Reb added, handing the money back to the wrangler.

"I only know what the man said, Mr. Peters."

"We better keep this quiet and not let on that Yellow Jacket's back home. But let me get you the money I owe you. You've damned shore earned it!"

Reb ran into his house and soon returned with $950 in gold. "There, that squares us. Now, would you like some supper before you ride off?" Peters asked.

"No sir, I'm in a hurry to get back. I'm bone tired, but thanks anyway," Keeps Eagle said, mounting up and gathering the lead ropes of the three remaining horses. "Don't go off half-cocked with them two, Mr. Peters. I believe Logan told the truth, but I could be wrong. Talk to Mr. Stuart before you make a move."

"That's probably good advice, Eagle. And from here on in, call me Reb. I owes you for this, son. I owes you big."

The following day, Reb found the papers Keeps Eagle had taken off the horse thief, and out of curiosity, looked them over for the first time. A letter from Logan's mother was found, which Reb didn't read after he discovered its nature; there was bill from a Leadville saddle shop for $3.25 in harness repair, and finally there was an address scribbled on a piece of paper. The address was for an Emil Rather, 610 Beaver Lodge, Denver, Colorado.

"So it's true! Damn them devils!"

Φ

In late June, while Keeps Eagle was pursuing the horse thief, Granville received a message from one of his informants in Wyoming Territory warning him that an outlaw named "Rattlesnake" Jake Fallon and his partner, Edward "Longhair" Owen, were soon to leave that territory bound for central Montana, "where the pickin's is easy." Granville and Harley decided they'd have a fair chance of finding the two men if they positioned pairs of raiders in various towns around the region. Therefore, Harley sent pairs of men to Billings, Junction

City, Miles City, Maiden and Lewistown. The raiders were told to wait and keep their eyes and ears open until Harley telegraphed them. This they did.

Lewistown was founded in 1879 by 25 families of Metis traveling with Red River carts, small two wheeled conveyances made entirely of wood, whose most notable feature was the awful squeal the un-greased wheels and axles made as they traveled. The squeal could be heard for miles across the prairie. The Metis were half-breeds of French-Indian blood originally from southern Canada and northern Dakota Territory, and were "considered progressive, well educated, devoutly Catholic and fond of dancing." Large flat brimmed hats and colorful waist sashes easily identified the men and many of the Metis women were quite beautiful, having the best features of both races.

On July 2nd, Dave Thomson and Dirty Bill arrived at Lewistown, and waited as instructed. The Fourth of July (Cowboy Christmas, as some called it) festivities were getting underway and they promised to be great fun, with picnics, horse racing, a turkey shoot, a box lunch social, a parade and a street dance. People from all around the area flooded the small town and the population soon tripled with happy revelers.

On the afternoon of July 3rd, horse races were held outside of town. These were straight-line races of 600 yards, the eventual winner taking a $300 top prize at the end of the day. As the festive crowd pressed up against the ropes that marked the course, everyone was in a joyous mood, many feeling little or no pain as a result of having sampled various refreshments from one of the several tents set up near the course for the purpose. Dave and Dirty Bill were in the crowd but neither man was drinking. They were on the lookout for the two outlaws, although neither man had ever seen them or knew what they looked like.

A local man, Bob Jackson, was dressed in costume as Uncle Sam and he worked the crowd, passing back and forth, starting cheers and encouraging everyone to have a good time. He was a popular figure, well liked and many revelers bought him drinks as he passed by. He had the misfortune of bumping into a man, who quickly pulled his Colt and pistol-whipped him to the ground. The bully then cocked his pistol and made the man slither through the dust like a snake and kiss his boots, with the bully and his partner laughing loudly all the while. One of the two men suggested they retire to Crowley & Kemp's

Saloon for some refreshment and "then clean out the town." These two men were "Rattlesnake" Jake Fallon and his partner, Edward "Longhair" Owen.

The comment about "cleaning out the town" was overheard by local townsfolk, and as the two hard-cases adjourned to the saloon, the local residents quickly organized themselves and formed a plan to protect the small town. Dave and Dirty Bill were on the edges of the activity, having seen the pistol whipping but being too far away to hear the outlaws boasting. They accompanied the crowd of townsfolk back to town, where many men entered Power Mercantile. There, Winchesters and ammunition were handed out to all who wanted them. The newly armed citizens then took up concealed positions around the saloon and waited for the action to begin.

"Well, let's find us a spot and see what develops, Dave. Looks like the town's going to do our work for us!" Dirty Bill said, as the two raiders walked down the street and found positions behind grain barrels in front of the feed store.

The two raiders each pulled their Colts and cocked the hammers, ready for action. Looking around them, they saw barely concealed men in doorways, behind boxes, lying prone in wagons boxes and behind the false-fronts of buildings. As the minutes tickled by, the atmosphere in the little town, which had been so festive earlier, grew thick with tension.

Rattlesnake Jake and Longhair Owen finally came out of the saloon, well lubricated and feeling full of fight. Jake seemed to sense something was amiss and looked around but saw nothing threatening. Owen looked around too, and saw Bill Donley standing in the door of the Mercantile, with his arms at his sides. In one hand he held a pistol. This was all Owen needed.

"It's a trap!" Owen shouted, pulling his Colt and firing at the man in the doorway, who quickly ducked back through the open door. When Owen fired that shot, it was as if a signal had been sent. Everyone began firing at the two outlaws and a storm of hot lead and powder smoke filled the air.

"Get to yer horse, quick!" Jake shouted, as he jumped into his saddle, wheeled his horse and made a mad dash down the street in a hail of lead. Although hit hard in the side, Jake turned in his saddle to see where Owen was. He was surprised to see his partner hadn't made it to his horse, having been wounded in the stomach and was unable to mount up. Jake spun his horse and raced back to Owen, where he jumped from his saddle, firing with one hand, as he grabbed his partner's arm and half-drug, half-carried the man down the street toward the raiders position. Lead continued to pour in, Dave and Dirty Bill's offerings among them.

Though wounded numerous times, the two outlaws kept firing. They finally made their way to a spot just outside the tent of a photographer, and made their final stand. When the action was over and the smoke cleared, 9 wounds were counted on Rattlesnake Jake and 11 were counted on Longhair Owen. Several of the wounds each man received would have proven fatal if given time. The outlaws had killed one over-confident townsman and wounded several others.

The photographer, Ed Clark, was quick to procure two crude wooden coffins, set the two desperados into them and propped them up for display outside his tent, where he sold photographs of the dead men. Business was good.

"Well, don't that beat all," Dave said. "We had a whole damned army helpin' out! And a good thing too. Them two was sure full of fight."

"We was lucky alright. Stay here while I telegraph Harley. He'll want to know these two coyotes is dead so he can call all the men back."

While Dirty Bill went to contact the ranch, Dave approached the photographer. "How long you gonna keep these two buzzards on display?"

Clark laughed. "Oh, 'til the big doings are over, I guess. Why?"

"You know what we does with bad men and rustlers in these parts I suppose?"

"Sure, you hang 'em! What of it?"

"We also decorates 'em with signs. Sort of a warning to other sneakin' coyotes about the end they gets if they don't mend their ways or move on," Dave said.

"Signs? What kind of signs we talkin' about?" the photographer asked, curious.

"We put signs around their necks with the numbers '3-7-77' painted on 'em."

"And that's a warning to other outlaws, huh?"

"Try it. Them two buzzards won't argue one bit."

Two days later, Dave and Dirty Bill returned to the DHS ranch with a photograph of two dangerous and very dead bad men.

Φ

The evening following Keeps Eagle's return, Reb Peters went to the DHS to talk with Granville. Katie answered the door and quickly showed the rancher into her father's study, where Granville was playing a game of checkers with his youngest son.

"I might have known I'd catch you taking some poor child's money!" Reb said.

"Hello Reb! But you got it all wrong," Granville said, "this tadpole's skinning me good!"

"Bear down son, bear down," Reb said to the boy.

The boy grinned, told his father he had been saved by Mr. Peters' arrival and said they'd finish the game later. Granville laughed as the boy quickly left the room. Granville was attentive to his children's needs, reading to them when they were young, buying the latest fashions for his daughters from Helena when they were older, giving them anything they wanted and trying to make them happy. He was a good father.

"What's on your mind, Reb?"

"Did Keeps Eagle talk to you about who was behind Yellow Jacket being stolen?"

"No. He only said he rode almost to Denver and killed the man that stole him. Why? Is there something more?"

"The thief said Ham Rather and Slocum paid him $500 in gold to steal my horse and deliver him to kin of Rather's in Denver. Keeps Eagle found the money on him, along with some papers. I got to looking through them papers and found this," Reb said, handing Granville a small piece of paper with an address on it.

"Emil Rather? I didn't know Ham had family in Denver."

"I didn't either, but this seems to confirm what the thief told Keeps Eagle, don't it? Rather and Slocum put the man up to stealing my horse and taking him to Denver where he was to be delivered to a brother or cousin of Rather's."

"That's the only way I can read it," Granville said.

"Well, knowing what we does to horse thieves and knowing these two sneaks was behind it, I figure we ought to take care of 'em," Reb said, "so I came to ask for your help. You got more experience at this than I do."

"It don't take experience to put a rope around a man's neck and hang him, Reb. It's as easy as tying your lace-up boots."

"I'm going to need some help catchin' these two polecats away from their ranch though. If I just go ridin' onto the Double S with a couple hands, there's likely to be more people hurt or killed than just them two skunks," Reb said.

"I see what you mean," Granville replied. "Slocum won't be a problem because he's often out on the range, checking the line shacks and such. Rather seldom leaves the ranch though."

"That's what I was thinking. Somehow we need to bait him out and catch him when he's alone."

"Let me do a little thinkin' on it and I'll let you know if I come up with anything. I assume you want to be there when we catch them?"

"I wouldn't miss it for nothing. I want to drop the rope around their necks and slap their horses from under 'em," Reb responded. "Let me know when you get her figured out Gran. Thanks."

Three days later, Harley and Jimmy rode down to Ft. Maginnis to talk with Orin Winkler, the post telegrapher. After a brief discussion, Winkler made out a false message as dictated by Harley. It was in Winkler's handwriting, on official paper with an official date and time stamp and put in an official envelope; it was the most authentic looking fake possible. Winkler was told to get the message to Ham Rather, which he did by way of his delivery boy, a young kid who helped out around the post and delivered messages when needed. Then Winkler was given $20 in gold and told to keep his lips tight in no uncertain terms.

Harley then rode to Reb Peters' ranch to tell him what was afoot, while Jimmy returned to the DHS to let Granville know the message was being delivered as planned.

On the Double S, the messenger rode into the yard, dismounted and walked up onto the porch, where he was met by Rather before he could knock on the door.

"What you want?"

"I got a telegram for you, sir. Mr. Winkler said I was to bring it right out," the boy said, handing the envelop over to Rather. The boy stood there waiting.

"Well, what is it?"

"Mr. Winkler said I was always to wait to see if there was a response, so I'm waiting. To see if there's a response?"

"Oh," Rather said, as he opened the envelope and looked the message within. It read: *"FOUND BUYER STOP SOLD FOR TWICE VALUE STOP WILL MEET YOU DEADWOOD FIVE DAYS STOP EMIL"*

Rather was both puzzled and elated. Puzzled because his brother had planned to race the stolen horse. Elated because "twice value" could only mean $10,000, twice what Peters had paid. $10,000!

Rather looked up from his reverie and saw the boy still standing there. "Well?"

"Is there any response, sir?"

"No, there ain't no response sir! Thank yer Winkler for me. I didn't know you delivered messages," Rather said, walking back into his house, leaving the boy standing there.

"Skin flint!" the boy muttered, as he got on his horse and began the ride back to Ft. Maginnis.

The following morning, Ham Rather saddled his best riding horse and headed south, skirting around Black Butte to the east. He had barely gone four miles when he saw two riders approaching. He felt some unease but knew he had nothing to fear. *Guilty conscience? Ha!* No one knew he was behind the theft of Yellow Jacket and the horse was now 600 miles away. What's more, the horse had been sold! He soon recognized the two riders as Reb Peters and Harley Denny. *What now?*

"Morning boys," Rather said, grinning. "What's up?"

"Your hands," Reb said, pulling and cocking his pistol. "Reach for the sky!"

"What's the meaning of this?"

"I said reach! Unless you want to die right here," Reb replied, as Harley rode forward and pulled Rather's Colt from its holster. Harley then shucked the man's Winchester from the scabbard.

"What's this all about?" Rather said, shocked that he had been rendered helpless so easily.

"It's about Yellow Jacket, a thief named Logan and the sum of $500 in gold. That's what it's about," Reb said. "Now, get moving you thievin' coyote!"

Rather rode off in the direction Reb had waggled his pistol. The two men were right behind him and any thought of escape was quickly forgotten. *They know everything! But how could they? Emil? Slocum? Logan?*

The three men rode west for several miles until they came to Little Box Elder Creek. There they met two more DHS wranglers who had a small fire going with a pot of coffee simmering.

"Get down," Harley ordered. "Jimmy, tie this skunk's hands behind his back and set him down. All we can do now is wait."

Harley and Reb poured themselves some coffee and squatted down next to the fire with Black Dutch to wait. There was little conversation and Rather was puzzled over just what everyone was waiting for.

Less than an hour later, Dirty Bill and Red Mack rode into sight with Lem Slocum in the lead. Gone was the fire and bluster the man normally exhibited. He too had been taken by surprise and stripped of his weapons.

As the men dismounted, Harley asked, "Any trouble gettin' this galoot?"

"None. This nine-fingered wonder came nice and peaceful, after we got the drop on him," Dirty Bill replied, chuckling.

"Well, you boys get some coffee and a smoke while I tie this rattler up."

Harley quickly tied Slocum's hands behind his back and ordered him to sit next to Rather. Reb walked over and knelt down in front of the two thieves. "You two jug-heads thought you had her all figured. But you didn't count on Keeps Eagle. He tracked your man Logan damn near to Denver and killed him, but not before he told your part in all this. So, I got my horse back, I got the money you paid Logan and I got you two coyotes in a sack. I'd call this a pretty neat package. Get ready to cross the divide."

Fifteen minutes later, amid Rather's curses and Slocum's tearful pleas, the two men were hung and signs were placed on them. Reb Peters was the man that put the rope around their necks and the man that fanned the horses out from under them.

On the ride back to the DHS, Jimmy asked Harley if the two men they just hung were involved in rustling all along.

"I don't think so, kid. I think they sorta slipped over the edge, recent like. They both let their tall talk get 'em into trouble and couldn't figure a good way out. Their solution was what killed 'em."

Φ

One day a man named Leonard Marshal and his son rode onto the DHS ranch looking for Granville Stuart.

"Are you Mr. Stuart?" Marshal asked.

"I am. What can I do for you?" Granville asked, as he took in the scene. The father and son looked tired and this was true of their mounts. The horses carried an unfamiliar brand and they rode different style saddles than those commonly seen in the northern territories. Granville assumed the men were from someplace south.

"My name's Len Marshal. This is my son Toby. We was over in the Pease Bottom of the Yellowstone when 5 men stole the horses we was herdin' up to Miles City. We had 50 head we was bringin' in from Nevada. We followed them to a cabin north of here where two rivers meet. We glassed their cabin and saw our horses in their corral. They was brandin' 'em. We come to ask for help gettin' 'em back," Marshal said.

Granville considered the situation. "How was it you got my name?"

"We run onto someone that calls hisself Floppin' Bill? He told us where to find you and said you might give us a hand."

Everything about the man and boy rang true. Turning to Harley, he said, "Go with this man and get his horses back for him if you can. Take anyone you need to do the job. Do whatever you think right with the thieves; I'll back whatever play you make."

Harley enlisted Black Dutch, Second Bob, Jimmy, Fargo, Red Mack and Terry for the hunt and with a pack horse laden with supplies, the group left the DHS, riding northeast with Marshal and his son as guides.

Two days later, just before sunup, the raiders approached a cabin near the mouth of the Musselshell on the Missouri River. They spotted a lookout at the same time the lookout saw them, and as the man turned and fled to warn the gang, Jimmy and Second Bob raced in at an angle to cut him off. This they did, sweeping down on the man with pistols drawn.

"Drop ur guns, senior," Second Bob ordered. The lookout quickly complied. "Tie hees hans, Yeemy."

As Jimmy was tying the man's hands, Second Bob noticed the brand of the horse he was riding; it was the **D-S** brand. As the other raiders rode up, Second Bob showed the brand to Harley.

"Well, well. Caught cold, huh?" Harley said. "Jimmy, gag this varmint so's he can't warn his friends. We'll take him with us. We gotta be close."

The raiders continued on for less than a mile, dropping down into the rough river bottom to a log cabin, stable and corral. Tying their horses off, Harley left Jimmy in charge of their prisoner and the other raiders advanced on the hideout.

As the men drew near the cabin, Harley signaled for the men to surround the building. He then leaned close to Marshal and his son. "You recognize them horses in the corral?" he whispered.

Both nodded their heads. "They's ours," the boy whispered.

"Take cover," Harley said, no longer whispering. Seeing that all the raiders were in position, Harley fired three shots from his pistol into the air.

"You in the cabin! You're surrounded! Come out with yer hands up! If you don't, we'll burn you out!"

All was silent for perhaps a minute, and then a voice shouted from within, "Who are you?"

"I'm the fellar that's gonna roast you turkeys fer dinner if you don't come out. Now get yer hind parts out here, pronto, or it's gonna get mighty hot awful fast!"

Slowly the cabin door opened and a man shouted, "We're comin' out. Don't shoot!"

Four men walked out into the early morning light, their hands high. The raiders quickly tied their hands behind their backs and sat them down on the ground. When the outlaws were secure, Harley turned to Marshal and his son, "Get whatever stock is yours from the corral and be on your way. We got business to take care of here."

The father and son recovered their saddle horses and then separated out their stolen stock in the corral. All the brands had been freshly blotted, making the original brands unreadable, the hair around the brands freshly burned. After offering their thanks to the raiders for a sample of "Montanie justice," Marshal and his son left with their horses, happy they'd been recovered.

"Dutchy? How 'bout you and Fargo gettin' a top rail off the corral and puttin' it between the roof of the cabin and the roof of the stable. Red, get us enough ropes for this bunch."

When the corral rail was set in place, spanning the gap between the two buildings, all five rustlers were hung from it, each kicking and jerking, fighting to remain on this side of eternity. The work was soon concluded, and the raiders recovered the 11 remaining horses from the corral. Driving the loose stock, the raiders were back on the DHS ranch two days later.

Φ

The Great Falls Tribune years later said, in explaining the need for Vigilante action: *"Isolated ranches, continually at the mercy of outlaws and rustlers, lived in daily fear of losing their stock and even life itself. No "nester" out of sight of his horses and cattle, could feel reasonably certain that he still possessed them. Some found it advisable to sleep in the mangers of their stables, rifles in hand to protect their horses. The region was losing heart under the curse of organized hordes of outlaws, against which the established agencies of law were well-nigh powerless.*

"The cattlemen, from purely selfish reasons, stepped into the breach and, becoming both prosecutor and judge, disregarded the law's prior claims against individuals and wiped the docket clean. There was no appeal. A few outlaws escaped, perhaps, but none returned."

Chapter Six- The Dude

One of the features common to many western ranches was the presence of dudes or visitors from back east or Europe. These were people who had heard and read much about the "wild west" and wanted to witness and experience it for themselves. These visitors fell generally into two categories, either tolerable, friendly, likeable folks or pests who asked lots of idiotic questions, caused problems and were a general nuisance.

Whichever group the visitors fell into, none of the ranchers looked forward to these interlopers because they were a distraction and required someone to "baby sit" them, show them around and keep them out of trouble. So it was with Granville. His partner, Conrad Kohrs, had friends back east who's son wanted to experience the west and had recently arrived in the "rugged frontier town" of Helena, where he quickly grew disappointed. He wanted to experience real ranch life and urged Kohrs to find him a ranch position. In mid-summer Granville received a telegram from Kohrs saying that he was sending the young New Yorker out from Helena to the DHS. He would be arriving at Lewistown on the stage from White Sulphur Springs.

On the designated day of his arrival, Jimmy and Red Mack were dispatched to bring the newcomer to the DHS ranch. It is understandable that the two wranglers were put out at having to assume baby sitting chores, when they could and should be taking care of ranch business or hunting down outlaws.

"What time's the dude s'posed to show up, Red?"

"I think the stage gets in from White Sulphur Springs in about a half hour. Let's us get a drink at Crowley & Kemp's, then wait for him to show," Red replied, after checking his pocket watch.

"Least this trip won't be completely wasted then. I could stand a drink for the grief I am about to receive," Jimmy groused, as the two wranglers tied their horses off to a hitch rail and stepped into the saloon.

Coming from the bright sunlight outside, the dark interior, with its tall 12 foot tin ceiling and dark wood furnishings, took a few moments for their eyes to adjust. As they stood at the bar, Jimmy surveyed the patrons in the back bar mirror. The crowd was a mix of wranglers, soldiers, miners, gamblers, townsfolk and a couple Indians sitting near the front door. At a table in the corner, five rough looking men sat playing poker, smoking cigars and drinking whiskey. One of the men caught Jimmy's attention because of three long scars on his face, running from near to one eye down to his chin.

"See that feller in the corner with wagon ruts for a face? Seems to me I seen him somewheres," Jimmy said in a low voice. "You know him?"

Red looked carefully. "Not me. Never seen him before."

"Hey Pete! How 'bout two more?" Jimmy shouted to the barkeep.

The barkeep walked down and poured the DHS wranglers two more shots.

"Pete, that fellar in the corner with the scars on his face; who is he?" Jimmy asked quietly.

Pete gave a quick look and then said, "I think his name is Tyler, or Wyler or Syler. Something like that. Why?"

"Seems like I ought to know him from somewheres, that's all. Who's he playin' cards with?"

"Never seem 'em before. They're a rough crowd though; insulting really. I wish they'd pull their freight outa here and go somewheres else," Pete replied, wiping the bar down and moving on.

"Let's throw these back and go find our dude," Red said. "It's bitter medicine but we has to swaller it. Come on."

The wranglers walked down the boardwalk and arrived outside the Lewistown Hotel just as the stage pulled up in a cloud of dust and commotion. "Whoa, whoa, you spavined lop-eared glue bags!" the driver shouted, straining as he pulled on the lines, bringing the rig to a cacophonous and dusty stop. "All out for Lewistown, the middle of Montana!"

The side door popped open and two women stepped out briskly, then a drummer and finally, the dude. Dressed in a very tall dome-topped white Stetson, a red and white satin shirt, yellow fringed gauntlet gloves, bright blue trousers, bright yellow and white boots with a pair of large-rowelled Mexican spurs, nickel plated and shining like the sun, the young man stepped to the ground and took in his surroundings. He was a wonder!

Jimmy burst out laughing uncontrollably, doubling over with mirth, barely able to catch his breath. Other onlookers laughed as well. Red Mack growled something about a "circus comin' to town," walked forward and asked the man if his name was Douglas Dinkins.

"Yes, yes it is. You must be the boys from Mr. Stuart's ranch. Very happy to meet you," Dinkins said. "My bags are in the boot. Please get them and put them in your wagon."

"Whoa mister! We ain't boys; we're men. And if you wants yer bags moved, you'll move 'em yerself. We ain't got no wagon 'cause we brung you a horse to ride," Red said decisively, "and that's flat!"

The youngster looked as if he'd been slapped, but went to the rear of the stage and began pulling his bags from the boot. Jimmy walked up next to Red, still chuckling; his eyes and cheeks still damp. "We can't go nowhere with that parade. We'd never be able to walk these streets again!"

"Oh, why me lord?" Red said, sighing deeply. "You're right, kid. We gotta get him some new clothes pronto," Red replied, as the dude came up, dragging his numerous bags.

"If you have no wagon, what am I to do with my bags?"

"Throw 'em in the hotel. They'll be alright," Red replied, disgusted.

After the bags were moved inside, and the dude returned, Red asked, "You got any other clothes or they all like what you got on?"

The dude looked as if he didn't understand, then said, "All my clothes are similar to this, yes. I understood this is what cowboys wear riding the range and punching doogies."

Jimmy burst out laughing again. After giving Jimmy a dirty look, Red Mack said, "You can't go nowhere lookin' like that; not if you wants to live. Come on; let's get you a proper outfit. And make sure you walk at least 10 feet behind me! I don't want anyone knowin' you're with me!"

As Red stomped off toward Power Mercantile, the young man looked around, confused, and lost. Jimmy was no help whatever, and burst out laughing every time he looked at him. Finally, seeing no choice but to follow the rough cowboy, he walked hurriedly after him, and followed the man into the store. There, much to the humor of Mr. Power, the dude was outfitted with a proper hat, two white shirts, two pairs of tight fitting canvas pants, a black vest, a pair of snug high-heeled riding boots and a blue silk bandana. DHS wranglers all wore boiled white shirts, instead of the usual plaids and calicos worn by other wranglers. This was something they'd adopted to set themselves apart from all the other outfits, and while they'd done it on their own, Granville was pleased and felt it added a certain espirit de corps. As one of the top outfits in the territory, the men were proud of the DHS and their involvement with the ranch.

When the dude had changed into his new clothes, Red picked up his circus clothes and asked, "How long was you planning on stayin' with us?"

"My plan was to remain with you until October, if that is acceptable with Mr. Stuart."

"You got any nickel plated guns and fancy dude holsters in your bags?"

"What? Err…no, I have no guns or holsters with me."

"Good." Red turned to the storeowner and tossed the dude's fancy clothes to him. "You better burn these."

Before the dude could voice an objection, Red dragged him over to the gun case, where he picked out a new Colt Single Action Army pistol with a 5-½ inch barrel and black rubber grips. Next, Red selected a decent holster, nothing fancy, but certainly functional. "Better give me ten boxes of shells while you're at it," he told Mr. Power, "He'll be wantin' some practice."

After the boxes were set on the counter, Red asked, "How much is all this?"

"The total for the clothes, boots, hat, pistol, holster and ammunition is," Mr. Power said, pausing as he tallied the bill, "is $93 even."

Red turned to the dude and said, "Pay him. I'll be outside."

The dude was flustered, but handed his money over. "Please don't burn the clothes I wore in here. If you would, please fold and bundle them, and I'll pick them up the next time I come to town," he said.

He buckled the holster around his waist and slipped the Colt into it, feeling its heft. In a large mirror, he admired his new duds. They certainly weren't like the clothes he'd worn in but they looked serviceable. In fact, the dude thought he looked pretty good in them, just like a real cowboy! Feeling somewhat less putout than he should have been, he tucked his remaining purchases under his arm, puffed up his chest and proudly walked out into the bright sunlight.

"You look better; at least I ain't embarrassed to be seen with you. Now, go pick out one bag you need to take with you right now, and stick your new things in it. We'll send a wagon for the rest of your things tomorrow. I'll meet you down the street in front of the saloon."

After the dude selected one carpetbag and tucked in his clothes and ammunition, he joined the two men. "Jimmy, tie this man's bag on his horse. Doug? You looks like you could stand a drink. If you can't, I damn shore can. Come on," Red said, walking into the saloon. "And don't say a word to anybody but me or Jimmy!"

With Jimmy bringing up the rear, the three men strode to the bar and asked for drinks. After Pete filled three glasses, Red hoisted his, turned to the dude, and said, "Welcome to the wild west, dude. Bottoms up."

"Thank you, mister…I don't believe I got your name."

"My name is Red Mack or Texas Red Mack or Texas Red or Red or Mack. Whichever you prefer. This laughin' hyeenie next to me is Jimmy Van Horn. Glad to meet you," Red said, shaking the young man's soft hand.

"I take it I looked somewhat the fool when I stepped off the stage. I do apologize. I was under the impression everyone dressed in that fashion. No wonder Mr. Van Horn couldn't compose himself."

"That's what comes of reading dime novels. No harm done, though. At least you weren't wearin' no hair pants or shiny pistols!"

"I guess the joke was on me. Thank you for helping me get properly attired. I hope I can show a better result than my first impression made on you two men," Doug said.

"What sorta of work did you do back east?" Red asked.

"Oh, I didn't work, I just graduated from Harvard."

"What's that?"

"It's a university," the dude replied, and then seeing Red's puzzled expression, quickly added, "A school. I plan on working when I return home."

"A man that don't work must be rich. What did you do to make yer money?" Red asked, being very forward. The dude couldn't have been more than 22 years old and Red was curious to learn how a young man could earn enough money not to work.

"My parents are quite well off, I'm afraid. My father is a banker and good friends with Mr. Stuart's business partner."

"Oh. Well, we can't hold havin' money against no man, I guess. Just don't wear no more of them circus clothes around here. The DHS ranch is one of the best outfits in the territory and we gots our reputation to think of."

"I am sorry, Mr. Red. It was an honest mistake and one I will not repeat. I promise. Now, how about another drink?"

"Just plain Red will do. I give you a hatful of names and mister weren't one of 'em."

"Yes, thank you. Red," the dude said, somewhat flustered. "Now, I believe it's my turn to buy?"

"Pete! Set 'em up again!" Red shouted to the barkeep.

As the three men were waiting for their drinks, Jimmy suddenly came alive. "Red! I know where I saw that galoot in the corner! That's the skunk that was pawin' Katie at the dance, the one she knocked over in Miles City!"

Red Mack looked at the man seated in the corner playing poker. "Well, what of it? The way I heard it, she pretty much trimmed his horns for him."

"Yes, but I got some trimmin' of my own to do," Jimmy said, turning and walking over to the seated man, then standing over him until noticed. Red Mack and Doug stood leaning on the bar, watching carefully for things to develop.

"When that tornado gets goin', don't say a damned word and don't pull that pop-gun on your hip, no matter what happens," Red whispered into the dude's ear.

"Glad to hear it. It's not loaded," the dude replied, in *sotto voce*.

"What? Don't *never* wear no gun unless it's loaded!" Red whispered excitedly, as Jimmy confronted the man.

"You're the skunk that likes to paw women at dances and force himself on them, ain't you?" Jimmy said, in a deadly voice. "And from them wagon ruts in your face, I'd say women don't likes you any better than I does!"

"I'll make you eat them words, you whelp!" Tyler shouted, and jumped up, overturning his chair.

As Tyler came up, Jimmy hit him hard in his left eye with a straight right, effectively closing that eye and knocking him backwards, over the overturned chair, into the corner. As the man struggled to get to his feet, Jimmy tossed the chair out of the way, reached down, jerked the man to his feet and hit him with a left hook in the other eye, closing that one too, and knocking him down again.

All the card players at the table stood up and backed away from the action. Just as Jimmy bending over to grab the man on the floor again, one of the poker players pulled his pistol, pointed it and prepared to fire. Suddenly, he felt a hard thrust in the small of his back, and heard the distinctive clicking sound of a pistol being cocked. "Drop it or die where you stand," Red said from behind him.

The man dropped the pistol as if it were on fire. "Get over by the bar and behave," Red said. "You three do the same. Shuck yer guns and step to the bar. Ain't gonna be no back-shootin' in here today."

The men did as ordered, dropping their pistols and sullenly walking to the bar. As Red kept them covered, he said over his shoulder, "It's your play kid. I got all his tribe up a tree."

Jimmy reached down again and grabbed the struggling man's shirt tail, pulling it up over his head, leaving him in the dark and his arms tangled up. Next, Jimmy jerked his pocketknife out, flicked it open and slashed at Tyler's waist as the man came to his feet. The man's gun-belt and pants fell to the floor, eliciting laughter from the patrons enjoying the spectacle. Grabbing the man by the shoulders, Jimmy shoved him hard toward the front door, but he tripped over his tangled pants and fell hard. Everyone laughed again. Jimmy jerked him up again and made a show of aiming him at the front door. When he was sighted properly, Jimmy kicked the man hard, launching him across the room, where he fell in a heap. More laughter. Jimmy repeated the process a couple more times, finally kicking him through the front door, over the boardwalk and out into the street in a cloud of dust. A big hoorah went up as everyone cheered, except the four men at the bar, who only saw humiliation and embarrassment at their friend's poor showing.

"That's one skunk that'll know better before he starts pawin' women!" Jimmy said, making a show of dusting his hands off. The theatrical movements brought on more laughter.

"You egg suckers!" Red said, waggling his pistol at the four sullen men at the bar, "Pull your freight outa here fast. And you, Mister Backshooter; if I sees you again, I'll kill you."

The men walked out, offering nothing more than surly looks and attitude. Red Mack and Doug straightened up the chairs and table, then collected the pistols and dumped them on the bar.

"Pete! That money over there's yours for cleaning up this hog trough. Hang onto these shooters 'til we leaves outa town. Don't want them babies havin' no acci-dents! Now, how 'bout another drink gents? Drinks for everyone on me!" Jimmy shouted. Everyone cheered and stampeded to the bar, slapping Jimmy on the back, laughing and hollering.

"I'll serve your drinks, but I won't take your money, Jimmy," Pete shouted over the din, laughing as he poured more drinks. "It's worth a few drinks to see the way you fellars buffaloed that bunch!"

After the men downed their drinks, Doug turned to Red and said, "Is this the type of thing that happens every day out here?"

Red laughed. "No, this was just a little show we puts on special sometimes for dudes, drummers and sky pilots."

"Ha! That certainly was some show all right, but speaking for the dudes in the crowd, I'd like to congratulate the winner. Good job, Jimmy! They were a tough bunch," Doug said, pouring fresh drinks and saluting the young wrangler.

"They was only half-tough, but thanks for the drink, dude," Jimmy said, chuckling.

Red laughed. "Blinded, hobbled and humiliated. That was some show, kid!"

"Well, let's head for the barn. I feels like punching some doogies!" Jimmy proclaimed, mocking the dude in a friendly way. The three men walked out of the saloon laughing.

As the men rode for the ranch, the dude asked what kind of man Granville was.

"He's about the fairest man you'll ever meet. And he ain't afraid of nothin'. Sorta bookish sometimes though," Red replied.

"Bookish?" the dude asked, "What does that mean?"

"Always got his nose in a book; reads all the time. A funny story I heard about him and his books happened while he and some other men was on a roundup or drive. Seems that Mr. Stuart took a sack-full of books along so the men would have something to entertain themselves with. They did, usin' any free time they had, which on a roundup is damned little, for readin'. Anyway, the cook complained to the roundup boss that the men was showin' up at all different times to eat instead of everybody eatin' at the same time. This made his job lots harder and he threatened to quit. Good cooks is hard to find in these parts so the roundup boss said he'd take care of it and he did. The next day, he grabbed Granville's sack of books and flung 'em into the river. I heard that was the first traveling library in Montana

Territory and the last time Granville ever tried to educate cow punchers."

Φ

Two hours later, they arrived at the DHS ranch, much to the relief of Granville. Following the pro forma introductions, Douglas Dinkins was shown a guest room in the big house.

"Excuse me, Mr. Stuart? Would it be acceptable if I were to stay in the bunkhouse with Red Mack, Jimmy and the other men?"

Granville was taken aback. "Them men must have had quite an effect on you!"

"Yes sir! They're everything I imagined cowboys to be! If possible, I'd like to work with them while I'm here. I think I could learn a lot and I certainly like their style."

"What you're askin' is risky. These men do dangerous work and I don't want to write someone's mother sayin' he was killed," Granville said, surprised at such a request from a dude. The request also earned a measure of respect for the young man.

"If those fellows will have me, I'm willing to take my chances. Why don't we leave it up to Red Mack and Jimmy? If they're game, I'd just as soon spend my time with them. If not, well, I do appreciate the hospitality and I'll stay wherever you say," Doug offered.

Granville sent Mary to find Harley. When he arrived in Granville's study, the situation was explained to him. Like Granville, Harley was surprised at the request. Neither Granville nor he had ever seen a dude ask to work alongside the wranglers. Harley walked down to the bunkhouse where Red and Jimmy were washing up for supper.

"What'd you fellars do to the dude? He asked if he could spend his time on the ranch workin' and bunkin' with you two tumble bugs!"

Jimmy burst out laughing. Red considered the request. "Well, he learns fast, don't he Jimmy? If we gotta baby sit him, he's welcome to spend his time with us if he wants," Red replied. "How 'bout you, kid. You mind if he sticks with us?"

"Not one bit! He's sorta entertainin'," Jimmy said, laughing, thinking of the dude as he stepped from the stage. "Like a circus! Bring him down boss. I think you'll like him."

Harley couldn't believe what he was hearing, given all the complaining Red and Jimmy had done before they rode off to retrieve the man. All Harley could do was shake his head in wonder and walk away. *Some things is beyond understandin'!*

As Harley walked into Granville's office, he and the dude were looking at Granville's extensive library. "Well dude, Red and Jimmy says 'let her buck', so you can bunk with us if you're still game."

Doug was happy the men accepted him. Granville however, was not. "Well, son, if this is the way you want it, I insist that you sit here and write your parents a letter telling them that you've asked to work alongside our ranch hands, that it's dangerous work and I recommended against it. When you're done, I want to read it and mail it for you. Will you do that?"

"Certainly! Where can I set and write?"

As the dude bent to his labors, Harley and Granville stepped into the parlor to talk.

"What's going on, boss? I'm startin' to think them two knot-heads we sent for the dude has lost their good sense!" Harley said, still at a loss to understand.

"Beats me, Harley. But you get with those two idjits and tell 'em to keep a close eye on the dude. I don't care what he writes or what he says. This is dangerous country and I don't want no tenderfoot hurt or killed!"

After supper with Granville and his family, Douglas Dinkins moved his gear into the bunkhouse. The heavy stink of mildew, sweat, dirty clothes, wood smoke, coal oil, body odor, tobacco smoke and filth created a pungent mix that assailed him as he entered the low structure. The dark interior seemed to suck the light from the very air, and no matter how many oil lamps burned; the interior would never be bright. The dirt floor was covered with an inch of dust and scattered in all directions when anyone walked through. Around him, the men were a bit reserved, except for Red Mack and Jimmy, but their opinion of the dude began to change when he joined four men in a friendly game of poker, and took most of their money. While playing cards, the dude noticed those men not playing or watching the game, were busy repairing their outfit. One wrangler was mending a set of broken reins while another was working over a worn saddle with a heavy needle and thread. Off to one side he saw a Mexican wrangler braiding an intricate rawhide quirt in a fashion he'd never seen before. It was beautiful.

When the card game finally broke up, Doug was shown where he would sleep. The crude bunk was a pitiful affair with packed straw for a mattress. It was hard as a rock and had long since lost its ability to conform to anything, and after he laid down, the dude was forced to seek the shape of the bed rather than the reverse. He fought to find a comfortable sleeping position, trying various attitudes, until he reached a compromise of sorts. Relaxing at last, he started to drift toward sleep until the bedbugs and mosquitoes made themselves known, feasting on him with abandon, buzzing and gnawing away with impunity. Itching and slapping in desperate defense, Doug counted his regrets, instead of sheep, before he finally slipped off to a restless and unrewarding slumber.

Φ

Doug arose stiff and sore the following morning, his frame having been racked and bent at unaccustomed angles. He ambled about in a fatigued stupor as he pulled on his clothes. Seeing his distress, one of the men told him to sleep with all his clothes on to avoid offering the bugs a meal and this advice he took to heart for future use. Outside near the cook shack, he "washed up" at the washstand, where he could find no soap and had to content himself with simply splashing cold water on his hands and face. When he reached for a towel to dry off, he could only find a filthy, much-used rag. Doug abandoned any thought of towel drying and, though dripping wet, followed the other men into the dogtrot that connected the bunkhouse with the cook shack. There, he discovered a rude dining room. Taking a seat on one of two long benches that bracketed the huge table, he surveyed the scene. Around him men were busily forking mountains of food onto their tin plates, arms and elbows flying in all directions, as they loaded up, each afraid he'd miss his share. The din was unimaginable: the babble of various conversations competing with one another, the cook shouting at some chastened miscreant, the clatter of tin in collision with knives and forks, the boisterous laughter. A couple of the ranch dogs skulked around the tumult, waiting for any offerings that might fall their way. When the two hounds both made a grab for a fallen ham bone, a vicious dogfight broke out, but no one seemed to notice. The growls and yelps only added to the pandemonium. Doug began to suspect the men were putting on a crude show for his benefit, sort of a prank, but this proved to be not so. What he witnessed during his first meal was typical of every meal he was to eat with these rough men.

After the men had eaten and everyone had cleared out, Red Mack waited patiently outside for Doug to show. Most of the men had already left to tackle their chores and when Red asked the few that remained, they said they hadn't seen him. Puzzled, Red went looking. He finally found him in the cook shack talking earnestly with Phonograph.

"Ah, there you are!" Red exclaimed.

"I was just tellin' the dude abou..." Phonograph started to say.

"Bill, yer probly the finest man in the territory when yer alone. But when you're with someone else, you acts like a damned 5 year old child!" Red said, with some heat.

"I was just talkin'!"

"Bill, yer *always* talkin'! Come on Doug, we got things to do that don't involve swappin' recipes and tellin' tall tales!"

Red Mack left the cook shack in a hurry, with the dude right on his heels. "When you talks to him, kid, you better make sure yer hat's on tight! He's the windiest man I ever know'd!"

"He seems like a good man," Doug replied.

Red stopped in his tracks and turned to face Doug. "He *is* a good man. Every man in this outfit is damned good at what he does, but Phonograph's paid to cook, not palaver! Why you think we calls him Phonograph? It's 'cause he can't shut up! He'd talk the legs off a senty-peed! Now, come on!"

Red led the dude into the tack room, where they got saddles, bridles and horse blankets. Next they walked out into the corral, where they found J.D. Flagg smoking a cigarette.

"Mornin' J.D. How 'bout ropin' Pickles and Stony for us?"

"No problem," J.D. replied, tossing his cigarette away. He grabbed a lariat and quickly returned with Stony on lead.

Red picked up a bridle and started to show Doug how to put it on the horse. "Excuse me Red, but I know how to do all that. You don't have to waste your time showing me," Doug said, smiling.

"You can, can you? Show me," Red responded, doubtful.

Doug took the bridle, slipped it onto Stony, flipped a saddle blanket in place and then grabbed the saddle, quickly putting it on Stony properly. Red could only shake his head.

Just then, J.D. walked up with Pickles on lead.

"Excuse me Red, but is Pickles for me?" the dude asked.

"That was my plan. He's a gentle old cuss, but a good ridin' horse," Red replied, patting the horse's neck

"I can ride, Red. And I can rope too," Doug said. "J.D.? Would you mind if I borrow your lasso?"

"Lasso?" J.D. replied, unfamiliar with the term.

"That's Texas talk for lariat, J.D.!" Red said, laughing.

"Here," J.D. said, handing his 60 foot lariat to Doug, smiling. He was confident the young man was about to make a fool of himself.

Called lariat, riata or lasso, the cowpuncher's rope had changed little from the earliest days in Texas, where they were first used to work stock. Originally made of braided leather or grass, a lariat had an eye called a honda, through which the body of the rope passed to form the loop needed for roping. Later lariats were made of braided horsehair. These were rough and prickly with the short stiff hairs sticking out; they were very rough on all but the most calloused hands. They were so rough that many wranglers would surround their bedroll at night with a horsehair lariat, believing a rattlesnake would not pass over the rough cactus-like surface. By the 1880's, imported fibers of tightly twisted hemp or manila were used. Most wranglers carried a 40-foot long lariat, this being the practical limit for all but the most expert, who used longer lengths, some few up to 70 feet in length. The trick to roping was to throw a loop out so the animal could run through it and then pull the loop closed around the animal's head or hocks. When roping horses, it was important to close the loop as soon as possible after it was past the horse's head so the animal was caught high on the neck. If the rope slipped down where the neck met the body, all leverage was lost and the horse could drag the roper around all day.

Doug took the lariat, shook out a loop and walked toward the horse herd standing nervously at one side of the corral, the loop carried low at his side. Twirling was not done because it would spook the horses. The jittery horses eyed the approaching man nervously, rightfully suspecting he would try to rope one of them and each was determined not to be caught. As the horses bolted and ducked away,

Doug stepped to head them off, watching their movements carefully. When he spotted the horse he wanted, he quickly fired a long overhand loop, called a hoolihan, which settled over a fiery 5-year-old buckskin gelding's head. As Doug took up the slack the loop tightened high around the horse's neck, he back-stepped to the snubbing post in the center of the corral and snubbed the horse off with a couple quick turns around the post. He slowly began working the buckskin closer and closer until the horse was on a short lead. Throwing two quick half hitches over the post, he walked over to retrieve the bridle, saddle and blanket. These he quickly put on the horse, removed the lariat, coiled it up and jumped into the saddle. The buckskin put on a brief aerial display, bucking and crow-hopping stiff legged but the dude stuck to him like a tick. After a couple minutes of useless protest, the horse calmed down, accepting his fate.

Riding over to an astounded J.D. and Red Mack, the dude handed down the rope. "Here's your lariat, J.D.. That's a good one."

The thick manila rope was used especially for roping horses. It's larger diameter and softer fiber was easy on the riding stock, causing few injuries no matter how hard the horse might fight it.

"That cayuse you got is one of Dutchy's string. Name's Tony. He's a good horse," J.D. said.

"Will Mr. Dutch mind me riding him?"

"I doubt it. Just take it easy and don't run his legs off," the horse wrangler said, walking off to attend to other matters.

"What are we going to do today, Red?"

"Well, I'll be dipped! Where'd you learn to ride and rope the way you does?" Red asked the young man, clearly impressed. If the Texan hadn't seen the demonstration, he wouldn't have believed it. A dude!

"I've wanted to come west since I was a boy. I learned all I could from cowboys that came east and I spent a lot of time practicing what they showed me."

"I guess you has. Come on."

Φ

Over the following week, Doug proved he wasn't the average addle-headed dude. What he didn't know, he quickly learned if shown. Those things he thought he knew, once corrected, he never repeated. The wranglers soon took to the likeable young man, and

131

when Granville asked Harley how the young man was working out, the foreman always made the same reply, "Holding his own."

One evening after supper, Harley and Doug rode several miles northeast toward Black Butte. As they dropped down into a dry wash, Harley told Doug to dismount and tie the horses up. As he was doing this, Harley set up several well shot-up and rusted tin cans on a fallen log. Stepping back 10 yards, Harley called the dude over.

"I understand your ridin' and ropin' is purty good. Did you learn to use that iron on your hip?"

"I know how to shoot and I'm fairly accurate," Doug said, "but I've never had anyone show me anything special."

"Well, if you wants to be a cow hand in this country, you gotta learn to shoot fast and accurate. Shoot them six cans I just set up over there."

Doug pulled his pistol, cocked it and took slow deliberate aim. Every shot fired hit home and Doug seemed fairly pleased with himself.

"Set 'em up again."

When Doug returned, Harley said, "I'm gonna show you some tricks you can practice when you gets the time. Watch."

Harley drew and fired a single shot in a blur. His hand moved faster than Doug could see and the dude only caught sight of the pistol as it was being slipped back into the holster. Harley was surrounded in cloud of gray powder smoke from the black powder propellant that fueled the Colt and all other cartridges. When Doug looked, one can was down. Harley then repeated the demonstration with his left hand; firing an accurate shot with a draw so fast it couldn't be seen.

"No matter how fast you are you can always get faster. The trick is hittin' what you intend," Harley said as he reloaded his pistols. It was an amazing demonstration of Harley's ability to shoot fast and accurately with either hand. "Remember that. The key is *intention*. Train yerself so yer body does exactly what you intend. Set 'em up again."

"Watch," Harley said and drew with his right hand, twice fanning the hammer with his left hand in a blur as the gun came level, firing three shots with each fan. Six cans were knocked down.

"Harley, how in the world did you do that? You fired six rounds in less than two seconds and you hit six targets!"

"When I fans a pistol, my thumb fans the hammer back first, then my middle finger, then my little finger. That way, with one fan, I fire three shots. If I fan twice, six shots. See?"

"I understand the numbers alright, but I've never seen or heard anything like it! That was amazing!" Doug exclaimed, shaking his head.

"Set 'em up again." Harley replied, brushing aside the compliments as if he were swatting flies, and began reloading his pistol.

"This is the last 'trick' I'll show you. It's dangerous, so be awful careful if you try to learn it. Watch close."

Harley's pistol seemed to leap from its holster with lightning speed and twirl around pinwheel fashion as Harley fanned the hammer as it passed. With each revolution, a shot was fired and a can was hit. It only took seconds for Harley to fire all six rounds. With a final flourish the pistol was back in his holster. It was magic.

"Judas priest! That's the most unbelievable thing I've ever seen! I'll be damned!" Doug exclaimed, jumping up and down in a small circle, astounded by Harley's shooting ability and gun control.

"Set 'em up again and we'll move back a ways."

After the cans were reset, Harley told Doug to pace off 100 yards. While the dude counted off paces, Harley reloaded his pistols as he walked along. When Doug had counted out 120 paces, he stopped.

"This it?" Harley asked.

"Yes sir, this is as near 100 yards as I can get."

"Good. Watch."

Harley pulled one Colt, gripped it with two hands, elevated the pistol to compensate for bullet drop and fired six slow aimed shots. Five of the cans were hit.

"I'll be damned! I never heard of anyone shooting a Colt at this range, much less being accurate with it!"

"It's tough to get six hits at this range. Today I'm about average. Run down and set them cans up again, while I back us up a bit more."

Harley paced off another 100 yards and reloaded his pistol while he waited for Doug to return. When the young man was by his side, he said, "I just paced off another 100 yards. It's tougher to get hits at 200 but with practice, you can do it. Watch."

Again Harley pulled his Colt, elevated the pistol considerably more this time and fired six more slow aimed shots.

"How many did I hit?"

"I can't even see them! Not at this range, I can't."

"Well, run down and get our horses and see what kind of a shooter I am today," Harley said, as he began reloading his pistol again.

A few minutes later, Doug came up leading the horses. "You hit three of them! I couldn't even see the damned things! How did you do it?"

"Magic, kid, just plain old Texas magic. The reason I showed you all this was so you would understand what's possible. With enough practice, a fellar can do damn near anything. Now let's get back to the ranch; no tellin' what's busted loose by now."

As Harley and Doug rode back to the ranch, the Ranger explained things that couldn't be shown. He talked about the difference between shooting at tin cans and someone who's shooting back. He stressed the need for accuracy over speed. He talked about carrying the hammer on an empty chamber so he wouldn't accidentally shoot himself. He told him about blackening the sights with lamp black under certain situations and he talked about two gun rigs versus single pistol outfits. He talked about tied-down triggers, extended hammers, open trigger guards, stoned actions, long-barreled pistols versus short barrels, various holster designs, the damage caused by dry-firing and a myriad of other arcane subjects very few men on earth knew. Finally, he talked about the need to always keep a weapon clean, because his life may depend on it working properly with no misfires, hang-fires or jambs.

When the two men arrived back at the ranch and put their horses up, Doug turned to Harley and said, "Before I came out here, I thought I was prepared and knew everything there was to know about being a cowboy. I see now I really didn't know a thing. Sure, I could ride a horse, and I could throw a rope, but with the real things that a man's life depends upon, I'm lost. I can't tell you how much I appreciate you taking the time to show me what a good pistol shooter is capable of. Thank you, Harley. As you men say out here, you're aces with me!"

Doug then reached out and grabbed Harley's rough leathery hand and shook it.

"Thanks dude," Harley said, embarrassed at the display. "I believe we'll make a wrangler outa you yet, if you got the time and don't give up when things gets tough. Now, go skin that bunch of roosters in there. They still got some money you ain't took yet."

As Doug walked away, he was immensely pleased with himself. In the short time he'd been on the ranch, he had learned so much; he was like a new man. He felt vital, alive for the first time in his life. He had immense respect for Red Mack, Jimmy and the other men, but they wouldn't make a patch on Harley's shirt in his estimation. What an outfit!

That night, he didn't play cards, choosing instead to clean his pistol and oil down his holster, rubbing neat's-foot oil into it to take some of the stiffness out. He turned in early and thought of the amazing shooting demonstration Harley had put on and all the things he told him. Harley had shared a lifetimes experience with him! A real Texas Ranger to boot! Tomorrow, he would have to write his parents again and tell them about this amazing man.

Φ

Two days later, a rare opportunity presented itself. Granville received word that a huge grizzly had been seen at the head of Dog Creek, 20 miles north. A small group of six riders was put together, including Doug, to go on the hunt, and after the party was properly outfitted, they set out.

The men passed Black Butte and rode onto a vast range that stretched away into the distance. As they rode, Red Mack explained they were following the same route taken by the Nez Perce Indians during their breakout.

"They come through here in the winter of '77. Indians hates to fight in winter, but the army had 'em on the run. They was tryin' to get up into Canada and damned near made it too, but they was caught near the Bear Paw Range. They put up one hummer of a fight. Chief Joseph was the only surviving chief, so he gets the blame, but he weren't the one leadin' 'em. The survivors was shipped to Bismarck in Dakota Territory, where the town put on a big feed for 'em, sort of a welcome home party. The next day, they was packed off to Kansas and finally to the Indian Nations."

"It sounds to me like you have a lot of respect for them," Doug said.

"I do," Red replied. "They weren't these reserve Indians you see today, they was the real thing. Proud and full of fight. There was lots of real Indians at one time. The Shoshone tribe, Mrs. Stuart's bunch, were a terrific people. And the Northern Cheyenne was some of the best fighters that ever sat a horse. The Blackfeet, Keeps Eagle's tribe, were terrific horsemen too. Awful dangerous and mean as snakes."

"What happened to them? I mean, aren't they still real Indians?"

"Some few are. We whipped 'em, wore 'em down, and killed most of 'em. The few that was left, they was packed off to the Indian Nations, many of the survivors died there. The Northern Cheyenne broke out and made a run at returning to their homelands. They finally made it and because there was so few, the government decided to let 'em stay. Something similar happened to the Nez Perce. And the Blackfeet still live on their traditional lands. Anyway, once they gets bottled up on a reserve, it changes 'em. They can't hunt like they used to or migrate with the seasons or follow the buffalo or do any of the things they know how to do. All they got is the government tit, if some crooked Indian agent don't steal most of what they was promised."

"Do you still have Indian trouble? I mean, when I came into Lewistown, I saw several Indians and they seemed harmless."

"The only trouble we has these days is stealin' horses and killin' cattle. Small bands get frisky, jump the reserve and raid the ranches, raisin' Cain. We gotta be on the lookout fer that. There's some that has taken to farming and ranching and they does fine, if no one bothers 'em. Like I said, some of them are good people," Red concluded.

Around noon, the party came to the head of Dog Creek, where they ate a quick meal. They soon saddled up and formed a line abreast, with the riders about 200 yards apart. Doug had been warned that if he spotted the bear to fire a pistol shot into the air and everyone would come running. The line moved slowly north, carefully sweeping Dog Creek bottom clean and the washes that joined it.

A half hour later, Doug heard a shot and shouts off to the west. He spun his horse and spurred hard, the horse jumping forward. What he found, excited and amazed him. Among stunted junipers and pines, Buster and Dirty Bill had roped a huge white-backed bear and he was giving them a fit.

"Don't be shy, dude! Jump right in!" Buster shouted excitedly.

Doug quickly added his rope to the enraged bear and dallied it off. It was perfect chaos as the three riders struggled mightily, the bear charging first one way and then another, the horses squealing, rearing and bolting, forced close to their mortal enemy. The action was fast and furious.

Suddenly, the bear charged forward, jerking Buster Burns and his horse to the ground. He'd tied his rope to his saddle, Texas fashion and was finally able to release it after some desperate handwork. It could have been disastrous because only Dirty Bill and Doug had their ropes on the bear! Doug was forced to bear down hard to keep the animal away from the fallen rider and horse, trying to anticipate the bear's next lunge. More riders soon added their ropes to the enraged animal, adding some insurance, much to Doug's relief. The maddened beast roared and bellowed. Riders whooped. Horses plunged. The air was filled with dust, the sounds of breaking trees, and pandemonium. Finally, the action slowed; the grizzly was exhausted and blowing, spent and broken without the strength for further protest.

Dirty Bill pulled his Winchester and killed the animal with a single shot and quickly set about removing the ropes. As he was removing the ropes, Keeps Eagle prepared to skin the dead animal. But before he started, he asked if Doug would like to help, to which the dude quickly assented.

"You got any cuts on your hands? Look close, no matter how small they are," Keeps Eagle said.

Doug studied his hands and wrists closely, and finally said, "I got two small wire cuts on my right hand. Why?"

The Indian pulled a small bottle of iodine from his saddlebags and dosed the two small cuts. "If you skin a bear and you got open cuts, sometimes it kills yer arm if you ain't been dosed. I've seen men crippled 'cause they didn't bother takin' care of themselves."

"You're sure this works?"

"Certain."

Keeps Eagle was speaking of trichinosis, a disease carried by bear, wolves and other animals that can destroy muscle movement in the body and on occasion prove fatal. The two men set to skinning and dressing the bear. And before long, the dude had blood up to his elbows and was grinning like a child with a new toy. Keeps Eagle showed him how to properly cape the large animal, saving the hide for tanning so a rug or clothing could later be made.

"I feels like I been jerked through a knot-hole," Buster replied when his friends asked about his condition. The wrangler was none the worse for wear after his spill, receiving nothing more than bruises, cuts and scrapes. He decided this was the last time he'd rope Texas fashion and set himself to learning to dally.

As the men looked on, smoking and talking quietly, Keeps Eagle and Doug finished their bloody work, finally rolling the hide into a tight bundle and securing it with leather strips. This was tied onto a nervous packhorse, along with a bundle of choice cuts of meat.

On the ride back to the ranch, Red rode up beside the dude and asked, "How'd you like yer bear hunt?"

"It was exciting! When Buster's horse went down, and just Dirty Bill and I had ropes on him, I thought that bear was going to have me for supper! I didn't realize how big and powerful grizzlies are."

Red laughed. "They can outrun a horse for a short distance and they can kill a man with one swipe. They're dangerous, so you has to be careful. Of course, they got weaknesses too. Grizzlies can't climb trees, so if you can shinny up a tree and get high enough, you're pretty safe, unless he knocks it down! And they can't run down hill very well without fallin' on their face."

"Why not?"

"'Cause their hind legs is longer than their front. Get 'em headin' down a steep hill and they're liable to roll past you."

"What else you know about bears?"

"Well, they hates to be stobbed in the butt or havin' their belly sliced open. If it's you and a big-assed bear that's dancin' and all you got is a knife, stob him in the butt or slice his belly cross-wise. It's the most painful hurt you can put on 'em and if that don't send 'em packin', nothin' will. If they do get you, play dead. Grizzlies usually bury a fresh kill so it can rot some; they likes their meat tender. Then's when you makes you getaway, if yer able."

"You sure know a lot about bears, Red."

"Keeps Eagle knows lots more than me."

"What's he planning to do with the hide?"

"He's tryin' to keep the old ways alive. I s'pect he'll have some ceremony when we gets back. Many Indians think of these bears as their cousins and they sorta honor 'em. The brains he'll use to tan the hide," Red replied, chuckling.

"I'm glad he asked me to help skin the bear out. I've never done anything like that before."

At the evening meal, the men attacked Phonograph's noble efforts. The cook used herbs and seasonings to cover the distinctive taste of the bear meat, and the mound of steaks was slowly whittled down, as the wranglers loaded up. Red Mack was sitting next to the dude and elbowed him in the side. Across the table and down a ways was Kenny Johnson, one of the DHS men who normally stayed at one of the remote line shacks. When the dude looked up, Red nodded down the table and said in a whisper, "Watch this."

"Hey, Kenny. How you likes the grub? Bet you don't eat like this ever' day," Red said in a loud voice.

"Phonograph outdone hisself! Yessir, this shore is good and worth the wait! *Hehehe.*"

"Shoot, I bet you'd eat anythin' after three months of beans and bacon ever' meal."

"Yer about right, Red! I eats anythin' but bear. No sir, I won' eat any of *that*, but I'll eat anythin' else! *Hehehe.*"

Kenny refused to eat bear meat and had made his objections known to Red several times over the years they'd known one another. Kenny was a good cowhand but couldn't keep a secret to save his life. Consequently, he wasn't asked to join the raiders and had been assigned to distant duties so he would be out of the way. He rarely ate with the men at the bunkhouse and this evening was a special treat for him.

"What, in the name of Hades, you think you been eatin'? Porky-pine?" Phonograph asked from the cook shack door.

"I'm eatin' beef, like ever'body else. What you think, you jug-head? You cooked it, didn't you?"

"That slab you's forkin' into yer pie hole is bear meat," Phonograph replied.

"Very funny, but I don't believe it. This here's beef. I knows what I tastes and I tastes beef. *Hehehe.*"

"Kenny, for a man what knows everythin', you shore got a lot to learn," Phonograph said chuckling, and ducked back into the cook shack.

"I damned shore know beef when I eats it, you grinnin' fool!"

"Well, this 'beef' shore *looked* like a bear. He jerked me an' Roscoe around like we was infants," Buster said, smiling. "We got five ropes on him 'fore he called her quits."

"Yer loco! This ain't bear meat; this here's beef! You fellars is tryin' to run a blazer on me, but yer trick won't work. Bear. Ha! *Hehehe.*"

"Well Kenny, you reckon these dogs is in cahoots with us?" Red asked innocently.

"What's them flea ranches got to do with it?" Kenny mumbled around a knot of steak. He'd continued to load up throughout the conversation.

"Let's see." Red thrust out his arm, stabbed a steak on the platter and flipped it over onto the floor as he let out a sharp whistle. The dogs jumped and raced to claim the prize, but as each dog approached and started to take a bite, it scented the bear, arched its frame and backed off, the hair down its spine standing straight up. Low rumbling growls carried through the room.

"If this bear is really beef, them dogs is really cats. Hear 'em purr?" Red asked laughing.

Kenny sat open mouthed, stunned. He suddenly spit out the plug he'd been worrying, and threw down his fork. Jumping up from the bench, he stomped toward the bunkhouse door. "I'll be damned! You is the cussedest varmints I ever seen!"

"Ain't we though? *Hehehe*," Red mocked. A wave of laughter and hoots swept the disgusted wrangler out of the room.

Φ

The following week, Granville asked Harley to get five men mounted up and ready to ride. Harley recruited Red Mack, Fargo, Dirty Bill, Black Dutch and Jimmy and waited for Granville outside the big house. When he came out he looked at his wranglers and then turned to Harley and asked if the dude was around.

"Shore, he's getting his ears pinned back listenin' to Phonograph. You wants him to go on this job?" Harley asked, surprised the boss would want the young man in the party.

"He might as well see what's happening out here," Granville replied.

Doug was soon rounded up and joined the party. As the men left the ranch, Granville rode next to Doug and gave him some history on what he was about to see.

"Earlier this summer, the army caught a band of Crow Indians stealing local rancher's horses. They were caught cold and the army knew the horses were stolen, because it was reported. Anyway, the soldier boys took the horses and Indians down to Ft. Maginnis. While they were there, a few of us ranchers rode over to the fort to claim the stock. The army refused to give 'em up, even though we could prove we owned 'em through our brand books. I talked 'til I was blue, but it didn't do any good. They said we'd have to talk to the Indian agent on the reserve if we wanted our stock back.

"Well, the soldiers took the horses, 29 in all, along with the Indians that stole 'em and headed down to the Crow Agency, where the Indians came from. Along the way, the stolen horses was so tired and played out, the army shot about 20 of them along the trail. It was senseless slaughter. If they'd simply turned 'em loose, they'd have survived and been fine. Anyway, when they got the Indians to the reserve, nothing was done to the thieves and the Indian agent refused to return the remaining horses.

"I got word earlier today that the army has more stolen horses they're taking down to the agency. We're riding out to get our horses back. I wanted you along so you can see what goes on out here. The papers back east tell a different tale, about the army and "cattle barons" abusing our red brothers. It's nonsense, but its got the army doin' all the wrong things for the sake of the politicians and eastern papers. Keep your eyes open and pay attention to what goes on out here," Granville concluded.

"I'm happy you asked me to come along and I appreciate the history of the situation. I'll keep my eyes peeled, Mr. Stuart," Doug replied.

It was late morning before Granville and the others caught sight of the cavalry detail driving 20 or so horses toward the Judith Gap. The wranglers quickly broke into a gallop and swooped down on the unsuspecting soldiers and surrounded them.

"What's this all about? Why have you stopped us?" a young lieutenant in charge of the detail asked with some heat.

"We heard you'd recovered some stolen horses and we want to see if any of them belong to us," Granville replied. "Harley, look over these brands."

Harley rode around the small herd, eyeing the various brands and taking a tally. When he was finished, he made his report to Granville. "Six of these is ours, five belong to Reb Peters, two are Bob Shepard's stock, three of 'em belong to Dave McHenry's outfit and two belong to Rather's bunch."

"The way I count, that's 18 horses you got that belong to us local ranchers. You will hand them over now," Granville commanded.

The lieutenant was shocked at the request. "Mr. Stuart, you're interfering with official government business. If any of this stock is yours, you can claim it at the Crow Agency. I warn you; do not impede this detail in the execution of its lawful duty."

"Well, I'm happy you know who I am," Granville replied, "because if you know anything about me, you know I mean business. Now, hand over them horses and be quick about it. If you don't, we'll take 'em at gunpoint. Which way you want to play it?"

The young officer was in a tough spot. If he followed his orders and refused to give up the horses, he would probably be shot, along with the four enlisted men with him. If he surrendered the horses, he would likely face harsh consequences when he returned to the fort and made his report. After some thought, he chose to live and face the commanding officer's ire, rather than die trying to protect horses from their rightful owners.

"Very well, Mr. Stuart. Take the horses," the officer finally said, resigned to the task of reporting to his commander how he lost the animals.

"Here's something to chew on, young man. Every time the Army finds our stock, we want them back. And I don't just mean quick; I mean in a hurry. If you soldiers *continue* to side with horse thieves, I guarantee you, trouble won't be far behind. Now, you know what we do to horse thieves in these parts. From now on, whether they wear blue or buckskin, all thieves will be treated the same. Good day, young man."

The wranglers gathered the horses and ran them back up the trail, toward home. The five soldiers in the detail were left with three horses to escort the many miles to the Crow Agency. Granville's group arrived at the DHS late in the afternoon. Harley assigned riders to deliver the recovered stock to the rightful owners and the men set off on their chores, riding in pairs as they loose herded the horses along their separate trails. Doug was assigned to work with Black Dutch delivering five horses to Dave McHenry's ranch. When that was done, the two men began their ride home.

"Mr. Dutch? Can I ask you a question?" Doug inquired. He didn't know Black Dutch very well and had only talked to him briefly.

"How 'bout just callin' me Dutch? Now, what's on your mind, dude?"

"When Mr. Stuart told the lieutenant about what happens to horse thieves, what did he mean? What *does* happen to horse thieves?"

"We either shoots 'em or hang's 'em, often both," Dutch said chuckling.

Doug was surprised, "But they're just horses! I haven't been here long, but I've seen quite a few wild horses on the range. Don't you think killing a man, for taking what is free, is just a little bit extreme?"

"You don't know how she lays, dude. Shore, wild horses is free, but, you gotta catch 'em first, and a man afoot has no chance whatever of catching one, none at all. Out here, miles from nowhere, if you take a man's horse, it's probly a death sentence. He'll freeze or starve or die of thirst before he can walk out and find help.

"We got no jails, no courts and no law handy, so when we catch a horse thief, we only got two choices; hang him or let him go. If we lets him go, he'll be back to steal again. Same thing goes for cattle thieves. You catch a man stealin' your cattle and you let him go, 'cause hangin' seems 'just a little bit extreme,' that man will be back to steal again 'cause he knows he can get away with it. And he'll keep stealin' yer stock 'til he's got it all and you got none. We been hoping the 'law' would come along and do its job, 'cause it shore would save us some bother, but it ain't happened yet and we has to survive 'til the day it does."

"I knew frontier justice was rough, but I thought everyone wanted it that way."

"Shore, it's rough, but no one likes it much. It's all we got though; ain't no other way to it. Would you work and sweat for a man that's too lazy to work for hisself? And if a lazy man wants yer horse or yer cow and will take it, what would you do? A child knows the answers to them questions. You'd protect what is yours. That's all we're doin', protectin' what we've worked hard to build up. But the thieves think the man that's worked hard owes 'em somethin' for free. We got organized gangs of rustlers and killers loose hereabouts and they're gettin' mighty bold."

"What do you mean, what are they doing?" Doug asked.

"They've killed men. They killed Duncan Sides, one of our hands, in a shoot-out north of here. Duncan was just a kid, a bit younger than you are today."

"What did Mr. Stuart do?"

"He didn't have to do nothin'. I tracked the man down what done it and killed him. What do you think should happen to them devils that rob and kill? Remember, all we can do is kill 'em or let 'em go."

"Given those two choices; I'd kill them," Doug replied. "It just seems like there should be a better way to dea—"

"Dude, you gotta deal with things as they is, not how they should be. This ain't no Sunday picnic we got out here."

Φ

The following day, Granville asked Doug if he wanted to go with him to the Indian reserves. The dude quickly assented, so, along with Keeps Eagle and Second Bob, the men left for the Assinaboine and Ft. Belknap Agencies to the north. The trip would be a long one so the party took two packhorses along to carry their food and a new Sibley tent Granville had gotten. This style of tent was new to the region, and resembled nothing so much as a canvas teepee 12 feet tall with a hole in the center of the conical roof for a stove, if needed. The design was simple but effective for keeping the elements off and was being adopted by many ranchers who camped on the open range, being easier to set up and carry than the more traditional wall tent because it could be erected with a single center pole or three external poles teepee fashion.

Indian agencies in Montana Territory were in a period of flux at this time. Established under the treaty of 1855, the Blackfeet Indian Reserve originally stretched north from the Missouri River to the Canadian line and east from the Continental Divide in the Rocky Mountains to Dakota Territory. Over subsequent years, the government reshuffled the deck and changed the rules repeatedly, and in 1887 abandoned the "Indian Reserve" and opened up vast tracts of land for settlement. The natives were moved onto successively smaller areas. Not only was the government reducing their holdings, but also gave portions of Blackfeet land to their historic enemies.

When the group arrived at the new Ft. Belknap Agency, Granville met with Tomas Workman, the resident Indian agent, who arranged a meeting with all the chiefs. When all were assembled, Granville had a strong message for them.

"I bring a warning to you today. Braves have been stealing horses from the Ft. Maginnis range for years. My horses have been stolen many times, as have those of my neighbors. There will be no more taking of horses. White men who take our horses are hung. We will hang any brave who steals our horses.

"Your braves will not hunt on our land. Your braves will not travel across it. We will not honor travel or hunting permits issued by any Indian agent on the Ft. Maginnis range. If we catch any braves taking horses or butchering cattle, they will be hung, just as white men are hung. Carry my words to your people and tell them what you have heard here today."

Granville's tone and demeanor left no doubt that he meant what he said. His steady gaze met each man's eyes so they would know he spoke the truth.

The following day, the party continued on to the Assinaboine Reserve, where Granville met with Donald Van Meter, the Indian agent, who organized a meeting with the chiefs of the reserve. The message Granville delivered was identical to that delivered at the other agency. No thieving, no travel, no hunting; rustlers will be hung. Period.

It was a stern message and one not particularly appreciated by the Indian agents, but Granville felt it was necessary. If the raiders were hanging white thieves, why would the Indian thieves be treated any differently? Granville's words were received and understood by those who heard them. The chiefs spoke to their bands and the message was soon passed to every Indian on all the reserves by the moccasin telegraph.

Incidents still occurred but they were few and far between. A few Indian rustlers were caught and hung, as Granville had warned, and these hangings underscored Granville's warning and put iron in his words. This effectively ended the predations of Indian raiding parties on the Ft. Maginnis Range, much to the rancher's relief.

During his visit to the reserves, Doug was able to see the living conditions of the various tribes. He was shocked at what he saw and wasn't prepared for the depressing conditions or poverty. On the return ride to the DHS, Granville had a long conversation with the young man about the reserve system and its impact on the Indians.

"The reserves are the single worst thing our government did to the Indians. The government beats them out of their land with lies and trickery, bottles 'em up on the reserves and says 'we will give you food and the things you need to live.' Half of these damned Indian agents are corrupt and the other half are usually incompetent. So, the fate of the 'noble Red Man' rests in the hands of swindlers and fools. Once put on the reserves, there's nothing much for them to do, so they sharpen their skills at stealing and drinking.

"The American government is making every effort to destroy their culture and doing a damned fine job of it, too. On some reserves, they're banning use of their language and won't let them practice their religious ceremonies. Their children are packed off to Indian schools and along the way, somewhere, they lose their identity; they forget who they are and where they came from and the damned meddling preachers have gotten involved, determined to make 'good Christians' of them, as if such a thing actually exists! Bunch of damned hypocrites and opportunists! Most of what you see on the reserves today are just shadows of what Indians once were," Granville said.

"If the reserve system is wrong, what should have been done?" the dude asked. He'd never heard the heresy that tumbled from Granville's lips and was shocked, having accepted the reserve system as a matter of course, a kind system established by a benevolent government, intent on helping the downtrodden aborigines.

"I think the Indians should assimilate, live next to whites so they can learn our ways. Them people on the reserves learn nothing. Their old ways are dead, a thing of the past. If they are to survive and prosper as a people, they have to learn our ways so they can get along in the world as it is, not as it was."

"But won't assimilation destroy their culture?"

"It might, but is what the government doing any better? Has assimilation destroyed the Russians, the Irish, the Germans, the English and all the other cultures that make up the States? And if it has, so what? Seems to me, this country is what it is because it's taken the best of each people and thrown it into the mix. Why should

Indians be any different? Don't you suppose the Indians have things they could teach us? The damned government views them as children, too lazy to work and too stupid to learn, incapable of adopting new ways, and unable to fend for themselves. The whole idea's insulting. They're just as capable and able as anyone else. When Lincoln set the slaves free, he didn't move them onto reserves and wet nurse 'em; he didn't treat them like ignorant children, too backward to learn. He treated them as men, fully capable of learning and living. Why shouldn't Indians be shown the same respect and given the same opportunities?"

"I thought the government was helping the Indians."

"Just how is the government helping? You saw the poverty on the reserves; it's pitiful. People stumbling around in rags, waiting for the next handout. But if you look at those Indians living off the reserves, they're mostly doing fine. They're good farmers and good ranchers. They understand things about nature no white man ever will. They understand working with the land and animals, not against it. I've been living amongst them since I was your age and I've found them to be resourceful, brave, compassionate and fairly industrious. What's more, they can take more hardship and do less complaining than any people I ever saw. The reserves are destroying all their good qualities and replacing them with the worst traits of the human animal. It's a damned shame."

"Is that why you married an Indian woman?" Doug asked, somewhat nervously. He was up against his own prejudices and knew it.

"That's it. White women complain and argue too damned much to suit me. Awbonnie has never complained, although she's had plenty of reason. Life ain't easy and there's no reason to pretend it is. Indians seem to accept that and don't fight it. That's a lesson all whites should learn," Granville concluded, and rode up to the head of the small party.

Granville's words gave Doug much to think about. It would be years before he realized just how much impact they would have on his life and how much they would affect his outlook. Like the passing of the buffalo, the Indian ways were also passing, shadows lost in the glare of advancing civilization.

The dude, Douglas Dinkins, spent the balance of his time on the DHS working as a common cowhand, a wrangler. There was much for him to learn about ranching and wrangling, yet he took to it with a will, enthusiastic and eager to learn all he could. He never complained and never flagged. Demonstrating more than just tolerance, the wranglers came to like him; through what was to follow, they came to respect him.

Chapter Seven - Dakota

|n Dakota Territory, the impact of the rustlers and outlaws was significant. During this time, in western Dakota, Billings County, in which the towns of Medora and Little Missouri were located, had no organization, and didn't have the benefit of a healthy local government. The law was represented by part-time officials, usually cattlemen who filled the breach temporarily. When petty offenders were caught, they were taken to Dickinson, the county seat of Stark County, 40 miles away, for disposition. Major offenders were taken to Mandan, the county seat of Morton County, 150 miles to the east.

The lawless environment in that portion of Dakota Territory prompted the Glendive Times, from Montana Territory, to comment: *"Little Missouri is fast gaining a very unenviable reputation. It seems as though what little law does exist in the place cannot be enforced, and the better class of citizens being in the minority a committee of safety* (Vigilantes) *is out of the question . . ."*

When the citizens of Billings County began to press for organization, their efforts were recognized and supported by the Dickinson Press, which commented: *"Medora is clamoring for a county organization in Billings County. We hope they will get it. If there is any place along the line that needs a criminal court and jail it is Medora. Four-fifths of the business before our justice of the peace comes from Billings County."*

In mid-summer, A.T Packard, editor of the Bad Lands Cow Boy, commented: *"From all parts of Dakota and Montana come reports of the depredations of horse-thieves. We think we are entirely within bounds in stating that in Dakota alone, there have been at least two hundred head stolen, and scarcely more than half dozen have been recovered. Several men have also been hung for horse-stealing, but the plague still goes on . . . We wish to be placed on record as believing that the only way to cure horse-stealing is to hang the thief wherever caught. The end, in this case, fully justifies the means."*

Φ

It was in this lawless environment that the Vallom-Brosa now found himself. While he wasn't in the cattle business per se, he had fenced feedlots and holding pens where cattle were kept prior to slaughter and shipment. The fencing of here-to-fore open range by the Marquis caused much rancor among the local cattlemen; these harsh feelings would eventually lead the Vallom-Brosa into trouble with the local citizens and the law. It was from these pens and lots that cattle were being systematically stolen and despite Vallom-Brosa's best efforts, the culprits could not be caught. Frustrated, he finally turned to the National Detective Agency for help.

"Your task is to catch these men. I want the entire area searched until the thieves are captured. Search as far east as Bismarck and west to Glendive. Go north to Ft. Buford and range south to the Black Hills. It's much territory to cover, but I feel certain you will find your man if you do," the Marquis told the detective standing before his desk. "You will have my complete support."

"My god man, that must be 50,000 square miles!" the detective exclaimed.

"Well, what of it? You will be paid for your efforts, have no fear of that," the Marquis replied stiffly, seeing no problem whatever.

"Well, I'll put an end to the rustling, but I'll do it in my own way, if you don't mind. I got my methods. If it's results you're lookin' for, I'm your man," the detective said confidently. "I wouldn't presume to tell you your business. Don't tell me mine."

Vallom-Brosa was stumped. Results *were* what he was looking for, yet he felt certain a thorough search would be needed. Finally, he told the detective to take whatever action he felt necessary, much to the detective's relief. *There's nothing worse than an amateur tellin' a man what knows what to do, what to do!*

Four days later, the detective was able to identify the rustlers. He felt certain the culprits were much closer to home than the Marquis suspected. While visiting a brothel in Dickinson, he interviewed a whore who was familiar with the situation and she quickly identified the five men responsible for the thefts. Based on this information, the part-time sheriff in Medora accompanied the detective and the suspects were captured without a shot being fired. Following a brief investigation, proofs were forthcoming regarding their guilt and they were promptly taken to Dickinson and jailed. When the detective reported to the Marquis that the case had been concluded and the rustlers in jail awaiting trial, he was shocked.

"But this is amazing! I will never understand this country! How did you do it? How was this done?" Vallom-Brosa demanded, incredulous. After making all the details known to the Frenchman, the detective was paid off, along with a healthy bonus, and went on his way. The rustlers were later moved to Mandan where they were tried and found guilty of rustling. All were sentenced to territorial prison.

Φ

Although the Marquis was the most notable victim of rustling activities during this period, he was not the only Dakotan losing stock. All the larger ranchers in the region were being raided and made to suffer. Several men had been shot trying to protect their herds and the situation continued to worsen.

Unknown to the Marquis or Teddy Roosevelt, earlier that spring, a group of influential Dakota ranchers telegraphed Granville Stuart for help, hopeful something could be done to stop the rustling. Granville made the long trip to a ranch outside Medora, where a secret meeting was held and the rancher's problems discussed. Granville assured them he would help after certain steps were taken. These included organizing an effective cattlemen's association, gaining the ranchers support for Vigilante activities and putting their range detectives in contact with Gus Adams or Floppin' Bill Cantrell, both of whom had proven to be very competent during the Montana raids. Subsequent meetings were held among the Dakota ranchers and the lists Adams had compiled were expanded, based on the new information.

Granville was buried in bookwork on the early fall afternoon when Gus Adams arrived at the DHS. Awbonnie quickly showed the detective into Granville's office, where he was warmly greeted. The two men discussed the problems of the Dakota ranchers briefly and then Gus asked if Granville had a good map of the two adjoining territories. After returning from his extensive library, Granville was embarrassed to report he couldn't locate any good maps.

"What? Three thousand books and you can't find a couple maps?" Gus asked, gently rawhiding the boss.

"Well, I know I got 'em somewhere," Granville said ruefully. Suddenly, he exclaimed, "I know where those damn maps are! Hold tight."

Granville left the room briefly, and quickly returned with a large portfolio of maps. Spreading the maps out on his desk, he asked, "What've you got in mind, Gus?"

Gus found the two most suitable maps and studied them carefully, all the time checking his outlaw lists before replying. "If you look at the ranches that's being hit in Eastern Montana and Western Dakota, and look at the suspected and known hideouts and then look at the route of the Northern Pacific Railroad, I think we can sweep that country clean of all those rats."

"I see the tracks come close to many of these operations but what of it?" Granville asked.

"If we were to put together a special train with a passenger car and one or two cattle cars, we could take it east towards Medora, stopping when we need to discharge raiders. Doing it that way, our men could cover a lot of territory and hit most of the gangs unawares. That sure would be surprisin' to them devils!" Gus said, pleased with himself as he uttered the plan aloud for the first time.

Granville studied the maps for a moment. Then he suddenly saw the beauty of the detective's plan, amazed by its simplicity and potential effectiveness.

"Well, I'll be damned! Hurrah! You're aces, Gus!" Granville exclaimed, excitedly. "This plan's a real hummer!"

"It's gonna take lots of planning to make her run straight," Gus warned, "but I think we can really clean up if we do it right."

"Let's get Harley in here and get at it then!" Granville replied, enthused at the prospect of cleaning out the rustlers from that region in one massive sweep.

The three men planned for several hours, defining what had to be done, who had to be contacted and what steps had to be taken to insure the success of the huge and complex operation. After the meeting, Granville made arrangements with the Northern Pacific for the make-up of a special train to be ready when needed. Gus began contacting the various detectives affected by the plan from Orin Winkler's telegraph office at Ft. Maginnis. Harley poured over the outlaw lists and maps to determine how many raiders would be needed and the sequence the raids would follow.

Fort Maginnis was established in 1880, shortly after Granville and his partners had started ranching operations. Despite Granville's outraged protests to the contrary, the army built the fort in one of his prime hay pastures and claimed nearly all the land surrounding it. This would be a bone of contention for several years, until the army finally relented and ceded the pastures back to the DHS ranch. Having the fort nearby was a mixed blessing though, because Granville did have access to the post telegraph and Broadwater & McNamera's sutlers store, which was handy for purchasing supplies.

A few days later, after Gus was satisfied he had the latest information, he met Harley and Granville again. The three men carefully studied Harley's plan of attack, confirming stops and raider discharge points, primary and secondary target locations, range detective rendezvous points, manpower assignments and re-supply ranches necessary for extended operations. Neither Gus nor Granville could find any fault with Harley's plans, which were thorough and complete, allowing for a variety of contingencies. The more Granville delved into the Ranger's plans, the more proud and satisfied he was with his selection of the man to run the show. Harley's plan called for discharging raiders from four points along the railroad to attack five primary hideouts; when these raids were complete, each group of raiders would move on to attack secondary targets before making their way back to the ranch individually.

Finally Harley asked, "You got an almanac around, Gran?"

"Got one right here," The boss replied, pulling the book from a shelf behind him. "You ain't gonna check the weather are ya?"

Harley laughed. "No, not the weather. I want to see when the next new moon is. We'll need to work at night if we're gonna catch these skunks by surprise, which we'll have to do because the rustlers will outnumber us in almost every situation. Given that, it'd be best if it was plenty dark. Less chance of discovery."

"You Rangers know all the tricks!" Gus remarked. "Damned if I don't learn somethin' new every time we get together."

Harley ignored Gus's comment, studying the book closely. "Here it is. Next new moon is on September 19th. That's 10 days away. Think we can get everything lined up by then?" the Ranger asked the detective.

"Should be enough time. It'll give the other detectives time to get things set and me to get my end covered," the detective replied.

"Well, let's do it. Our men can hop the train on the 17th and start the raids the morning of the 18th," Granville said, with a tone of finality.

Gus made arrangements for the detectives, who were to act as guides, to be available at certain locations on the proper day, while Granville contacted Samuel R. Ainislie, Superintendent of the NPRR, and made arrangements for the special train. He also contacted the possible layover ranches and the ranches where fresh mounts and supplies would be available. Once again, Terry and Jimmy carried messages to and from Orin Winkler's telegraph office at Ft. Maginnis. The next day, all the necessary arrangements were confirmed by telegram.

That afternoon, Harley called all the raiders together in Granville's office.

"We got another series of raids planned. This time we're workin' in eastern Montana and western Dakota. In eight days, we're gonna meet a special train at the Hathaway siding, west of Miles City about 20 miles," Harley told to the group. "There'll be a passenger coach for us and a cattle car for our horses. The train will pass through Miles City and then start makin' stops along the way to Medora in Dakota Territory. Each of you will be partnered up with one or more of this outfit, so we'll always have at least two men on a raid, usually more. If we can, all the raids'll take place at sunup or after sundown, depending. Even though you may be outnumbered, you'll have the advantage of surprise, and if possible, the men you're after should be bottled up nice and tight. Things can and will go wrong though, so we gotta stay flexible and play it the best we can."

"We gonna have a guide like we did the first time?" Black Dutch asked. "That Adams and Floppin' Bill was mighty handy to have along."

"Glad you mentioned it, Dutch. Each group will have a range detective to work with, who'll act as your guide and be an extra gun. Me and Granville haven't met any of the other detectives yet, but Gus swears by 'em and that's good enough for me," Harley answered.

"From Hathaway to Medora is more than 150 miles. The train will make four stops along the way. You'll move to your different targets from your stop. Now, this is a big operation. We're tryin' to pull off five lightening raids, as near the same time as possible. After your first raids, you'll move to local ranches for more supplies and fresh mounts. Each team will then move to their second target. This whole plan is mighty complicated. We got over 75 men on our list and we probably won't get 'em all, but I'm willing to bet we'll get most of 'em."

"What we gonna do if these men ain't home?" Andrew Fergus asked.

"You go hunt 'em up, if you can. But remember, in all cases you will probably be outnumbered, so it's important that you use your heads and take 'em by surprise. We don't want no prisoners either. We wants 'em hung or shot. And make certain you hang signs on everyone, like we been doin'. That's a powerful warning for those we miss, and who knows, maybe they'll get religion and leave the country."

The wrangler nodded but said nothing.

"Dirty Bill? You'll be responsible for the first raid. You and Dave will be getting off near the Powder River. You'll be met by one of the range detectives, who'll lead you in. Your first attack should be made that evening. There's six rats in the first bunch that needs killin'. After that, you'll head to a local ranch for more supplies and fresh mounts. Your range detective will spell out the next raid."

"Red? You're leadin' the second raid. You, Fargo and Ed Spencer will be gettin' off just after a water stop in Fallon, at Cabin Creek. Follow the crick south 'til you come to the O'Shea ranch, where one of the range detectives will be waitin' for you. You'll lay over for the night and make your raid the following morning, just like we did at Stringer Jacks. There's about eight or nine men in that gang, so it's important you surprise 'em. Just like Dirty Bill's raid, you'll get supplies and remounts locally.

"Dutchy? You're the boss of the third group. You, Buster and Terry will be gettin' off just past Mingusville, at Beaver Creek and head north along the crick about 25 miles to where Elk Creek runs into it. There's an abandoned dugout and a range detective will meet you there. Like Red's bunch, you'll spend the night and attack the following morning. Near as we can tell, there's twelve rustlers in that nest, so be damned careful. Done right, the four of you should be able to handle the situation. Your detective will help you get supplies and fresh horses after the raid.

"I'll be leading the last group. Jimmy, Second Bob, Keeps Eagle and Andrew Fergus will be riding with me. We'll get off at the first water tank past Sentinel Butte, where Gus Adams will meet us. There's two outfits that need to be stomped out, so we'll split up once we get the drift of things. One bunch has eight men and the other has seven. We'll wait and see how we want to divide up. Following the raid, Gus will help us get setup and make the second attack.

"The numbers I've given you are the best we can come up with. There could be less men, but we don't think there'll be more. Whichever way she goes, don't make your raids 'til you got the advantage of surprise and have 'em bottled up, plain and simple. Any stock recovered, drive it to the nearest ranch and let them folks figure it out. Now, before anyone asks any questions, and I figure there's a plenty, I'd like to meet with Dirty Bill, Red Mack and Dutchy to lay out each unit's job in detail. It'll make things lots easier for everyone."

On the appropriate day, the raiders started leaving the DHS ranch in two's and three's, taking different routes to their common objective, Hathaway siding.

Φ

The small train, consisting of an engine, a tender, a coach, a livestock car and caboose stood hissing on the siding, smoke slowly rising from its stack. All the rolling stock was of the older single axle truck design. The engineer, fireman, brakeman and the conductor were crowded into the engine cab, talking, speculating and wondering what force was behind the special makeup of the train. Both the men and the engine idled, ready for action. Off to the Northwest appeared a group of riders, thirteen in all, riding in at an easy lope. As they drew near, the railroaders could see the men were cowboys of the common variety. In attire and demeanor, the men were unremarkable; lean, youthful and weathered with alert eyes and a suppleness of movement that bespoke a vigorous life in the outdoors. "Here comes our bovine steerers," the engineer said, with a chuckle.

As the riders pulled up at the livestock car and began to load their mounts, the leader of the group rode up to the engine and addressed the men within the cab. "You fellars ready to roll?" he asked, patting his horse's neck.

"We're ready when you are," the engineer replied, "soon as you get your horses loaded and get aboard, we'll be moving."

156

"Well, let my get shed of my horse and I'll join ya," Harley replied, turning his mount back toward the livestock car, where he dismounted and ran his horse up the wooden ramp his men had positioned at the loading door. When all the horses were loaded, the ramp was pulled back and hung on the side of the car. The wranglers quickly stepped aboard the coach, while Harley joined the men in the cab. It was a tight fit.

"What you're doin' up here with us, anyway?" asked the puzzled engineer, put out at having a stranger in his "office."

"*I'm* the boss of this outfit. We'll be makin' several stops. I'll tell you where," the foreman replied, in a tone that established immediately just who was in charge. The brakeman gave the conductor a knowing look before stepping down and going back to the coach. As soon as some room was made in the cab, the fireman grabbed his shovel and bent to his labors, charging the boiler with coal. The engineer began working various valves and levers and the train started forward, slowly accelerating until it was clipping along, clickity-clack, at a swaying and noisy 25 miles per hour. Half an hour later, the train slowed as it passed through Miles City, and then returned to its previous speed. No one spoke. The engineer alternately watched his gauges and the tracks ahead; the fireman fed the boiler and Harley surveyed the vast landscape as they moved slowly through. Every 15-20 miles, the train stopped to take on additional water and coal. Harley was amazed at the complexity of operation and gained some slight degree of respect for the men who where in control. After a time, the train passed over the low Powder River trestle and pulled to a stop beside a wooden water tank and coaling tower. As the tender was being replenished, the wranglers unloaded two horses, and when Dirty Bill and Dave Thomson mounted up, they were met by another rider, and together the three men rode south toward Alkali Springs.

Levers were thrown and valves were turned and soon the odd train once again pulled out and continued on its journey. After making a water and coal stop at Fallon, Harley told the engineer to stop just before the small trestle at Cabin Creek, 12 miles to the east. There, Red Mack, Fargo and Ed Spencer unloaded their horses, mounted quickly and rode south along the stream bed, careful to stay near the creek bottom, so as not to skyline themselves.

At Harley's orders, a third stop was made at Beaver Creek, and three more men, Black Dutch, Buster Burns and Terry Beard, pulled their horses off and left the train. Once mounted, the men rode north along the creek bed and were soon lost behind folds of the land.

Shortly after the water stop at Mingusville, Harley spotted Sentinel Butte and knew the train would be stopping for the final coaling and water stop before reaching Medora. "Well boys, we appreciates your service. Good luck!" Harley said, as he stepped down from the engine and helped the remaining men unload their horses. Soon, they had closed the loading door on the livestock car and returned the ramp to its rack. Mounting up, they crossed the tracks and rode off to the north, where another rider was waiting for them in the distance. Together they disappeared into a coulee and weren't seen again.

"I wonder what them 'Terrors of the Plains' is up to?" the conductor asked, as he joined the engineer and fireman in the cab.

"Don't know and don't care. They's up to no good, if I had to guess, but I ain't no guesser and neither is you," the engineer replied. "I didn't see nothin'. It's a wonder I made it this far, me bein' blind like I is."

"Well, take one more little peek and get us to Medora. I got an itch to stop at The Senate, and drown my fuzzy memories in red-eye," the conductor said, laughing.

The Senate was a saloon and pool hall located in Little Missouri, across the riverbed from Medora. Though the small town was older than Medora, it didn't have a train station or sidings as Medora did.

"Hang on tight, then. This here speed wagon is some tough," the engineer announced. Everyone laughed as the train crept forward, with Medora in its future.

Φ

As Dirty Bill and Dave Thomson rode along, the range detective introduced himself as Marcus Adams. He was an older man, somewhere in his 40's, who'd been in the detecting business for several years. As they rode south, the land grew more rugged, with high bluffs on both sides of the river, forcing the men to pass through the heavily wooded and brushy creek bottom. Following game trails when they could, by late afternoon they had ridden about forty miles south of the tracks. At last, Marcus led them into a narrow draw, where they came upon the detective's small, well hidden, campsite.

"We'll stay here 'til just before sundown," Marcus said, dismounting. "We're too close for a fire, but I got us some jerked elk and canned food in the tent. Grab what you want."

The men stripped the saddles and bridles off their horses and put hobbles on them. Once the stock was tended to, the two raiders decided to get something to eat and in the tent the raiders discovered a box that held cans of Red Seal sugar corn, Muscantine String Beans, Baltimore Green Peas, dried peaches, Arbuckle Coffee and gunpowder tea.

"Cats! Looks like a general store in here!" Dave said. "How long was you plannin' on stayin' Marcus?"

Marcus laughed. "Well, to tell you the truth, I ain't sure. You ain't complainin' are you?"

"Shoot no! I'm just surprised you're livin' so high on the hog!"

After the men had selected their fare and opened their cans, they dug in with a will and discussed the upcoming raid between mouthfuls. Finally, with the meal behind them, they relaxed, checked their weapons and other equipment. As twilight settled in, the men saddled their horses, and mounted up. Marcus led them up out of the draw and onto a long section of bench land that stretched away to the east, where a string of low buttes could be seen in the distance.

"The bunch we're after are setup on O'Fallon's Creek, just on the other side of them buttes," Marcus said. "We got about four miles to go."

The men rode easily through the evening and passed through the buttes as darkness closed in around them. The detective led them to the top of a dry wash that dropped down into the O'Fallon creek bottom, and after picketing their horses, they removed their spurs and chaps. Carefully, they made their way down the ravine to the creek bottom, and after 10 minutes of slow advance downstream, Marcus halted, crouched down and whispered, "Their dugout is just around the next bend. If anyone's home, there'll be smoke comin' out the chimney and you'll see some light slipping out around the door and windows. Now, be extra quiet. Let's go."

Moving cautiously by starlight, for the moon was only a slight sliver, the men crept forward, rifles at the ready. When the low structure came into view, the men were gratified to see light spilling

159

out into the yard and the faintest hint of wood smoke lazily drifting up from the chimney. By prior arrangement, Dirty Bill passed the front of the hut and took up a position 20 yards away behind a woodpile. When he was in position, Marcus handed his rifle to Dave and eased forward to a stack of short unsplit logs. As Dave and Dirty Bill covered him, he carefully hefted an 18" long log and quietly carried it to the dugout. There, he gently set it down in front of the door. He could hear low conversation and the sounds of men eating their supper coming from within. *Sounds like hogs at the trough.* This was what he had hoped for. Marcus carefully moved four more short logs, stacking them in front of the door to form a low barricade. He quickly returned to Dave's position and grabbed an old saddle blanket he'd brought along. Creeping up the embankment to a point where the roof of the dugout met the cut-bank, he stepped cautiously onto the roof and slowly walked forward until he was able to drop the blanket over the chimney, blocking any smoke from escaping. Carefully, Marcus eased off the roof and returned to Dave's side where he waited for the action to begin.

The voices from within grew louder and coughing could be heard. Dirty Bill pulled the hammer back on his Winchester, cocking it with a soft series of metallic clicks and waited. Dave and Marcus did the same, knowing the show was about to begin.

"Come out with your hands up!" Marcus shouted. "You men are under arrest!"

"Who's out there?"

"Santee Clause! Throw out your guns and come out with your hands up! And make it fast! I want to make this picnic short," Marcus shouted, taunting the outlaws.

Low voices were heard from within the structure. Suddenly the door was thrown open and the rustlers burst out, silhouetted by the light from within and firing blind as they moved forward, only to stumble and fall over the low log barricade. Tumbling and sprawling to the ground, the knot of men tried in vain to get themselves untangled and regain their feet, but the raiders opened fire, shooting as fast as they could operate their weapons, cutting the men down as they struggled. The last two men still in the dugout, seeing what was happening to their comrades, jumped to the side of the door as soon as they were outside, avoiding the barricade. But it was no use; those that hugged the wall were quickly shot and collapsed just a few feet from their friends.

In less than a minute, it was over. Dead and dying outlaws sprawled before the dugout were wreathed in a low hanging fog of powder smoke. When the shooting stopped, Dave started to stand, but Marcus quickly grabbed his shoulder and pulled him back down. "Not yet," he whispered. "Might be others inside. Let's have a smoke first and give this nest of snakes time to cool."

Marcus rolled himself a smoke, lit it and enjoyed the quiet after the excitement. Across the yard, Dirty Bill did the same. The only sound that could be heard was the low rattle of a lunger who was stepping slowly into the void of the eternal. Because Dave didn't smoke, he had nothing to distract himself and slowly reloaded his rifle. "I'm gonna pull that blanket off the chimney. Be right back," he said softly.

As soon as Dave returned, Marcus set his rifle down and stood up. "Stay right here and keep me covered," he whispered, and slowly moved forward, his Colt cocked and ready. Carefully stepping around and over the pile of outlaws scattered around the door, Marcus made his way into the hut, where he remained for a few moments. Finally, he brought an oil lamp out and held it above the rustlers, lighting the scene in the yard and looking closely at each man. "This bunch is all dead," he said.

Though it took some time, the raider's horses were recovered, the bodies of the seven dead rustlers where hung from the cottonwoods in front of the dugout and signs bearing the numbers "3-7-77" were placed on each man. When all was complete, the raiders spent the night at the dugout, so they might recover any stolen stock the following day.

Next morning, a careful search was made for spent rifle brass. This was a relatively simple task because the men had maintained their positions while the attack was in progress. Following this, the raiders searched for stolen stock and recovered more than 170 horses. These they herded some twenty miles to a local ranch and turned the herd over to a very surprised foreman.

"Where in the world did you get this bunch?" the man asked.

"Oh, we finds 'em growin' outa trees," Dirty Bill responded, chuckling. "How 'bout seein' they gets back to their owners?"

161

"I wish that was my only problem," the foreman replied, shaking his head. "I'll see they're taken care of."

As the men rode away, Dave said, "That business last night was plum simple. Puttin' that log jamb in front of the door shore was a real hummer!"

"It did make things sorta easy, didn't it?" Marcus replied, laughing.

"I hope our next raid is this easy," Dirty Bill added, happily. "Them rustlin' wolves turned out to be nothin' but coyotes!"

Φ

Red Mack, Fargo and Ed Spencer rode single file, Indian fashion, along the Cabin Creek bottom, careful to stay as concealed as possible. The men had a tough thirty-mile ride ahead of them and were intent on reaching the O'Shea ranch before sundown. The distance wasn't a problem, but the precaution of following the rugged creek bottom, with its myriad twists and turns, made for slow going. Mile after mile the men struggled along the irregular landscape, ever mindful of the need for secrecy.

Just past noon the wranglers stopped for a hasty dinner of jerked beef, cold biscuits and water from the stream. Sage hen and grouse were abundant in the area and shooting a few for a meal wouldn't have presented a problem, but the raiders couldn't risk the gunshots, the campfire or the time it would take to make a meal.

"I shore hopes we gets there soon," Ed Spencer said, "this country is tough on men and horses."

"I guess we're 'bout half way, maybe a bit more," Red Mack said, carefully checking his horse's feet. All the raiders had checked their horse's feet before they left the train, but Red wasn't one to take chances. "No way to get there, 'less we go there," he said, climbing into the saddle. His friends quickly did the same, and they began the slow arduous ride toward their destination.

Finally, as the riders came around a bend, they saw the O'Shea "ranch," which wasn't a ranch at all, but an abandoned homestead. Riding up the gentle slope to the weathered sod house, the men saw smoke rising from the chimney and wolf hides stretched and drying on crude wooden frames. A horse was corralled near a collapsed stable. "This must be the place," Red said, stepping down from his horse. As his friends were doing the same, a young half-breed stepped out the door of the house with his Colt drawn, covering the three men.

"Tell me somethin' I wanna hear," the breed said, cocking his pistol.

"Gus Adams and Granville Stuart mean anything to you?" Red asked.

The young gunman uncocked his weapon, holstered it and smiled. "Can't be too careful," he said, by way of an apology. "The name's Able Michaud. Glad you boys could make it. This late in the day, I was beginning to wonder if you'd show."

The raiders quickly introduced themselves. As Fargo and Ed put the horses in the corral, Red shook hands with Able and said, "This is quite an outfit you got here. You a wolfer?"

"Not really. I'm play actin'. It's the only way I could get close to those men you're after and not cause any suspicion. They don't expect trouble from a breed wolfer," Able replied, chuckling. "I been killin' wolves for show." Grey wolves were plentiful in the territory and were a scourge to livestock, particularly sheep, calves and foals.

"Are you Metis or is that play actin' too?" Red asked.

"No actin' there. I'm the genuine article. How'd you know I was Metis?" Able asked chuckling.

"The French name, for one thing. And I know quite a few Metis over toward Lewistown. With your sash and flat-brimmed hat, you don't look like no Blackfoot," Red replied, chuckling. More than half the local population around Lewistown was half-breed of one sort or another and Red had many Metis friends.

When Fargo and Ed returned from the corral, the men went into the old soddy, where the wranglers were surprised to find a iron stove with a pot of something cooking away, a rough table and four tired but serviceable wooden chairs. "Whatever you got cookin' shore smells good," Ed told the young detective, "I hopes you got enough for the rest of us. We stuck to the crick bottom all the way in and worked up an appetite."

"Well, that's one thing I *can* guarantee!" Able responded, chuckling, "But while it's cookin', I'll explain the layout and what we got to work with.

"About eight miles east is a tradin' post on Beaver Creek. They sell a few things there, along with rotgut whiskey. I been watching 'em since March and they move a goodly amount of stock through

163

there. They got a couple corrals and a stock shed where they doctor the brands. After the brands are worked over, they hide the stock in dry washes close by until they're healed up. There's usually six or eight men around there, sometimes more."

"How many more?" Fargo asked.

"Two days ago I counted fourteen saddle horses around there," the young man said.

"Jumpin' Jeezus! We was told there was only eight or nine men there," Ed exclaimed.

"Takin' that many won't be easy with just four men," Red said. "Can you lead us in nice and quiet?"

"I can get you in and put you in a rockin' chair on the front porch but the layout will be a problem 'cause there's doors front and rear and windows on all sides. We got too few men to cover everything tight, specially if they come pourin' out of them windows and doors like rats," Able responded.

"Well, we gotta figure a way to bottle 'em up or bait 'em out. It would be good if we could at least put 'em all afoot," Red Mack said.

"How 'bout if I cripple the horses?" Able asked.

"Why not just run their horses off?" Fargo asked.

"Cause they'd hear them horses and we'd lose our surprise," Red said. "How you gonna cripple 'em? I'd rather not see them horses ruined if we can help it."

"I got a pair of hoof trimmers. If I notch a hoof close to the quick, the horse would be too tender to walk for a couple days. Notch each horse and they won't be riding when they leave there. And it won't ruin them horses permanent," Able said, pulling a pair of steel trimmers from a shelf behind the stove.

"That sounds like a winner, if you can do it without the horses raisin' a ruckus," Red said. "They got any dogs around?"

"I ain't seen any. These men ain't exactly the kind to keep house pets," Able replied, checking on the stew. "Grub pile! I think she's ready to go."

After a good supper of beef stew and corn bread, the men set about cleaning their weapons and readying their equipment for the following day. Finally, using Able's hides as blankets and their saddles for pillows, the men quickly fell asleep.

Well before sunup the following morning, Able and Red Mack roused the other two men, and after a hasty breakfast of cold stew and coffee, the horses were saddled and the men were on their way, crossing Cabin Creek to the east, across the rolling prairie. No one spoke. After an hour-long ride, the party came to a heavily wooded depression, where they dismounted. The night was black as pitch and the men moved cautiously.

"Take off your spurs and chaps," Red whispered, "and pin your horses." When that was done, Able led the men along the top of the bench for a half-mile until they were immediately above the log trading post, which they could see faintly below them.

"There it is," Able whispered. "Anybody got any ideas how to handle this nest of hornets?"

The raiders studied the layout, walking first one way and then another. As each man developed an idea, he walked to get a better view and finding some limiting factor, which spelled doom for the idea, struggled to find another. After 15 minutes of mental wrestling, Red whispered, "If we cover the windows, they'll come out the doors and if we cover the doors, they could come out the windows, but I think I got an idea."

The other men quickly gathered round. "Those ain't glass windows down there; they's rawhide, which means they won't be able to see how many of us there is. If we was to put a man opposite each corner of the cabin, he could cover two sides from his position and every side would have two men covering it, if we all take a corner. Once we get in position, Able, you lame their horses quick as you can without disturbing anyone inside then hurry back to your corner," Red whispered, waiting to see if his ideas would hold water.

"That's good thinkin'," Fargo said quietly, "damn good thinkin', Red."

"That ought to work. Just make certain you boys are covering me while I'm working on the stock," the detective whispered, "I'd hate to get caught out with no one watchin' over me."

"That sounds like the way to play her then," Red said softly, "Anybody got anything else?" When no one responded, Red said, "Let's go then. Able, you and Fargo take two corners nearest the corral. Me and Ed will take the other two. I'll start this circus when we get set."

Able waited until the other men were in concealed firing positions before he moved quietly toward the corral. Inside were thirteen horses, aware he and the other men were about, but so far, showing no alarm or making any disturbance. Horses have extremely good sense of smell and hearing, making it nearly impossible to sneak up on one. Donkeys were even better than horses for guard duty, as the Apaches in the Southwest had proven. They always kept a few burros in their horse herds for that reason. Burros were seldom seen on the northern ranges however.

Able quietly slipped between the corral rails, moving slowly. Once inside, he slowly walked to the nearest horse, whispering, talking to it, as he pulled the hoof trimmers from his back pocket. Running a hand down the horse's rear leg, he tapped just the right spot and the horse lifted its leg. He quickly gathered the leg between his own and used the trimmers to cut a deep V-notch into the hoof. The horse jerked his leg, but made no noise. Able repeated this process, again and again, until every horse in the corral was lame, standing with it's newly injured leg pulled up off the ground. He quietly retreated through the fence and took up his position opposite Fargo and Red and waved a signal.

Many Indians had a remarkable touch with horses, a sympathy of spirit that allowed the animals to trust them. Perhaps it was because the lives of Indians were so closely intertwined with the animals. Whatever the nature of the relationship, it was considerably different from that of all but a few white men. In wounding the animals, Able took no enjoyment in his actions, but knew the horses would soon recover.

As the sky began to brighten in the east, someone stirred within the cabin and could be heard moving around, yawning and soon, a candle or oil lamp lit the interior, adding a yellow glow to the thin rawhide window coverings. The door of an iron stove could be heard squeaking open and then closed and soon a plume of smoke from a freshly built fire rose from the chimney.

The raiders braced themselves, knowing action was close at hand. Suddenly, the back door opened and a man wearing long-handled underwear and cowboy boots walked out toward the woodpile to gather firewood for the stove. After gathering an armload, the man turned back toward the cabin, but was met by Red Mack's pistol touching his nose and brought up short. Red put one finger to his lips, signing for the man to be quiet, and then waggled his pistol to let the man know he was to walk where Red indicated.

The fire-starter did as directed, moving away from the cabin, still holding his armload of firewood. When Red and his prisoner were some distance from the cabin, Red whispered, "Talk quiet and speak true or I'll kill you. How many men in the cabin?"

"Twelve," the frightened man whispered immediately.

"I want you to go back in there and tell them boys there's a U.S Marshall out here that wants them to come out, hands up. Can you do that?" Red asked quietly.

The man couldn't believe his luck! "Shore, I can do that," the man said softly, bobbing his head up and down.

"You take your wood in there and tell 'em then," the raider whispered.

As the man turned toward the cabin, Red clubbed the man over the head with his pistol, dropping him like a rock. *He won't be goin' nowhere for a while.* Red had no idea if the man spoke the truth but he didn't have time to worry about it. Red quickly returned to his firing position and ducked down just as the backdoor opened again.

Out stepped another man in long johns, slowly making his way toward the outhouse, thirty yards behind the trading post. When he was well past the two raiders guarding the corners of the building, Red hand signaled to Able to follow the man and knock him out. Quietly and quickly, Able moved on moccasined feet up behind the sleepy man, bringing his pistol down with a dull whap just as the man was stepping into the privy. Able caught the man as he fell and quickly shoved the unconscious man into the outhouse and let the door close. As he turned to move back to his firing position, another man stepped from the cabin, walking to the outhouse. The men met less than twenty feet apart; their eyes locked. "You're that breed wolfer ain't you? What in the name of hob are you doing out here?" the outlaw demanded, looking around, now fully awake and suspicious.

"Oh, I had to take a sit-down so I stopped in to use your privy," Able replied, somewhat stupidly.

The unarmed man couldn't believe what he heard. "What did you say?" he asked.

In a flash, Able pulled and cocked his pistol. "Get over here, nice and careful."

As the man debated on how the play the situation, Able pointed the Colt at the man's head, and waggled it toward the outhouse, making the man's mind up for him. As he walked past the raider, and opened the outhouse door, Able dropped his Colt across the rustler's skull and he fell onto the man already stretched out on the floor. Red gestured for the young man to return to his position, which he quickly did, leaving the unconscious rustler where he fell, with his legs sticking out of the privy.

After a quick look at Ed and seeing that Able was back in position, Red fired a shot into the chimney, knocking a brick off the top, which tumbled down the tin stove pipe into the stove with a loud racket. "You in the cabin! Come out with your hands up. This is the law and you're surrounded!" he shouted.

Suddenly someone opened the backdoor a crack and fired a shot, which was quickly returned by Red and Able. At the same time, the front door was thrown open and two half-dressed men emerged, pistols in hand, making for the horse corral. Fargo and Ed fired at the same time, dropping the man in the lead. The second rustler quickly jumped back into the cabin and slammed the door shut as bullets struck the door and its frame.

There was no more movement from within the cabin for nearly a minute. Suddenly, the entire gang made a break out the front door, firing as they ran. Hidden behind a tree, Ed began firing as soon as the outlaws came into the open, dropping a man as he turned toward the corral. Fargo was blazing away and also dropped a man as he ran past. Fargo's pistol soon ran dry and he began reloading. Ed fired into the pack of fleeing men, dropping another outlaw. Two more fell as they came under fire from Able's rifle. Fargo, now reloaded, rejoined the fray, firing into the fleeing mass.

Three outlaws made it to the corral, threw open the gate and each jumped on the nearest horse they could find, but their mounts refused to move. A quick look at the horse's hind legs would have told the tale. The wounded leg was pulled up, off the ground, the animal refusing to put any weight on the notched hoof. As the men struggled to motivate their mounts, Able and Fargo ran to the corral.

"Them ain't rockin' horses and you buzzards is too old anyway! Drop your guns and get off them horses. You three look plum stupid!" Fargo shouted, laughing. Having no means of escape and with weapons pointed directly at them, the three dejected men did as they were told.

While Able and Fargo were herding their catch back toward the cabin, Red entered the cabin through the back door as Ed went in the front. They quickly determined no one else was in the cabin and walked out to join the men with their prisoners.

"You boys got some catch there," Ed said, chuckling at the bedraggled rustlers, all of which were wounded and bleeding.

"Yeah, they been playin' horsie," Fargo said, laughing.

"Keep an eye on these bronc-busters, Fargo, while we get them sore-heads out back," Red ordered, chuckling.

Red, Able and Ed walked around behind the cabin where they recovered the three dazed outlaws and marched them at gunpoint to join their friends at the front of the building.

"Ed, why don't you and Able see if you can find six good horses that ain't buggered up? No need for saddles, just bridles. Might be some in that second corral or the stock shed. I'll tie these boys up and get 'em ready to ride," Red said.

As Red went to work with his rope, cutting short sections and tying each man's hands behind his back, Fargo kept the men covered, chuckling softly. "You boys been throwin' a long loop. Didn't your mamas tell ya thievin' don't pay?"

"You got the drop on us now, but it won't be forever. Where you takin' us?" one of the rustlers asked.

"See them cottonwoods down by the crick? That's where we're takin' you and it *will* be forever." Fargo said.

Suddenly, the fire-starter spoke up, "I'm just the cook here, mister. All I did was cook for this outfit. I didn't have no part in their thievin'!"

"That true?" Red asked the other bound men.

They sullenly nodded, confirming what the man said.

"Well, if you sleeps with thieves, you dies with thieves," Red said.

Ten minutes later, the two raiders led six horses up to the cabin where the six outlaws were each put on a horse and led into the trees by the creek. Ed walked up with ropes and started making loops in their ends, which were placed around each man's neck and pulled tight. When he went to drop a loop over the cook, Red gave him a subtle sign not to. Ed tied the loose ends of the five ropes off to the base of a nearby tree, and when all was ready, Fargo slapped the horse's rumps and they bolted forward, leaving the men to twist, kick and slowly strangle to death.

The cook looked on the scene with a mixture of revulsion and relief.

"I've known some cooks I *wanted* to hang, but since you ain't burned *my* biscuits, I guess you deserves a chance," Red said, as he untied the man. "You got twenty-four hours to get out of the territory. If we sees you after that, we'll kill you." Red slapped the man's horse and it leaped forward, ridden hard by a man wearing red long johns and cowboy boots. That was the last they ever saw of him.

After the rustlers who'd died in the shootout were hung, signs were put on each of the dead outlaws. For the next half hour, the raiders carefully swept the area for spent rifle cartridges. When they were certain all the spent brass was accounted for, they recovered their horses and went in search for stolen stock. More than 200 horses and 150 head of cattle were recovered. After setting fire to the trading post, the raiders drove the mixed herd to Tower's and Gudgell's OX brand ranch, south of Medora, where it was turned over to a surprised by pleased foreman.

"I don't know who you men are but I appreciates your help! Who do you ride for?" the foreman asked happily.

"We rides for the Apocalypse brand, 'bout a quarter mile this side of hell, down Oklahoma way," Able said, as the raiders rode away, anxious to begin their next raid.

"Packy lips brand? Where did that come from?" Fargo asked.

"Church school," Able replied, saying no more about it.

Φ

Black Dutch, Buster Burns and Terry Beard crossed under the Beaver Creek trestle and began their long ride north down the creek bottom. The land grew steadily more rugged and became more difficult to traverse. Riding until noon, the men dismounted where Little Beaver Creek joined the main stream and had a quick meal of cold canned fruit, pickled meat and stream water.

"Wonder how much further we got before we run onto Elk Creek?" Buster asked. "I ain't been in this country before, so I got no idea where we are."

"I'd guess we're pretty close but no way to know for sure. We come a fair piece so far," Black Dutch said.

"Shore hope I get in on this play," Terry said. "All I did was hold the horses in that last game."

"There's supposed to be twelve of these buzzards roostin' here, which is a bunch for four men to handle, so there ain't gonna be no horse-holdin' this trip," Dutch replied.

"After what they done to Duncan, I shore got some catchin' up to do," Terry said.

"We best get at it then," Buster said, as he mounted up. The other men did the same and the small party was quickly on its way. Three hours later, they came to a small stream that joined the Beaver from the south. "This must be Elk crick," Dutch said. "Let's ride up and see if we can spot that dugout. Oughta be close, if this is the right crick."

Rounding a small bend, an abandoned dugout was set on the west side of the creek bottom, facing the east. A short distance upstream, three hobbled horses grazed quietly. Nearby, a man slept in the shade of a cottonwood tree. Black Dutch and his men rode over to the sleeping figure and dismounted, stretching their tired legs.

"Stickin' to that crick bottom shore ain't much fun," Buster said. "I'm gonna sleep solid when I turn in."

The sleeping man opened one eye and looked up from under his hat. After he checked the men's outfits, he sat up slowly and pushed his hat back on his head. "You fellars who I think you is? I didn't know what time you'd show, so thought I'd take a nap. Stayed up late watching that bunch yer after."

"No harm done. I likes to see a man enjoy his work," Dutch said, chuckling.

"Why don't you men set up your bedrolls next to mine, over there by the crick. Then I'll explain what we got," the detective said.

The raiders led their horses over to the detective's campsite and set up their beds. The man was well setup, with a small tent stocked with supplies and everything he would need for an extended stay outdoors. As the men spread out their gear, the detective walked up and introduced himself. "My name's Jesse Roberts. I been workin' with Gus for several years now. We sorta works together when we can."

The wranglers introduced themselves in turn.

"Well, let me explain what we got," Jesse said, "About ten miles north, on Prairie Dog Creek, is a wolfers dugout. That's where these guys your after hang out, but they ain't there."

"Where is they then?" Buster asked, indignant at the thought the rustlers wouldn't be around for the party.

"I been watchin' that bunch every night since I got word you boys was comin'. Just past sunup this morning, the whole bunch lit out. Except for the cook that is," Jesse replied.

"Well, let's go get that biscuit-burner and see if he knows where they is," Terry said.

"Ain't gotta go nowhere 'cause I got him hog-tied upstream," the detective said, walking away. He retrieved his horse and led it upstream. "Come on."

Following a narrow game trail, Jesse led the men fifty yards upstream. Coming into a small clearing, they found a man tied to a massive cottonwood tree backwards, with his arms tied around the tree behind his back.

"I tried questioning him earlier, but he claims he don't know anything," Jesse said. "So I think we'll just hang him. If he starts talkin', he'll go on breathin'. If not, he's one less thief we gotta concern ourselves with. Get him off that tree and tie his hands behind his back."

As the raiders set about their task, Jesse threw a loop over a sturdy limb above them and placed it around the outlaw's neck. He mounted his horse and dallied the rope around his saddle horn, pulling most of the slack out of the rope.

"I want to know where the rest of your pack of coyotes is. If you talk, you'll live. If not," Jesse said, as he slowly backed his horse, tightening the rope around the cook's neck.

"Well?"

"You can go to hell!" the man said.

"I was sorta hopin' you'd say that," the detective said, as he backed his horse again, applying more tension to the rope, finally lifting the cook off the ground. The DHS wranglers watched as the man's face turned red and breathing became difficult. Slowly his face turned blue, his breathing gurgled and raspy, and his legs beginning to kick violently. All the while, Jesse calmly rolled a cigarette, unimpressed with the man's struggles as he dangled at the end of the rope.

After lighting his smoke, he eased his horse forward, and the suffocating cook fell to the ground, gasping and fighting for breath.

When he'd recovered enough to talk, Jesse asked if the man had anything to tell him.

"Go to hell, I says!"

Jesse laughed and backed his horse again, pulling the man off the ground by the neck and repeated the crude procedure. He repeated it again and again, each time taking the man close to death and then letting him recover. The man was a wreck. His neck was bleeding from the repeated applications of the rough rope, and his lungs rattled like a box of marbles when he breathed.

"Enough! I'll talk!" he finally declared, croaking like a bullfrog.

"Where did them boys light out to this morning?" Jesse asked the shattered cook.

"Burning Mine Butte! They's deliverin' some stock and then goin' to Medora tomorrow drinkin'," the man replied, his breathing strained and difficult, bloody drool flying from his mouth with each word.

"Where 'bouts in Medora?" Jesse asked, impatient.

"They goes to Little Toms. Always," the cook said, as tremors racked his body.

"How many of them is there?" Black Dutch asked.

The cook gave Dutch a contemptuous look but didn't answer. Jesse jumped from his horse and stomped the man three times in his chest as hard as he could, breaking several ribs. "One more stomp and yer ribs will be through yer lungs! You heard my friend here. Answer him!"

"There's eleven of 'em!" the cook screamed, curling into a fetal position and coughing, blood and snot running from his mouth and nose.

"Who's leadin' the outfit? What's he look like?" Dutch asked the sobbing man.

"Rawhide Larson! Wears a serape, Mexican style."

Jesse and the wranglers dragged the broken cook back to their camp and again tied him to a thick tree.

"Well boys, I don't see no reason to go chargin' off. Let's spend the night here, then ease into Medora tomorrow morning and find them buzzards. Anybody think different?" Jesse asked. When no one raised any objections, Jesse said, "Good. Let's fix us some supper then. With them coyotes off chasin' the bottle, no reason for us not to have a fire and get a hot meal."

Following a good supper, Jesse asked if anyone knew how to catch skunks.

"If you mean the four legged kind, I do. I ate lots of skunk when I was younger," Dutch admitted. "If yer starvin' there ain't much a man won't eat."

"Can you catch 'em without getting stunk up?"

"If you got some heavy sacks and know where they den up or feed, I can. We gotta keep 'em in the dark and treat 'em gentle if we don't wanna get hit. And we'll need somethin' fer bait. Bacon grease works good. Eggs, fish, honey, lard, any of them things works. Skunks'll eat damn near anything."

"We're in luck, then. I saw some gunnysacks in that old dugout over there and I got a skillet half full of bacon grease. Also got some stale biscuits to sop it up. Any of that work?"

"That'll work good," Dutch replied, chuckling softly. "If we use three bags, one inside the next, it'll be dark enough they won't get us."

"Good. I know where a few dens are and they been feeding on bull berry bushes something awful. Let's get our outfit together and go catch us some polecats," Jesse said, chuckling to himself.

As Jesse and Black Dutch rode off, Buster and Terry could only wonder.

"What you reckon that fellar wants skunks for, Buster?" Terry asked.

"Beats me. Jesse shore is some tricky though. Chokin' that pot wrestler was somethin' to see. That old buzzard had more sand in him than I woulda thought. Whatever them skunks is for, I figure Jesse's got his reasons."

Jesse and Black Dutch managed to gather up three skunks that evening. When the men returned late to camp, the other wranglers had already turned in. The cook wasn't fed or even given a blanket, but was left tied to the tree during the night. Early the following morning, the men ate a quick breakfast and broke camp. Dutch took the two sacks of skunks and tied them to his saddle.

"You gotta do anything special to keep them skunks from goin' off?" Jesse asked Black Dutch, eyeing the two bags somewhat nervously.

"We dasn't shake 'em up or talk loud. If we treats 'em gentle and rides easy, they'll be fine."

174

"I sure hope yer right. I'd hate to have one of them critters go off!"

The cook was put on his horse and his legs tied together under its belly, making it impossible to get off unless someone untied him. If he tried to untie himself, he would slip down the side of the animal until he hung upside down. Riding up out of the creek bottom, the small party rode slowly southeast toward Medora.

Just past noon, the raiders and their prisoner rode into Medora and quickly spotted Little Toms Saloon. Out front, tied to the hitch rails, the raiders noticed close to a dozen horses. The men pulled up short and rode down an alley next to the Hotel De Mores to the livery stable in the rear. After Dutch pulled the sacks of skunks off his horse, the raiders turned their mounts over to the liveryman. Buster untied the battered cook and marched him into the barn.

"How much you charge to guard a coyote for a spell?" Dutch asked the sweating and dirty shovel wrangler.

"With no feed, $2 suits me," the liveryman said, looking at the raw abraded flesh of the cook's neck. "We don't have to stand guard on horses."

"Well, I'll tie him up, so you don't strain yerself," Jesse replied. "And this rustling coyote better be here when we gets back. If he ain't, we got cures for that too."

Moving to the rear of the barn, Jesse quickly tied the man between two sturdy timbers on opposite ends of a stall, arms spread-eagled, so he was unable to move.

"If he starts hollerin', you got my permission to bust him with that shovel you're ridin'," Jesse told the man. "If you don't like his looks, feel free to give him a taste."

The raiders adjourned to the front of the stable to make their plans. When all was understood and each man knew his job, they set to work. Jesse and Buster took the bag with two skunks and carefully carried it to the front of Little Tom's, as Black Dutch and Terry went to the rear of the building. Then, while Terry held the sack with the lone skunk, Dutch walked into the saloon, bellied up to the bar and ordered himself a beer. Just as the barkeep finished pouring a mug, Buster entered through the front and did the same, standing apart from Dutch, pretending not to know him. As the two men stood drinking, they each studied the other patrons in the mirror behind the bar. They quickly identified Rawhide Larson by his serape. The rustlers were gathered around two tables, playing poker, talking loud and drinking heavily. They were the only customers in Little Tom's.

Dutch called the barkeep over. "All them boys over there from the same outfit?" he asked in a low voice.

"They all come in together, so I guess they is," the man said. "They been playin' cards and drinking since before lunch."

"This your place?"

"Little Tom, the festive barkeep, that's me. Why?"

"You got a key for that back door?"

"Shore, what of it?" the barkeep asked, suddenly suspicious. He was the boss of this outfit and was determined to retain his dominance.

"Well, here's the way she lays," Dutch said, as four metallic clicks of a Colt Single Action Army being cocked below the bar were clearly heard by the barkeep. "In about two minutes, there's gonna be some unhealthy ruckus in here. If you gives me the key, you won't be caught in the middle of it. If you don't, well, I can kill you where you stand. You savvy?"

The barkeep swallowed hard and quietly slid the key across the bar. "Here, here's another beer. I'll be right back," the barkeep said, and headed out the back door without another word.

Dutch caught Buster's eye and nodded, then followed the barkeep out back. Buster casually walked out the front, grabbed the bag of skunks Jesse held, and waited. He was in a position where he could look through the saloon at the back door, but not be seen by the men at the tables.

At the rear of the building, Dutch took the skunk sack from Terry. Relieved of the sack, Terry quickly moved to a buckboard the two men had positioned nearby. After he was in position, Dutch nodded his head and walked back into the saloon, dumped his striped prisoner onto the floor and quickly backed out, closing and locking the door behind him. Then the two raiders rolled the buckboard to block the door and ran around to the front of the building.

When Buster saw Black Dutch reenter the saloon, he quickly carried his sack through the front door, upended it and quickly backed out the door, closing it behind him. Once outside, the raiders ran to firing positions across the street, covering the front and sides of the building with their rifles.

Inside, the outlaws had paid little attention to the two strangers at the bar and somewhat belatedly became aware of the skunk's wandering about. Once the alarm was sounded however, they were quick to react, jumping up, shouting, overturning one table and then another in their haste. The skunks were scared by all the noise, and lost no time in firing their own brand of weaponry, as the locoed outlaws bolted for the exits.

The men who stampeded for the backdoor were sprayed by Dutch's skunk and a couple were temporarily blinded when sprayed in the eyes. Arriving at the door, and finding it locked, the rustlers panicked. One man decided to try the front door and ran back past the skunk and was dosed again. Those who remained clawed at the latch, shouting and kicking the door as the atmosphere became ripe, trying vainly to reach the fresh air outside. Finally, the knot of panicked men gave up and charged to the front, firing their pistols at the skunk as they ran. Those men who were blinded by the skunk spray, fired indiscriminately, wounding their fellow outlaws in the legs and feet, as they desperately sought a target they couldn't see.

Those men who ran for the front door, Rawhide Larson among them, were also firing at the skunks as they ran. One skunk was finally killed but the remaining skunk perceived the charging outlaws as aggressors and hiked tail, firing at close range. Several more men were splashed in the face and eyes and were blinded. They too began shooting blind, wounding one man in the stomach, who' had earlier tripped and fallen in his haste to get away. In the blind frenzy they were running into each other, stumbling over upturned furniture and fallen men. In total panic, one man ran full force into the pot-bellied stove, knocking it over and bringing down several sections of soot-filled stovepipe, clouding the air with a thick black haze. It was a perfect hell for the men trapped in the saloon.

Finally, some of the outlaws made it to the front door and stumbled out into the street, where they ran into the raiders and were ordered to drop their weapons. Some did. Those who refused to surrender and chose to fire on the raiders were immediately shot down. Inside the saloon, the shouting and firing continued. Chairs were thrown through windows in an effort to escape and reach fresh breathable air. The men who dove out the windows were quickly disarmed and marched to the front of the building to join their compatriots who'd been made lie down in the middle of the street as townsfolk gathered around and looked on in amazement.

When all the commotion was over, seven of the outlaws were captured alive, three of these were wounded. One was killed in the saloon by his fellow outlaws and three were shot dead in the street when they refused to surrender. The saloon was a shambles; two of the four windows were knocked out, all the tables and chairs were toppled over, money, broken glass, whiskey, beer and blood was spilled across the floor. The mirror behind the bar was shattered, much of the potable stock had been destroyed and a thin layer of black soot covered everything. The heavy scent of skunk was overpowering and nauseating.

The captured rustlers had their hands tied behind their backs and were searched. The raiders recovered more than $1300, which was given to Little Tom before he could start squawking. After all the spent brass was recovered, the outlaws were put on their horses, the dead as well as the living, and taken south of town where they were hung along the Little Missouri River. The surly cook was taken from the livery stable and hung as well. The bodies were labeled with the appropriate signs and the raiders departed, confident a strong message had been sent regarding future rustling activities.

"We gonna look for stolen stock at their hideout?" Terry asked the group. "Seems like we oughta return whatever we find."

"There ain't no stock. From what the cook said, they took all their stock to the river yesterday. This bunch didn't even bother to rework the brands. They just stole the stock and turned it over to someone else," Jesse said.

"Why don't we go after the outfit they was turned over to?" Buster asked.

"No need. Some of your group will already be paying their respects. We gotta move on to the next bunch," Jesse replied.

"That skunk business was the funniest damn thing I ever seen," Black Dutch said, laughing as they rode out of town. "Lord! Listening to them boys try to get shed of them varmints was something I'll never forget! What caused you to think of it?"

"Gus Adams and I tossed a hornets nest into a cabin down in Wyoming one time and it got results quick," Jesse replied. "I figured skunks oughta work and thanks to you, Dutch, we was able to catch us some. The idea of two legged skunks fightin' four legged skunks appeals to me somehow. Ironic, you might say."

"Wait 'til the boys hear 'bout this," Terry said, laughing. "All them rustlers whipped by skunks! Yes sir, yer play's a real hummer!"

Φ

As the five DHS wranglers rode up, Gus greeted the men. "Hello Harley. Hello boys. Glad to see you made it. I know it's late in the day, but we got better than 60 miles to cover before we get to where we're needed. I figured on hittin' them coyotes at sunup day after tomorrow, so we best get at it."

The six men began their long ride, heading north toward Twin Buttes off in the distance. The party rode along in silence, each man surveying the territory, lost in his own thoughts. Because the group was so far from the outlaws they sought, they didn't feel it necessary to skulk through draws and creek bottoms. The following day would be different however, and as they drew closer to their targets, they would have to be more careful and circumspect in their actions.

The raiders rode 25 miles before they halted and made camp in a depression next to a thin stream. It was near dark when camp was finally set up, horses watered and hobbled, wood gathered and bedrolls laid out. The sky was clouding up to the northwest and the wranglers knew a storm was on the way. Little energy was wasted on talk, all the men being tired from the long day they'd already put in.

Sometime past midnight, it started raining; softly at first, then growing in intensity until it became a full-scale blow. The horses scattered, but there was nothing for it. It would be impossible to find them in the heavy weather and all the men chose to remain warm and dry inside their bedrolls.

It was still raining, though the wind had died down, when the men awoke. Andrew Fergus and Second Bob hiked off in the direction the storm had taken, looking for their horses as the other men broke camp, breakfasting on jerked venison and canned beans. Before the men had had their second cup of coffee, the two absent wranglers came riding up bareback, leading the missing horses. As the last two men ate a quick meal, Gus explained the situation to the men.

"One of our detectives, Ned Jessup, is supposed to meet us near Burning Mine Butte and we got a long way to go before we reach

179

him. He's been keeping an eye on the two outfits we're aiming to raid. Today, we'll need to stick to draws as much as possible. The problem is, they mostly all run kitty-corner to the way we need to go. We'll just have to try our best to stay outa sight and hope we're not spotted going in."

"How much further we got to go?" Jimmy asked.

"As the crow flies, 'bout 35 miles, though I expect we'll cover more than 50 miles before the day's out. If we can, we'll make our raids tomorrow morning at first light, depending on what Ned has to report. We may split up and attack them separately or work together on first one outfit and then the other. Any other questions?" Gus asked.

When there were none, the men saddled their horses, tied their bedrolls and other gear on and mounted up. All the men were wearing slickers, trying to stay as dry as possible in the drizzle. Riding over the soggy ground was tedious, the horses slipping frequently. It seemed as if the men spent all their time making switch-backs, dropping down into one draw heading west and then dropping into another draw heading east, slowly making their way north. Back and forth, zigzag fashion, the men rode, and hour after long hour. Some of the larger draws had become raging torrents because of the rain and couldn't be safely crossed, forcing the raiders to travel considerably out of their way until they found a safe crossing. The rain continued throughout the day and showed no signs of letting up. Late that day, the damp and weary men made a hasty cold camp while darkness closed in around them. They had yet to reach Burning Mine Butte and had seen no signs of Ned Jessup. The rain continued throughout the night, and while there weren't the high winds of the previous evening, the constant rain made camp life cold and miserable.

Early the following morning, the men saddled up after another cold meal, and continued their journey through the drizzle. Around dinnertime, Gus halted the file of raiders and all dismounted. Ahead, a conspicuous butte could be seen two miles away.

"That's Burning Mine Butte. We're supposed to meet Jessup there but if he was around, he'd have seen us coming in and would have met us by now. I'm worried. After we finish eatin', let's spread out and form a line. If we can't find him, maybe we can cut some sign," Gus told the chilled and damp raiders.

A short time later, the men mounted, spread out at intervals and moved slowly north toward the butte, each man studying the area carefully, looking for any sign of the detective's presence. Suddenly Keeps Eagle shouted, waved his arm then pointed at something on the ground. The raiders quickly rode up as Keeps Eagle dismounted and knelt next to a clump of bunch grass. The grass had been tied in an overhand knot and the top twisted to point east. The strange configuration couldn't occur naturally. Muddy hoof prints could be seen here and there, though barely. The continuing rains had washed most of the sign away. There was no way of knowing who'd made the tracks or tied the grass off. The grass marker was the only clue the raiders had.

"This make sense to you?" Harley asked Gus.

"One of the outfits we're after is almost straight east from here. They got a hideout down on the Little Missouri. If Jessup had to pull his freight, and work in close to them, that sign would make sense," the detective responded. "It's thin but I think we better follow it; right now it's all we got."

The party quickly turned toward the distant river. The direction of the draws and ravines was now in the raiders favor, running toward the river bottom and the party was able to drop down into a draw and follow it all the way to the Little Missouri River. Approaching the river, they entered rugged Bad Lands; the landscape became more treacherous and difficult to travel. Finally Gus called a halt above the river bottom and the men gathered to discuss the operation.

"The hideout we're lookin' for is north of us, downstream a ways," Gus said. "We're a day late and we got no idea what we'll find. Jessup was our eyes and ears in this game, and without him, we're workin' a cold deck. Let's make camp right here, eat some supper and then scout it out to see what's what."

The drizzle finally stopped as the men were setting up their camp. Food was getting scarce and the raiders pooled their rations, so all might share the meager repast. Six men supped on a couple pounds of jerked meat and the last three cans of vegetables. When the sparse meal was over, Andrew Fergus, Jimmy and Keeps Eagle rode out of camp to scout the rustler's hideout.

Well past sundown, the weary wranglers returned; their report wasn't good. The rustlers were nowhere to be found and appeared to have pulled, leaving their hideout standing empty. The raiders did manage to retrieve some groceries though, so the raiders were back in clover regarding supplies.

Keeps Eagle reported the outlaws were driving their stolen stock upstream. "We crossed a muddy trail of horse and cattle sign headed south. Looks like they're movin' a good sized herd someplace."

"Upstream? South? That don't make sense," Harley responded. He was under the impression the outlaws would move the stolen stock north into Canada.

"It might, if they're planning to ship their stock out of the territory by train," Gus replied. "If they cooked up some counterfeit ownership papers or had someone workin' for the NP, they could move the stock easily."

"All that's south is Medora, ain't it? They wouldn't dare ship stolen stock outa there. Too many folks around to see what they's doin'."

"There's pens and a siding at Sully Springs, west of Medora a couple of miles. It's remote and seldom used but they might be heading there," Gus said. "If they are, they'll stay in this river bottom until the last moment so they won't be discovered. Then they'll want to get up on the flats so they can avoid the Elkhorn and other ranches south of here."

"We gotta get busy then. I wanna see that dugout for myself. Gus, first thing tomorrow morning, let's us go take a look. Might find something they overlooked. The rest of you men head south and keep an eye on these devils. And make sure you ain't seen. We'll catch up after we look around a bit," Harley said, happy they knew where the outlaws were but concerned that Jessup hadn't been heard from. He was also concerned that the rustlers weren't doing what was expected.

The following morning, the raiders broke camp and split up. Harley and Gus rode to Burnett's hideout and began a thorough search of the dugout while the other raiders rode south in pursuit of the outlaws and the mixed herd.

After considerable scratching around inside the dugout, Gus found two account books hidden under a false floor. Carrying them outside into the sunlight, the detective was amazed at what they contained.

"Harley! Come look at this!" the detective shouted, excited at his discovery.

The Ranger ran from the low cabin. "What'd you find? Buried treasure?"

"Something better. See these two books? I found 'em hidden inside. They're account books or ledgers with dates, shipping points, numbers of stock delivered, prices paid and money due. I can't believe Burnett would keep something like this around! According to this, he's been dealing with an outfit called the Minnesota Star Cattle Company since '82. Ever hear of 'em?"

"Not me. You said 'shipping points'. Do them books say anything about usin' the railroads?"

"Looks like it," Gus said, pausing as he scanned the columns carefully. "They shipped from Sully Springs last August and they shipped from somewhere called Sunnyside the following month, next was Glen Ullin, then Judson. It doesn't say but these must all be sidings with loading pens! They been shipping from different sidings all along the Northern Pacific line!"

"Well, hang on to them books. Let's look around a little more, then go find the others. I don't want this show to be a bust."

While Harley was searching the outbuildings, he discovered the body of a man in a low stock shed past the corral. The man had his fingers and his toes cut off and then what was left of his hands and feet were chopped off. A bloody axe lay near his body. Various body parts were scattered about on the ground. Whoever the man was, he bled to death. Harley called to Gus, who came on a run.

"It's Jessup! My god…they killed him Indian fashion," Gus exclaimed, kneeling next to the ravaged body. He was referring to the Blackfeet Indians taste for dismemberment of captured white men in years past. "If I get my hands on the man that did this, I'll make him wish he'd never been born!"

Harley left Adams and walked outside to get some air. A few minutes later, he retrieved his ground tarp from his horse and returned to the shed. He and Gus began collecting the detective's parts and body, which they rolled into the tarp. Next they tied the ends off with leather thongs so nothing would fall out and the bundle was thrown over the back of Harley's horse. Gus was silent, whether from shock or rage, Harley didn't know.

"Come on Gus, let's go get the devils that did this," Harley said, snapping the detective out of his daze.

It was late afternoon before the two men found the other raiders. Two of them were sitting in the shade of a large cottonwood relaxing, as Gus and the Ranger rode up.

"What's going on?" Harley asked, dismounting.

"Them skunks is upstream a few miles from us," Andrew Fergus said. "Keeps Eagle and Jimmy are watchin' 'em. What's that you got on the back of your horse Harley?"

"That's what's left of Jessup. That bunch we're followin' chopped his hands and feet off and let him bleed to death. Come on, let's move up and figure out a way to wipe 'em out."

The men followed the churned and muddy trail of the herd. A short time later, they met Jimmy and Keeps Eagle riding back to report that the outlaws were setting up camp for the night and were bedding the cattle down south of their camp.

"How many is there?" Harley asked Keeps Eagle.

"There's fifteen, boss."

"What do you make of it, Gus? I thought the bunch we was after was lots smaller," asked Harley.

"Sounds to me like the two outfits Jessup was watchin' have joined up and are workin' together," Gus replied. "That's gonna make it tough; six of us against fifteen of them."

"They camped in the bottom?" Harley asked Keeps Eagle.

"Yep, they're loose herding the stock about a quarter mile past their camp. I imagine they'll bed 'em down right there."

"Good. I got an idea," Harley said. "When we was trailin' cattle up from Texas, desperados in the Indian Nations would sometimes stampede our herds at night, then peal off a small bunch as the herd lit out. If we was to stampede them cattle back the way they come, downstream through the outlaw camp, the livestock might just thin them buzzards out for us. At the least, the stock will be scattered from hell to breakfast, slowing 'em up considerable."

"Damnation!" Gus exclaimed, "That's a good idea!"

"All them critters running through their camp sure would raise hob with them devils!" Jimmy said excitedly, imagining the chaos and destruction.

"Si, amigo!" Second Bob said, laughing. "Aaaayyyy de mi!"

"How we gonna get the cattle on the prod?" Gus asked. "I doubt we could get 'em moving without gettin' shot up some."

"Well, it don't take much if the cattle is nervous; a popped blanket, a rattled pot or a match being lit late at night can do it. But we gotta scare the devil out of 'em if we want to make sure they stampede and set a good pace," Harley said.

Keeps Eagle jumped to his feet. "Wolves!" he exclaimed. "Wolves would make 'em bolt!"

"You hit her plum center!" Harley said, laughing, happy someone had figured it out. "Them bushwhackers along the Texas trails sometimes used wolf scent to drive our cattle loco. They didn't have to pop no blankets or take many risks. Once the herd smelled wolf scent, they might run twenty miles before we could mill them."

"Where in Hades we gonna get wolves?" Gus Adams asked.

"We'll buy 'em. All we gotta do is find some wolfers," Harley said, "and buy some fresh kills or fresh pelts. I bet there's three or four wolfers within fifteen miles of where we are right this minute. If we spread out and go searchin', I bet we could find us a few."

Camp was set up on the dry ground of a small rise above the river bottom and after a cold but filling supper, five men left camp, leaving an angry Gus Adams to stand guard. *Imagine them jaspers leavin' me here to guard some damned blankets!* It also gave him time to consider the situation. What the outlaws did to Jessup still troubled him and he swore he'd kill the man that killed the detective. *Chopped him up like firewood!*

Just before sundown the wranglers began drifting back into camp with mixed results. Three of them had failed to find any wolfers, but two of the men carried dead wolves or fresh pelts across the back of their saddles. This was a difficult thing to do because wolves are a horse's natural enemy and it was all the two men could do to keep their horses from bolting after they scented the wolves and hides being tied on. After the men dismounted and had a chance to water themselves and their horses, the men circled up to discuss the next move.

"We got one wolf and three fresh skins, which is plenty. Three of us will circle wide 'round the herd, so we come at 'em from the far side. When we gets close enough, we'll dismount and drag them wolves on lariats as close to the herd as we dare. Once we're close, we start draggin' 'em cross-wise, so the scent is all across that end of the river bottom. I can't see 'em coming any way but back downstream through that bunch and their camp. And God knows how far they'll run; they may not stop runnin' 'til Christmas!"

Harley, Jimmy and Keeps Eagle elected themselves to carry out the evening's activities and mounted up just as darkness fell. With only a sliver of a moon showing, the three rode up out of the river

185

valley, and after circling some distance around the herd, they dropped back down into the river bottom. Riding slowly toward the herd, Harley finally signaled for a halt and the three men quickly dismounted.

"Take off your spurs and chaps," Harley whispered. "Leave your rifles with your horses when you hobbles 'em. After we get 'em runnin', don't leave your pelts behind. We may have to do this again tomorrow night. Savvy?"

Both men softly affirmed their understanding.

"I'll take the side next to the river. Jimmy, you take the middle and Keeps Eagle, you take the other end. We'll go straight in until we're right on top of them cattle. Then I'll walk toward Jimmy. Jimmy, you walk towards Keeps Eagle. Eagle, you walk back toward me. It probably won't take that much moving around, but it may. Keep as quiet as you can, walk soft and stay low. There ain't much moon out but they gotta have nightriders out and I don't want anybody gettin' shot. Let's go."

The wranglers split up and began walking slowly toward the bedded-down herd, dragging their wolves behind them parallel to the river. Soon, they heard the mournful tones of a nightrider singing to the cattle as he circled the herd. Moving cautiously forward, the raiders came within twenty-five yards of the cattle and then turned perpendicular to the river, walking across the front of the herd. As the nightrider approached, each man in turn would drop to the ground until the man was well past, then continue with his drag. Just as the rider was approaching Harley, the cattle suddenly scented the wolves and jumped to their feet as one, bellaring and spinning away from their dreaded enemy, charging off down the river valley.

"What the hell?" exclaimed the nightrider. Just then, Harley grabbed the horse's bridle and jammed his Colt into the outlaw's side.

"Get down nice and easy. If you gets frisky, I'll kill you," Harley shouted over the thunderous rumble of the fleeing cattle.

As the man stepped to the ground, the boom and crash of stampeding herd filled the air. Harley quickly disarmed the outlaw and said, "I'm missin' one of my friends. A fellar named Ned Jessup. What've you devils done with him?"

"I don't know nothin'," the rustler said.

Harley shot him in the knee. He screamed and collapsed onto the ground, writhing in pain and holding his wounded knee to his chest.

Harley bent low, grabbed the man's hair and jerked his head back, and said into his ear, "I'm missin' one of my friends. A fellar named Ned Jessup. What've you devils done with him?"

"You go to hell!" the man shouted.

Harley shot his other knee. The man's screams again filled the air as he clutched his crippled legs to his chest, writhing in pain.

Harley repeated his question for the third time. When the man was slow in responding, Harley cocked his pistol and prepared to shoot the man again, but before he fired, the outlaw suddenly shouted, "Burnett done it! We caught him snoopin' around and Burnett killed him with an axe when he wouldn't talk!"

"That weren't so tough was it?" Harley said and walked away, dragging his wolf back toward his horse.

"Help me, don't leave me like this!" the outlaw shouted.

The Ranger stopped and addressed the rustler, "You left Jessup, didn't you? Chopped him up and left him to bleed to death? You're on yer own. If you wants help, yer goin' to have to walk out and find it. Or, you can stay there and bleed to death. Your choice."

As Harley returned to his horse, Keeps Eagle and Jimmy, each with their wolves in tow, soon joined him. In the distance, the low rumble of pounding hooves could still be heard.

"Shore glad there ain't much of a moon," Jimmy said. "I thought that night rider was gonna find me shore!"

"He won't be findin' nothin' but the gates of perdition," Harley commented, suddenly realizing the thunder of the stampede had covered his confrontation with the nightrider.

The stampede had happened so quickly; the rustlers in camp had little time to react. There'd been no warning, nothing to spook the cattle. They simply started running. Why had they gone loco? The cattle charged blind through the night. Those that smelled the wolves panicked, and their panic was infectious; instantly it spread through the herd and basic survival instinct took over. Running for their lives, the herd couldn't be turned or slowed, although the few outlaws on horseback tried futilely to turn them. The herd charged through the rustler's camp at full speed, running down anyone and anything in their path. The thunder and bellow of the wild-eyed cattle, mixed with the shouts and screams of men, drew further away into the night, until the bed ground was quiet as a graveyard.

At dawn the next day, the raiders rode along the bench until near the remains of the rustler's camp, where they dropped down into the river bottom. Three saddle horses lay dead on the flats and two more, broken and battered, stood eyeing the raiders helplessly as they approached. Dead cattle littered the chewed up ground, trampled by their mates during the mad run. The camp looked like a cyclone hit it. The remains of two wall tents, along with knots of bedrolls, crushed coffee pots, a broken dutch oven and two misshapen frying pans were trampled and half buried in the dirt and debris. The bodies of six rustlers were found in the wreck, stomped into oblivion, looking like they'd have to be collected with a garden hoe.

The river valley had served as a conduit for the locoed cattle, channeling their mad run along a narrow corridor of bottomland. The rustlers didn't have a chance. Harley found the dead night rider he'd shot during the night and using his horse, dragged the body to the devastated camp, where other raiders were busy moving bodies to a nearby stand of trees. There, all seven outlaws were hung and signs placed on them proclaiming to the world a message no living man knew the meaning of, yet many understood.

Harley found a rustler's horse that was still serviceable and loaded Jessup's body on it as the raiders mounted up and rode downstream, searching for the remaining rustlers and the stolen stock. During the morning, three more rustlers were found dead, men who apparently had suffered internal injuries but were able to flee, only to die later. Their battered bodies were hung and marked as the others had been. Later that afternoon, Jimmy and Keeps Eagle came riding back to Gus and Harley at the rear.

"We spotted them boys up ahead. They're collecting stock and still heading downstream!" Jimmy said excitedly. "They shore are a sorry outfit!"

"How many is there?" Harley asked.

"They's four of 'em," the kid replied. "How you want to play it?"

Harley whistled and called all the raiders in. As the men gathered around, he presented the facts as Jimmy had related them. "Since there's only four, I think we should simply ride in and kill 'em. Go in fast and hot and start pluggin'. After last night, I doubt they got much fight in 'em. I ain't in no mood for pussyfooting around so let's just go kill 'em.

"We'll form a line abreast and start in at a lope 'til we spots 'em. When we do, go to yer spurs, guns blazin'. Don't quit 'til they're all dead or surrender. You see someone needs help, jump in and lend a hand."

The men quickly spread out across the narrow river bottom, bringing their horses up to speed. Gus was the first to spot a rustler and quickly urged his mount into action. Then, Jimmy and Second Bob spotted another outlaw and rode in hard, firing on the surprised outlaw. Keeps Eagle spotted a man just as he saw the raider and after a good chase, the Indian was able to knock him out of his saddle. Harley and Andrew Fergus spotted the fourth outlaw making tracks up out of the river bottom and set off in pursuit. Harley had to abandon the chase when the horse carrying the body of Jessup came up lame. Andrew continued on and finally caught his man holed up in a dry wash, where he used his rifle to settle accounts.

All the rustlers were returned to the river bottom where they'd been found and after they were hung and marked, the raiders continued downstream, gathering the stolen cattle and horses as they went. More than eight hundred head of cattle were recovered, along with better than seventy horses.

Driving the herd south along the river, Harley said to Gus, "That buzzard I shot last night said Burnett killed Jessup."

"Hap Burnett's the skunk that led this bunch! I didn't see his body anywhere, though some of them was hard to tell. I got some unfinished business when we get shed of this livestock then," Gus said, again swearing an oath.

"*We* got some unfinished business, Gus. I'm on this trail 'til she plays out."

Two days later, the raiders drove the herd of recovered cattle and horses onto Theodore Roosevelt's Elkhorn ranch, twenty miles north of Medora.

"Where'd you get this bunch?" the foreman, Bill Merrifield, asked.

"We found 'em out skylarkin'. Is the boss around?" Harley asked.

Merrifield noticed Harley leading a horse with a body wrapped in a tarp thrown across the saddle. "I'll get him," he said.

A few minutes later, Merrifield and Roosevelt stepped out of the large log home Roosevelt had built for himself.

"Hello," said Roosevelt, happily, "I see you've brought in considerable stolen stock. We're most appreciative and we'll see it's returned to the rightful owners." Roosevelt studied the scene, recognized the **D-S** brand carried on the men's horses, but said nothing. He then noticed the tarped form slung across a horse Gus was leading.

"Who is that you have there?" he asked, walking over to the limp form.

"Ned Jessup. You know him?" asked Gus Adams.

"Of course I know him! He's been working on our rustling problem for some time now. What happened to him?" T.R. asked.

"That rustlin' problem killed him. See that he gets back to his family. He was a good man and game 'til the end," Harley replied.

Roosevelt looked first at Harley, and then at Gus, before finally turning to his foreman. "Bill, help me get him down. Ned worked for us and deserves better than this."

Roosevelt and his foreman quickly untied the tarped body and lowered it to the ground, where they removed the thongs and carefully unwrapped the dead man, until the full light of day shown on the mutilated and tortured form.

"My God!" shouted Roosevelt, "What happened to him?"

"He was tortured for information. But he wouldn't tell them rustlin' skunks anythin', so they used an axe on him," Harley said.

"But this is despicable!" Roosevelt shouted, his face turning red, his anger growing volcanic. "Didn't you catch the men that did this? I don't see any prisoners in your party!"

"No sir," Harley said, "This here is Dakota, not New York. We don't make prisoners of men who do this sorta thing. We kill 'em like the rats they are."

Roosevelt studied the six raiders carefully, and finally said, "I may have misread the situation, but I take your meaning. After seeing what they've done to Jessup, I most heartily concur with your methods. Please excuse me my ignorance and thank you for spelling it out plainly for me. I say bully for you men! Bully!"

T.R. then bent low to the ground, where he knelt over the body and said a silent prayer. He picked up the mutilated body of his range detective, slowly carrying it onto his front porch. Merrifield rolled the tarp up, with the remains of the man's life inside, and followed his boss.

The raiders continued their journey south into Medora, where they arrived well past sundown and quickly took rooms at the Western House, a local hotel. "$1.50 for a bed? This ain't Denver you know. This is Medora!" After cleaning up, they had a good meal at The Elk dining room and proceeded to look the town over. They passed Little Tom's Saloon and noticed it was completely empty, though the barkeep, presumably Tom himself, was on duty cleaning glasses. Walking through the door, the men were assailed by skunk scent and made a hasty retreat back out the door.

"Damnation! What happened in there?" Jimmy asked.

"Maybe they has a different class of skunk that drinks in this town!" Harley said, laughing, as the men moved down the street to the Pioneer Bar.

Harley ordered drinks all around. As the barkeep was pouring, Harley asked, "What's the story on that skunk palace down the street?"

The barkeep laughed. "Little Tom's? We had some excitement here two or three days ago. Some Vigilantes cornered a bunch of rustlers in there and ran 'em out with skunks!"

"Skunks?" Jimmy exclaimed, "How many skunks does it take to stink-up a place like that?"

"I don't rightly know, but I was told a small herd came streaming outa there. I didn't see the skunks; just saw the gunplay outside. It was the damnedest thing you ever saw! The Vigilantes shot several men down in the street and hung the rest south of here along the river."

"Any idea who them Vigilantes was?" Harley asked innocently.

"Don't know. Someone said they's man-killers from Oklahoma. A determined lookin' nigger was leadin' 'em. There was four men all together but no one recognized their brands. Yes sir, it was some excitin' here for a spell."

"How many men did these skunk herders hang?" Harley asked, curious. He signaled for another round of drinks and the barkeep promptly complied, pouring as he became more enthused.

"Mister, there's twelve men hangin' outa them trees! Even hung men that was already dead! And hung another man they musta hung six times before 'cause his neck was all eat up by a rope. Then they put signs on 'em all; '3-7-77' they says. Any idea what that means?"

"I reckon it means don't do no more killin' and rustlin'," Harley said.

The following day, with a good night's rest behind them, the group split up. After questioning the ticket agent closely, Harley and Gus boarded the morning train for St. Paul. They were fairly certain Burnett had taken the eastbound train the day before and were anxious to catch up with him. If the outlaw couldn't be found, the two men were determined to bring the owners of the Minnesota Star Cattle Company to justice in one form or another. Harley had taken the precaution of sending a telegram to Granville, informing him of the sudden side trip.

Φ

While Harley and Gus were absent, the remaining Vigilantes and their guides conducted their second series of surprise attacks. These were of a much smaller nature, and usually involved the capture and hanging of two or three outlaws in each raid. In one instance, Black Dutch discovered the man he sought was visiting a neighbor and rode to the nearby ranch, where he walked the outlaw out of the shocked rancher's home at gun point. As the rancher and his family looked on, Dutch and the outlaw mounted up and rode off without another word. That was the last the rancher ever saw of his visitor, but over subsequent years, he swore the man was innocent of any crime, and charged the Vigilantes with killing an innocent man. He was not privy to the evidence that motivated Black Dutch, however; evidence that unequivocally proved the man's guilt.

A total of eleven outlaws were captured and killed in the second and final series of raids. Following these actions, all the DHS men were remounted on horses borrowed from nearby ranches sympathetic to their activities. From these outfits, the men rode the nearly 300 miles singly or in small groups, and finally made their way home a week later. Almost a year passed before the borrowed stock was returned to the proper owners.

Chapter Eight - Minnesota Star

Hap Burnett fled for his life, riding blind into the pitch-black night, pursued by the thundering herd of fear-stricken cattle close at his heels. The rumble of hooves pounded in his ears, driving him on a terrifying ride pall-mall through the night, never knowing what would happen the next instant. At first he simply rode to save his own skin, knowing any misstep of his horse, any gopher hole, any stumble, would cost him his life. It was too much for his already taut nerves. It was time to find another source of income, another form of employment. The discovery that someone was sneaking around his camp put his nerves on full alert, and although he'd gained no hard information while torturing the man, Burnett took the man's presence as a sign. And now this stampede! He'd missed death by a hair's breadth, and was fortunate to have been in the saddle when the stampede mysteriously began. He decided that if he got out of this scrape alive, he wasn't going to press his luck any further. It was time to clear out and settle accounts.

As he charged into the blackness, the thunder of the fear-struck herd behind him slowly fell away and he was finally able to check his terrified horse into a slow walk. He listened closely for the rumble that would strike fear into any cowhand's heart, but it was gone. He heard nothing but the blowing of his exhausted horse and the pounding of his own heart. As he rode north, he considered his situation. He'd heard of the mysterious Vigilantes known as "stranglers." Maybe the sneak was working for them? He'd known several of the men who'd been hung, and he knew them to be a fairly hard-boiled bunch. Burnett realized if that sort of thing could happen to them, it could certainly happen to him. No, it was time to quit this business. Burnett decided he'd go to St. Paul, collect the money Al Harris still owed him and then? Then he could do anything he wanted. Anything in the world. Maybe strike out for Mexico till things settled some?

Burnett turned west and rode up onto the bench land for several miles before turning south, avoiding entirely the river valley. If the stampede was the result of Vigilantes, he didn't want to be anywhere near the river bottom. This would make his ride to Medora much longer, but it couldn't be helped if he was to survive. Three days later, he arrived in Medora early in the morning and was forced to wait until the ticket agent's window opened. When it did, he bought a ticket on the next eastbound train, destination St. Paul. It wasn't until he was seated and the train was moving out of the small station that he relaxed for the first time. Two days later, he arrived at the booming midwestern city located on the banks of the Mississippi River and quickly made his way to the offices of the Minnesota Star Cattle Company where he was promptly shown into Al Harris' office.

"You're early," Harris said, smiling, "I wasn't expecting you for another week. How many head did you bring this time?"

Burnett frowned. "I ain't got no cattle. We was wiped out a few days ago. My cattle rustlin' days is over and I wants to get paid up."

"What?" Harris exclaimed, studying the outlaw carefully. "What's got you so spooked? We've done good by you haven't we? My partners and I've always treated you right, haven't we? And you've gotten rich with our little arrangement."

"Can't spend that money if I'm dead, can I? I caught a someone snoopin' around and figure this game's up for me. Over in Montana, the Vigilantes has been hangin' men for rustlin'. I ain't gonna stretch no rope for nobody; I'm done," Burnett said.

"Yes, yes, I heard about that," Harris said, with honeyed words, trying to sooth the man, "Why didn't you simply take care of the sneak; make him disappear? No one would ever know. Men disappear all the time."

"Oh, I took care of him alright! Something or someone stampeded the herd I was bringing in, right through our blasted camp! If I hadn't been headin' out to check the nightriders, I would've been stomped into dust! I don't know how many of my men survived but I figure most of 'em is dead. Them cattle didn't run just 'cause they got the itch to see some new country," Burnett said.

"In all the time I've known you, I've never known you to run scared," Harris said.

"You ain't listening! Don't you read the damned papers? The men that was hung in Montana was strangled to death! They even hung men that was already dead! Then they put signs on 'em with '3-7-77' written on 'em! That means Vigilantes!"

"Those numbers don't mean a thing to me!" Harris said.

"They'd damn sure mean somethin' if you was in my line of work! Now, give me my money and quit foolin' around," Burnett replied. "It's quits for me and that's flat."

"Very well, if you're determined to quit, I can't stop you. It'll take me a few days to get your money though. We don't carry that kind of cash and it'll take time to raise it. Get yourself a room over at the Merchants and come back in three days. We owe you," Harris paused as he pulled out a ledger and studied the entries, "we owe you almost $15,000. Come back in three days and I'll have it ready. In the mean time, relax and have some fun."

"I'll relax when I have my money and I'll have fun leaving this country," the rough man said with a scowl. "I'll be back in three days. Just make damned sure you have it ready. If you try to cheat me, I'll show you some of what I showed that sneak!"

A ripple of fear shot through Harris' body at Burnett's threat, chilling his spine and making his face flush at the same time. After Burnett left the office, a shaken Harris hurriedly telephoned his three business partners and scheduled a meeting. Each of the men had various commitments and the hastily called meeting of all four owners couldn't be arranged until late the following afternoon.

The Minnesota Star Cattle Company occasionally bought legitimate herds of cattle as well as horses and hogs as a cover for their illegal operations. The majority of the stock they purchased was stolen in Dakota, Montana, Wyoming or Canada and shipped in by rail to the company's pens and slaughterhouse in North St. Paul. Burnett's methods were typical. He and his gang stole cattle and horses, drove them to a secluded spot, picked only marketable beef and horses from the herd and ran off what couldn't be sold. Once the brands were reworked, they were then given time to heal because freshly branded stock was easy to identify by the singed hair and the fresh wounds. Some rustlers branded through a wet burlap bag to eliminate the problem of burned hair but Burnett found this to be tedious. Once healed, the stock was driven to a remote rail siding and loaded into livestock cars.

Brand and stock inspectors were the biggest threat to these illegal operations but there were few such men in Montana and Dakota Territory, and none in Minnesota. If legitimate inspectors found someone driving or shipping stock, they were required to prove ownership. Burnett altered the brands of stolen stock to ones he was registered as legal owner. But this wasn't always possible. When the original brand couldn't be altered to a brand he owned, he and his men would "blot" or burn over the brand to make it unrecognizable and then re-brand in another location. The only way to determine the original brand was to kill the animal and skin it so the brand marks could be studied from the inside of the hide of the animal. If Burnett didn't have everything set as he wanted, he would try to control or distract the inspectors using whiskey, cards, whores, bribes, blackmail, coercion, intimidation and threats. In the two years Burnett and Harris had been working this deal, he'd never been caught.

Φ

The day after Burnett arrived in St. Paul, Harley and Gus stepped off the train in in the same city. Harley carried his pistols, holsters, lariat, the account books and a couple changes of clothes in a carpetbag he'd purchased in Medora. Gus carried a similar bag. At the train station, Gus found a city directory and looked up the address of Minnesota Star Cattle Company. All towns and cities of any consequence had directories and beginning in the early 1880's listings also carried telephone numbers if available. Harley knew of telephones because Col. Nelson Miles was responsible for establishing a small telephone system at Ft. Keogh in 1879, and in 1881 a small public telephone exchange was established in Miles City. Although service was poor, it marked the beginning of telephone service in eastern Montana Territory. He was surprised at the size of the directory however. The city boasted a population of nearly 100,000 inhabitants.

St. Paul had many amazing sights for Harley's eyes. Tall buildings (seven stories high), gas street lights, paved streets, horse drawn trolleys, fancy carriages and high toned businesses were all a wonder, not to mention the shear size of the sprawling metropolis. As the two men took a hired hack to the cattle company offices, Harley couldn't help staring at his strange surroundings. Gus was more traveled than his companion and enjoyed watching the rough Ranger's reactions to the various sights.

They finally arrived at the address and took up a position kitty-corner from the Minnesota Star Cattle Company offices in a neighborhood saloon. They sat near a front window and ordered two beers, which they barely touched. Carefully, they watched and noted who came and went. They soon identified one man as the likely owner by his fancy trappings, manner and dress. They'd seen him come and go several times that afternoon in an expensive carriage with a fancy liveried driver.

Late in the day, when most of the neighboring businesses were closing, three men arrived in separate carriages within ten minutes of one another and entered the Minnesota Star offices. While their carriages remained at the curb, the drivers walked across the street and entered the bar where Harley and Gus sat.

"Looks like a pow-wow to me," Harley said. "You reckon them three fancies is owners too or just other business men?"

"I'd hate to guess," Gus replied, "but we'll know for sure after I talk to those drivers. Hold tight."

Gus made his way to the bar, where the three liveried drivers were standing and chatting. He quickly insinuated his way into the group by pretending to be a rich buyer from Milwaukee looking for a beef supplier. The fact that he kept buying the drinks didn't hurt the flow of information. Twenty minutes later, he returned to the table where Harley kept a close eye on the Star offices.

"Nothin's moving over there. You do any good?"

"I got the names of all four owners of the Minnesota Star Cattle Company. We can grab a city directory and find out where each lives if we want. All we gotta do now is connect Burnett with them and we'll have 'em in a sack."

"You do good work, Gus!"

Φ

As each partner arrived, he was met by Harris and shown into his large office. When all four men were present, Harris explained the situation with Burnett. While the rustler wasn't their only supplier of stolen stock, he was consistent and had turned over more than 10,000 head in the time they worked together.

After Harris finished recounting Burnett's story of losing the herd and the possibility of Vigilantes in his area, William Warren, one of Burnett's partners exclaimed, "Vigilantes? That's the last thing we need! Seems to me something was in the papers not too long ago about some rustlers getting hung! What if those brush-poppers come for us?"

"Are you kidding? I'm not worried about some 'pirates of the plains' 700 miles away. Burnett's spooked, that's all. Besides, there's nothing that ties us to him. Nothing. In the eyes of the law, we're legitimate and above board. He's coming by the office in a few days to get the $15,000 we still owe him. After that, he's gone and I doubt we'll ever see him again," Harris said.

"Why bother to pay him at all? If he ain't going to be supplying us with cattle, we don't need him. Why don't you take care of him? I don't think he'll be missed by anyone," Warren said, chuckling.

"Why don't *you* take care of him? You're such a big man, go ahead! He's a killer and I don't want to get sideways with him. If you think it's so damned simple, go at it!" Harris said, daring Warren to back up his tall talk. He didn't rise to the bait.

"Looks like we better pay Burnett off then," Max Hoffstedter said. "Anything else we need to look at?"

The men continued to discuss their joint business interests for nearly an hour. When the meeting was finally concluded, each man went his own way. Across the street, Harley and Gus connected names with faces, burning each man's features into their memory.

Φ

That evening, Gus and Harley took a room at a nearby hotel. Following a fine supper, the two men took a cook's tour of St. Paul in their rented hack as they discussed plans for the following day.

Harley entered the Minnesota Star Cattle Company office shortly after it opened and asked to see Mr. Harris. After a short wait, he was shown into the boss's office and had a seat as Harris concluded a phone conversation.

Looking up finally, Harris said, "Ah, Mr. Jessup, is that it? I didn't know if my secretary got your name right. How can I help you today?"

"I been back east on business and thought I'd stop by on my way home. Me and Hap Burnett are in the same sorta business, and some time back he said it might be in my interest if I was to talk to you, if I ever had the chance. Well, I got the chance, as I said, and here I am."

"And what business would that be, Mr. Jessup?"

"Like Burnett, you might say I'm a beef supplier. I specialize in findin' strays and bringing them to market," Harley replied.

"I see we speak the same language. By the way, when was the last time you saw Hap?" Harris asked innocently.

"I ain't seen him in nearly a year. Why?"

"What would you say if I told you Hap is getting out of the business?"

Harley chuckled. "I'd say good for me and too bad for him. My setup is different than his though and I'm lookin' to grow. If he's gettin' out, that suits me down to my boots."

"What kind of 'strays' are we talking about and how many could you deliver?"

"Mostly I finds Herefords. No longhorns, that certain. As to quantity, I can ship 3,000-4,000 head per month by rail," Harley replied.

"That many? How's that possible?" Harris asked, surprised. Burnett was aggressive in his activities but never managed to ship more than 1,000 head in his best month. If this man could deliver what he claimed, losing Burnett would be of little consequence and Harris would grow rich as Midas!

"I specialize in government strays. I sorta borrows 'em before the Indians get their thievin' hands on 'em. I have a partner in the Indian Bureau and the way we work it, no one knows they're even gone. All you gotta do is tell me where you want 'em delivered."

"Err, our pens and slaughterhouse are at the Union Stockyards in North St. Paul. But aren't you worried about Vigilantes?"

"Them 'stranglers' got nothing to do with us. We only ship government strays, nothing from individual ranchers. That's why our setup and Hap's are different. Vigilantes aren't the slightest worry to us, unless the government has Vigilantes!" Harley said laughing. "We do have terms though."

"And what would those terms be?" Harris replied, bracing himself for the worse. Just when he thought things were looking up, a snag!

"We gotta be paid cash on delivery. The way I figure it, you're probly payin' Hap half of market value, so you can sell the beef before he gets his money, but for cash on delivery, we'll take a third of market. But if these terms are too rich for you, well, there's other buyers around," Harley said, standing as if to leave.

"Wait, please!" Harris said, relieved and shocked at the generous terms, "I must be frank. I have partners, Mr. Jessup. I'll need to get their approval before I can commit to such a proposal. But in principal, I accept your terms and I feel confident we will be able to work something out that will be beneficial to both of us. By the way, where are you staying?"

"Well, ain't stayin' no place. I just got in," Harley replied.

"As it happens, Hap is in town and has taken a room at the Merchants Hotel. Why don't you get yourself a room and look him up while I contact my partners? I'm sure we can work things out. Just give me twenty-four hours," Harris said, elated with the possibilities. *Did Jessup say 4,000 head a month? That's 48,000 head a year! I'll be rich, rich, rich!*

"Good idea! If he's gettin' out of the business, I'd like to buy him a drink or two! I'll call again tomorrow afternoon. What time do you close?"

"We close at 5:00, but I'm usually here until after 6:00."

"Fine. See you tomorrow evening then," Harley said, and left the grinning cattle thief's office on a note of fellowship and good will.

As soon as Harley was gone, Harris began making phone calls. "You won't believe what just happened…"

Φ

"Did he take the bait?" Gus asked when Harley had returned.

"Took it like a baby reachin' for a sugar-tit," the Ranger replied. "I told him my name was Jessup and I was an old friend of Hap's. Harris sorta got into the mood of things and told me where we could find him. Let's get us some supper and then look the man up."

Following a good meal, the two raiders collected their belongings and checked into the Merchants Hotel on Bank Street. Gus explained to the clerk that Hap Burnett was a friend and requested a room near his. The clerk was very accommodating and quickly gave them a key to room 520, just down and across the hall from 517, Burnett's room. As the men ascended the open stairway to the fifth floor, the huge building was a wonder to Harley's eyes. The huge lobby with its vaulted ceiling, the sumptuous furnishings and rich décor were something the Ranger had never seen before.

"At least the devil won't be jumping out the window," Harley whispered to Gus as they stepped onto the fifth floor landing.

With a bellboy in the lead, they quickly found their room. As Gus tipped the boy, Harley strolled to the window and looked out over the city with its gaslights and brilliantly lit businesses, restaurants, theaters, clubs and saloons. He wouldn't have believed it if he hadn't seen it for himself. And yet, for all the city had to offer, he already missed the open spaces of the prairie and while he found St. Paul interesting, he would never want to live there or anyplace like it. Never.

When the boy was gone, Harley said, "Let's see if Burnett's in his room."

"Not yet," Gus replied, "first we need to figure what we're going to do with him. After what he done to Jessup, I figure I owe him something special. And we gotta figure out what we're gonna do with them crooked cattle buyers."

"I saw a saloon down stairs. I'll go rustle us a bottle of good whiskey and some cigars. We might as well make this pow-wow comfortable," Harley replied

The two men planned and plotted for more than an hour. Each had different ideas of how things should be worked out. Gus wanted to make Burnett pay for what he did to Jessup, and Harley had no problem with that. As to the four partners, Harley was for simply hanging them one at a time in their homes. Gus felt there would be too many witnesses; each man must have a wife and possibly children, after all. The various possibilities were discussed and looked at from every angle. Finally, they settled on a plan agreeable to both men.

Although it was nearly midnight, Burnett was still not in his room. After several knocks at the door and receiving no answer, Gus picked the simple lock and entered room 517. Burnett's few items were on the mirrored dresser but the man was gone. Gus quickly went back to his room and spoke with Harley.

"That buzzard must be out drinkin' or playin' cards or chasin' women."

"Go back to his room and wait. I'll stay here with the door cracked. When he comes back, we can grab him," Harley replied.

Back in Burnett's room Gus turned down the gas wall lamp, pulled a chair up behind the door and sat down to wait. He was more accustomed to the boredom than Harley because his profession often involved long hours of waiting. His only fear was that he would fall asleep before the outlaw returned. Harley also fought to stay awake, though his room wasn't darkened, and several times he went to the washbasin and splashed water on his face. He knew that once the action began, he would be wide-awake; the waiting however, was difficult after the day he'd put in. He wasn't used to sitting and doing nothing for long, tedious hours at a time.

Just past 12:45 in the morning, Gus heard footsteps come up the stairs and approach down the carpeted hallway. He quickly stood up and waited. As the footsteps drew nearer, he pulled his revolver and held it poised above his head, ready to strike. The footsteps moved past the room and continued down the hall until they stopped. He heard a key inserted into a lock, a door open and close, then all was quiet. False alarm.

He resumed his previous position, hoping that Harley hadn't succumbed to the siren's call of sleep. At 1:10 Gus again heard footsteps coming up the stairs and move down the hall until they stopped just outside. He heard some mumbling and the rattle of coins, as though someone were looking through their pockets for a key. A key was inserted into the lock and turned. The door was shaken as someone tried to open the door while it was still locked. Again the sounds of mumbling were heard as a key was again inserted into the lock and turned. This time the door swung into the darkened room and a drunken man entered, staggering toward the oil lamp that sat on the nightstand. Just as the man found the lamp and lit a match, Gus's pistol came crashing down on his head, knocking him unconscious.

Gus lit the oil lamp using the freshly lit match. After replacing the globe, he turned to the man lying face down on the bed and rolled him over. Hap Burnett. He quickly left the room and walked two doors down to get Harley. The door was ajar and as he walked in, Harley jumped to his feet, startled, pistol at the ready, eyes blinking rapidly.

"You get him?"

"Yep, he's taking a nap and won't be givin' us no trouble," Gus replied. "You got the bag?"

Harley grabbed his carefully packed carpetbag from under the bed and quietly followed Gus to Burnett's room. Gus patted the unconscious men down and found a .44 caliber derringer in the man's coat pocket. From another pocket he retrieved a wad of folding money and $300 in gold.

"Look what I found! Ill gotten gains, I'd say."

"Might as well keep it. Where Burnett is goin' they don't take currency."

Gus quickly stuffed the money into his pockets and grabbed the outlaw. With a raider on each side, Burnett was dragged out the door and down the hall toward the door to the back stairs. Once outside, moving the man down five flights of stairs wasn't easy, but they finally arrived at the alley behind the hotel and let Burnett slump down next to the building.

"Hold him here while I get the hack. You ain't gonna fall asleep on me again are you?" Gus asked, chuckling.

"I weren't sleepin' damn it; just restin' my eyes! Now that I got this buzzard fer company, I'm ready as a ruttin' buck," the Ranger replied softly, as he set his carpetbag down and retrieved his trusty Colt.

Fifteen minutes later, as Burnett was starting to come around, Gus drove the hack down the alley and pulled to a stop beside the two men. Although barely conscious, Burnett was forced into the hack and made to sit between the two raiders. While Gus drove, Harley held the man erect with his right hand, as he held his pistol in the side of the murderer with his left. He warned Burnett repeatedly not to say a word or it would be his last. Gus brought the horse up to a trot and the men set off for North St. Paul at a good clip; not so fast as to raise suspicion but fast enough to get them to their destination within half an hour.

They arrived at the Minnesota Star Cattle Company slaughterhouse and stock pens without incident. As Gus pulled up outside the street entrance, Harley jabbed the Colt hard into Burnett's side, so there could be no doubt who was in control. The Ranger grabbed Burnett roughly by the neck and they quickly stepped down from the carriage and walked to the locked door. Gus joined them carrying the carriage lantern and a pry bar. Using the bar, Gus levered the door and soon the heavy padlock and hasp came apart with a rending and splintering sound of shattered wood.

"What is it you men wan?" asked Burnett, slurring his words. "You can haf all my money, all my money if you wan-wants; no need for rough stuff!"

"Get in there and stop your yappin'!" Harley ordered, as Gus kicked the door hard, springing it open. Burnett sullenly did as he was told, staggering into the darkened building and when all three men were inside, Gus closed the door, and led the way with the carriage lantern as they worked their way through the darkened offices, and into the slaughterhouse proper. The stench of the still air was overpowering.

Noticing a flight of stairs at the rear of the building, Harley said, "Let's take him upstairs. We'll use the balcony so no one can miss him."

Harley prodded Burnett, and the drunken man slowly stumbled up the stairs onto a narrow balcony that ran around the perimeter of cooling room, where cattle carcasses were hung to cool before butchering and packing.

"Tie his hands and feet," Harley said. As Gus was tying Burnett's hands behind his back, Harley said, "Danged! I forgot to bring my bag in. You got him?"

"He's too drunk to give me much trouble. Go ahead, I'm alright."

"I'll be right back."

As Harley made his way through the darkness to the hack out front, Gus used the carriage lantern to check Burnett's bound hands. The man could barely stand and slumped against the wall as if made of rubber. "This ought to hold you," he said, satisfied with his rope work. Gus retrieved another short length of rope, and as he bent to tie Burnett's feet, the outlaw suddenly came alive, spun around, and kicked the detective hard in the face, knocking him over onto his back. Gus saw stars, and fought to retain consciousness. Though dazed and bleeding heavily from his broken nose, Gus got to his feet as quickly as possible, but Burnett was gone. *The devil was playin' possum!* In the distance, Gus could hear pounding footfalls fading away. Grabbing the carriage lantern, he ran along the balcony to a side door that now stood open, and leaped out onto a landing, where steps led down to an elevated walkway. He could hear the sounds of Burnett in the distance, running along the wooden structure.

Gus bounded down the steps, and ran along the walkway. As he ran, he heard the sounds of cattle, and realized the walkway was built above the stock pens of the slaughterhouse. Suddenly, he came to a crosswalk-intersection where the walkway branched off in four separate directions, and he was forced to stop, and quiet his breathing, listening for Burnett. Off to the left, he again heard the faint footfalls of someone running down the boardwalk. Gus quickly changed direction, and charged toward the sound, worried that Burnett would escape the justice that was his due.

After Burnett had smashed through the outside door and fallen onto the landing, he quickly scrambled to his feet, and plunged down the stairs into the darkness, with no idea of where he was going. His only desire was to escape the two men who'd kidnapped him. Below, he could hear the sounds of cattle, and occasionally hogs, that were being held for slaughter. He'd delivered cattle to the yards many times, but after changing his direction of travel several times in the darkness, he was thoroughly lost, and had no idea which way to run. Each time he came to an intersection, he had to decide which way to go; forward, turn right or turn left. Making his choice quickly, on he ran. Coming to another crosswalk, he stopped to listen, and could plainly hear the sounds of someone chasing after him. This spurred him on to greater exertions, his fear singular in his mind, making it difficult to pay attention to his path. Again he changed direction and charged forward, running blind into the night. Once more he stopped, and listened carefully, and again heard the sounds of his pursuer. Were the sounds growing closer? The sounds *seemed* closer, but he couldn't be sure. Despite his labored breathing and near exhaustion, he urged his body onward once again, hoping he could find a way out of the maze to safety. The adrenalin was rushing now; he was running for his life! He'd played possum with the two men, pretending to be more drunk and incoherent than he really was. But his cleverness had only bought him a temporary stay if he couldn't find his way out of the puzzle.

Panic filled him as he ran, when suddenly his foot caught on something, and tripped him, bringing him almost to his knees. By shear force of will, he scrambled to regain his feet and charge forward, only to suddenly run into a low wooden handrail and topple over the walkway into the void below, where he was jerked to a stop.

Disoriented, slowly Burnett realized he was hanging upside down, suspended by one leg. He'd gotten tangled in a workman's rope somehow. He had no idea how far he was above the ground. The rope had prevented him from breaking his neck, but now he was hanging with his hands tied behind his back. He jerked and twisted, trying to free himself, but the detective had done his work too well, and the knots that bound his hands refused to yield. After a brief struggle, he was forced to abandon the idea of freeing his hands, and decided to try to use his free leg to shuffle out of the rope that held his leg. Burnett knew if he succeeded, he would drop some distance, but thought he might control the fall by pinching the rope off between his feet and legs. Frantically, he tried to free himself, but because his entire weight was on the rope, he couldn't get the slack necessary for it to slip free. After some time, a noise that seemed to be in the back of his brain suddenly became more demanding, and he was horrified to realize the sounds he was hearing were hogs. Were they in the same stock pen he was suspended above? If so, how high above them was he? He had no way of knowing. He could be inches or several feet above the ground. All around him was black.

Gus lost his man! He slowed his pace to a cautious walk, and listened carefully, but could hear nothing. The footsteps he'd heard earlier were gone and he had no idea where the man was. He finally stopped and leaned against the handrail, his breathing labored and coming in gasps through his open mouth. His shattered nose was clogged with blood and starting to swell shut, and although it was extremely painful, he knew it would heal. His only true regret was loosing his prisoner. *I lost him! Damn!*

"What happened?"

Gus jumped a foot, shocked and surprised. He recognized Harley's voice, and turned the lantern to see the Ranger step out of the darkness. Frustrated and embarrassed, Gus replied, "Burnett jumped me and ran out onto the walkway. I been chasing noises for the past ten minutes! I can't hear him anymore, and I'll be damned if I know where he could be. I reckon he's escaped, Harley."

"Well, let's look around some. Maybe he stopped to rest."

"I'd like to give him a rest with an axe handle!" the detective said.

Just as the men were about to begin their search, they heard a shout. As they walked toward the noise, the shouts became more insistent, finally rising to screams. As the men drew closer, Harley noticed a taught rope running along one side of the walkway toward the frantic screams. Moving forward, screams, squeals and grunts grew louder, and suddenly the light from the lantern fell on the busted railing at the end of the walkway. Easing forward, Harley and Gus stopped at the end of the walkway and Gus shined the light down into the void. There, they saw Burnett hanging by one leg, his head almost touching the ground, his hands still tied behind his back. Helpless, he was pitching and jerking desperately, frantically trying to keep the huge hogs that surrounded him at bay. But, it was no use; grunting and squealing, the ravenous hogs were pressing so close to the outlaw he could feel their breathing. One of Burnett's ears had been torn off and presumably eaten, the bloody stump the only reminder. The outlaw's screams, and jerking movements, continued as the hogs pressed in, ravaging the soft tissues of his face and throat, biting and tearing chunks of flesh from the suspended outlaw.

Pigs are omnivorous and will eat flesh as well as vegetable matter. Early pork producers fed their stock meat that had gone bad and was of no value for human consumption, until it was discovered that meat-fed hogs had an unusually high incidence of trichinosis, a disease that attacks the central nervous system in humans. In 1889 laws were passed to prevent the practice. Hogs could only be fed vegetable materials and grains after passage of the new law.

"Jeezus! If there's a rough way to go to hell, Burnett's shore takin' it!"

"Go ahead and bellar, you son-of-a-bitch!" Gus shouted down at the outlaw. "Did Jessup scream like that when you was choppin' him up?"

Burnett suddenly became aware of the men above him, and begged to be saved, as the hogs tore at him greedily. "Help me! Please! You can't let me die like this! HELP ME!"

"Save you from being killed, so we can kill you? That don't sound reasonable! Go ahead and die, you black-hearted bastard!" Gus shouted again.

Harley pulled one of the account ledgers from his carpetbag and set it on the walkway above the dying outlaw. Next to it, he placed a numbered sign. Then, he and Gus slowly began working their way out of the yards, with the pitiful entreaties of Burnett continuing, as the hogs ripped and tore at the outlaw. The grunts, squeals and screams filled the night air. By the time the raiders worked their way back to the slaughterhouse, the pleading, shouts and the screams had stopped. The hungry hogs squealed and feasted until Burnett was disemboweled, picked clean to the waist. He was eaten alive.

Φ

When Harris arrived at his office the following morning, a familiar figure was waiting for him. "Ah, Captain Linderman, a little early in the month to see you isn't it?"

"This ain't about that. We got a call that a man had been murdered at your packinghouse. I've just come from there to pick you up. I want you to see if you know him. He had certain 'evidence' with him that implicates you and your partners," the captain said smiling.

"What are you talking about? What man and what evidence?"

"Come along and I'll show you."

As the two men rode along, the captain explained the situation. "We found a man hanging in one of the hog pens in your stockyards. His hands were tied behind his back. He was hung head down just above the ground, helpless. The hogs ate him alive. There was a sign on the walkway above him with the numbers 3-7-77 marked on it. Next to the sign was an account book, more of a journal really, that documents deliveries of cattle and horses; the deliveries were made to your company. It also gives dates, quantities, payments and it names you personally," the captain explained, grinning at the panicked man.

"My God! Do you have the book? I mean do we have it?" Harris asked, a cold icy chill running down his spine. He was shocked and stunned by the implications.

"We have the book, but it's going to cost you. You been making regular payments so we'd look the other way concerning where your cattle were coming from. This is something entirely different. A murdered man, a sign suggesting Vigilante activity, the account book. You see what I mean?"

"Yes, yes of course. How much will it cost us to keep this out of the papers and keep everyone quiet?" Harris asked, trying to gain some control yet dreading the answer.

"The newspapers already have it. There were three reporters there when I left to get you. They know about everything. Everything except the account book. No one knows about that except me and a few of my men. It'll cost you $10,000 to keep this quiet. And you'll get the book back when we have the money."

"Christ! That much?"

"You should be happy we was the ones that got it! Otherwise, you and your partners would be headed for jail right now," the captain said with confidence.

"I see what you mean. You're right, of course. Who was the hanged man, by the way?" Harris asked, even though he felt he knew the answer already.

"Based on the ledger, I'd say his name was Burnett. I'd like you to confirm the identity, though because the man's head, neck and upper body were stripped nearly to the bone, that may be difficult. If you can confirm the man's identity, we should be able to wrap this up. The boys at City Hall like to see things tied up nice and neat. If we can verify who he was, well, there shouldn't be too many questions after that."

When Harris and the police captain arrived, Burnett's lifeless and ravaged body had been pulled up onto the walkway. The reporters were still interviewing the men who discovered the body. Harris looked on the grisly scene, and then looked closely at the man's hands. Burnett always wore a Mexican silver ring and Harris identified the body through that.

"I've seen this man, captain. His name is Burnett. He wore this silver ring here," Harris said pointing at the swollen hands still tied behind the man's back. "Told me he was from Montana. He came to my office a couple days ago with some cattle to sell. We didn't buy them because he couldn't prove ownership. This is a brutal murder, captain. Have you caught the men who did it?"

"We have no suspects yet. The front door was broken open and the building entered sometime last night. That's all we know for certain," the captain replied, playing his part equally well for the benefit of the reporters nearby. "I'm curious why you don't have a night watchman or a guard?"

"Because we keep no money here. There isn't anything of value, except our livestock, so we never felt the need," Harris replied. "We lock up more as a matter of routine than anything else. After this, I think a night watchman would be a good idea."

When Harris finally returned to his office, he quickly telephoned his partners and called an emergency meeting. The three men dropped everything they were involved in and arrived at Harris's office within the hour. When all were present, Harris told them about Burnett's murder and the grisly method used, the 3-7-77 sign and the secret ledger.

"Harris, it was just yesterday that you sat there calmly and told us we had nothing to worry about! Them 'pirates of the plains' as you called them, wouldn't be a problem you said!" James Lund exclaimed.

"That damned sign proves the Vigilantes did it. And the fact that Burnett was killed on our property proves Vigilantes know who he was supplying cattle to!" William Warren added. "We're next! They know who we are and we'll be killed too!"

"Shut up, damn it! Stop your damned whimpering and show a little backbone for a change. You knew there were risks before you got involved," Harris said, disgusted.

"Sure, I knew there were risks; *legal* risks. I didn't think there was a risk I'd be murdered!" Warren exclaimed. "And I'd like to see how much backbone you got while hogs are eating you alive! Jeezus H. Christ!"

"There is not a chance, not a single chance you or any of us will be murdered; none whatever. Think about it," Harris said calmly. "You're over-reacting."

"Al's right. Burnett was killed as a warning, nothing more. If the Vigilantes were after us, we'd already be dead. The real question is, what do we do now?" Max Hoffstedter asked. Harris was relieved to see someone had some sense and was able to stay cool in this situation.

"Well, Linderman has Burnett's account book and says it'll cost us $10,000 to get it back and cover everything up. That book is all we got to worry about because it's the only thing that ties us to Burnett. Once we get it and destroy it, we're in the clear," Harris said.

"$10,000! That's too much damned money! We can't pay it!" Warren shouted.

"What kind of a fool are you, Warren? If Linderman and his bunch hadn't gotten that book, we'd all be headed for jail! The Vigilantes left it there to implicate us. Besides, we won't have to pay Burnett his $15,000 now, so after we pay the $10,000 to Linderman, we're still $5,000 ahead on this deal. Wasn't it you that said Burnett ought to be killed? Well, he has been, so quit your carping! You sound like an old woman, for Christ sakes!" Harris said, berating the big man.

"That's right. Burnett's out of the picture and we're $5,000 ahead after we pay Linderman off. I'd say we made out just fine. The papers will report the murder and although it gives us some press we don't want, it can't be helped. This whole thing will blow over in a month or so," Hoffstedter said happily. "We should be glad we're not in jail or worse."

"That's right. It could've been lots worse any way you figure it. And we got a new supplier. Right Harris?" James Lund asked.

"That's what I said but the timing sure makes me nervous. Jessup shows up just before Burnett gets killed? For all I know, Jessup is one of them 'stranglers' himself. And I'm the one that told him where Burnett was staying!" Harris said, growing more suspicious as he reasoned things out aloud. "Right after I tell him about Burnett, the man is murdered?"

"It does seem a little too convenient," Hoffstedter agreed. "Then again, this new man may be exactly what he says. When are you supposed to meet with him again?"

"Today around closing time. I told him we'd talk it over and let him know today."

"Well, let's agree to his terms. If he is on the level, we could sure use a new supplier and that government beef angle sounds too good to pass up. Those Indian agents are crooked as snakes," Lund added. "We'll have time to have someone check his story and make certain things are as they seem."

"We just gotta play it real careful; if he's square, we all stand to get rich. Just imagine what almost 50,000 head a year at one third of market value will mean!"

Φ

That morning, following a late breakfast, Gus and Harley returned to their lookout in the saloon. While Harley kept a close eye on the office, Gus took the hack to the Salvation Army soup kitchen and looked up the boss, a woman named Major Margaret Sweet.

"I'd like to make a contribution to your cause, ma'am. But you gotta do something for me in return," Gus told the stern looking uniformed woman.

"Why should I do anything for you?" the Major asked.

"Well ma'am, I have more than $1100 to donate. That money would buy a lot of soup bones and beans. See this ledger?" Gus asked, as he set the book on her desk, "All I ask is that you deliver this ledger to the editor of the St. Paul Herald day after tomorrow. That's all."

"You should know better than ask me to do anything illegal!" the Major said in a huff. "The Salvation Army would never be involved in anything like that."

"Delivering a book to a newspaper isn't illegal. See here," Gus said, as he opened the book and fanned the pages, "this is just an accounts book. That's all, and there ain't nothing against the law about it."

The Major was silent. Finally, she asked, "Why don't you give it to the newspaper yourself? Why involve me?"

"I gotta leave town later today. I left another book just like this one for the police to find, but they covered it up. It looks to me like some of them are taking payoffs. But, if the newspaper folks ain't fools, this book will help put some powerful men and some crooked police where they belong, in jail.

"I came to you because I believe you folks are honest. I've heard of you. Sure, I could pay some kid or a drunk $5 to deliver the book, but first, I can't trust them to get the job done, and second, that still leaves me with this money. And yes, this is money they stole or killed to get. I'd like to give it back to whoever it came from, but I have no way of knowing who they were. All I know for certain is it doesn't belong to the people named in this accounts book. Since I have no way to return it to the lawful owners, I could think of nothing better than to see it put to some good use, such as yours, ma'am. Will you do this for me?"

"Will you swear to me on a Bible, under threat of everlasting hellfire and damnation, that this is not illegal, and neither I personally, nor the Salvation Army, will be involved in any sordid activity?"

"Certainly. You gotta a book handy?"

The bargain was quickly sealed, and Gus left the Major's office, $1,179 poorer. He made his way back to Harley's position and sat down in front of a cold beer he'd grabbed from the bar.

"It's done. The other ledger will be delivered to the newspaper day after tomorrow, and I gave Burnett's money to charity. Anything stirring across the street?"

"Shore is. A policeman dropped Harris off, just after you left, and a short time later, his partners showed up. It looks like Burnett's body has been discovered, and Harris is spooked. We'll have to see," Harley replied as he got up to get himself a fresh beer.

Thirty minutes passed before three of the partners left the office, looking a little nervous, but not particularly frightened.

"Well, I'll be damned! If the law was onto them tinhorns, they'd be scattering like a covey of quail. Looks like you called it right, Gus. Those rascals got the law in their pocket. I wonder what it cost 'em to get the ledger?"

"Not enough to pay for Jessup, I'll wager," the detective replied.

"Them rats gotta be thinkin' they got everything covered. It'll shore be surprisin' when the newspaper starts workin' that claim!" Harley said, chuckling. "But, if nothing happens, I guess we'll just drift back this way, and wrap this mess up Montana fashion."

"I hope it works out. I like the idea of those crooks losing everything they own, and serving prison time in the bargain. If the state can prove their loot came from stolen beef, they'll confiscate everything they own."

"Shore hope you're right," Harley replied. "I just ain't got much faith in the law doin' its job."

Many of the town sheriffs in the American west were "saloon" sheriffs, bought and paid for by a powerful saloon owner. Consequently, the sheriff worked the law to suit his boss in every case. It was a perversion of justice. Despite Harley's Ranger experience, he had seldom seen local law enforcement work the way it was supposed to. Too often, he'd seen the guilty go free, while some innocent fool paid the price for someone else's greed or enmity.

"Well, we got us a train to catch. Shore will be nice to get back to the DHS. Granville will be happy to hear Burnett's been taken care of, and the other men will have finished all their raids by now. It's too bad about Jessup though," Harley said, finishing the last of his beer, and heading for the exit.

Φ

The uniformed woman charged through the front entrance as if on a mission. Her hair was pulled back in a severe bun, she wore no makeup of any kind, and she walked with a determined military bearing. At the reception desk, she asked the woman who sat behind it if she could see the editor-in-chief.

"That would be Mr. Horace Samples. Who are you and what is this about?"

213

"My name is Major Margaret Sweet. My mission concerns thieves and police corruption. I believe I have evidence your newspaper would be most interested in."

"Please have a seat, and I'll let him know you're here," the woman said, quickly rising and walking back into the myriad of offices, as Major Sweet took a seat on an oak bench, and sat stiffly at attention, not allowing herself to relax for an instant.

Soon the receptionist returned and announced, "Major Sweet? Mr. Samples will see you now. Please follow me."

After Major Sweet and Samples completed their introductions, the Major explained how she had come into possession of the account book she now held to her chest. She also explained the large donation that had accompanied it. She then handed the book across to Samples for his inspection, and he immediately began leafing through it.

"The man that gave me this book said a similar one had been left for the police but he feared they were as crooked as the men responsible for the account book," Major Sweet said. "He swore on a Bible before me, that what he said was true, and I would not be in trouble for delivering this book to you. I believed him and felt he was telling the truth."

"This is the damn— err, excuse me, Major. This is the darnedest thing I've ever seen. It's an account book all right, but it's also sort of a journal. It belongs to someone named Hap Burnett. Looks to me like it names names, gives dates, loading points, quantities and sums of money for stolen cattle delivered to the Minnesota Star Cattle Company here in St. Paul. I think we just did a story that involved them. Excuse me a moment, Major. Morgan! Get in here!" the editor shouted out the door of his office. Instantly, a harried man in shirtsleeves appeared in the doorway.

"Didn't you do a story a couple days ago that involved the Minnesota Star Cattle Company?"

"Sure, boss. There was a particularly grisly murder in their stock yards the day before yesterday," the young man replied, puzzled at the question and hopeful he had done nothing wrong.

"Do you know anything about an accounts book or a ledger being found?"

"When I interviewed the men who discovered the body, they mentioned a book but I didn't see it. I asked the police about it, but they said it wasn't 'germane.' Why?"

"Well, looks like we got one just like it. And I'd say it's about as germane as you can get. Dig up everything you can on this cattle company, the owner or owners, their operations, the police officers involved in the investigation, the whole thing. And tell Jacobs we got a new front page for tomorrow's run and be quick about it," Samples said, turning to Major Sweet.

"What you've just given me will sure make a mess of some powerful men's lives in this city. Them, and the police. I want to thank you for bringing the ledger to me. It's sure going to shake things up some."

Major Sweet was silent for a moment. Finally she said, "So the man who gave this to me was telling the truth? I am gratified to hear it, and I'm happy to have been able to play a small part in bringing these men to justice. Thank you for your time, Mr. Samples. Good day."

After the Major marched out of the office and was gone, the crusty editor started stirring the pot, marshalling his forces, investigating everyone involved, and after working late into the night, he sent his tired staff home while he put the finishing touches on the next day's edition. It promised to be a red-letter day for the newspaper.

Murder! Police Corruption! Stolen Cattle! Crooked Businessmen! The paper was able to milk the story for a solid week, each day presenting new revelations, new inquiries, and new details. Circulation jumped 500% before the week was out, and the newspaper's standing rose sharply within the city and its environs. All other city papers were at a loss as to where the Herald was getting its information, and could only parrot what the Herald printed. For three days the paper actually had to print extra editions! At the end of the week, Horace Samples was visited by Jefferson Lane, an assistant states attorney, who launched a grand jury investigation into the reported wrongdoings.

When Harley and Gus arrived back at the DHS, Granville warmly greeted them. After the two men made their report of the trip, Granville said that as a result of the train raids, sixty-three rustlers had been killed, a staggering number of men. Some of the outlaws had fled and couldn't be found. All the raiders were accounted for, with no serious injuries or deaths, except Jessup.

Months later, Gus and Harley learned the owners of the Minnesota Star Cattle Company had been convicted of cattle rustling, conspiracy and receiving stolen property. Albert Harris was deemed ringleader and was sentenced to a minimum of fifteen years in federal prison. William Warren and James Lund received twelve and nine year sentences respectively. Max Hoffstedter turned state's evidence and was sentenced to time served. All the men's property was confiscated and sold at public auction with the proceeds going into the city coffers. Captain Linderman was charged with corruption, and found guilty as a result of Hoffstedter's testimony. He was sentenced to nine years in state prison. Five other officers were charged and also found guilty. They were sentenced to four years each. The assistant states attorney who tried the case, Jefferson Lane, was elected Minnesota States Attorney the following year. Based on her ability to generate donations, Major Margaret Sweet was promoted to Colonel and given responsibility for all Salvation Army operations in Minnesota, Wisconsin and Michigan.

Chapter Nine - Powder Smoke

With the fall calf roundup nearly over, Granville and Harley were visiting James Fergus at his ranch north of the DHS to discus the current situation. Outlaw activities had been greatly reduced following the raids of the summer, but Granville believed some gangs still remained and continued to operate. The men also discussed Fergus' letter writing campaign supporting the Vigilante activities and the various newspapers' editorial stance with regard to public opinion. As he promised Granville following Duncan Sides' funeral, he wrote articles for the Rocky Mountain Husbandman, among other newspapers, defending Vigilante activities as being necessary to maintain order. The degree to which he helped sway public opinion is unknown, yet it was generally felt his writing campaign had a favorable impact. When their business was finally concluded, Granville and Harley began their 25-mile ride back to the DHS ranch.

Suddenly off to the west, Harley noticed tendrils of smoke beginning to crawl skyward. The smoke was billowing up and whisping into long streamers, becoming diluted to a haze as the wind took it.

"Fire!" Harley shouted.

Granville turned suddenly to see where his foreman was looking and immediately his blood chilled. Prairie fire was a dreaded force on the open range, one that threatened every rancher's property. The high winds of Montana and Dakota Territory drove the fires at amazing speeds, easily out-pacing the swiftest horse and were often impossible to outrun. Spring and fall were the worst time of year for such fires because the prairie grasses were tinder dry and burned easily. Once started, men came from many miles away to help with the prairie fires, which were nearly impossible to stop and often had to burn themselves out. Large prairie fires were up to 40 miles wide and ravaged areas up to 200 miles in length. Ranchers downwind from the fire would try to save their outfits by setting controlled backfires or plowing firebreaks if they had the time, which depended upon wind speed, the density of the grass and distance of the ranch from the blaze. If conditions permitted, cattlemen sometimes killed cattle, split them down the brisket and dragged the flattened carcasses through the

217

fire with their horses. This was done to smother the blaze and while no rancher liked to kill his cattle, it sometimes stopped the fires and saved their outfit. Days were sometimes spent fighting fires in this way, working toward the middle from the edges, the wranglers working frantically past the point of exhaustion, their skin blackened by the smoke and ash for months following the incident.

"We'll never make it to the Judiths!" Granville said.

"We'll never out-run it either," Harley replied. "We better try a backfire!"

Harley jumped from his horse and grabbed the reins from both horses as the rancher stepped down, and moved downwind. Granville quickly knelt and pulled some matches from his pocket, striking one and setting the grass alight at his feet. When the grass began to burn and the fire leaped into the air, he moved off several feet where he repeated the process again and again until he ran out of matches.

"You got any matches?" Granville shouted to the Ranger.

"Got a few," Harley shot back, "Hold the horses!"

After the two men traded positions, Harley continued setting small fires until all his matches were gone. Harley noticed when the fires caught, they left a distinctive wedge shape as the flames caught and spread outward as the fire moved downwind. The small fires the two men set soon joined into a single wall of living flame, racing east, driven by the high winds, burning a 150 foot wide swath as it swept away into the distance, leaving blackened and scorched earth in its wake.

"Quick! Let's ride!" Granville shouted, nervously eyeing the firestorm sweeping toward them. The two men mounted quickly and rode into the blackened area behind the fire they'd just set. They'd created a safe zone, an area that wouldn't be consumed by the huge fire, the grass having already been burned. This safe zone would be effective if the area they'd burned was wide enough to keep them away from the intense heat of the oncoming flames.

The two desperate men rode quickly forward until they judged they were in the widest part of their burn-off. There, they hurriedly dismounted and put their horses side by side into the smoky wind. Harley pulled a canteen from his horse, jerked his silk scarf off and wet it down thoroughly. He retied it around his neck and lifted the front up over his nose like a mask, so only his eyes were visible between his hat and the scarf. He hoped this would make breathing easier and protect his face during the next few minutes. Granville did the same, following the Ranger's lead. When both men were masked, they stood between their horses, holding their mount's bridles firmly, and braced themselves for what was to come.

The scene they beheld was terrifying. The wall of fire rushed toward them nearly as fast as the wind, which was gusting to thirty miles per hour. The flames were leaping twenty feet into the air, arcing and clawing at the sky, twisting, writhing like an enraged serpent. The roar of the wind and swirling flames was incredible, and the hot air, thick with smoke and ash, made breathing difficult and painful, even through their masks, which quickly dried in the super-heated air.

As the two men desperately tried to shield themselves, through the smoke they could see the Hades part before them, skirting the area they had so recently burned off. As the inferno drew closer on either side, the heat and smoke became unbearable, the terrified horses tried to bolt and it was no small task keeping them in check, holding them against their most primal fear. As the heat increased and the roar became deafening, the smoke choked out all air, making breathing impossible. Although they were more than seventy-five feet from the nearest flame, the searing heat was intense.

Just as they felt they couldn't last another moment, it was over; the hellish fire swept past them on either side, roaring like a freight train and sped off into the distance. The air quickly cleared and breathing became easy again, the impossible heat suddenly gone. Looking around, the two men could only marvel and thank the heavens they were still alive. Each man appeared sunburned where his skin was exposed and both men had red raccoon-like masks around their eyes. Their ears, necks and the backs of their hands were bright red from the heat and their clothes were smoking. Like the men's clothing, the horses coats were smoking as well, singed by fire, their hair curling and white with ash, their eyelashes, manes and tails denuded, giving them a bizarre sickly nude appearance.

"My God! I though we was cooked fer shore!" Harley exclaimed.

Granville chuckled. "Dante's Inferno wouldn't make a patch on this! Watch it go!"

The men turned and watched the receding wall of fire sweep down into a creek bottom, engulfing everything in its path and racing up the opposite side of the coulee and across the prairie like a hellish tide. It was beautiful and terrifying, an immutable force wreaking havoc and destruction, seemingly with a life all its own destroying everything before it.

"I shore hope folks can get out of the way of this runaway," Harley commented. "Our roundup should be way north by now, so I thinks they're safe."

"I just hope our horses are alright. Damn! What a fire!"

"Mine looks like a damned cactus, with his hair stickin' out like this! Well, let's see if we can find where this thing started," Harley said, mounting up. "Can't be too far away." He and Granville were both relieved to find their horses hadn't been seriously injured in the inferno, and aside from looking peculiar with spikie manes and thin broom-straw tails, they were unhurt.

The two men rode west; following the blackened earth for several miles as it tapered down, finally coming to the western-most scorched area. There they discovered the distinctive wedges of scorched grass where the fire had been deliberately set. Two sets of tracks were found leading away from the starting point and without any words being spoken, the Ranger and his boss began tracking the fire-starters. The trail was plainly seen in the tall grass and tracking was easy. The men galloped north, each aware the men who had set the fires were relatively close at hand.

The stiff breeze felt good as they hurried along, their eyes alert, searching the horizon, hoping to catch sight of the vandals. Suddenly ahead of them, they again saw smoke beginning to fill the sky, and a sense of urgency gripped the men as they spurred their horses forward at a run, demanding greater efforts from their animals. Topping a small knoll, they looked down on the scene where another fire had just been set. The telltale wedge shapes of burnt grass were again seen.

Granville and Harley rode past the freshly scorched and smoldering earth, and two miles further on, just as the raiders topped another rise, they saw two Indians below them. One man had dismounted and was handing his reins to his companion.

"Let's take 'em from here!" Harley shouted, reining his horse to a sudden stop, jerked his Winchester from its saddle scabbard and quickly jumped to the ground, where he knelt and adjusted the rear sight of his weapon for the range. The Indian was walking forward and reaching into a pouch at his waist. Cocking the hammer on his rifle, Harley brought the weapon up to eye level and drew a bead on an Indian, careful to adjust for windage.

"I make it about 420 yards," Harley said, as he slowly squeezed the trigger. The roar of the huge round was quickly followed by the bark of Granville's rifle, the two shots fired in quick succession. Harley's shot found its intended mark, catching the mounted man square in the back, blowing a huge hole through his chest, lifting him off his horse and slamming him to the ground.

Granville's hurried shot missed its mark and the startled fire-starter suddenly ran past his dead friend for his horse. Just as the man jumped into his saddle, Harley's rifle barked again and the man's head pulped, the air around him misted red and he slumped to the ground, dead. The heavy 500-grain bullet had entered above the man's left ear, launching him instantly into eternity.

"There's two mischief-makers that won't do no more foolin' around," the Ranger said, mounting up. "Let's see who they is."

"That was some fine shootin' Harley," Granville said, stepping into his saddle. "Glad we got 'em before they could get another blaze going."

"I wonder what they were tryin' to do? Why would they be settin' prairie fires?" asked the Ranger, as they rode forward.

"Not a living soul would benefit, as far as I can see," Granville said. "They were doin' it just for meanness I expect, trying to terrorize the ranchers in these parts. It ain't gonna work though. This is our home and we're here to stay. It's cost us too damned much to duck out now."

The raiders rode down to the dead men, studying their faces to see if they could be identified, but neither raider had ever seen the men before. The bodies were loaded onto their horses, carried into a distant creek bottom and hung, strangler fashion. On the ride back to the DHS ranch, Granville wondered that the renegades and outlaws were still bold enough to keep at their mischief.

"You know, I figure we've killed damn near a hundred men since we started last fall," Granville said.

"Yer count's about right."

"I'm surprised they still hang on. Each man convinced he won't get plugged or strung up. It's amazing, the power of self-delusion."

"I understand things has cooled down considerable over in Dakota. Looks like we did a lot of good over there," Harley commented.

"I don't doubt it. I'm just wondering how long this is going to continue," Granville replied. "Gus Adams and Floppin' Bill are still out nosing around, but so far they haven't cut any trail. That makes me suspect all the larger gangs have been busted up and we're just seeing the stragglers and mischief makers."

"That sounds right, too. I think we're still getting' robbed by a few of the small outfits, sleeperin' and such. Maybe this would be a good time to pay 'em a visit and remind 'em what happens if we catches 'em doin' it."

"Good idea. Why don't you and some of the others make it your business to warn them then? If they aren't guilty, there'll be no harm done. If they are, remind them we take a dim view of thieving."

Over following weeks, the DHS wranglers set out in small parties, visiting every small rancher, nester, wolfer, wood hawk, settlement and town on or near the Ft. Maginnis, Moccasin and Power Ranges, warning them of the consequences of stealing horses or cattle.

Some of the recipients were indignant over the warning but these were few. Granville's efforts to help the settlers and small ranchers were well known. He pitched in whenever asked, branding their stock at roundup prices, giving them feed when he hadn't enough for his own stock and generally looking out for their welfare. He was responsible for the first school in that locality, dedicating one room of his home for this purpose. He hired a teacher from back east and purchased books and other supplies at his own expense and let it be known the school was open to all children who wished to attend. By these actions and others, most of those who knew him or came in contact with him had only the highest regard for him and the men who rode for him.

He'd been determined to prevent conflicts between cattle and sheep interests too. Cattlemen and sheep men often were at odds over use of the open range, and sometimes these animosities boiled over into gunplay, as they had down in Colorado and Wyoming Territories. Granville was determined not to let that happen in Montana and encouraged a level of tolerance and acceptance not seen in other areas. For this reason, men like James Fergus could run both sheep and cattle and need have no fear of any ill will or bad feelings from other ranchers.

Φ

Winter was coming on; river bottoms and creek beds took on a brilliant golden color as the quaking aspen and cottonwood leaves turned bright yellow, creating a beautiful contrast with the dark green of spruce and pine trees. The native prairie grasses had turned brown earlier, giving the open range a dead look, yet this was deceptive. The rich bunch grasses still held valuable nutrients close to their roots and the livestock continued to find life sustaining nourishment as they grazed.

It was early November; the fall calf and beef roundups were now complete and all marketable beef, four-year-old steers, were trailed to the nearest railhead for shipment to the booming markets in the east. Men were still stationed in the line cabins keeping careful watch over the herds, but would be returning to the ranch when the first snows fell. Granville was still concerned with rustlers and for this reason, other men patrolled the open range searching for outlaws.

Ranch life on the DHS settled into the annual routine as the wranglers prepared for the cold weather to come and extra supplies were laid on in anticipation of the pending sub-zero temperatures. Late one morning, Phonograph and the dude took a wagon to the mining town of Maiden to pick up supplies. Doug had planned to return to his home in New York by now, but found life on the ranch difficult to walk away from. The west was interesting and invigorating, and he now had a healthy tone and taut muscles beneath his shirt he hadn't possessed when he arrived.

As Doug and Phonograph headed out in a spring wagon, Jimmy and Dirty Bill saw them leave from a small rise above the ranch.

"Looks like Phonograph and the dude is headed out for more supplies," Dirty Bill said. "What say we follow along and give 'em a hand? Maybe the dude will buy us a drink with his poker winnin's!"

"That rascal's been feedin' on me for months! Let's go," Jimmy replied.

As the two wranglers rode along, they discussed the dude, remarking on the positive changes he'd made since coming to the ranch. Everyone knew Doug had stayed longer than intended but he was well liked by the DHS wranglers and would be missed when he finally departed. He was of the same age as Jimmy and some of the other pranksters and had quickly joined in the practical joking, giving as least as good as he got.

"That thing with the jack-rabbit was the derndest thing I ever saw. I wouldn't have though it possible!" Dirty Bill said, laughing as he recalled the incident.

"He shore is a lot better with a rope than I ever suspicioned," Jimmy agreed. "I thought Red was gonna choke!"

Φ

Just a month earlier, the men were playing cards in the bunkhouse one evening and discussing various subjects. Red said that Buffalo Bill Cody had once challenged a group of wranglers to rope a jackrabbit and offered to pay $100 to the first cowboy that did. In Red's telling of the story, one of the men successfully roped one and earned himself the prize money. All the DHS men had strong opinions on the subject. Some doubted the story outright and felt it was just a tall tale. Most believed the bet had been made but were doubtful anyone could actually rope a jackrabbit. A couple felt it could be done if the situation was right. A heated discussion ensued and finally, Red said he'd be willing to pay $20 gold to see someone do it, believing a jack rabbit was impossible to rope. Several men agreed and made the same offer, feeling their money was safe as Dolly's drawers.

"I can rope a jack rabbit," the dude offered. "And I'd be willing to bet anyone here $20 gold that I can."

The entire outfit broke into good-natured jeering and laughter. No one believed the dude was serious or that he could do it. Impossible! The very idea was ridiculous. Some thought the dude was just spouting off and others felt he wasn't aware of the difficulty of roping the fast-moving flop-eared animal. Finally, Red looked at the dude smiling, and said, "Yer teasin', right Doug?"

"No sir, I believe I can do it. And I'm willing to let you men win back some of your poker losses…if you want."

The dude's words were met with silence as each man considered the money he'd lost to the dude over the poker table. The idea of suddenly recouping their losses made a lot of sense to some and soon seventeen men accepted the bet, each throwing $20, half a month's wages for most, on the table.

"Gentlemen, I'll take your bets. That means I have to put $340 into the pot," Doug said, walking to his bunk. He returned with that amount in gold and handed it to Harley. "We'll let Harley hold the stakes. I don't want any of you scamps getting forgetful after I do it!"

Everyone guffawed as the foreman raked the money from the table into a basket, counted it carefully and announced that "the pot's right."

"When you gonna do it, Doug?" Terry asked, anxious to see the show.

"Yeah, when you gonna do it?" Jimmy seconded.

"First thing tomorrow morning before breakfast," the dude said. This was met with more disbelief. No one thought the dude could even find, much less rope a rabbit before breakfast. Most of the men went to bed, happily anticipating finally skinning the dude and winning some of their money back.

The dude smiled as he went to sleep, safe in the knowledge that he knew where rabbits could be found and fairly confident he could win the jackpot. Phonograph had complained long and often to him about rabbits getting at his truck garden behind the cook shack. What's more, Doug had put considerable time into his rope work, practicing often, and his skills had improved steadily. The following day would tell the tale.

Next morning, under the watchful eyes of all the wranglers, Doug rode out from the horse corral, rope in hand and ready to back up his tall talk. He had chosen a soft thin rope because it was more flexible and would throw faster than the heavier ropes commonly used for working cattle or horses.

"I'm gonna show you boys how we ropes rabbits in New York," Doug said smiling, deliberately using the local speech patterns. He turned his horse and rode toward the cook shack and then disappeared around behind it, out of sight of the anxious men. There he saw several rabbits thinning the scant remains of Phonograph's truck garden. Doug quickly cut a big buck from the herd and came flying out from behind the cook shack with his thin rope twirling above his head, his horse on a dead run, hot on the heels of a gray streak! With each jog the rabbit made, Doug's horse made a corresponding move, much as a good cutting horse would when working cattle and within

225

hundred feet, Doug pulled the trigger, firing his loop at the low swift target. Jerking the rope tight at exactly the right moment, Doug snagged the hare just in front of its hind legs and it immediately set to squealing to high heaven, as if it were mortally wounded. Despite the frantic cries, the dude reeled the struggling rabbit in and slowly rode over to the astonished men, the kicking rabbit held high above the men.

"Anyone want rabbit for breakfast?" Doug asked, grinning at the open-mouthed group of stunned cowboys. Suddenly the spell was broken and the group rushed forward, shouting their congratulations and amazement. It was quite a scene and no one begrudged him the loss of their money. Phonograph looked on from the open door of the cook shack, smiling and happy Doug was able to surprise the men.

"Grub pile!" the cook shouted, banging on a steel wagon wheel rim, calling the men to eat. What followed was one of the noisiest meals ever held on the DHS, the rowdy and boisterous wranglers excited and amazed at the dude's roping display.

Φ

"I lost $20 on that deal, but it was worth it just to see it done," Dirty Bill said, laughing as he recalled the incident.

"That was sure amazing' all right," Jimmy said, chuckling. "I think he's the only dude that ever come out here and made money!"

The two wranglers were now within sight of Doug and Phonograph. The wagon ahead was just entering the rolling foothills of the Judith Mountains. Following the lay of the land, the twisting road the wagon followed dropped into depressions only to be seen coming up onto a rise, giving the two wranglers only occasional glimpses of the cook's wagon ahead.

To the surprise of some, Doug had become friends with Phonograph and the two men were often seen together. While Phonograph was at least 20 years older than the dude, they hit it off for some reason and spent much time in each other's company. No one could guess what the connection was and while it was somewhat odd, it was no one's business who someone picked for a friend.

As Phonograph Bill and Doug eased along the hilly road, ahead of them, five rough looking horsemen approached from Maiden. As the group drew closer, Doug noticed one man in particular, a man with distinctive scars on his face. "Say, isn't tha—!"

"Quiet!" the cook replied under his breath, "Take the reins and hush!" Handing the reins to the dude, Phonograph rested his hand on his ever-present 8-gauge shotgun that sat beside him and eyed the riders closely. He too had noticed the scar-faced man.

From behind them, Jimmy and Dirty Bill saw the group of riders closing on their friends, but lost sight of the men as they dropped down into a dip in the road.

As the two parties passed one another, Zeke Tyler noticed the **D-S** brand on the team of horses and stared at the men in the wagon. Phonograph felt the hair on the back of his neck rise as he came under the man's hard look. Janie's run-in with a scar-faced man was well known to him, and after the two groups passed, he casually hefted his scattergun and cocked the twin mule-ear hammers.

Once again, Jimmy and Dirty Bill topped a rise, and saw the riders pass the wagon and continue in their direction. And again they dropped into another depression and lost sight of their friends and the group of riders.

Looking over his shoulder, Phonograph watched the group of men stop in the road fifty yards behind them and scar-face speak excitedly to his fellow riders, his arms gesturing wildly as he spoke. Two of the men turned to look at the retreating wagon and then turned their attention to scar-face.

Just as Jimmy and Dirty Bill crested another rise, they saw the riders ahead spin their horses and start firing at their friends in the wagon as they charged forward in hot pursuit, fogging their horses and putting a ton of dust in the air. "Let's go!" shouted Jimmy, though Dirty Bill was already in motion, spurring and slapping his horse with the reins, bringing the animal up to a dead run in three jumps.

"Let 'er rip Douglas, that bunch of crooks is chasing us!" Phonograph shouted over the sound of gunfire from their rear. Doug needed no further encouragement and popped the reins vigorously. As the wagon plunged forward, Phonograph turned his body around on the bouncing wagon seat, bringing an unsteady aim on the men behind them.

Doug frantically whipped the horses into a run, shouting for more speed. "Hee-Yaw! Yaaww!" As he applied more motivation to the team, Doug heard Phonograph's shotgun answering the gunfire behind them. Just as the cook fired his first round, Phonograph saw Jimmy and Dirty Bill come flying over a rise behind their pursuers, passing through clouds of powder smoke as they fired their pistols at Tyler and his men.

"The cavalry just showed up, Doug! Pull up and we'll make these slab-sided varmints jump! We got 'em trapped!"

Doug struggled to bring the plunging team of horses to a halt, rearing back on the reins and setting the brake with his foot, as Phonograph fired again and reloaded. Zeke Tyler and his men were suddenly taking fire from the front and rear, as two men suddenly appeared behind them, firing as they dashed forward. The attackers were confused and halted their charge on the wagon to turn and fire at the men behind them. As Tyler and his men began firing on the two approaching DHS wranglers, Doug finally wrestled the team to a halt in a cloud of dust and noisy protest.

Phonograph jumped from the wagon and threw the shotgun to his shoulder, firing both barrels at once. The blast was deafening and the cloud of smoke nearly hid the targets, but some of the shot hit home, peppering the attackers and their horses with stinging pellets. Although no real damage was done because of the range, a couple of the attackers horses bucked and reared, distracting the attackers and wrecking their aim at Jimmy and Dirty Bill, who continued to bear down on them.

"Take some of this medicine, you sons-of-bitches!" Phonograph shouted, reloading and firing again.

Doug was suddenly by his side, delivering slow aimed fire as Harley had shown him. As Doug began firing, Phonograph hastily retrieved a box of 8 gauge shells from the floor of the wagon and stuffed his pants pockets full of the large brass cases. Moving back to Doug's side, he reloaded and fired again at the attackers, stinging them once more.

"You wants more? Come an' get it, you cowards!" Phonograph shouted, fairly dancing with energy and venom.

Zeke Tyler and his men were overwhelmed and confused. It should have been easy to take care of the two men in the wagon. Now they were suddenly under attack from front and rear! Tyler quickly made up his mind. "Let's run them two down in the wagon and light out!" he shouted, turning his horse toward Phonograph and Doug and leaping forward, his men close behind. Firing as they charged, Tyler hoped to overwhelm the two men and force them to flee.

"Here they come! Them yeller-bellied snakes ain't got the stumick to fight real men! Come on, you sons of Sodom!" Bill shouted gleefully.

Neither Phonograph nor Doug had any quit in him, and as Tyler's men rode down on them, the cook unexpectedly walked forward to meet the attackers, firing and reloading as he went. This surprised Doug, but he quickly joined Bill and they moved forward as a team, firing at the oncoming riders as they went. Doug didn't feel his shirt being tugged at or his hat when it was jerked from his head; he was too busy to consider the matter. When his pistol ran dry, he steadied his shaking hands and reloaded, all the while Bill continued firing on their attackers.

"Still wants it?" Bill screamed, "I'll damn shore give you thumpers a belly full!"

As Tyler came in on the two men, he was cheered to see the younger man reloading his pistol and fired on the man as he swept past. The older man was still shouting and blazing away with his shotgun but Tyler wasn't concerned; after all, it was just a shotgun. As Tyler raced past the cook, Phonograph brought his shotgun up and fired on the rider behind him, catching the man fully in the chest, making daylight where none should exist. He turned his remaining barrel on the next rider in line, firing at point blank range as the man swept past, catching him in the thigh and nearly blowing his leg off. The rider screamed and tumbled to the ground, where he lay, wreathed in powder smoke and dust, watching his life-blood ebb into the dust with each beat of his heart.

Now reloaded, Doug brought his pistol to bear on one of the two trailing riders, firing once and missing, then firing again and hitting the man in the head. He somersaulted off the back of his horse, bounced to a stop, and lay still. Suddenly Doug felt as if he'd been kicked hard in the fanny and turned to find the culprit. He saw Zeke Tyler had reined to a stop and was firing at Bill as the cook was reloading. Before Doug could bring his pistol to bear, Tyler fired again, hitting Phonograph in the chest. Bill folded up and collapsed to the ground, his shotgun dropping into the dust beside him.

Doug tried to reach Phonograph but found himself unable to move properly; it was as if he were walking through thick mud and he had great difficulty making his legs do as he commanded. He finally reached his friend and dropped to the ground beside him, cradling the Bill's head in his lap. The action around him receded to a distant blur, forgotten, as he held his friend close and repeated, "You'll be alright, Bill, you'll be alright."

Phonograph's eyes had a distant, glazed aspect as he looked up. "We showed them yeller devils, didn't we Doug? We showed 'em we's real men!"

Doug looked at the wound in his friend's chest and somewhere in his mind realized the wound was fatal; blood pumped from the wound in gushes and flowed into an expanding pool beneath him. He placed his hand over the wound, desperately holding his friend's life together, refusing to let Bill's essence slip out, but it was no use. Phonograph became ashen, his lips and eyelids turning blue as his life seeped into the dust.

"Yes, we showed 'em alright. We showed 'em good," Doug said to his unhearing friend. He watched helpless as Phonograph eased over the Great Divide and suddenly found he was crying over his friend's damaged and lifeless body. He slowly reached down and closed his friend's eyes, and as if in a trance, he pulled himself from beneath the man and tried to stand. It was the most difficult thing Doug had ever done. Through a veil of tears and grief, he couldn't make his legs work as they should. *What's wrong with me?* He could only wonder as he finally stood on tottering legs and looked around. Four men lay dead on the road but Doug barely noticed. No one else was around. The battle had moved on.

Toward Maiden, forty yards away was the wagon, the horses standing quiet. Doug slowly made his way there and grabbing the bridle, led the team back to his friend, where he slowly lifted Phonograph into the wagon after much struggle. *Why am I so weak?* Slowly, he got himself up onto the seat and started for town. As he drove, he was surprised at how tired he felt. "I gotta get Bill to a doctor and then I'll rest," Doug said to himself, as the wagon rolled on through a dimming haze. "It's getting dark, but I gotta get Bill to the doctor before the sun..."

Doug awoke in a strange bright place; a radiant place he'd never seen. He was lying in a mountain stream with his back resting against the creek bank. Confused, he looked at the towering pines around him and the shorter willows that hugged the bank. Out of a beautiful blue sky a dazzling sun shown down, bringing a welcome warmth, and he felt no pain. *How did I get here?* Across the stream was a small well built cabin with smoke curling lazily from the chimney. In front of the cabin, a young deer grazed and watched him, unafraid. To his right was an intricate wooden footbridge spanning the stream. *What is this place?* The musical trills of a meadowlark could be heard in the distance, and from further away the caw of crows and the skree of a distant hawk came to his ears. The yellow leaves of the cottonwood and quaking aspen shimmered and danced in the light breeze. The burble of the stream sounded almost musical and he could hear the faint buzzing of insects. The whole scene was one of tranquil beauty and he felt a detachment he had never known. *Am I in heaven? Is this what heaven looks like?* He sensed someone behind him and turned to see a beautiful young girl in a white dress silently watching him, a look of serenity on her face. *This must be heaven.*

"I'm ready," he said to her. "I never thought it would look like this; it's so beautiful here." He tried to set up, but as he did, darkness swept in around him and he was falling.

Doug awoke to the sound of distant voices. As they drew closer, he opened his eyes to see Granville standing next to his bed talking with a man he'd never seen before.

"…want to know how soon he can be moved back to the ranch. Doc, I don't want him recuperating in some strange place; I want him home where he belongs. We can take good care of him and I think he would mend faster."

"Mr. Stuart, I agree completely. All he needs now is plenty of bed-rest and good food. That bullet I pulled out of his rump may have caused some nerve damage when it hit the bone but I don't think he'll be a cripple. And that tumble he took into the crick didn't help him neither but a broken collar bone ain't serious and if he doesn't move around, he should hea…"

At the DHS that evening, Dirty Bill told the other hands what happened. "Just as we topped a rise, we saw Tyler and his bunch lay into Phonograph and the dude, blazin' away. Them two jumped off their wagon and went at 'em, Phonograph walkin' forward, firin' as he went, with the dude right by his side. When them polecats charged 'em, them two didn't bat an eye, but kept layin' the lead down. We could barely see them for all the damned smoke! It was some scene!"

"Yes sir, the dude shore is some surprisin'! You boys shoulda seen it, lead whistlin' all around 'em and steady as you please, he's reloadin' and getting' ready for more!" Jimmy said, laughing. "I shore hope he pulls through alright. The doc said he might be a cripple."

The dude slipped in and out of consciousness over the next few days. When Doug finally awoke, he was lying in a featherbed in a sunlit room. He was confused and couldn't make much sense of anything, but soon recognized Red Mack, Jimmy and Harley standing near his bed.

"How you feelin' Doug?" Jimmy asked, grinning down at him.

"Yeah, we's tired of you loafin' while we takes care of this outfit," Red said, chuckling softly.

"I don't know if I'm a man or a train wreck," Doug confessed. "Where am I? Is this heaven?"

The three men burst out laughing. "Not hardly; yer back on the DHS, in Granville's house. This is the room you woulda had if you'd played dude, 'stead of bunkin' with us hard cores," Harley said, smiling at the young man.

"What happened? I remember Phonograph and I were shooting at some men, and Bill was hit and I could hardly get to him. I remember being in heaven and sitting in a stream and a cabin and a beautiful girl and a deer, and then I remember Mr. Stuart talking to someone. Where's Phonograph?"

"He was killed in the shootout, Doug; he's dead," Harley said solemnly. "Zeke Tyler was the trouble that attacked you and Bill on the road to Maiden. You two fought 'em off and killed three of them, before Phonograph was killed. You was shot too, hit in the fanny actually! Luckily, Jimmy here and Dirty Bill was followin' close behind and saw most of it. They ran Tyler down and killed him and another one of his gang."

"I remember holding Phonograph and talking to him. Next thing I remember, I was in heaven."

"Well, you loaded Phonograph into the wagon and started for Maiden. Along the way, you passed out and fell off the wagon, tumbled down a steep bank and landed in the crick. Broke yer collarbone in the fall. Glenda Jameson found you and got help. They carried you to Dr. McDonald and he pulled a bullet outa yer butt and patched you up. That's all that happened."

"I thought the girl was an angel. What happened to Phonograph? I mean, where is he?"

"We got him in the ice house. We'll have the funeral for him tomorrow, if yer able. We sorta been waitin' for you to wake up 'cause we know'd you was close," Red said. "You gonna be up to it tomorrow?"

"Yes. I'll be able and I'm happy you waited for me."

The following afternoon, 'Phonograph' Bill Doughty was laid to rest on the knoll above the ranch, next to Duncan Sides' grave. The short service was again presided over by Reverend Moss, the missionary from the Blackfoot reserve. Following the service, everyone adjourned to the Stuart's home for a proper wake, where the memory of Phonograph Bill was toasted with good whiskey and colorful recollections. The men of the DHS would doubly miss the man.

Two weeks later, as Doug was finally starting to move around on his own, Granville spoke with him. "Doug, we ain't gone through Phonograph's belongings because I sorta thought it would be more proper if you did it. He had no next of kin that I know of, so we got no one to send his things to. Would you like to go through his stuff and clean his nest out?"

"Yes sir, I'd like that very much. I appreciate your consideration, sir. I really do."

Doug limped down to the cook shack with an apple crate under his good arm and at the rear found Phonograph's nest. There, he slowly went through his friend's belongings, placing items he felt were significant on the man's cot. There wasn't much. At the bottom of a wooden trunk, under a stack of well-worn clothes, he found a thin hard case covered in dark blue fabric. Turning it over and studying it carefully, Doug found two small pins at the corners opposite a thin hinge. Pulling each pin out, the case made a soft popping sound as the internal catch was released. Carefully lifting the cover, the interior was dark blue velvet with a depression in the center. In the depression, a United States Medal of Honor rested. The medal itself was quite striking, with an upside down five pointed gold star surrounded by a laurel wreath. Two points of the star were suspended from a gold bar on which an eagle with wings spread sat, clutching in its claws bundles of arrows. The eagle was suspended from a satin ribbon with tiny white stars on the blue field. On the reverse side of the medal was an image of a man holding serpents that were attacking a beautiful woman. Below the image were the words: *Secessionists Attack the Nation.* Doug didn't know where Phonograph could have gotten such a thing. Pulling a small ribbon tab at the bottom of the case revealed a hinged panel, under which was a folded piece of paper. Doug carefully removed the paper and unfolded it to reveal a U.S. Army citation.

It read: *This Medal of Honor is awarded to Sergeant William Doughty, Co. F, 1ˢᵗ Missouri Light Artillery for meritorious service and bravery in action. To wit: At Perryville, Missouri, remained on duty though severely wounded. While procuring ammunition from the supply train at Chester, Illinois, was captured, but made his escape, secured ammunition, and in less than an hour from the time of his capture had the batteries supplied.*

Doug sat staring at the citation and the medal, numbed by what he was seeing. Phonograph Bill was a real war hero, yet he never spoke of it, never let on. In fact, he was one of the most humble men Doug had ever met. He returned the citation to the case and closed it. Setting it aside, he continued to go through his friend's things. When he was done, on the bed rested the Medal of Honor, an old .36 caliber Navy Colt percussion pistol, a few tintypes of people he didn't know, a well used straight razor and strop, a small hand mirror in a silver frame, a tortoise shell comb and $667 in gold and currency. Looking at the bed with its few holdings, Doug felt hollow; these few things weren't much to show for a man's life, what he felt, what he thought or who he was. It was sad.

Doug put everything in the crate and hobbled off to see Granville. He found the boss working in his study, pouring over account books; distracted from all worldly concerns except what was contained by the books he loomed over. Doug knocked on the doorframe, hobbled into the room and set the crate on a chair. From it he pulled the medal and set it on the desk in front of Granville.

He looked at it carefully and then looked at Doug. Lifting the case, he turned it over and saw the marking: *William Wilson and Son, Philadelphia.* He opened the case and looked at the impressive medal and then opened the hidden compartment and read the citation. Following his perusal, Granville returned the citation to it's hidden compartment and closed the case. "This is the second one of these I've seen. It takes a rare man to earn it."

"Outside of this medal, an old Navy Colt and some money, there isn't much to show for his life," Doug said.

"I'd say that's quite a lot; far more than most leave behind to prove they were ever here. Bill won this medal saving other men's lives, and he died saving yours. If you want to honor him, take his things, keep them safe and don't forget him."

"It seems so sad."

"What do you remember about him?"

"I remember him walking forward, firing at those men as they charged and cussing them with every step of the way. He was...magnificent."

"Magnificent isn't sad."

"No sir, it's not."

Φ

There was a knock and Keeps Eagle stepped through Doug's door, dusty and sweat stained from a hard days work.

"I hear you're leavin' us tomorrow."

"Yes, it's about time I went home. I was going to stop by the bunkhouse tomorrow after breakfast and tell everyone goodbye," Doug replied.

"I made something for you so you wouldn't forget us," the Indian said, holding out his hand with something hanging from it.

Doug took it and was amazed. It was a necklace made from four-inch long bear claws and small teeth of some sort. The other decorations Doug didn't recognize. Everything was strung on a braided multicolored cord.

"This is beautiful. What is all this? I recognize the bear claws but what's it all mean?"

"The claws are a sign of bravery. After Phonograph, well, you earned 'em. These small teeth in between are elk ivories. They mean eternal life to my people. An elk only has four of 'em, so you got three elks worth there. That round silver thing in the center is a 7th Cavalry uniform button that came off one of Custer's soldiers the day they was wiped out. I put it on there to remind you of the balance of life between life and death. The silver disk below it is a medicine wheel and represents the four elements of life; earth, wind, fire and water. The cord I braided from hairs from everyone's horses. This necklace is strong medicine."

Doug was silent, reining in his emotions before he could speak. "Thank you. You honor me," he said with in a strained voice. "I'll keep this always. Thank you very much."

"How 'bout havin' yer last breakfast with us tomorrow mornin'? I think that'd be a good idea."

The following morning, Doug ate a hearty breakfast with the DHS wranglers and then said his goodbyes. That the men no longer called him dude was singular in his mind and told him he'd earned their respect. Doug rode into Lewistown alone. Prolonging his parting from the people at the DHS was painful for the young man and he wanted to make a clean break from the outfit he'd come to love. Harley, Red Mack, Jimmy, Phonograph, Keeps Eagle and the other men would hold a special place in his heart. He would never forget their kindness and friendship. Later that morning, he would take the stage to Billings and catch the eastbound train for home. That he now carried only one bag was a reflection of how his life had changed, slimmed down to only what was necessary, reduced to only the things that mattered in his life. Gone was the showy and extraneous, banished to some other world, some other time.

Riding into town, Doug couldn't help but remember the day he'd arrived. He seemed to have been a different person then; someone else stepped off the stage that day, not this Doug. He grinned as he remembered Red's embarrassment. And Jimmy's laughter. Ropin' doggies. Ha! The comical fight in Crowley & Kemp's Saloon. Harley's amazing demonstration with his Colts. Playing poker with the boys. Skinning the grizzly with Keeps Eagle. Shocking everyone by roping that jackrabbit and winning their money. And he remembered Tyler shooting Bill. And his friend looking up at him as his life seeped out. So much had happened in just a few short months! Doug marveled at the changes wrought in him, and knew no matter what path his life followed in the future, his heart would always be here in the west.

Arriving in Lewistown, Doug tied his horse off in front of Power Mercantile, and limped into the store, where he found Mr. Power fiddling with something behind the counter.

"Mr. Power, do you remember me?"

The man looked at him carefully. "Oh yes, you're the young man who wanted me to save his clothes," Mr. Power said chuckling, and retrieved a wrapped bundle, setting it on the counter. "Here they are," he said proudly.

"Burn 'em."

Chapter Ten - The Final Chapter

On the Northern Plains, winter came late in 1884, the first snows falling in early December, locking the land in its icy grip. As usual, most of the riding stock had been turned loose to fend for themselves. The horses would be collected the following spring, when the weather broke and ranching operations returned to normal. Horses were usually able to paw through the snow to the rich grasses below, which, despite the brown and withered appearance, were still nutritious. Unless the winter was particularly harsh, the riding stock would be fine until spring.

Cattle lacked the ability to dig through the snow and were forced to feed on the slopes of hills, where the snow didn't collect heavily. Here, the grass would poke up through the white dusting, and by this means, the cattle survived through the long frigid months. Water for the stock was normally available at various places along the streams and rivers where open areas and air holes could be found. If the winter was particularly severe and no open water was available, cattlemen were forced to chop holes in the ice and maintain them until open areas became available. Thus, all range stock, whether horse or cow, was normally left unattended.

Throughout the winter, Granville remained concerned with rustlers, feeling that this was a prime opportunity for their thieving activities, with few people about and most ranching operations suspended. Consequently, he sent riders out in pairs to ride the range on the lookout for outlaws, but none were found.

Φ

Theodore Roosevelt shared Granville's suspicions, and in the early spring of 1885, he set his riders combing the range on the lookout for rustlers. It was during one of these patrols, just as spring was breaking, that one of Roosevelt's men discovered six men driving a herd of Elkhorn brand cattle north toward the Missouri River. The rider quickly fanned his horse for the ranch, where he found Roosevelt sitting in his rubber tub, enjoying a hot bath. When the situation was explained, Roosevelt jumped out of the water, dressed quickly and assembled a group of eleven riders to pursue the thieves and recover the stolen cattle.

The Elkhorn wranglers collected their gear for the hunt, tying their oversized bed-rolls on the back of their saddles, getting extra ammunition and bundling up for the work ahead of them. Although daytime temperatures crept above freezing, the men knew a sudden winter storm could strike at any time and were thus prepared for whatever they may encounter. Roosevelt had two packhorses made ready, with food and equipment necessary for several days on the open range. When all was in readiness, the party of twelve men set forth and soon picked up the trail of the missing herd and the rustlers.

As the party rode north, they found the small creeks to be nearly open, the wintry covering of ice having been swept almost entirely downstream, where it occasionally formed ice dams. Roosevelt's party slowly caught up with the rustlers, and two days later they came within sight of the stolen cattle in late afternoon. The rustlers were driving the herd west along the banks of the Missouri River, heading toward Montana Territory.

Roosevelt considered the situation. If he and his men rode in on the rustlers now, some were sure to escape in the approaching darkness. This he could not abide. Choosing a more conservative method, he decided they would apprehend the rustlers the following day, and so the group pulled back from the river valley some distance to prevent their discovery. At their cold camp that evening, Roosevelt and his men planned the next day's activities in detail, with each of the twelve men assigned to a particular role and placement.

Early the following morning, Roosevelt's party divided into two groups. The first group left camp and rode parallel to the river for some distance before turning north and dropping down into the river valley, where they were to wait until the stolen herd and rustlers came within sight. Roosevelt and the remaining men were to follow the herd at a distance until it met the blocking force. Then, Roosevelt's group would close in from the rear and have the rustlers trapped. Any escapees would be handled individually.

Roosevelt and his group rode north until they came to the bed grounds the herd had used the previous night, where they turned west and followed the churned trail along the riverbank. This required careful riding; they had to remain out of sight yet close enough to lend support when the blocking element struck.

At a little past ten o'clock, the rustlers came up against the blocking force, six men who rode in a line abreast, moving forward with their rifles across their saddle swells or propped on their hips, ready for action. On seeing a force equal to their own, the rustlers fired a couple hasty shots in the blocker's direction and retreated quickly downstream, abandoning the stolen herd. They were quickly brought up short by Roosevelt and his men closing in from downstream, riding in at a gallop with their rifles at the ready.

The outlaws suddenly realized they were trapped and decided to make a stand. When the rustlers began firing on the advancing wranglers, Roosevelt's men returned fire, steadily moving forward, closing the trap. One of the rustlers was killed within the first few minutes, and another tried to make a break between the incoming riders, but was cut down. The remaining rustlers decided to make a break across the mush ice that covered the Missouri river. As the outlaws rode out onto the ice, the two men in the lead plunged through the soft slush and disappeared under the ice where they drowned. The two remaining men, seeing that escape was impossible, dropped their weapons and surrendered.

After the herd was gathered, Roosevelt and his men drove the stolen cattle back to the ranch, with two rustlers in custody and two dead men across their saddles. The bodies of the two outlaws who fell through the ice were never found. The prisoners were taken to the sheriff in Dickinson and jailed, later to be transferred to Mandan for trial. Found guilty of cattle rustling, the two men were sentenced to territorial prison.

Three weeks later, Roosevelt had another run-in with outlaws. When he first moved into the Medora area and commenced his ranching operations, he brought his own men from back east. Two of these, Sewall and Dow, were rugged Maine woodsmen who Roosevelt put to work over the winter building a fine lap-strake rowboat Roosevelt intended to use for his hunting trips on the Little Missouri and Missouri Rivers.

Just a few days after the beautiful craft was completed and set near the water's edge, it was stolen. Roosevelt and his men immediately suspected three rough looking men who lived ten miles upstream toward Medora. The three were suspected rustlers and were known to be anxious to leave Dakota Territory; for these reasons, they were the most obvious suspects. Roosevelt ordered his woodsmen to build another boat, a crude chink-built craft, hastily made but suitable for the purpose. After gathering supplies, Roosevelt and his two woodsmen set off downstream in pursuit of the thieves.

Three days later, they came upon the missing boat beached on a muddy riverbank. Quickly pulling ashore, the three men followed the muddy tracks into the thick undergrowth along the riverbank. Taking pains to move as silently as possible, the men discovered the thieves camped in a clearing two hundred yards from shore. Roosevelt signaled for the woodsmen to split up and encircle the thieves, which they did.

When all was ready, Roosevelt stood and boldly walked into the outlaw camp, his rifle cocked and ready for action. He shouted for the men to put up their hands.

The men jumped, surprised at the sudden appearance of a stranger, each reacting according to his nature. One man raised his hands immediately. Another tried to bolt towards the undergrowth, while the third made a grab for his rifle, which was leaning against a small cottonwood sapling. Roosevelt fired a shot over their heads and all three outlaws froze in their tracks, resigned to the fact that the stranger had the drop on them.

At Roosevelt's command, Sewall and Dow stepped out from their hides, weapons at the ready, further discouraging any thoughts of escape. The men were quickly disarmed and their hands tied behind their backs.

Rowing upstream against the current, with the three thieves in tow, would be an impossible task and the boats were left for recovery at a later time. If Roosevelt were to get his captives to the nearest lawman in Dickinson, he would have to do it overland. When the outlaws were secured, Roosevelt and his party moved up, out of the river bottom, onto the adjacent prairie where they saw a settler's ranch in the distance. With the bandits in the lead, they walked the mile or so to the ranch. There Roosevelt bought a small wagon and two horses for transporting the party south to Dickinson, fifty miles south.

The bandits were put in the back of the wagon while one of the woodsmen drove. Roosevelt and the other woodsman were forced to walk along side because there was no room for them in the wagon. The ground was muddy from frequent spring rains and recent snow melt, and walking quickly built up a thick layer of mud that added several pounds to each man's boots. Even though Roosevelt and his men traded off driving and walking chores, it was an exhausting journey for all concerned.

After walking all day in this fashion, they at last came to another small ranch and asked to spend the night. When the situation was explained, the rancher was incredulous. He was amazed anyone would take the time to transport three outlaws to the law instead of simply hanging them.

Roosevelt would have no part of hanging the thieves, saying their fate was a matter for the law to determine. After some debate, the mystified rancher gave his approval and the six men were fed and then shown into the stock barn. While the men slept under cover of thick buffalo robes, Roosevelt's biggest fear was the outlaws would escape during the night. Consequently, he determined to stay awake all night and guard his charges. And so he did.

Following a scant breakfast the next morning, the party continued on their journey in the same fashion as the day before. At the end of the day, the exhausted men finally arrived at the sheriff's office in Dickinson, where the prisoners were turned over to the deputy, the sheriff being absent. Roosevelt took two rooms in town and the three worn out men were finally able to clean up, get a decent meal and a well-deserved night's sleep.

The next day, Roosevelt and his men returned to his ranch, where the whole thing had begun nearly a week earlier. After sending two men and a wagon to fetch the boats, Roosevelt and several of his wranglers rode upstream to the thieves' rough cabin. After a careful search of the surrounding area, more than forty horses were found in a temporary corral. The stock belonged to several local ranchers and were subsequently returned to the rightful owners. Word was carried to the sheriff in Dickinson, adding further evidence of the men's guilt. The rustlers were soon transferred to Mandan for trial, where they were found guilty and were sentenced to territorial prison.

During Roosevelt's time in the region, he acquired the Maltese Cross, Elkhorn and the Triangle ranches and helped organize the Little Missouri Stockmens Association, modeled after the Montana Stockgrowers Association. In 1886, at the peak of his ranching operations, he owned 5,000 head of cattle. The severe winter of 1886-1887 effectively ended his career as a cattleman, although he continued to run small herds until 1898. Roosevelt returned to his ranches for short visits during the summer or early fall in 1887, 1888, 1890 1892, 1893 and 1896. The stark beauty of the region had claimed his heart and soul, profoundly affecting him, and he would never forget his days in Dakota Territory. During his initial stay in the Badlands, he wrote to a friend: *This country is growing on me more and more; it has a curious, fantastic beauty all its own.*

Originally Roosevelt divided his time between his ranching interests and his political pursuits, but as the years passed, he was drawn to the political arena, where he served successively as New York State Assemblyman, Delegate to the Republican National Convention, U.S. Civil Service Commissioner, Police Commissioner of New York City, President of Board of Police Commissioners, Assistant Secretary of Navy, Lieutenant-Colonel of the 1st US Volunteer Cavalry Regiment (Rough Riders), Governor of New York State, Vice President of United States and finally President of United States following President McKinley's assassination. At 42 years of age, Roosevelt was the youngest man ever to become president.

During his time as president, Roosevelt was responsible for forty-five antitrust suits against big business interests, creation of five national parks, initiation of twenty-one major irrigation projects, creation of the Panama Canal, mediation of regional strikes, mediation of international disputes, creation of the Departments of Commerce and Labor, establishment of fifty-one national bird sanctuaries, creation the National Forest Service, mediating Russo-Japanese War (for which he was awarded a Nobel Peace Prize), signing the National Monuments Act creating monuments such as the Grand Canyon and Devils Tower, signing the Pure Food and Drug Act, and sending the Great White Fleet on a circumnavigation of the world. While not otherwise engaged, Roosevelt found the time to author twenty-four books. He remained active until the end of his life, when he died of a coronary embolism on January 6, 1919 and was buried in Oyster Bay, Long Island, New York.

Φ

Sentiment against Antoine-Marie-Vincent-Manca de Vallom-Brosa grew progressively more hostile during his residence in Medora. The local cattlemen were upset because he'd fenced his property, thus blocking portions of the open range from travel by the herds that grazed freely. The claim that Vallom-Brosa was a nobleman also stuck in the craw of many local inhabitants, and the feeling was he tried to override the local custom of equality established in the earliest days of the west because of his title. As tensions developed between the established ranchers and the Marquis, rustlers and the outlaw element sided with the Marquis, hanging around him and his men. This made the ranchers even more angry and many heated words were exchanged between Roosevelt and Vallom-Brosa, nearly leading to a duel between the two men before friends of both intervened and cooled tempers.

The Marquis heard of threats to drive him from the territory and on June 24th, 1885, Reilley Luffsey, Frank O'Donald and John Reuter repeated the threats while drinking in Medora and proceeded to shoot up the town to underscore their threats. Their feelings were generally supported by the local inhabitants.

Vallom-Brosa was an experienced military officer and big-game hunter of some repute. He was not frightened by the threats but when the three men shot up the town, he feared for his staff at the chateau and went to Mandan where he talked to Sheriff G.W. Harmon, asking that the rowdy men be arrested. The sheriff was otherwise engaged but sent his brother, Deputy Sheriff Henry Harmon, to Medora the following day to make the arrests.

When Harmon arrived at a small station east of Medora, he received a message from the Marquis telling him that if he were killed in making the arrests, Vallom-Brosa and his men would consider themselves deputized and would prevent the escape of the murderers. Henry was not the bold and experienced man his brother, the sheriff, was and the message terrified him, rendering him nearly useless for the errand ahead. Continuing on to Medora, he braced the three rowdy cowboys, but when they confronted him with their rifles, he made no attempt at an arrest. After bluffing the timid deputy, the men jumped onto their horses and, guns blazing, left town.

While Harmon was confronting the three rowdy men, the Marquis and his men had each taken up positions at the various passes leading from town, intent on stopping the troublemakers if they should kill the deputy and try to escape. Hearing the firing, they assumed the deputy had been killed, and steeled themselves for a confrontation with murderers. The charging riders rode directly at the pass blocked by Vallom-Brosa, who stepped out and held up his hand to halt the men.

The three men immediately opened fire with their repeaters. Under a hail of gunfire, the Marquis returned fire with his single shot rifle. He quickly fired and moved to a new position, reloading as he ran, and stopped only long enough to take aim and fire again. By this manner, the only time he offered a stationary target was when he stopped briefly to sight and fire. With his accurate and deliberate fire, Vallom-Brosa killed Luffsey, seriously wounded O'Donald in the leg and killed all three of their horses. Reuter promptly threw his hands up and surrendered.

The Marquis had several holes through his clothing and his rifle had been struck by a bullet but he was uninjured. He marched his prisoners into Medora where he was surprised to find Deputy Harmon alive and well. The prisoners were then turned over to the deputy.

Shortly after this happened, Vallom-Brosa and his two men were arrested for the murder of William R. Luffsey. Following a preliminary hearing in Mandan, the charges were dropped and the Marquis and his men were set free. Their release exacerbated the animosity felt by the ranchers and they clamored for the charges to be reinstated, outraged that a rich foreigner was riding roughshod over the fine law-abiding people of Dakota Territory and getting away with murder. As the uproar and outrage grew, the Marquis and his men were rearrested and another hearing was held before a different judge. Again the men were released and no charges filed. These dismissals added more fuel to the fire and after loud demands were made, a grand jury was convened and Vallom-Brosa and his men were indicted for murder and arrested for a third time.

The Marquis engaged the law firm of Allen & Allen from Bismarck for the defense and prepared for trial. In the meantime, sentiment west of the Missouri River was running at a fever pitch against him. People were deliberately fanning the flames, inciting passions and the region was in an uproar. Seeing this, Vallom-Brosa and his lawyer, Frank Allen, felt it would be impossible to obtain a fair trial and asked for a change of venue to Bismarck, immediately across the Missouri River from Mandan. The change was granted and the trial was held in Bismarck beginning on September 12th before the Honorable William Francis presiding as judge. The trial was notable for the degree of false testimony made against the Marquis, but the jury was not deceived. On September 19th, the jury returned with a verdict of not guilty, and the Marquis was acquitted of all charges.

Infuriated, the District Attorney, T.K. Long, polled each juror to confirm the decision, and when the decision was confirmed by all jurors, Vallom-Brosa was set free.

Coincidental to the trial, the Marquis realized his beef packing business was doomed to failure because of lack of customers, and soon after made arrangements to shut down all slaughter and packing operations. Earlier, in 1884, he had created the Medora-Deadwood Stage Coach Line using four new coaches to make the thirty-six hour, two hundred fifteen mile run between the two western Dakota Territory towns. This too proved to be a failure and operated for only one year. As a result of his two expensive business failures, and the ill-will created by Luffsey's death and the subsequent trial, he and his wife Medora, along with their two children and household staff, left the territory for New York and then on to France late in 1886, never to return.

Upon arriving in France, the Marquis bought a chain of newspapers where he criticized the French government severely and made comments particularly offensive to Jews. A Jewish sword master from the French army, reputed to be the best swordsman in all of France, named Meyers, challenged Vallom-Brosa to a duel, which the Marquis eventually reluctantly accepted. While the sword master's skills were impeccable and above those of the Marquis, he had never fought a man to the death, all of his experience being in training and demonstration only. During the duel, Meyers foolishly exposed himself, and with a fatal thrust, Vallom-Brosa killed him. A second officer immediately offered himself, which the Marquis promptly accepted, and wounded the man but refused to finish him. Some time later, while leading an expedition into interior Africa to resolve a land dispute between the French and English governments, the Marquis was killed by his traitorous French guides who were in league with his enemies. The Marquise had her husband's body returned 2000 miles to France, where he was buried at Cannes. Determined to have justice done, at great expense, the Marquise had the murders tracked down and tried for her husband's death. One murderer was subsequently executed and his accomplice was imprisoned.

Φ

During the spring calf roundup of 1886, the DHS branded ten thousand calves, which represents a total herd population of forty thousand head of cattle. Following a severe drought that summer, one of the worst winters in recorded history struck the territory with a vengeance. Record snows fell and one blizzard followed another, week after week, month after month, filling some draws with snow ninety feet deep, effectively sealing the cattle off from their feed and water. Where they could, the cattle resorted to eating the bark off young cottonwood trees, but this last resource was quickly depleted. The animals began to starve in huge numbers or drown as they fell into the few air holes on the rivers. Many hundreds of thousands of cattle died in Montana, Dakota, Wyoming and Colorado Territory that winter, and when the spring thaw finally came, the ranchers were shocked and stricken at the degree of desolation. Thousands and thousands of dead cattle littered the ranges, choked the draws and floated downstream in the rivers, creating a sight and stink that those who experienced it would never forget. It was a catastrophe of unparalleled dimensions. After seeing the rotting carcasses piled in the coulees and washes, Granville later said: *I never wanted to own again an animal I could not feed and shelter.*

Final proof of the magnitude of the disaster came during the spring calf roundup of 1887, when only a hundred calves, just 1% of the previous year's tally, were found and branded. The huge herd of DHS cattle was reduced to just seven thousand head, mostly steers and dry cows. Granville and Conrad Kohrs lost more than 90% of their herd; what had taken years to build up was suddenly was gone. Before the disaster, there were nearly one million head of cattle in Montana Territory, but the cumulative effects of over-grazing, drought and severe winter weather was horrendous. Average stock losses in the territory were approximately 60-80%. The Mandan Pioneer estimated the stock losses in Dakota Territory as 75%, and other neighboring territories were impacted in a similar fashion. This disaster marked the end of the huge open range cattle empires in the American West.

Granville Stuart was forced out of the cattle business because of his losses and subsequent failure to meet his payments on notes signed for the purchase of his share of the DHS outfit. His wife, Awbonnie, died in late 1888 of infection following childbirth. A little over a year later, in early 1890, Granville, then in his fifties, married the 26-year old Allis Belle Brown Fairfield, a one-time teacher at the ranch school Granville established. In 1891, he was appointed State Land Agent for the newly created State of Montana.

In early 1894, President Grover Cleveland appointed Granville as U.S. Envoy to Paraguay and Uruguay. While the appointment brought him some financial stability, he hated the responsibilities that came with the appointment and commented in a letter to a Montana friend: *"The social duties of a Minister are just awful and as you can well imagine that sort of thing comes about as natural to me as climbing a tree does to a fish."* Granville died of heart disease in October 1918, while living in Butte, Montana. His wife Allis died of cerebral hemorrhage in March 1947, while living in Hamilton, Montana.

Whatever may be said of Granville Stuart's failings, he remains the embodiment of the rugged western rancher and chiefly was responsible for bringing order to a wild and lawless land. While financial success always eluded him, it wasn't for lack of trying. Like Roosevelt, Fergus and Vallom-Brosa, Granville Stuart lived more in one lifetime than most men could in ten.

Rancor and animosity exist to this day between the descendants of Granville Stuart and those of the men who were hung or shot. Relatives of the victims continue to work their petty spites, unwilling to believe their ancestors were guilty of rustling, and therefore, deserving of death at the hands of the Vigilantes. Were mistakes made? Were innocent men killed? No one can say with absolute certainty.

Montana has a long history of Vigilante activity, yet it should not be confused with lynch mob violence as practiced by the Ku Klux Klan or other groups who specialize in hatred of race, religion or ethnicity. The Stranglers and the Vigilante Committee of Virginia City and Alder Gulch had only one goal in mind; to stop the lawlessness, thievery and murder, no matter who the perpetrators were. Be they Mexican, Indian, Chinese, African or whatever, all men were subject to the same standards of behavior, no matter who they were, where they came from, what their beliefs were, what the color of their skin or what language they spoke.

The most cited problem with any Vigilante activity is the concern that innocent people will be killed, whether as a result of honest mistakes or dark ulterior motives by those who hold the rope. This was true in early Montana and Dakota Territory, just as it is true today. But the question of guilt or innocence can seldom be guaranteed. Whether men must face Vigilantes or today's legal system, innocent men are almost certainly wrongly accused and must pay the price; this is the fallibility of all human endeavors. It is not uncommon today to pick up a newspaper and discover someone has been freed from prison because DNA evidence proved their innocence. Too often, this happens after the poor soul has spent many years in prison and his life has been destroyed. How could an innocent person be found guilty of a crime, after having had the full benefit of our legal system, and having been tried before a group of his peers? Just as with the Vigilantes, "honest mistakes or dark ulterior motives by those who hold the rope." Often police are unwilling to search for the "one armed man" or they develop tunnel vision, convinced of a person's guilt, despite evidence to the contrary. The table is tilted. The legal process subverted. Evidence is suppressed or ignored, witnesses are coerced, justice is bent and society's best efforts are corrupted. Legal has *nothing* to do with right and wrong. Ask any lawyer.

Granville and the men involved with him were well aware of the consequences of their actions. They knew there was a possibility that some of the men they hung or shot weren't guilty of anything more than associating with the wrong class of people. Yet all those involved felt something had to be done and were willing to "hold the rope," thereby taking responsibility for what was to follow. If they hadn't, well, who knows? Granville, for one, never denied his part in these activities or tried to shift blame. Teddy Blue, a famous Montana cowboy and Granville's son-in-law, said that Granville was in town one day and was accosted on the street by a woman who accused him of killing thirty men.

"Yes, ma'am, and by God, I done it myself," he replied, tipping his hat.

Φ

Of the Vigilante efforts, The Bad Lands Cow Boy said: *"Whatever can be said against the methods adopted by the "stranglers" who came through here last fall, it cannot but be acknowledged that the result of their work has been very wholesome. Not a definite case of horse stealing from a cowman has been reported since and it seems as though a very thorough cleanup has been made."*

Φ

The cleansing effects of the Vigilante's efforts lasted approximately ten years. In the 1890's an outlaw gang called the Wild Bunch or the Hole-in-the-Wall Gang robbed trains and banks, stole mine payrolls, rustled livestock and murdered people throughout the west. Members of this powerful gang included the Sundance Kid, Butch Cassidy and Kid Curry. The gang, which included as many as forty outlaws, was finally broken up in 1901. Ironically, Kid Curry, whose real name was Harvey Logan, worked for Granville Stuart as a wrangler on the DHS ranch, as well as other outfits in the Judith Basin, during the 1880's. Some time later, the Kid turned outlaw, and once turned, the transformation was complete. He became known for being especially trigger-happy, killing with little provocation and was dissuaded from killing needlessly by Butch Cassidy on at least one occasion. The Kid was captured and jailed repeatedly during his career, only to escape and renew his profession. Finally, in 1904, after being seriously wounded and surrounded by a particularly aggressive posse, Kid Curry killed himself rather than be taken alive.

BIBLIOGRAPHY

General Western History and Perspective

River of the West: The Adventures of Joe Meek, Frances Fuller Victor, Mountain Press Publishing Company

Westering Man: The Life of Joseph Walker, Bil Gilbert, University of Oklahoma Press

Trails of Yesterday, John Bratt, University of Nebraska Press

Tales of the Frontier, Everett Dick, University of Nebraska Press

Figures in a Western Landscape, Elizabeth Stevenson, The Johns Hopkins University Press

Forty Years on the Wild Frontier, Carl Breihan and Wayne Montgomery, Devin-Adair Publishers

Charles Goodnight: Cowman and Plainsman, J. Evetts Haley, Houghton Mifflin Company

The Log of a Cowboy, Andy Adams, University of Nebraska Press

Life of Tom Horn: Government Scout and Interpreter, Tom Horn, The Lakeside Press, R.R. Donnelley & Sons Company, Chicago

The Cowboys, Time-Life Books, New York, New York

A Texas Ranger, N. A. Jennings, The Lakeside Press, R.R. Donnelley & Sons Company, Chicago

Montana History

Children of Grace: The Nez Perce War of 1877, Bruce Hampton, Henry Holt and Co

This Last West, Dr. Lorman L. Hoopes, SkyHouse Publishers, Helena, Montana

Centennial Roundup: Miles City 1887-1987, Miles City Star, Miles City, Montana

The First 100 Years: A History of Lewistown, Montana, Roberta Donovan, Central Montana Publishing Company, Lewistown, Montana

Custer County Area History: As We Recall, Helen Carey Jones, Curtis Media Corp., Dallas, Texas

Pioneer Trails and Trials, Madison County History Association, Madison Co., Montana

Brand Book for Roosevelt, Daniels, Valley, Richland, Sheridan and McCone Counties, State of Montana, The Estrayed Cowbelles, Wolfpoint, Montana

The Bloody Bozeman, Dorothy Johnson, Mountain Press Publishing Co.

James Fergus: The Grand Old Man of Montana, John R. Foster, Published by the author

Trails Plowed Under, Charles M. Russell, Doubleday, Doran & Company

The Road to Virginia City, The Diary of James Knox Polk Miller, Andrew Rolle, University of Oklahoma Press

Prospecting for Gold: From Dogtown to Virginia City, Granville Stuart, University of Nebraska Press

Pioneering in Montana: The Making of a State, Granville Stuart, University of Nebraska Press

The Frontier Years: L.A. Huffman Photographer of the Plaines, Mark H. Brown and W.R. Felton, Henry Holt and Company

Before Barbed Wire: L.A. Huffman Photographer on Horseback, Mark H. Brown and W.R. Felton, Henry Holt and Company

We Pointed Them North: Recollections of a Cowpuncher, E.C. "Teddy Blue" Abbott & Helena Huntington Smith, The Lakeside Press, R.R. Donnelley & Sons Company, Chicago

Montana: The Magazine of History

The Central Montana Vigilante Raids of 1884, Jan. 1951 Vol. I No. I, P23-35, Montana State Historical Society, Helena, Montana

Judith Basin Top Hand, 1953 Vol. III No. II, P18-23, Montana State Historical Society, Helena, Montana,

Montana: The Magazine of Western History

Granville Stuart of the DHS Ranch 1879-1887, 1981 Vol. XXX1, P14-27

Granville Stuart, Cowman "To Struggle Against an Adverse Fate" 1981 Vol. XXX1, P28-41, Montana State Historical Society, Helena, Montana

"Mr. Montana" Revised: Another Look at Granville Stuart, 1986 Vol. XXXVI, No. IV, P14-23, Montana State Historical Society, Helena, Montana

Dakota History

North Dakota History: Journal of the Northern Plains
Various Editions, North Dakota Historical Society, Bismarck, North Dakota

The Bad Lands Cow Boy, Medora, Dakota Territory, Vol. I & II (1884-85) Various Editions

Theodore Roosevelt: An Autobiography, Theodore Roosevelt, Da Capo Press

Roosevelt and the Stockmen's Association, Ray Mattison, The State Historical Society of North Dakota, Bismarck, North Dakota

The Land of the Dacotahs, Wallis Huidekoper, The Montana Stockgrowers Association

Ranching in the Dakota Bad Lands, Ray Mattison, The State Historical Society of North Dakota, Bismarck, North Dakota

The Way It Was: The North Dakota Frontier Experience, Everett Albers and D. Jerome Tweton, The Grass Roots Press

Marquis De Mores at War in the Bad Lands, Usher L. Burdick, Ye Galleon Press

Dakota Cowboy: My Life in the Old Days, Ike Blasingame, University of Nebraska Press

The Author and the Editor
Cousins, Madison Valley, Montana
1952

About The Author

Born in Whitehall, Montana, and raised on a ranch in the Madison Valley, the author understands western culture as few writers do. His earliest memories concern a grizzly that was marauding the ranch and killing the stock, calving, lambing, haying and riding hogs when he was too young to set a horse.

The author defines a good book as follows: "A book should transport the reader to another place, and hopefully, teach something along the way. It should be authentic in every respect. Too often, writers don't do their homework or check all the details. Simple errors rob the work of its credibility and sour the reading experience. Readers deserve the author's best efforts."